Murder
in South Bend

By John Bridges

M. T. Publishing Company, Inc. ™

P.O. Box 6802
Evansville, Indiana 47719-6802
www.mtpublishing.com

Library of Congress Control Number: 2016944942

ISBN: 978-1-945306-09-9

The materials were compiled and produced using available information. M.T. Publishing Company, Inc.™ and the author regret they cannot assume liability for errors or omissions.

Graphic Designer: Thalita A. Floyd-Wingerter

Printed in the United States of America

CHAPTER 1

Wolfsburg, Germany
August 5, 1944

The siren seemed to scream louder than ever before sending a chill through me. After the damage caused by previous raids, the factory couldn't stand much more. Would this be the end of the KdF, "people's car" program? It might be the end of all of us. I grabbed my valise packed with blueprints of the car we were yet to manufacture and headed for the shelter. Within seconds, the rumble of the American bombers competed inharmoniously with the siren's wail. Taking one last look at the nearby production machines, I noticed several were still running but the workers were gone. I glanced out a western window. The bombers were getting closer. There must have been a hundred or more. They had fighter escorts. I ducked into our tiny aboveground shelter. Most of the other engineers and supervisors were already there. Being only twenty centimeters thick, the walls offered little protection. Once Porsche and Hitler decided to build the plant in a swampy area, everything had to be built above ground. Being inside that dark moldy enclosure offered little feeling of security. With the drawings tucked against my chest, I sat on the damp floor with my head between my knees. The roar of the bomber engines made the ground quiver. My whole body vibrated. I covered my ears to deaden the noise of the screaming bombs and the nearby explosions. One could tell by the way the ground jumped that the bombs were close, too close. Between blasts, I could hear walls outside collapsing. The one small electric bulb in our shelter flickered and died. The darkness heightened my fear. Ever since I was a small boy, I had been frightened by darkness. For good reason, this time. Putrid smoke swept through the dank, dark enclosure. I closed my eyes tight so they wouldn't burn so much. Everyone around me was coughing and gasping for breath. I pulled my shirt over my mouth and nose and breathed small and shallow. The raid would last no more than ten minutes, but that's a long time to go without adequate oxygen.

Finally, the ground stopped shaking and the drone of the bombers started to fade. We all rushed for the small shaft of light that showed the way out. Once in the open, I shielded my eyes from the afternoon sun and looked around. Much of the plant's roof and walls lay smoldering on the ground. Roof girders hung precariously ready to fall on some unlucky victim. I wondered if the barracks where my mother, sister and I lived had been damaged. I rushed to check on them. On the way, I looked to see if the presses and welders were damaged. Without them, there would be no more production. I stepped over the body of a Polish laborer. His intestines had spilled onto the dusty concrete. His open eyes were set in fathomless sockets, looking but not seeing. He must have been too weak to make it to his shelter or had chosen death over the horrid life of working twelve-hour days on scant rations. From out of nowhere there was a loud roar and then the terrible rattle of machine guns. Bullets dug a path near me. With the bombers homeward bound, American P-47 fighters dove down seeking targets of opportunity. I dove behind a pile of rubble and stayed there until I was sure the fighters were gone.

Soon, the incendiaries burned out and the few fires they had started were being brought under control. Rubble was everywhere. Shattered Ju.88 wings were scattered about like plucked feathers of a giant goose. I picked my way through the debris and smoke. On my way to the bridge across the canal to check on my mother and sister, I had to pass through the Kubelwagen production area. Those military scout cars used the KdF chassis, the heart and soul of the future "people's car." I had been obsessed with Porsche's automobile design, which he showed to Herr Hitler the last day of April, 1938. I was sure it was just what the country needed to help raise the standard of living for the average German. I was hired to work on the civilian passenger car but the war had diverted my efforts to Kubelwagen production.

What I saw next stopped me like a brick wall. Twisted steel and mangled parts were everywhere. A bomb must have made a direct hit on the Kubelwagen assembly line. Incredibly, the largest press had escaped serious damage. I rubbed my burning eyes. Is this the end of the Volkswagen?

"Hans, why are you crying? Get hold of yourself! We've got work to do!" I turned to see the plant manager, Otto Haniel standing there like Mussolini, with his hands on his hips and his barrel chest and round midsection stuck out. A tiny fringe of black hair surrounded his baldhead. His holstered MP38 hung low on his hip like an American cowboy. Thick spectacles coated with oily dust hung on the end of his red bulbous nose.

"I'm not crying, Otto," I said. "How can we ever get production started again? Do you know if the turbines were knocked out?"

"Can't you see that conveyor over there is still running? Open your eyes, Hans." By now, I had become accustomed to Otto's gruff, sarcastic ways. His manner didn't bother me anymore. "We were lucky, boy," he snarled. "A 500-pounder fell right between our two turbines. If it had exploded, that would have been the end of all production and probably all of us.

I stood up and faced him. An intense fear gripped me. I had to leave and check on my family.

"I'll be back soon, Otto." Without waiting for permission, I ran as fast as my legs would take me the 200 meters from the plant to the civilian barracks. My heart sank as I crossed the canal bridge to the residential area. The whole block of apartments where my mother, sister and I lived was leveled. All that remained was a pile of smoldering rubble. Several small fires were being extinguished. Hopefully, Mother and Eva made it to the shelter. I walked closer to the ruins. Where was my family? (What was left of my family, anyway.) Father was killed in May on the eastern front. Poor Father. He hated this crazy war. He especially hated the Reds. Unfortunately, it was a Russian bullet that took his life. They didn't even tell us where he was buried. No one seemed to know or care. He was just gone, gone like our home.

At the site of our building, I climbed the pile of splintered wood framing, slate roofing and cracked plaster. Hoping I would find nothing human, I pulled several boards back and cautiously looked underneath. Dust and foul odors filled the air. I could smell sewage. About a meter down I saw a woman's face. Her unmoving eyes starred back at me. I recognized Mrs. Klasmeyer, our upstairs neighbor. Why was she still here when the bombs were falling? I was afraid to look further.

Suddenly, shouts and cries from behind me grabbed my attention. I looked around to see dozens of people running in my direction. I frantically searched the crowd.

"Mother, Mother, Eva!" I shouted. "Oh Mother, where are you?" I searched for Mother and Eva until it was too dark to see. Exhausted, I went back to my office and fell asleep on my little cot.

Early the next morning I went to the company hospital to see if they had any word on Mother and Eva.

A young girl who appeared to be still in her teens manned the reception desk. I ask if she had any news about my mother and sister.

"Are you Hans Werner?"

"Yes, I am." She wiped her streaked face with the back of her hand. Her clothes were tattered and filthy. She looked as if she had been crying. Her index finger pointed at a spot on the wrinkled paper she held.

"Hans Werner, nearest of kin to the deceased, Freda Werner and daughter, Eva Werner. Is that correct?"

"They found my mother and sister? Is that what you're telling me, fraulein?"

"Yes, sir. I'm afraid so. I've been instructed to tell you that you can identify the remains here at the hospital morgue. You'll have to remove the bodies within two days or they will be buried in the company cemetery.

Would you sign here?" I stood for a moment trying to absorb the news. I couldn't think straight. "Sir?"

"Uh....... What am I signing?"

"That I informed you." Her dirty finger pointed to the spot. I didn't choose to see my mother and sister dead so I walked back to my office in a haze. Yesterday, in ten short minutes, my world crumbled. The emptiness consumed me. I felt I was losing control. I hoped no one would come in my office and see me sobbing like a child. It would take a long time to get past the grief I felt. The loneliness, the all-consuming fear of the future tore at my heart. With my family gone, all I had left was my work. Even that now seemed trivial. All we worked on were military projects of which I had little interest. The plant was a wreck. My ambition of helping develop an affordable car for the ordinary German family now seemed nothing but a shattered dream. Ferdinand Porsche didn't come around anymore. With the war going badly for Germany, I guessed that Herr Hitler had given up on the Volkswagen concept and his vast plans for a nationwide autobahn. I was just thirteen when Hitler became Chancellor of the Fatherland. I was impressed by his persuasive, almost hypnotic, speeches. He promoted national pride and patriotism. Who could disagree with his "collective good takes precedence over individual good" statement? If the automotive engineering bug had not already bitten me, I would have gladly joined the German Youth movement.

My best friend, Karl Heinz was my roommate at the Berlin Technical Institute. He and I both felt learning English was important so we practiced on each other. We both graduated in 1937. He wanted to get into rocket science and I chose automotive engineering. We were both very lucky. He got a job working on rocket development under Dr. Werner von Braun. During the early forties, he was at Peenemunde on the Baltic Sea. I got a job at die Autostadt (later called Wolfsburg) under the great automobile designer, Ferdinand Porsche. My work was wonderful at first. Unfortunately, our "people's car" program was soon put aside so all efforts could be devoted to war work. Karl and I stayed in touch most of those seven years after graduation, but I hadn't heard from him in almost a year.

The BBC, my only reliable source of war news, said the British and Americans were in the suburbs of Paris. The Russians were steadily pushing our army back on the Eastern front. Even with von Braun's V-1 rockets causing chaos in England, I suspected the war would eventually be lost. But I was sure der Fuhrer had no intention of surrendering or negotiating a peace treaty. With nowhere to go, I decided to stay at the factory. At least I had a place to sleep (in my office). And I could get two adequate meals a day. If I left, I would probably be picked up and sent to the Eastern front. I figured staying was the smartest thing, at least, until the enemy got closer.

I wondered how Karl was doing. Was he still alive? On August 18, 1944, I wrote a letter bringing him up to date on all that had happened in the past few months. The letter continued:

From what I hear, the V-1 flying bombs have been quite successful. Is it true that 2000 exploded in London in June?

I also heard about the big British air raid on Peenemunde last August. How bad was the damage? One report said the scientists' living quarters were wiped out. I hope you had time to reach a shelter.

The BBC said the Russians have now reached the Baltic Sea west of Riga. How long do you think it will take them to reach you? If you decide to leave Peenemunde, please let me know. I could join you somewhere. There is nothing to keep me here except the dream of the Volkswagen and I fear that dream is gone. Please let me know your thoughts. I promise confidentiality. Our mail here is not yet censored so you can speak freely. I'm open to anything, except the Russians.

Your friend forever, Hans

Just as I finished the letter, Otto Haniel stuck his head in my office. One of the unfortunate things about living where you work is lack of privacy.

"Who are you writing to, Hans, the Pope?" Otto chuckled as if he had said something funny. I tried to ignore him. I didn't even turn around. To get my attention he shouted, "Actung, Hans! I want to inform you that there are rumors that the prisoners working in the plant may soon revolt. Since most of our guards have been sent to the front, we have a dangerous situation on our hands. The prisoners greatly outnumber us. This could be disastrous!" With no response from me, he turned and was gone.

Two Months Later

Otto's prediction of a worker revolt had not come true. But the workers had slowed down. Also, there seemed to be a more belligerent attitude, if that were possible. Although there was little backtalk when an order was given, their quiet sullenness was somehow more menacing than outright hostility. I suspected something ominous was going on. Otto burst into my office and confirmed my suspicions.

"Hans, we're in great trouble with the SS! Representatives from the high command will be in next week to get a report on sabotage at our factory."

"What are you talking about? Sabotage? Here?"

"Yes, and it is not minor. A Ju.88 on its first mission crashed when a wing that was made here simply ripped apart. An investigation showed that many of the rivets had not been secured. The rivets looked all right from the outside but did not hold together in flight. Experienced airmen and a valuable bomber were lost." Otto paused and glared at me as if the problem was my fault. "And that is not all, Hans. A number of Kubelwagens have stopped running on the front lines. Seems the fuel systems were contaminated. As a result, petrol tanks, fuel lines, fuel pumps and carburetors have to be replaced before the vehicles can be used again. The vehicles in question were in service on the Eastern front. The maintenance men there do not have the time or the parts to repair them. Management here is blamed. I can only imagine what our punishment might be! We must locate and stop the sabotage at once. Hans, I am transferring you from engineering to final inspection for both the Ju.88 wing and the Kubelwagen assembly areas." Otto stormed out without waiting for a response. He had given me a direct order. I sat for a few moments considering my options. I immediately realized that Otto had put me in a position to take the blame for someone else's mistakes. I had no choice but to obey his order. I put my drawings away and headed for the Ju.88 area.

All the workers must have known what was going on. Suspicious eyes followed my every move. The finished wings were stored in horizontal racks awaiting shipment. By visually inspecting a finished Ju.88 wing, it was impossible to tell if the rivets were secure. And since the inside of the wings was inaccessible, I had to come up with a way to check from the outside. With my pocketknife blade, I tried to dislodge random rivets. I could feel a hundred eyes watching. I found nothing wrong. And then I started checking rivets on wings made several weeks earlier. On one wing, a whole line of rivets easily popped loose with my knife blade test. I pushed the rivets back in place and gave no outward sign that I had found anything wrong. I simply checked more wings and then stood for several moments scratching my head. I made a mental note of the defective wing numbers so we could determine who the riveters were that made them.

I caught up with Otto later that day and told him what I had found. He checked his worker schedule and determined that Polish prisoners number R678 and R972 were the riveters on the defective wings. I followed him to the assembly line wondering how he was going to handle the problem. R678 and R972 were busy riveting the thin aluminum panels together as we walked up. The two prisoners looked up at Otto and then quickly looked back to their work. Otto casually walked up behind R972, unbuckled his holster, placed the barrel of his MP88 against the base of the prisoner's skull and pulled the trigger. Blood, brain matter and bone chips splattered on the shiny wing surface that he had been working on. His bloody head slid down the wing leaving a wide red streak. He fell to the floor in a heap. I couldn't believe what I had just seen.

"Otto! What are you doing?" I shouted. Otto ignored me. R678 looked at Otto with eyes like saucers. He stood frozen. At point blank range, Otto shot him in the chest. The prisoner fell backwards and tried to scramble away on his hands and knees. Otto followed and put another bullet into his back. R678 was still. The other workers in the area crouched behind their machines. Otto reholstered his pistol and motioned for me to follow him back to his office. I thought I might vomit. I had never seen a cold-blooded murder before. Otto showed no emotion. Once we reached his office, he called the guard station and told them to dispose of the bodies and clean the area.

"Otto, are you sure you executed the right prisoners?" I asked.

"It does not matter, Hans! The other workers probably knew of the sabotage and therefore knew why those two were shot. My objective was to discourage future sabotage. I think the workers got the message." Otto and I agreed on some things; the need for a people's car and the autobahn, elimination of the communist-run unions and reigning in the power of the Jewish bankers, but I strongly disagreed with him on Nazi military aggression and slave labor. I especially disagreed with his method of dealing with the saboteurs. But I had to put those differences aside for the time being. For my own self-preservation, I had a job to do.

I worked late that night checking rivets. I found three more wings with loose rivets. This time I boldly marked them with red paint. Dead tired, I made my way back to my office, hoping to get some rest before I tackled the Kubelwagen problem the next day. I shivered under my musty blanket. After the last air raid, the factory's open walls made heating impossible. It was now nearing November. My office had no door, just a layer of canvas draped across the opening. I could not go to sleep. But it wasn't from the cold. The Kubelwagen fuel contamination problem was more complicated than loose rivets. I pictured the assembly process in my mind. The last things that happen after a Kubelwagen is assembled are the addition of petrol, startup, adjusting the carburetor and timing. Without clean petrol, the vehicle will not run properly. I figured some contaminator must have been added after the cars were loaded on the train. But that did not make sense. Those railcars are under constant guard. Besides, the report from the front said the Kubelwagens ran well for a few days. I tossed and turned and finally eased into a fitful sleep.

The prisoners watched as I approached the Kubelwagen assembly area the next morning. I was sure the workers knew that I was the one who identified the defective Ju.88 wings and named the two workers that Otto shot. It occurred to me that I might be the next to be killed. I walked about the area, hoping for inspiration. Nothing. At the end of the line, petrol is added to a finished Kubelwagen, I wet my finger under the nozzle and brought it to my nose. Nothing unusual. I tasted it. Not very scientific, but since I had no chemistry laboratory at my disposal, I resorted to simple methods.

"Hans, what's causing the Kubelwagens to stop running in the field?" Otto shouted.

"Otto! Don't sneak up on me like that. You scared me!"

"Well, here is something that will scare you even more. The SS will be in next Tuesday. More and more Kubelwagens on the Eastern Front have stopped running. The SS wants answers, NOW!"

"It's not that simple, Otto. Every vehicle that leaves the line is running perfectly."

"Well, the fuel systems are contaminated somewhere along the way. You are a university graduate. Are you telling me that the saboteurs are smarter than you?" I shook my head and stared at my feet. "Find the problem, Hans, and find it quickly!" Otto sucked in his stomach, adjusted his belt, and pushed his thick spectacles up as he marched away.

I walked back to the beginning of the fuel system assembly. One huge press stamped out a variety of parts depending on what die set was installed. That day it was Kubelwagen floor pans. Usually, I avoided this area. The downward crunch of the press made the ground shake and the ears ache. There were no safety guards on the press. A careless worker could easily lose a hand. The two loaders seemed unconcerned as they removed the sharp greasy shells. Blue lubricant smoke hovered around the press. It was not a pleasant scent. I soon found the storage area for the petrol tank stampings. The halves were stacked in two columns ready for degreasing. Nearby, the degreased halves were being trimmed and welded together. The finished tanks were stacked along a wall, the fill-tube with cap installed pointed skyward. A worker picked up a single tank and carried it to the assembly area as needed. I saw nothing suspicious. Believing that the petrol tank could be the source of the contamination, I followed the tank along the line searching for places where something might be added. But a big question remained. Why do the Kubelwagens run well for a period of time?

Two SS officers showed up at my office unannounced. They were both dressed in immaculate black uniforms with tall highly polished black boots. The taller of the two spoke.

"Are you Hans Werner?"

"Yes, and who are you?" I asked.

"Herr Werner, we will ask the questions. We understand that the Ju.88 problem has been solved. Is that correct?"

"We can not be sure unless we check every rivet and…"

"Werner, we demand answers. How did this happen in the first place? You were responsible, were you not?"

"Oh no! I was only recently assigned to inspect the Ju.88 wings."

"Our records show that you were responsible at the time of the sabotage."

"No, that is not correct!" I said.

"Records don't lie, Herr Werner. But we are reasonable men. We are willing to give you another chance even though an expensive airplane and several lives were lost due to your negligence. Tell me, Werner, has the Kubelwagen problem been solved?"

"No, not yet, but I am working on …"

"Not good enough! You have two days. Hiel Hitler!" The two clicked their heels in unison, turned and were gone.

I hoped a good night's sleep would give me inspiration, but I couldn't sleep. I worried about what might happen to me if I didn't solve the fuel contamination problem. I tossed and turned and then around midnight, I suddenly sat upright on my cot. Perhaps I should somehow try to duplicate the situation at the front. I slipped on my trousers and coat and headed for the Kubelwagen assembly line. The night shift workers were working at a snail's pace. I went to the petrol filling station. Instead of the normal two liters, I ordered the worker to fill the tank on one of the vehicles. I then drove it outside and around the complex several times. Stopping and restarting repeatedly, I continued to drive on and on and on. The Kubelwagen continued to run smoothly. I drove several hours and nothing happened. Was I wasting time and precious fuel? On and on I drove. As the sun started to show itself over the eastern horizon, the vehicle started to run rough. By the time I returned to the plant entrance, it was missing badly, heaving and jumping like a nauseated dog. I had not found the cause of the problem, but I suspected it had something to do with a full petrol tank. And then it hit me! The petrol must have to touch the contaminating substance before it could dissolve into the system. In my mind, I pictured tanks sitting on edge waiting to be bolted to the frame. I ran toward the area where the tanks were lined up against the wall. Stopping by the maintenance shop, I wheeled out an oxyacetylene cart. By this time, the morning shift workers were taking their places. All eyes were on me as I fired up the cutting torch. I had to find the problem, fast! Sparks flew. With the two halves separated, I examined the inside. I looked carefully at the interior of both halves. They looked clean. I grabbed another tank from the stack and started to cut it in two.

"Are you mad, Hans?" Otto shouted from behind me. "Why are you destroying perfectly good petrol tanks? Stop at once. Stop, I say!" I continued to cut. "I gave you an order, Hans. I command you to stop at once." I completed the cut. The two halves fell apart. One half looked clean. In the seam of the other half there was a puddle of what appeared to be dried varnish.

"There's your contamination source, Otto. It only gets into the fuel system when the petrol contacts it for several hours. That couldn't have happened by chance. Some saboteur has been pouring varnish into the tanks when they are setting on edge. It dries enough not to run before the two liters of petrol are added. I do not know if the saboteur is very clever or just lucky. In any case, all these tanks must be destroyed. After new ones are made, they should be guarded day and night. I suggest you have the petrol tank dies installed in the main press right away." Otto stood frozen with his mouth slightly open. I fired the torch again and continued to cut the remaining tanks in two. Most were contaminated.

The two SS men never came back. I suspected Otto contacted them and took credit for solving the problem. I really did not care. I just wanted to get away before the inevitable next crisis.

February 1945

I continued to worry about Karl. The BBC reported the Russians were within a few kilometers of Peenemunde. Since Karl had not answered my last letter, I feared the worst. Finally, the mail girl delivered a letter to my office. The envelope was dirty and torn. It looked as if it might have been opened and resealed. My heart beat fast as I ripped it open.

21-Feb-45

My friend Hans,

Please accept my apology for not writing sooner, but the workload at Peenemunde has been horrendous. Sometimes we slept at our workstations. It was grueling but exciting. Because of the advancing Russians, we have now left. When you told me that your mail was not censored, I felt envious. Our mail has been censored almost from the beginning. When your letter came, the SS called me in and asked me to explain who you were and why you had suggested we meet somewhere. The problem finally blew over but responding to you was out of the question, until now.

A few days ago, Werner von Braun called his scientists and engineers in for a secret meeting and explained our options. He said that since we were under the direct control of the SS, he feared that General Hans Kammler might use us as a bargaining chip or even have us all killed to keep us from being captured. We all decided if we were to be captured, we wanted it to be by the Americans. Perhaps, we could even continue our work in America.

I put the letter down on my table for a moment and thought about what Karl said about continuing his work in America. I had become very discouraged about the situation here at the plant. Food was becoming increasingly scarce and the prisoners more hostile. Allied bombings were now killing German civilians by the hundreds of thousands. Just a few days earlier, twenty thousand were killed in one raid on Berlin and one hundred thousand were killed in Dresden. With Germany in shambles, trying to get to America sounded like an excellent idea. I continued to read.

> *Just before we left Peenemunde, we were ordered to remain there and fight the Russians as soldiers. The next day, General Kammler changed his mind and ordered us to move to central Germany to the Mittelwerk factory. Although von Braun does not trust Kammler's intentions, it seemed the best option and so that is where we are headed. Since this letter would be censored at Peenemunde, I will drop it off at the post office in some village we pass through.*
>
> *If you want to try to join us, I suggest you come to the underground Mittelwerk factory. I have no idea how you can get there or how you can get inside the complex if you make it. But if you are successful in reaching us, I might be able to pass you off as a rocket engineer. Please bring your identification papers and your graduation certificate. If our work is to continue, it must be somewhere other than the Fatherland.*
>
> *Good luck, your friend, Karl*

I folded the letter carefully and hid it in my shoe. I feared if someone read the letter, I might be watched closely in the future. If I were to make a move, it had to be soon. My biggest problem was how to get to Mittelwerk without getting caught.

During the next couple of days, I paid close attention to Otto. He seemed less surly than before and even friendly at times. Had he read my letter from Karl or had he been told of its contents? If he knew I might leave, why didn't he just turn me in and let the SS or the Gestapo deal with me? I knew why. He needed me as an inspector. If I left and there was more sabotage, he would be the one to take the blame. Besides, who else did he have to solve his technical problems? I figured he was not going to let me get away if he could help it. But I was determined to leave. Unfortunately, other than my bicycle, I had no transportation to travel the 250 kilometers to the Mittelwerk factory. I thought of stealing a Kubelwagen. But I wasn't willing to take that chance. I'd surely be shot if caught. And getting caught seemed probable given it was known that I was headed for Mittelwerk. Besides, I'd probably be stopped at the factory gate. What to do?

It was an unusually cold night that February 28, 1945. Although my office had no door, the canvas across the opening kept out some of the cold air. I was able to grab one of the small kerosene heaters we were making for the eastern front. That helped a little. I had already turned my small light off and was listening to BBC news broadcast. The report told of American and British progress along the Western front. At the rate they were moving, they would be here in Wolfsburg in just a few days. I knew I should leave right away. But how?

There was a heavy knock on the wall outside my door opening. I got out of bed, went to the door and pulled back the canvas. There stood Otto. I had never seen him look so frightened.

"Otto, what's wrong? You look like you've seen a ghost."

"Herr Hitler has ordered that our plant be destroyed before the enemy arrives. All civilians, and plant workers are to be moved east. He orders that nothing is to be left standing. You'll be required to help in the destruction."

"That makes no sense at all, Otto. I won't be a part of it!"

"You cannot disobey der Fuhrer. You'll be shot."

"By whom?"

He pointed his stubby finger at my face and shouted, "You cannot disobey der Fuhrer, Hans!"

Not knowing how to respond, I looked at my watch and said, "It's late, Otto. Can we discuss this tomorrow?"

"There is nothing to discuss! It's an order." Otto turned and was gone.

I was certain I could not wait any longer to leave. Gathering my few belongings, I wrapped them in my old blanket. My valise containing the KdF drawings was already packed. I knew getting out of the main gate without a pass was impossible. So I walked my bicycle down to the canal. A light coating of snow covered the ice-crusted ground. About twenty meters ahead the canal flowed by. This was the only way I knew how to get out of the complex without being seen. I put my valise and blanket roll on the ground next to the canal. I held the bicycle high as I walked down the embankment and into the waist-deep canal. The water was freezing cold and foul smelling. The icy water took my breath away. I stumbled along, trying to keep my bicycle dry. Near the center of the canal, the water was up to my shoulders. Should I go further? Would the water be over my head? There was no turning back. Progress was painfully slow. The water was so cold; my only thought was getting to the other side. Finally, I made it. While pulling the bicycle onto dry land and trying to catch my breath, I considered returning for my belongings and the valise. But I was so fatigued and cold I didn't think I could make it. First priority was to somehow dry off and get warm so I decided not to go back. I hurried along the road going south toward Nordhausen. The road was icy and I was exhausted. Riding the bicycle was impossible so I decided to just push it. There was no traffic. The dim moonlight offered little visibility. If I didn't find some shelter soon, they would find my frozen corpse on the road tomorrow. I walked and shivered until spotting a small house just a few meters off the road. There was no light inside. I stepped onto the squeaky planks of the wooden porch and pounded on the door. No answer. As expected, the door was locked. Again, I pounded.

A weak voice from inside said, "Who is there?"

"Hans Werner, an engineer at Volkswagen. I fell in the canal and I'm freezing cold. Please let me in!" There was silence. Then the door opened slightly. In the dim shaft of light from within I could see an elderly man with a white beard pointing a shotgun at me. He looked me up and down with the gun pointed at my chest.

"Are you drunk?" he asked.

"No, sir. I lost my way in the dark and fell in the canal. May I come in and warm up?" The old man stood there for a long time and then finally lowered the shotgun and stepped aside. The coal fire in his fireplace had been banked for the night. The old gentleman poked it until it flamed. "Oh, thank you," I said as I started stripping off my wet clothes. I wanted to wring out the water but the outer garments were already frozen hard. "You have saved my life, sir. I will never forget your kindness."

"What are you doing out on a night like this? he inquired.

"I had started toward Nordhausen on my bicycle when I had the accident."

"Nordhausen? That's 250 km from here! Where is your bike?"

"It is on your porch. May I bring it inside?

"Alright. But be quick about it." I was already down to my underwear. Being quick was not a problem once I opened the door. I hoped the bicycle was still functional. I leaned the bike against the wall and hurried back to the fire. Twisting like a rotisserie, I let the flames warm all sides of my frigid body. Maybe I'll survive after all, I thought. The old man sat in his rocking chair with his shotgun laying across his lap as he watched me. Uneasiness filled the room. No one said anything for a long time. I looked over at my savior. The old man was snoring. I relaxed and laid on the tattered rug in front of the fire. Using my arm as a pillow, I drifted into a sweet sleep.

CHAPTER 2

As the first streams of a weak winter sun leaked though an eastern window, I was awakened by a tinkling sound. I looked to see my host with his back to me urinating in a chamber pot. I felt my clothes. They were warm and dry. After dressing, I thanked the old man for his kindness. Without a word, he disappeared into the next room. He returned with a sausage and a piece of bread. He wrapped them in a newspaper and handed the package to me. I again thanked him and left without knowing his name. I straddled my bicycle and rode away. I knew of the dangers of traveling in broad daylight but I figured I had at least two hours before I would be discovered missing.

The cold wind on my face stung like a million needles. The road was slick and treacherous. It had snowed again during the night. A clean white blanket covered the rolling countryside. On I peddled. In about two hours I arrived at the village of Haldensleben. I parked the bicycle near a petrol station and unrolled my sausage and bread. Nothing ever tasted so good. I hoped that someday I could repay the old man for his kindness.

With the national shortage of petrol, there were no customers at the station. Rationing had limited petrol's use to government officials or those willing to pay black market prices. I put my bike out of sight and waited for someone to come along. After a while, I was so cold that I went inside to get warm.

A rosy-cheeked middle-aged frau in oversized coveralls rose from her chair. "What do you want?" she barked.

"I'm just trying to stay warm until I can catch a ride to Nordhausen," I replied.

"This is not a hostel, young man. In any case, your chances of catching a ride are better outside than in here. Why do you want to go to Nordhausen? The place is crawling with French and Polish slaves. I hear they work in underground tunnels like moles."

"Yes madam. That is what I hear. But I have a friend who works there and I am going to see him." At that moment, a small army truck pulled up next to the petrol pump. The bed had a canvas cover supported by bows. It was of standard color and markings, nothing unusual.

"You come with me," the frau said. I walked out with her hoping the driver wouldn't ask any questions. I large soldier in a dinghy corporal's uniform walked up to us.

"Ten liters," the driver shouted.

"This is a private station, soldier. You know the regulations. I can't give you fuel unless you pay for it."

"Ten liters, and make it quick. I am already late," the corporal with a ruddy face, repeated.

"Show me your money first."

"I'll show you the sole of my boot if that petrol is not in this truck in one minute!" The frau looked at me as if I should intervene. I had no intention of crossing this cross soldier. We all looked at each other until I spoke up.

"Give me a ride in the back of your truck and the petrol is yours." The frau looked at me with daggers. I peeled off several slightly damp Reichmarks and tucked them into her top pocket. She pumped the petrol and I went to retrieve my bicycle.

"How far are you going?" I asked.

"Nordhausen, if it is any of your business. Did I say you could ride?"

"I'll be in the back behind the canvas. I won't cause any trouble. After all, didn't I pay for the petrol?"

"Alright. I'm going to the factory inside Tunnel A. You must get out before we get there. I'll tell you when." I couldn't believe my good luck, a ride all the way to the factory at Nordhausen. I threw my bicycle inside the bed and climbed in. The bed of the truck smelled horrible, like something dead. I kept my head outside the canvas so I could breathe. The truck sped away. It weaved and spun on the slick road. I tried not to think about the danger.

Four Hours Later

The truck slid to a stop and the driver shouted out the window.

"You get out here and make it quick!"

"Alright, just give me a moment!" I answered. I pulled back the canvas and lifted my bicycle over the tailgate. I walked the bike to the ditch and shouted, "Danker, der Freund." He nodded. I gave him a wave and moved behind the truck. As he started to move, I grabbed the tailgate and swung my leg over. I was inside again. We drove for another couple of minutes and then stopped. I could hear the driver talking to someone. We started up again. The echoing sound of the engine told me we were inside a tunnel. I peeped out beside the canvas. Through dim lights I saw hundreds of dirty men with bones stripped of flesh working on what appeared to be huge rockets. Smoke and fumes filled the air. The first time the truck stopped, I jumped out. There was so much activity I don't think I was noticed. None of those faces resurrected from the dead even looked up. The truck pulled away. The tunnel stretched as far as I could see. I walked along as if I had a mission. After passing several branch tunnels, I approached a desk set against the wall. It appeared to be an inspection station.

"Excuse me, sir," I said to the bespeckled man. "I am looking for the office and staff of Dr. Werner von Braun. He looked over his glasses and stared at me as if I were from another planet.

"Von Braun? Are you serious?" he said with a chuckle. "You won't find him in this hell hole. I hear he was in Nordhausen a few weeks ago, but as far as I know, he never came inside this stinking tunnel. Why do you ask?"

"Oh, I have a friend on his staff that I am trying to locate."

"Well, they're not here. From what I hear, they are all over at Bleicherode." "Where is Bleicherode?" I asked.

"It's about 20 kilometers southeast of here. Look, young man, I don't know who you are, but if I were you I wouldn't be asking so many questions about the whereabouts of Dr. von Braun. That could get you in trouble. What is you name, anyway?"

"I am Franz Buckner. Thank you for your help, sir." I headed back in the direction I had come from. I felt his gaze following me. The entrance to the tunnel was visible ahead. I walked faster.

At the tunnel entrance, I saw the guard station manned by two SS soldiers. How was I going to get by those two without showing identification, I wondered? By this time it was possible Otto had reported me to the guards here at Mittelwerk. Outside, snow was falling. It was starting to get dark. I stood at a safe distance from the entrance waiting for some opportunity to make my escape. Behind me a small military truck approached. He had his night 'blackout' lights on. As he slowly passed, I glanced up and saw that it was the same driver that had picked me up at Haldensleben. He looked at me and tapped his brakes. I looked away and ducked behind the truck. As he pulled away, I again grabbed his tailgate and swung my leg over. I gasped out loud when I realized I was on top of a pile of dead bodies. The driver again applied his brakes. When his door opened, I took a deep breath and dug my way underneath one of the corpses. I was very still when he pulled the canvas back. The next few seconds seemed like an eternity in hell. I held my breath and waited. When his door open again, I took a small breath and worked my way free of the dead man on top of me. The stench was overpowering. I knew I had to get out of there soon. Damn the risk! As soon as I was sure we had cleared the guard station, I crawled over the tailgate. By this time, we were going too fast to safely drop to the ground, but I couldn't stay with those dead men a second longer. I hit the snow-covered road skipping like a flat stone over a frozen lake and ended up in a ditch, bruised but not broken. I stayed in the ditch until the truck was out of sight. Even in the open air, the smell of those dead men clung to me. I scooped up hands full of snow and wiped it on my face and clothes. That didn't help. Having no idea where my bicycle was, I limped back toward the tunnel searching the ditches. My bicycle was nowhere to be found. Getting closer to the guard station, I saw what appeared to be supervisory workers lined up getting their passes checked. I got in line.

"How can I get to Bleicherode from here?" I asked the man ahead of me.

He stepped back from me and said, "Catch the #34 der zuj. It leaves here at eight, about thirty minutes from now."

"Where is train #34?" He fanned his nose and pointed at a group of rail cars parked on a nearby siding. I stepped out of line and headed for train #34. I climbed aboard a dark and cold car. Several other passengers were already inside. All were sleeping or trying to. Good idea, I thought. Knowing how badly I smelled, I took a seat far away from the others. I did my best to ease my bruised body into a comfortable position. There was no such position. My dozing was interrupted when I felt an engine bump against the car. I hoped the man in line at the guard station had told me the right car. Snow was still falling as we rumbled through the night. The car heaved and its wheels squealed as it bounced over a wavy track. I suspected a derailment at any moment. We were going so slow that I hardly noticed when we stopped beside a dimly lit sign that read Bleicherode. Most passengers got off and walked toward the town. I stood beside the track and watched. As the pitiful train pulled away, the quaint little village stretched out before me. Black coal smoke from a hundred frame houses blanketed the still air. Dim light escaped from a few windows. There appeared to be no electricity in the village.

Icy cinders crunched beneath my feet as I approached the main street of the town. I cocked my head to listen. Was it singing? If so, it meant a beer hall must be nearby. Although nearly out of money, I was willing to spend my last mark on a tall stein of the dark and foamy brew. As I got closer, I could hear stamping feet and I recognized the tankers' song, *Panzerlied*. I started to sing along. I could feel the warmth of the beer hall and its inhabitants even before I opened the door. I walked inside. The place was crowded! With the enemy approaching and an uncertain future ahead, drinking was about the only thing that made any sense, at least that's how I explained the large crowd. Squeezing between two young men at the bar, I ordered a stein.

"What's the occasion?" I asked the man at my right.

"It's our last night in town," he said.

"Where are you going from here?"

"Who wants to know?"

"Oh, just curious. Are you with Dr. von Braun's group?"

"I don't know who you are but you better have a good reason for asking that kind of question. What is your name and when is the last time you bathed?"

"I'm Hans Werner, and I'm looking for my friend and university roommate, Karl Heinz. Ever heard of him?" The man stepped back from the bar, held his nose and looked me up and down.

He scratched his chin, and pointed, "your smell is overpowering. Please take it elsewhere. Karl Heinz is sitting at the table in the corner with that buxom fraulein. As you can see, he's rather busy at the moment." Yes, it was Karl all right. I'd recognize him anywhere. His shiny black hair was combed straight back like in the old days. Karl's rugged good looks always attracted the girls. I watched for a while not wanting to disturb him. He had one hand inside the girl's peasant blouse as he kissed her. Her left hand was behind his head. Her right hand was under the table. Karl leaned his head back and looked at the ceiling. I watched and waited. Soon the girl whispered something in his ear, kissed his cheek and left the table. I walked over, stood in front of him waiting for him to notice me.

"Well, how was it, Karl?" I inquired. He looked at me and wrinkled his brow. His mouth dropped open as he tried to speak. He started to stand and then quickly sat back down.

Finally, he said, "Hans! Oh, my God, is it really you? You caught me at a rather awkward moment." He fumbled beneath the table.

I smiled and again asked, "Was it good?"

"Yes, you bastard! As good as it could be inside a crowded beer hall."

"I hear you're leaving tomorrow, is that true?" I asked.

"Yes, we are. That's why we're celebrating."

"Do you know where you are going?"

"I'm not sure. I hear it may be Austria. With the Americans approaching, we know we have to move somewhere. The American bombers have now found the Middlewerk tunnels and we are so close that Bleicherode might be bombed next. We have much to discuss, Hans. Let's get out of here. You can sleep in my room tonight. But first we've got to get you cleaned up." Karl pinched his nose. "What the hell have you been rolling in anyway?"

"Would you believe dead men?"

Karl shook his head. "Let's get out of here. Tomorrow, I'll get you on the train with us somehow."

We were up before dawn. Since Karl and I were about the same size, he gave me clothes to wear on the trip. Thankfully, I was able to discard the tattered, smelly ones I had been wearing.

"Hang on to me and act like you're drunk," Karl said. "When they ask for identification, let me do the talking." A large crowd of men lined up at the door of each car. Guards were checking identification. Our guard was just a youngster, no older than sixteen or seventeen. After checking Karl's, he held up his hand for my pass.

"You can't board without a pass," he said as we attempted to board.

"My God, man. Can't you see my friend is sick! He got robbed last night here in Bleicherode." At that moment, an American observation plane swooped low over the station. The couple of half-hearted pistol shots from SS soldiers were more symbolic than serious.

"Hurry up, up there!" someone shouted from the rear.

"You'll be the next one the SS will be shooting at if you hold up this train insisting on papers from my drunk friend. I told you he was robbed last night," Karl shouted at the guard. Seeing the logic of Karl's words, the guard stepped aside for us to pass. About two hundred rocket scientists finished boarding the train before daylight. We rumbled down the track to some undisclosed destination. Along the way, Karl told me what to say if interrogated. About an hour into the trip, we heard the unmistakable roar of fighter planes. Looking out the windows we could see the wide white stripes painted on the wings and knew they were enemy aircraft. That was a reasonable assumption anyway. I hadn't seen a German fighter plane in weeks. Three P-51 fighters with belly-tanks made a single pass and peppered the train with 50 caliber bullets. Everyone hit the floor. Several cars were hit. Only two windows were shattered in our car and no one was injured. The Mustangs must have had another destination because they flew away without making a second pass. Karl explained that trains moving during daylight hours were prime targets for the American planes.

With air superiority since early 1944, the Americans could pick and chose targets as they pleased.

"Since ours is clearly a passenger train and in retreat, we probably were considered unimportant. I guess they didn't know the train is filled with the best rocket scientists in the world," Karl said.

The train ride was a long one passing south through beautiful mountainous country. It was a part of Germany that I had never seen. Without a map, I didn't know where we were. But eventually it became obvious that we were in the Bavarian Alps. The train slowed as we wove back and forth between snow-covered mountains. Our engine strained as it climbed. Soon deep snow was all around us. The air was sweet and clean. I'd never seen any place quite so lovely and unspoiled. The war seemed far away. I shuttered to think that this and the rest of our country would soon be in the hands of our enemies.

We finally stopped and unloaded in the village of Oberammergau, still in Germany but only a few kilometers from the Austrian border. We were escorted to the Hotel Wittelsbach, right on the main street, only 500 meters from the rail station. It had forty-six rooms. The higher-ranking officials got private rooms some with balconies. The rest of us were four or five to a room. Some of the other scientists asked questions about the man they didn't recognize. Karl was able to cover for me. Luckily, most of von Braun's men had survival on their minds and had little time to worry about a stranger.

The view was spectacular from every window. The hotel lounge had a very high ceiling. A chandelier-hung restaurant was where we took our meals. Although the old hotel was luxurious by any standard and the staff was pleasant, it was surrounded by barbwire and was heavily guarded. We were prisoners of the SS. It was a strange feeling. Since we were forbidden to leave the hotel grounds, we spent many hours in the ground floor dining room talking and looking out at the snow covered mountains. Large front windows offered a spectacular view.

During our time in Oberammergau, Karl and I caught up on what had happened since we were last together. We also reminisced about our days back in Berlin. On campus at the Berlin Institute, Gleichshaltung (bringing citizens in line with Nazi beliefs) was not rigidly enforced. But on those days when we strolled around Tiergarten Park, we had to be careful to give Hiltergruss (the Hitler salute) if we met a soldier, otherwise, we might get arrested. But we freely sang Deutschland uber Alles (the national anthem) whenever the opportunity presented itself.

Karl told me of his development work on V1 and V2 rockets. He seemed very proud of the progress they had made. He then asked about my work at the Volkswagen plant.

"I really didn't have much time for development work, Karl," I said. "The closest I came to automotive engineering was solving problems that saboteurs caused on the Kubelwagen."

"When we were roommates I remember you telling about your development work on a zinc-air battery? Have you done any more on that concept? What was the principle there, anyway?"

"You may remember that I was working with Professor Kurt Gottmann on advanced battery concepts. We discovered that under certain conditions, the electrolyte in a battery can covert gasses from the air into electrical energy. This was possible when we added zinc particles to a solution of potassium hydroxide. The resultant battery recharged itself but it was highly sensitive to moisture. In time, I hoped the organic electrolyte that I added might evolve and help solve the moisture problem." Karl leaned forward.

"Organic electrolyte? What are you talking about?"

"At the institute, I found in my study of microbiology that the mutation rate of some living organisms was far faster than others. My microbiology professor said that he had gotten certain microbes to mutate and evolve a thousand times faster than other microbes. He even gave me a copy of his research detailing how the fast-mutating microbes could be grown. He warned me that he didn't know how to control the speed of mutation or what would happen if the microbes became adaptive enough to change form. I'm glad I memorized the critical steps of the process because I lost that paper during my escape from Wolfsburg."

Karl frowned and rubbed his chin. "That's an exciting theory, but how does it relate to the zinc-air battery?"

"Well, it may sound strange, but I believe that just as evolution has improved higher animals' ability to solve problems relating to survival, a battery might solve its own problems if fast-mutating microbes were introduced into the electrolyte. Millions of years of mutations might possibly be compressed into months. After all, microbes are living beings. Who's to say given millions of mutations, they wouldn't develop sufficient intelligence to solve the moisture problem? Surely reasoning can exist in a form other than a brain."

"Hans, that's a fascinating concept and if it works it won't be limited to batteries. My God, man, this could be a major scientific breakthrough. But what makes you think it can work as you hope?"

"Well, I found that the introduction of a tiny bit of moisture speeded the mutation process. But too much stopped the mutation. So it stands to reason that the microbes are using the moisture to survive." Karl scratched his head and raised his eyebrows.

"If the microbes get smart enough to solve the moisture problem in the battery, perhaps they could continue to evolve and have other useful functions."

"That's what I'm hoping," I said.

* * * * * * * * * *

The Americans and British continued to advance. The BBC reported that they had captured the Volkswagen plant at Wolfsburg as well as the underground plant and tunnels at Mittelwerk near Nordshausen. Although not specifically mentioned, the village of Bleicherode was surely captured too, it being so close to Mittelwerk. The biggest news was that Berlin fell to the Russians and Hitler was dead. But the war was not over. We were still prisoners of our own army. Our guards knew the situation was hopeless, yet they obeyed their previous orders to hold us. Finally, at von Braun's urging, the guards agreed to let us go into town, which meant for all practical purposes, we were free. Still, we worried that the advancing Americans might shoot us if our guards didn't surrender.

Since his brother Magnus could speak a little English, von Braun sent him over to the American lines to surrender. About one hundred of us milled around the heart of the village. There was nothing to do but wait. The weather had moderated a bit so standing outside was not unpleasant. Not knowing what to expect, everyone seemed tense. Smokers smoked and there was little talk. Karl and I stood like statues awaiting Magnus' return. After about an hour, we heard vehicles approaching. A U.S. Army Jeep with a 30-caliber machine gun mounted behind the front seats led the convoy. Magnus sat on the bonnet pointing the way. A soldier swung the gun around and pointed it in our direction. Were we about to be shot? An American captain wearing camouflage and a steel helmet swung his muddy combat boots out and was on the ground even before the Jeep had stopped.

"Doctor Werner von Braun!" he shouted in a loud commanding voice. von Braun with his left arm held horizontal by a huge cast, stepped forward and with the help of his brother negotiated our surrender. I couldn't hear the details but we soon were ordered to retrieve our belongings and climb aboard one of the ten 2 1/2 ton Studebaker trucks that were behind the

Jeep. We traveled the winding little road to the near-by town of Reutte, Austria. All during this ordeal, I stayed close to Karl and out of von Braun's sight.

To our relief, the Americans treated us well. The food was good and our beds clean. Best of all I got my first good look at a Willys Jeep. I was very impressed with the simplicity and utility of the design. It made our Kubelwagen look rather primitive by comparison.

Karl and I decided from that point forward to speak only English in private. After several days of interrogation, we were sent to England and put aboard the Queen Mary. The ship had been converted to a troop carrier early in the war and was now taking U.S. soldiers home. The boat was so crowded; I wondered how it could still float. Laughing soldiers scuffled and played games to pass the time. Almost everyone was joyful and smiling. Why wouldn't they be? They had won the war and were going home. We Germans were kept in a special section in the bow of the boat. With an escort, we were allowed to go up on deck for a couple of hours every day.

CHAPTER 3

After we arrived in New York, we were immediately loaded in C-47s and flown to Ft. Bliss, Texas with stops in St. Louis and Dallas. This was my first airplane ride and I must admit, I was a bit apprehensive. I was surprised how bumpy the trip was. Passing through clouds was particularly rough. I was told this was the same aircraft that was originally designed as a commercial passenger plane, the DC-3. At Ft. Bliss, American Army officers and scientists interrogated us separately and in groups. Karl and I stayed together most of the time. During the interrogations, I claimed not to speak English. That way I didn't have to answer as many questions. We were then loaded on buses and sent over to White Sands, New Mexico where we were again questioned on every subject imaginable. I was afraid it would be discovered that I was not a rocket scientist and would be sent back to Germany. But somehow, I was able to use enough engineering terms to bluff my way through. My first impression of White Sands was the heat. I had never experienced such.

Karl and I were roommates at White Sands but he was gone much of the time. Although I enjoyed working with Karl, I spent my free time alone, listening to the radio and practicing my "American" English. I considered my chances of getting to Detroit to work in the automotive design field almost impossible at that point. I had little American money, no social security card, no driver's license, no U.S. citizenship papers and little knowledge of American ways. Yet I had a strong urge to design cars, particularly small inexpensive ones and after the war America was the place to be. I read everything I could about the U.S. auto industry and subscribed to *Automotive News*. Karl understood my obsession and advised me to pursue my dreams even if my chances for success looked slim. I suspected he also wanted me out of his room so his new American girl friend could stay overnight. She was a secretary to one of the American scientists and lived on base.

I dreamed and schemed and evaluated alternative plans for my future. I knew that Americans were much more affluent than Germans, especially after the war, and would not be the largest market for a simple, small, inexpensive car. But all U.S. auto manufacturers exported cars worldwide didn't they? In the developing countries, my car would be like the Ford Model T was when it was introduced in America. Only my new "people's car" would be much more advanced yet still simple and low-cost. Germany and many countries around the world needed the car I wanted to develop. And later, if gasoline prices rose, Americans might want to buy an economy car. Since Studebaker seemed to be the most innovative in design, they would be my first choice of American car companies. The '39 Champion was certainly impressive compared to other American cars, although it was bigger and more complicated than the car I envisioned. Maybe I could even develop my zinc-air battery at Studebaker. I could dream, couldn't I?

In order to sound more American, I listened to the six o'clock news daily and practiced mimicking the accent of Edward R. Morrow. Since so many of our civilian workers were from nearby El Paso, I also tried to speak "Texan."

Not being an American citizen among other problems kept me from leaving White Sands and traveling freely across the U.S. Outside that fence, I would be an illegal alien-maybe even a German spy. And like the others, I signed a contract for a year's work at White Sands. Anyway, I doubted I could get employment without a social security card and other identification. It had been hinted that we might be given U.S. citizenship in about five years if all went well. I couldn't wait that long.

In the past, when passing Dr. von Braun in the hall, I avoided eye contact. But one morning in the spring of '46, we collided when he was reading some documents on his way to the men's room.

"Es tut mir leid (I'm sorry, sir)," I said in my most respectful German.

"Sprechen sie Englisch?" he asked.

"Ja, I mean yes. I forgot, sir. Sorry."

"What department do you work in?"

"Guidance Systems, sir. I'm Karl Heinz's assistant." He frowned and looked suspicious.

"I don't remember you at Pennemunde. Were you there?"

"Yes, sir."

"What building?" he asked.

"I don't remember, sir." He studied my nametag. He wrote something and walked away. I knew I had been discovered. As soon as my shift was over, I left the laboratory and hurried back to our room. I was sitting at the kitchen table drinking a Lone Star and wondering what to do when Karl walked in. When I told him what had happened, he slammed his fist down on the table and shouted.

"Goddammit, Hans. You have not only gotten yourself in trouble but me as well. You're going to get us both sent back to Germany."

"I'm sorry, Karl," I said. "I've caused you enough trouble already. You have done so much for me. If you'll grant me just one more favor, I'll never ask for another. Loan me fifty dollars and I'll leave tonight."

"Where will you go? How will you survive?"

"I don't know, but if I stay here, they'll send me back to Germany. I have no family or prospects for work there since the Volkswagen plant is in ruins. My dream is to go to Detroit or South Bend and design cars. I know it's a long shot, but I'm determined. Wish me luck and loan me fifty bucks, please." Karl looked at his shoes and shook his head. His long black hair fell across his face. He looked at me as if I were a stranger.

He stood silently for a few moments and then said, "O.K., Hans. Lucky I got paid today. Here, consider this a going-away present." I took the money and shook his hand. I packed my handbag, signed out at the guardhouse and boarded the shuttle bus into Alamogorda, the nearest town. We were allowed that privilege but were required to be back before midnight. At the Greyhound Bus station, I got a copy of their schedule. The next bus to leave was headed for El Paso and then on to Ft. Worth, Texas. I bought a ticket and climbed aboard. Figuring the authorities would soon be searching for me, I felt lucky to have gotten out of the front gate without being detained.

The bus rumbled along through the night. I tried to sleep but couldn't. There was just too much on my mind. I felt alone and helpless. Thinking positive didn't work. The bus made short stops in El Paso, Pecos, Odessa, Midland and Abilene. Texas is a big state. I stared out the window into the lonely night. The only light was from an overcast quarter moon. On and on we traveled. I finally made friends with the drone on the bus engine, sleeping and dreaming of South Bend.

"We're in Ft. Worth, Texas, folks," the driver announced. "Everybody gets out here!" I grabbed my handbag and headed to the men's room. It was already turning daylight. After washing my face and combing my hair, I walked through the waiting room toward the front door. In one of the empty seats I spotted a Ft. Worth *Star Telegram*. The date on the front page was April 2, 1946. I picked up the day-old paper and headed for a nearby coffee shop. The cool morning air smelled especially refreshing compared to the fumes of the Greyhound station. My cup of strong hot coffee smelled even better. The paper told the same old stories: strikes, problems with the Russian occupation forces in East Germany, unemployment and

President Harry Truman's falling popularity. The comic section was a bit more entertaining; Mutt and Jeff fell into a swimming pool, Wimpy ate six hamburgers, Dagwood made a foot-tall sandwich while sleepwalking and Popeye saved Olive Oil from the clutches of that evil, Blutto.

For some strange reason I scanned the obituary section. One death notice caught my eye.

> HOFFMANN, Van J., 26 years old, victim of a tragic accident on Jacksboro Highway yesterday morning. Young Mr. Hoffmann was a recent graduate of the University of Texas in Austin with a Masters Degree in Mechanical Engineering. He is survived by his parents, George and Stella Hoffmann of Richland Hills and a younger sister, Janet, a student at Texas Christian University. Visitation will be tomorrow from 4 to 6 p.m. at the Haltom City Funeral Home at the corner of 28th and Belknap. Burial will be 11 a.m., April 4th at Trinity Cemetery on Camp Bowie Boulevard.

I tore the death notice from the paper and stuffed it in my pocket. The coffee shop waitress gave me directions to the city bus terminal. Luckily, it was only five blocks away. When I got there, I studied the bus route map and found Belknap. I boarded a bus marked Belknap N.E. and paid my fare. It was a little after noon when I saw the 28th Street sign ahead. I pulled the buzzer cord and got off. There it was, the Haltom City Funeral Home. I dug in my bag and fished out my cleanest shirt. I changed right there on the street in the blazing Texas sun. People in passing cars stared. I hid my bag under a nearby bush.

The funeral home lobby was cold. Back at White Sands I was told that movie theatres and funeral homes were the first to get refrigeration air conditioners. Evaporation units had been popular in hot dry climates for years, but these new refrigerant units could really cool you off. In Germany, we didn't have this scorching heat problem.

"I'm Franz Buckner," I said to the receptionist. "And a very close friend of Van Hoffmann. I'm aware that visitation is from four to six today, but I have to work until six thirty. Also, tomorrow I have to work and my boss won't let me off to go to the funeral. I was just wondering if there's any way I could say goodbye to Van while I'm here. I know I'm not dressed properly, but I think Van would understand. I have to be back at work soon."

"What was your name again? I'll need to check with the family to see if it's all right."

"My name is Franz Buckner, but I'd sure hate for you to bother George or Stella at this sad time, them having just lost their only son. I won't stay long, please, let me see Van?" The lady sat for a few moments and then rose and motioned for me to follow. She opened the door to one of the rooms and there was a coffin on a stand surrounded by flowers. She lifted the lid to reveal Van J. Hoffmann. She walked back to the doorway and stood there, waiting. Van was a good-looking boy. He had auburn hair and a clean-shaven face, very smooth and unblemished. Although a few pounds heavier, he looked a little like me. I suspected his face was torn up in the accident and had been reconstructed. It didn't look natural. It was waxy and shiny. I put my face close to his and whispered the pledge to the American flag. I had been memorizing it all week. I then recited the multiplication tables from eight to eighteen. I rubbed my eyes hard then turned and walked quickly to the door with my face in my hands. As I passed, the lady put her hand on my shoulder and patted.

"Thank you so much," I said with a whimper. "He looks so natural. I'll remember him like that always. Since I won't be able to see George and Stella this afternoon or tomorrow, I want to write them a personal letter to offer my condolences. Do you have their address handy?"

"Sure, just a moment." She wrote the address on the back of a Haltom City Funeral Home card and handed it to me. I thanked her again and stepped back out into the hot Texas sun. I took another look at the death notice torn from the *Star Telegram*. Without a map, I didn't know exactly where I was. I grabbed my bag and walked north for a few blocks until I happened upon a small grocery store.

"What can I get to eat for fifty cents?" I asked. A quarter's worth of baloney and a quarter's worth of cheese," the proprietor said. I nodded O.K. Without hesitation, the old man in a dingy white apron cut off three thick slices of the pungent red loaf on a foot square sheet of wax paper. He then took the cover off of his cheddar block and cut three more sizable slices. He didn't bother to weigh either.

"The crackers are in that there barrel, son. Help yeself," he said and pointed me in the direction of the cracker barrel. I took out exactly twelve large squares. The old man looked at me disapprovingly but said nothing. An electric fan blew across a rocking chair near the door. I figured that would be a good place to have my lunch/supper.

"Whoa! That there's my cheer," he said.

"Oh, sorry," I said and sat on a Coca-Cola case also near the door. I munched on my bologna and cheese and finally asked, "How far is Richland Hills from here?"

"Oh, not far, maybe a mile or two. That there's a ritzy section of town, son, mostly German decent. You know somebody living there?"

"No, sir. I just thought I might pick up some grass-cutting jobs or something up there.

"Well, maybe. Where you from anyhow? You don't talk like nobody from 'round here." I pointed at my mouth full of baloney and didn't answer. I finished my food, wiped my mouth and started walking toward 1525 Highland Street in the Richland Hills community. By the time I found the house, it was getting dark. The temperature had dropped to what I estimated to be about eighty degrees Fahrenheit. I walked up and down the street watching the Hoffmann house. During the next hour, a cavalcade of cars unloaded dozens of visitors. I had plenty of time to think about what I planned to do. Surely Van Hoffmann's personal papers were somewhere in that house. All I had to do was to sneak inside and find them. I figured the best time to do that was when the family was at the funeral the next day. I found an overgrown vacant lot nearby and prepared to spend the night. I didn't sleep much. The ground was hard and the mosquitoes plentiful.

By morning, I was itching and scratching like never before. Sleeping on the bare ground in a dry thicket was an open invitation to every insect in Texas. I was hungry and in need of coffee but I tried not to think about it. All I could do at that point was watch and wait. At ten o'clock, a new 1946 Buick Roadmaster sedan pulled out of the driveway. There was a man driving, a woman beside him and a young lady in the back seat. When the car was out of sight, I hid my bag in the woods and walked around to an alley behind the house. I first tried the two back doors. Both were locked. All downstairs windows were locked too. I noticed that all the upstairs windows were open. I climbed up a pine tree that was only about four feet from one of the upstairs windows. Near the top, I rocked and leaned until the tree bent enough for me to reach the window. I tried to remove the screen but it wouldn't budge. I remembered my comb. Hooking it into an edge of the screen, I ripped a gash large enough for me to pass through. Once inside, I went from room to room, opening drawers, looking for Van's papers. I had never been inside an American home before. By the expensive furnishings, I guessed the Hoffmanns were wealthy. I tried to replace everything that I moved so as not to alert the family of my visit. Of course, the torn screen was a dead giveaway. I searched and searched until I opened a desk drawer in the downstairs study. Then I found a brown envelope labeled "Van's papers." Inside dozens of papers including college records and various award certificates. Tucked in the back of the stack was what I was looking for. I took Van's birth certificate, social security card and driver's license, replaced the envelope and started back upstairs. I glanced out a front window and saw a police car parked in the street. It was empty. Did a neighbor see me or did Mr. Hoffmann ask the police to keep an eye on the house while they were at the funeral? I ran upstairs hoping to somehow disguise the tear in the screen before the officers saw it. Peeping beside a drape in another room, I saw two policemen. One was pointing at the broken screen. One officer left, the other remained. I ran downstairs again and looked out the front window. The officer was using his car radio. My heart beat fast. I envisioned myself inside a Ft. Worth jail. That would surely lead to deportation. Time was short. When the officer got out of the car and walked back around the house, I walked out the front door, closing it quietly and then quickly walked across the street. I noticed a neighbor, two doors down was standing on his porch. I presumed he was curious about the police car or maybe he was the one that called them. When he saw me, he stared yelling and running toward the Hoffmann's house. I ran to the lot where I had spent the previous night and retrieved my bag. I ran through alleys and back streets, knowing the area would soon be swarming with police. I finally made my way back to Belknap Street. Sirens wailed in the distance. At Belknap, I stayed out of sight until a bus approached. I flagged it down and rode it back to downtown Ft. Worth.

Getting out of Ft. Worth was a high priority. I was sure the authorities at Whites Sands had found out about my bus ticket to Ft. Worth. The Ft. Worth police probably talked to the Hoffmann family and searched their house for clues. The neighbor who saw me leave the house would have described me to the police. The lady at the funeral home certainly told the Hoffmanns about the visit of Van's close friend, Franz Buckner, whom they never heard of. With her description of Franz, the police would surely suspect that I was also the burglar.

I walked the five blocks to the Greyhound station trying to blend in and not look suspicious. A police car was parked just outside the station. I watched from across the street. After a few minutes a uniformed officer came out of the station and got into the car. The car's siren screamed as it sped away. I approached the counter to purchase a ticket on the next bus to Dallas. The agent starred at me as I paid him. I wondered if the police would be waiting for me in Dallas.

The trip to Dallas seemed longer than the scheduled sixty minutes. The physical and mental stress of the day had drained me of energy. What I needed most was a good meal, a bath and a good night's sleep. Without money, where was I to get those precious things? I left the Dallas Greyhound station and looked in both directions. No police were in sight. I felt a certain amount of relief. Night was falling. Scarecrow-like men in dirty clothes gathered on a nearby corner. They passed a sack-covered bottle between them. Where do these men sleep? How do they eat? How do they bathe? Maybe they don't. I watched for a while and then like birds going to roost, they all started to move in the same general direction. Being unfamiliar with the ways of American poor people, I followed. After a couple of blocks, I saw the attraction that was drawing these unfortunates, The Dallas Union Rescue Mission. Although I felt completely out of place, I followed the odorous mob getting in line at the door. One man who was too drunk was turned away. He hurled curses and threats at the doorman before rejoining the crowd at the end of the line. I was allowed to come in. I was also able to take a shower before the hot meal was served. How different was the life of these men and that of the Hoffmann's. Using my handbag as a pillow, I slept soundly that night except when a poor soul who was having an alcoholic nightmare screamed and woke me.

The next morning, I was surprised to find out how easy it was to get a job in Dallas. The first restaurant I went in gave me a job washing dishes and only asked for my name. I said it was Van Hoffmann in case they asked for I.D. They paid me in cash. It wasn't much, but I was able to save almost all of all. The place was called Big D Steaks and Chops. The best part of the job was the food left over from the dinner crowd. While I worked at the Big D, I alternated between sleeping at the mission and in a wooded area down on the banks of the Trinity River. I preferred sleeping in the open but if it was raining or I needed a bath, I went to the mission. I kept that job for ten days. I then had enough money for a bus ticket to Chicago.

On the morning of April 16, 1946, I boarded a Greyhound for Chicago, Illinois, with intermediate stops in Little Rock, Arkansas, Memphis, Tennessee, St. Louis, Missouri, and Springfield, Illinois. It was a long tiresome trip but fortunately the weather was good and I got to see just how vast the United States is. I was surprised at the size of the farms. They were much larger than in Germany.

I didn't have the money or energy to do any sightseeing in Chicago. When I walked outside, the hot wind off Lake Michigan almost knocked me down. Even though I was sick of riding a bus, with what little money I had left, I bought a knockwurst and a ticket over to South Bend, Indiana. As we neared the city, a billboard announced South Bend , home of the Notre Dame's Fighting Irish.

It seemed to me all Greyhound Stations were the same. They were smoky and not very clean. As a result, when I stepped off the bus at the South Bend terminal, it was my hope that I'd never have to travel by bus again. The streets of South Bend were quiet, almost lonely. I saw buildings of several stories but there were few people outside.

"Hey Buddy, could you spare some loose change for a fellow down on his luck?" I looked around to see a thin beggar with his grubby hand outstretched in my direction. He reminded me of those slaves in the tunnels at Mittelwerks. Thinking of them brought back memories of that night in the back of an army truck full of dead men. Knowing my total wealth was a little under four dollars, I shook my head and walked away. "God bless," he slurred.

I walked the streets at random and eventually came upon a factory complex of very old buildings. Rusting automobile frames were stacked on open gravel lots. Workers carrying steel tool boxes walked in and out of one of the buildings. A flatbed Studebaker truck slowly backed up to a huge sliding door. What appeared to be a large punch press was on the truck's bed. Two men in dingy coveralls directed the driver. I soon realized that this was part of the Studebaker Corporation, hopefully, my future employer. Was this real? Had I finally made it to Studebaker? But, I must admit, I was a bit disappointed. From what I saw, the buildings looked little better than the bombed out Volkswagen factory I had left six months earlier.

"So this is Studebaker," I said to one of the overweight workers. He ignored me. "What does a cheap hotel room cost in this town?" I asked. He pointed to a side street. "Try the LaSalle 'bout three blocks down that way. I think their rooms start at two bucks, or a dollar an hour," he said with a chuckle.

"Thanks mister. Has Studebaker started back making cars yet?"

"Yep. They dusted off the old '42 for a while and called it a '46. But they shut the production lines down last week to get ready for the '47 model. That's what these tools are for."

"They hiring any new workers or do you know?" I asked.

"They laid off most of the workers when they shut the '46 down. So they'll call them back first when they start the '47. Why? You lookin' for a job?"

"Yes, I am. Where is the employment office?" He pointed to the four story brick less than a block away.

"That's the Admin Building. Check over there in the morning. Now if you'll excuse me, bub, you're cuttin' into my break time." He lit a cigarette and walked away.

"Thanks mister!" I shouted to his back.

The LaSalle Hotel lobby looked like it had been opulent many, many years ago. An elderly desk clerk looked me up and down as if to check my worthiness. After stressing my need for an inexpensive room, the surly clerk admitted they had a room for $2.00 per night. I was given the keys to room 3A. Ah, almost clean sheets, a bathtub full of hot soapy water and no worry about insect bites or smelly drunk men. It had been over two weeks since I had a decent night's sleep and I planned to take full advantage of the opportunity. I washed my dirty clothes in the bathtub and hung them around the room to dry.

I slept until about ten o'clock the next morning. After packing my clean dry clothes and checking out, I started to walk back to the Studebaker Administration Building. On the way, I passed the St. Joseph County Public Library. Since I knew little about the city and less about Studebaker history, I decided to stop in. A pretty young girl sat behind the checkout desk dutifully stuffing cards into little pockets glued to the inside back cover of books. She seemed pure and innocent. Her hair was shinny auburn and her eyes were sky blue. When one is in a library the old rule "don't judge a book by its cover" should apply, I suppose. But there was something about this girl that was irresistible. She seemed so trouble-free and unencumbered with the stresses of life.

"Pardon me," I said. "I'm new in town and want to know more about South Bend and the Studebaker Corporation. Do you have anything I might read that would help me?" Oh, what a lovely smile. Little dimples appeared on each side of her lips. Her smile reminded me just how long it had been since I had enjoyed female companionship.

"Sir, if I pulled everything we have on those two subjects, you'd have a least a year's reading to do. Could you be more specific?"

"Well yes, I suppose. Do you have any newspaper articles on recent Studebaker activities? I hope to get a job there and I need to know what my chances are."

"I can pull a couple of newspaper articles for you, but I know from talking to my father that until the new model is in production they won't be hiring many new factory workers. Do you have any special skills?"

"Yes, I'm a mechanical engineer." She raised her eyebrows and pursed her lips. I followed her over to the card catalogue file. She thumbed through the well-worn cards and pulled one out. "I could send you to the newspaper file room, but you'd waste a lot of time trying to find what you are looking for there. I remember just last week there was an article written by Roy Branson, Vice President of Engineering concerning plans for the new post-war models. I think I can find it for you."

"That sounds perfect," I said.

"If you're new in town, I guess you don't have a library card. I'll help you apply. What is your name?"

"Van J. Hoffmann."

"And your address?"

"I don't have one yet. I just got in yesterday. I stayed at the LaSalle last night. Frankly, I'm low on money, I have no job or a place to stay."

"Well, that could be a problem, Mr. Hoffmann. I can't issue you a card without an address." I stood there like a fool wondering what this nice young girl was thinking. Did I look like a vagrant? I told her I was an engineer. Did she believe me? She looked directly into my eyes as if deciding if she should trust me. "Are you willing to do manual labor for a while?" she asked.

"Sure, I'll do anything to tide me over until I can get a job at Studebaker."

"Let me call my father. I think he's home this morning. I know he's looking for someone to paint our house and those out of work Studebaker guys expect to be called back any time and besides, they want to be paid the same wages as the plant."

"If your dad will feed me and give me a place to stay, I'll paint his house for nothing. By the way, what is your name?"

"Mary Burgdorf." She handed me the paper with the news article written by Roy Branson and directed me to a table where I could read. As soon as I was out of earshot, she picked up the phone. After about five minutes, she walked over to my table. "If you can stay here a few minutes, my father is free right now and wants to come by and talk to you."

"That's very nice of you," I said. "I'll be right here reading this article. Thanks, Miss Burgdorf." She smiled and went back to her work. It was less than fifteen minutes when a neatly dressed man who I guessed to be in his forties walked in. He was tall with thinning hair and a bit heavy around the waistline. He walked over to Mary's desk and gave her a kiss on the cheek. She pointed in my direction.

"Van Hoffmann?"

"Yes, sir." I stood and accepted his firm handshake. He motioned for me to sit.

"My daughter tells me you are an engineer and are hoping to secure a job at Studebaker."

"Yes, sir, that's true. But that might take a while and I'm short of money and have no place to stay."

"I see. Where did you get your engineering degree?"

"University of Texas in Austin, sir. I have a masters degree."

"What's the name of the University of Texas football team?" I hesitated. I could make up something, but he probably knew the answer.

"I don't know, sir. I was always too busy studying to follow sports."

"Even so, how could you go to a school four or five years and not know the name of their football team?" I didn't answer. "I have some friends from Texas and you don't sound much like a Texan."

"Well, my family is of German decent. We only immigrated to America in 1932. I was twelve at the time, so I suppose I still have an accent." Mr. Burgdorf took a 3x5 card out of his shirt pocket.

"Tell me this, Mr. Hoffmann, what are the Fahrenheit equivalents of zero and one hundred degrees Celsius?"

"At sea level, thirty-two and two hundred twelve degrees, the freezing and boiling points of water."

"O.K. What is the square root of 256?"

"Sixteen," I quickly answered.

"And what is 16 times 18?"

"Two hundred and eighty-eight, sir." Luckily, I excelled in mathematics, but I hoped his questions didn't get any harder.

"In a right triangle, what is the cosign of an angle?"

"The adjacent side divided by the hypotenuse."

"What is Ohm's law?"

"Ohm's law defines the relationship between power, voltage, current and resistance. There are several combinations of the formula, examples are; ohms equal volts divided by amperes and watts equal volts times amps."

"You are a very quick and clever young man, but one thing bothers me. How come you have no money?"

"To be honest, sir, I left home rather suddenly. I have an alcoholic father who has disowned me. He says as far as he is concerned, I'm dead. I'm sorry to burden you with my family problems, sir, but that's why I'm broke. I barely had enough money to get here."

"May I see some identification?" I reached in my pocket.

"Yes, sir. Here's my social security card and Texas driver's license." He studied each carefully and then looked at me. He appeared to be in deep thought.

"Says here you weigh 165 pounds. Have you lost some weight?"

"Yes, sir. About 15 pounds."

"Ever done any painting?" I nodded. "Well, I tell you what, I'm gonna take a chance on you, son. Come with me and I'll get you started on the house-painting job this afternoon. It's a big house and will probably take several days. We will provide your meals and you can sleep in the garage. I'll pay you three dollars a day if you're doing a good job. You still interested, Mr. Hoffmann?"

"Yes, sir! Very interested. I'm ready when you are and you can call me Van."

"Alright, Van. You can call me Mr. Burgdorf," he said with a smile. He stood and waved at his daughter. "See you for supper, Sweetheart." I fanaticized that someday I'd be able to say the same thing to Mary.

CHAPTER 4

At about three o'clock, Mrs. Burgdorf brought me a ham and cheese sandwich and a tall cold glass of milk. It was delicious and I was hungry. This was my first experience with a real American family. All the Americans I had met up to that time were only casual acquaintances, soldiers, scientists or trades people. But this was a real family, normal and genuine. I liked what I saw. But I felt a little guilty lying to them about who I was. I knew it was necessary if I was to continue in the field of automotive engineering. Besides, what would they think if they knew I was an alien who had stolen a dead man's identification papers?

The Burgdorf's house was in a very nice section of South Bend and was as luxurious as anything in the neighborhood. The two-car garage where I slept even had a small room with toilet and sink. This allowed me to stay reasonably clean and made it unnecessary to bother the family to use their facilities. The first day's painting went well and at precisely six o'clock Mrs. Burgdorf brought my dinner tray. It held a huge bowl of steaming beef stew and several sticks of corn bread. I hoped that eventually Mary would bring my tray.

"I'll pick up your tray in the morning at 6:30 when I bring your breakfast," Mrs. Burgdorf said.

"Danker schon, I mean thank you. I hope I'm not too much trouble."

"Oh, no, not at all. I have to fix Mary and George's meals anyway. One more is no problem."

The next morning, it was Mr. Burgdorf who delivered the tray at precisely 6:30 a.m. I was already dressed and was outside getting ready to paint.

"Good morning, Van. Here is your breakfast. Looks like the painting is coming along well. Any problems?"

"No, sir. But one thing does concern me. I was wondering how I might get by the Studebaker employment office to fill out an application."

"My commercial real estate business takes me to that neighborhood quite often. I can pick up an application for you today if you'd like."

"Thank you, sir. That's very kind of you. And thanks again for giving me the opportunity to get back on my feet. I realize you know very little about me."

"Oh, in my business, Van, you have to be a good judge of character. At first, I wondered about your accent and the fact that you were broke, but you seem like an honest fellow. I'm not worried." If he only knew, I thought.

That afternoon at six o'clock when Mrs. Burgdorf delivered my dinner, there was an envelope on the tray. It contained a Studebaker employment application. I was surprised and pleased to see in the "references" section; the name of George Burgdorf and his address was already filled in. It seemed unusual that he would give his name as a reference when he hardly knew me. About an hour later, Mr. Burgdorf came out to the garage.

"Van, after breakfast in the morning, if you'd like, you can ride into town with me and deliver your application to the Studebaker employment office in person."

"Well, that's wonderful, sir, but I've got about one more day's work before I finish the house."

"That's alright," he said. "It'll be here when you get back.

When we arrived at the employment office, Mr. Burgdorf walked in with me.

"Hi ya, George. Haven't seen you since yesterday," the man at the front desk said with a chuckle.

"Good morning, Hamilton. Ham, this is Mr. Van Hoffmann, the young mechanical engineer I was telling you about. Van, this is Mr. Hamilton Majors, interviewer for salaried positions here at Studebaker." I shook hands with Mr. Majors, handed him my application and waited for instructions.

"Come around and have a seat, Mr. Hoffmann." I was seated in a straight-back wooden chair with cracked leather upholstery. It was well worn, as was everything in the office. "Let's see, it says here that you have a master's degree from the University of Texas at Austin but no business experience. Can you obtain a copy of your transcript for our files?"

"Yes, sir. It may take a few days."

"In the 'position wanted section' it says you are looking for a job in vehicle design engineering. Our body design and styling here at Studebaker is done by Raymond Loewy Associates of New York City, so they hire their own designers. However, all engineering comes under the direction of Roy Branson, our Vice President of Engineering. I know that Mr.

Branson's Industrial Engineering Department has an opening for a time study man. But with a masters degree you may be a little over qualified."

"That's not a problem, sir," I broke in. "I'll take it. I'm willing to work my way up." As soon as the words left my mouth, I realized that I was coming across as overanxious.

"Not so fast, son. You'll need to be interviewed by the department manager, Mr. Benny Goodall before we can even consider making you an offer. Let me call him and see when he'll be available." Mr. Majors spun around in his ancient wooden swivel chair. It groaned under his considerable weight. With his back to me, he told the operator to ring Mr. Goodall. I looked around to see Mr. Burgdorf. He smiled and stuck his thumb skyward.

"Mr. Goodall can be here in about fifteen minutes. Can you wait?" I again looked at Mr. Burgdorf and he nodded.

"Of course," I replied. Majors and Burgdorf chatted as if they were old friends. I felt that everything was moving in a positive direction. But how to get a copy of Van Hoffmann's transcript was dominating my thoughts. I wondered if the university was aware of Van's untimely death. Even though the university is in Austin and Van was from Ft. Worth, a request for his transcript for employment might raise red flags. It would be taking a big chance for me to reveal that "Van Hoffmann" was in South Bend. Suppose Van's parents had discovered his social security card and driver's license missing and then found out someone in Indiana was using his name to apply for a job? I would be in big trouble! I could be deported. I couldn't take the chance. But what if my employment depended on the transcript? My thoughts were interrupted when a short stocky man exploded through the front door like he was escaping a fire.

"Where's the time study guy, Ham? I could use him today!"

"Benny, this is Van Hoffmann. You want to talk to him?"

"I didn't come runnin' all the way over here just to see your ugly puss."

"Oh, Benny, when are you ever gonna be nice to me?"

"I'll be nice to you when you send me some qualified people. Up to now it's been mostly 'nit-wits'." Mr. Majors smiled and shook his head. Goodall shook my hand motioned for me to follow him over to a bench near the front door. Goodall asked me many questions about production problems, but few theoretical questions. A person without manufacturing experience could not have answered his questions. As an example, he asked me to list the pros and cons of using outside parts vendors. I was able to discuss vendor quality, costs, and scheduling and reliability considerations to his satisfaction. Fortunately, I had gained much knowledge and a good practical background at the Volkswagen plant in Wolfsburg. "How do you know so much about automotive manufacturing, Hoffmann? They don't teach you that stuff in school, do they?" Goodall asked.

"Much of it is just common sense. And back before the war, my dad took me on some plant tours in Detroit. I love automotive manufacturing. I read all I can about the subject."

"You're from Texas huh? You don't talk much like them cowboys down there. What gives?"

"My family is of German decent and I spent my childhood in Germany."

"Interesting! In your opinion, Mr. Hoffmann, what would you say is the biggest problem in automotive manufacturing today?"

"Labor unions," I replied.

"Whoa! Careful, son. Not so loud. Anti-union talk can get you fired here and you're not even hired yet. Not that I disagree, but you gotta be real careful what you say. But, if you can keep you mouth shut, you and I are gonna get along just fine. As far as I'm concerned, you're as good as hired." He shook my hand and escorted me back to Mr. Major's desk. "Sign him up, Ham. You finally got me a man I can use."

"Well, that was fast. Don't you want to see his application?"

"No, that's O.K. Can you start Monday, Mr. Hoffmann?" Goodall asked.

"Hey! Wait a minute, Benny," Majors said. "I'm the one who hires salaried people at Studebaker." Majors handed me a sheet of paper with the salary printed on it. He then said, "Can you start Monday, Mr. Hoffmann?" Everyone laughed and we all shook hands again.

"I'll see you at 8 a.m. Monday morning right here in this office. Don't be late," Benny Goodall said before he stormed out the front door.

I knew that Mr. Burgdorf was a busy man and yet he sat patiently waiting for me to be interviewed and for Mr. Majors gave me my badge and company booklet.

Finally, Mr. Majors smiled and said, "I think Benny likes you, Hoffmann, and that's unusual. Good luck. Don't forget to get me a copy of your university transcript for my records as soon as you can. See you Monday."

As soon as we were back in the car, Mr. Burgdorf turned to me and said, "Congratulations, Van. I've never seen anyone hired so quickly at Studebaker."

"It wouldn't have happened without your help, sir. I'll be forever grateful." I continued to wonder why he was taking so much interest in me.

"Now we'll need to find you a room close by so you can walk to work," he said. "I know a little boarding house over on West Sample Street that's within easy walking distance." Four blocks away, we stopped in front of a large two-story frame house. It needed a bit of paint and the front porch had some loose planks, but it looked clean enough and the landlady, Mrs. Kirchall, seemed nice. Mr. Burgdorf's recommendation was enough for her to waive any advance or deposit. Since it was Friday, I suggested I could finish painting Mr. Burgdorf's house the next day and move in Mrs. Kitchall's place on Sunday. That was agreeable to all concerned.

If this wasn't already the best day of my life, what Mr. Burgdorf said as we were driving back home put mustard on the bratwurst.

"Van, would you like to join me and the family for a dinner out tonight? I think a celebration is in order."

As Burgdorf's long black Cadillac came to a stop underneath the awning, a smartly dressed young man rushed to open the rear door on the passenger side. Mrs. Burgdorf and Mary exited like royalty. I had never seen such courtesy for ordinary people. I was beginning to think the Burgdorfs were anything but ordinary. The gold-leaf sign on the beveled glass front door read; "Indiana Café, where food, wine and service warms hearts." I felt naked in my short sleeve shirt and cotton pants. Although the weather was warm that evening, Mrs. Burgdorf had a dark chestnut-colored mink stole loosely draped around her shoulders. Mary looked beautiful in her maroon satin dress. Her long auburn hair cascaded onto her shoulders. Her hair sparkled. She must have brushed it a hundred times or more. I couldn't keep my eyes off her. Occasionally, she glanced my way and smiled.

I didn't talk much during dinner, thinking the less I said, the less chance I would say something that might cause suspicion. When the dinner was over, the valet pulled the Burgdorf's Cadillac under the awing. To my disappointment the seating arrangement going home was the same as before, men in front, ladies in back. In some ways, I regretted the house painting was almost done and I would be leaving the Burgdorf's on Sunday. That meant I might never see Mary again. On the other hand, I looked forward to my new job at Studebaker.

At ten 'til eight, I walked into the employment office. Benny Goodall was there pacing back and forth.

"Good morning, Mr. Goodall," I said with a smile.

"Oh, hello, Van. Please call me Benny. If you're ready to get started, our first order of business will be a plant tour. This is a very special day, Van. The new '47 model is just starting up."

Walking through the 100-year-old plant was like stepping back in time. The high ceilings and oil-soaked wooden floors looked like something from the middle ages. Huge timbers supported the roof. Even if I closed my eyes, the smell of oil and old oak made me know I had entered another world. I realized that this was the same plant that built wagons and buggies in the 19th century. But oh, that new '47 model was ten years ahead of any car I had ever seen. It was too bad the plant wasn't as advanced as the sleek new Studebakers.

Various components of the new model came together in a most unusual way. Whole car bodies were trucked outside and then lifted to the second floor for the "body drop." It reminded me of hay bales being lifted into a barn loft. The speed of the workers was much like our prisoners back in Wolfsburg. There, they worked just fast enough to avoid punishment. Some Studebaker workers just stood around talking. Maybe they were waiting for the "kinks" to be worked out in the assembly of the new model. Often, I saw two or three people doing what appeared to me to be work that could easily be done by one.

"Hey, Benny," I said. "Why does Studebaker have more workers than is really needs to do a job?"

"Well Van, the local union has always called the shots here. Whenever we challenge inefficient work practices, someone files a damn grievance. If we insist, they call a wildcat strike."

"What's a wildcat strike," I asked?

"It's a small unauthorized strike usually by just a few workers. But if the weather is nice, sometimes the whole shift walks out. The local union never takes any action and neither does top management. Victor Harper, our president, brags that Studebaker has never had a strike. Hell, he even sends a letter to all new hourly workers urging them to join the union. During the war, it was awful. With lucrative government contracts to fill and big penalties for delays, the union got away with murder. So much for patriotism. Of course, Ford, GM and Chrysler had the same problem but after the war, they all took strikes to get the wages and work practices under control. Not here at Studebaker. But let me stop right here and make something very clear to you, Van. Everything I've told you must never be repeated. Everyone who has made war with the union in the past is no longer with the company."

"I had no idea, Benny. How do you do your job in that environment? Time study sets standards for how much work is to be done at each workstation. What happens if the worker involved disagrees?" Benny laughed.

"That always happens. The work rate is negotiated every time. That is why Studebaker workers are the highest paid in the industry. Our engineering designs are excellent but any one of the 'big three' could build our exact cars $250 cheaper than we. If something doesn't change, we'll be out of business in six or eight years. Oh, we'll sell everything we make until the pent-up demand caused by the war is satisfied, then we're in trouble." My head was spinning. If what Benny said was true, what chance did I have to work on a small inexpensive "People's Car"? I figured it might take several years before I could even get into design engineering. First, I had to prove myself as a time study man. The company may be out of business by the time I've enough power to dictate design policy. By that time, some European company may have built a car for the masses. But since I had come this far, I decided to do my job as best I could and see what happens. I'd just have to work around the union. In Germany in the early '30s, communists ran the unions. When Hitler came to power, he simply abolished the unions.

After the tour, Benny led me back to the final assembly line. My first assignment was to study the assembly of components into a finished grille ready to be mounted on a car. The various bright metal parts came in large tote-boxes with cardboard dividers separating multiple layers so the parts didn't get scratched. Benny introduced me to the two assemblers at that station.

"Van Hoffmann, this is Willie Wyatt. Willie has been with the company for ten years. Willie, Mr. Hoffmann is our new time study man. He's going to be studying the operation here and trying to make the process more efficient." I stuck out my hand. Wyatt ignored me and continued to work. We walked to the next assembly station. "Van Hoffmann, this is Jason Hughes. Jason is an evening student at Notre Dame and works here during the first shift. He's been with us three years now." Again, I offered my hand. This time it was met with a firm handshake. "Van, I'm gonna leave you here for a couple of hours so you can become familiar with the operation and get to know the workers." Benny walked away. Even though ignored, I felt conspicuous.

I watched for a while and soon noticed that Jason was assembling about ten percent more grilles than Willie, yet the write-up on the job that Benny had given me showed that Willie was working at the standard speed. I suspected the standard was set too low and Willie had slowed down for my benefit. When I was gone, he would probably speed up to make more money. Another thing caught my eye. Both operators spent a good portion of their time taking the parts out of the tote-boxes and handling the dividers and stacking the boxes. This gave me an idea I would talk to Benny about later.

Finally, I approached Willie Wyatt again and asked, "Mr. Wyatt, it's been my experience that the best ideas for improvement come from the workers doing the job. Do you have any suggestions as to how this operation might be made more efficient?"

Willie thought about it for a few seconds and then replied, "Yeah, I got a suggestion. These piece work jobs should be reserved for senior workers."

"What do you mean 'senior workers'?" I asked.

"You know, workers with at least eight or ten years seniority."

"How would that help efficiency, Mr. Wyatt?"

"Older operators are more experienced. They know how to pace themselves. These young 'whippersnappers' may go like a bat-outta-hell for awhile, but sooner or later, they'll burn themselves out."

"Thanks for the suggestion, Mr. Wyatt. May I call you Willie?"

"Sure, if you can get the kids off our piece work jobs, you got a friend for life."

"Well, Willie, you know this is my first day. I'm just learning." I then approached Jason. "Hi, Jason. I was just talking to Willie and asked him if he had any ideas that might improve the operation. How about you? Any ideas?"

"Well, Mr. Hoffmann, I'm pretty happy the way things are now. Except Willie and some of the other guys sometimes give me a hard time, but I just ignore them and do my job. I make real good money and being in college, I need every dollar I can get. So I'm pretty happy." I realized that Jason's answer related to worker satisfaction and had nothing to do with efficiency.

When Benny returned, he slapped me on the back and said, "How's it going, Van?"

"Oh, O.K. I guess. Benny, can we go somewhere quiet? I want to ask you about something." We walked back to the office and I pulled a chair up to his tattered old wooden desk. "Benny, it's obvious to me the work rate at the grille assembly station is set too low. Jason puts out 10% more than Willie without any trouble."

"No, that's not right, Van," Benny interrupted. "Willie is actually faster than Jason and is one of the top paid employees at this plant. He hates that Jason works steadily which tends to prove that the production rate for that operation is set too low."

"Yes, I recognized that. With only three years seniority, how did Jason get such a good job?"

"Good question, I think he had some pull upstairs."

"Didn't the union object?"

"Oh, top management and the union scratch each other's back, it's all politics. Like I said, Jason probably knows someone important."

I sat quietly for a moment and then said, "O.K. Maybe there's another way to lower costs of that operation. Who manufactures those grille parts?"

"Standard Stamping and Plating, over in Mishawaka. Why do you ask?"

"Well, why don't we send them a finished grille and ask them what they would charge to ship the parts to us, assembled and ready to mount on the car? We could then compare that cost to what the parts and labor cost Studebaker now and pick the least expensive method." Benny wrinkled his forehead and rubbed his chin, walked in a circle, then stopped and smiled.

"Damn good idea, Van. I'll call purchasing right now."

My next assignment was on the chassis assembly line. Benny explained that the workers there were paid based on what is called "group incentive." He said that a certain output rate for the line itself is agreed on and all workers on the line were paid the same. He said the rate on the chassis line was set before any increases in line speed were made. I wondered why there was an incentive rate when management set the speed of the line and the workers had no control. To get more production, I guessed Studebaker management chose to add more workers to eliminate any bottleneck in the process. The line would therefore move faster yet the base pay rate stayed the same resulting in higher pay for everyone on the line.

Several possible improvements seemed obvious after a few hours of observation. I saw great variations in the time necessary to perform certain functions. As an example, installing a master cylinder was much faster than running the brake lines, yet both functions were done at the same station. Also the line moved steadily forward. Workers wasted motion trying to keep up with the moving line. After a week of observation and making notes, I was ready to make a report to Benny. I scheduled a meeting. It was at 8 AM, my third Monday on the job. I had spent all weekend making drawings and a detailed analysis of the chassis assembly as it was and as I proposed.

When I walked into his office, Benny was leaning back, feet on his desk and a huge smile spread across his face. "Before we get started, Van, I have good news. Purchasing got the quote from S S & P and we stand to save $3.85 per grille by letting them assemble it. The union will probably scream but the change is being implemented this morning.

"That's great, Benny. What happens to Willie and Jason when their jobs are eliminated?"

"Oh, they'll get bumped over to one of the group incentive jobs on the assembly line."

"Won't that cut their pay?" I asked.

"Yeah, so? Look Van, cutting costs is our job." I sat motionless. Benny broke the silence. "Let's see your new proposal, Van." For the next hour, I explained my plans for rearranging the workers and indexing the line to stop for a predetermined time before advancing to the next position. He seemed open to the idea and suggested we discuss it out by the chassis line. When we arrived, I saw the last thing I expected. Willie Wyatt was sitting on a rolling stool hovered over a right front wheel. His face was drawn and he was mumbling something. It was obvious, he was not happy. I understood why. Even with proper tools, brake assembly is a tough job. He looked up.

"Well, well, well. If it ain't Benedict Arnold and his sidekick, Judas the Jerry," Willie shouted. "You turds got a lot of nerve eliminating my job in grille assembly without even talkin' to me. You can bet your ass, you ain't gonna get away with it! 'Big Mike' is gonna hear 'bout this soon as my shift is over, maybe sooner!"

"You'd better watch your mouth, Willie," Benny shouted. "Why don't you just do your job and quit making trouble." Willie spun around and released a brake spring from his assembly tool. It made a swishing sound as it sailed like a bullet past Benny's left ear. It must have flown thirty feet before it hit the outer wall and ricocheted into a storage bin.

"What the hell? You son of a. What did you do that for?" Benny shouted.

"Opps," Willie said with a smile. "Accidents happen." We walked away. As soon as we were out of sight, I asked, "Who's 'Big Mike'?"

"Oh, he's a cheap hoodlum who's worked his way up to President of Local # 9 of the UAW-CIO. His name is Michael Levy. He's a big ex-boxer who got where he is by threats, intimidation and a surprising ability to be charming when the need arises. The workers love him because he's been able to get them just about everything they've ever asked for including sky-high wages. He struts around the plant like he owns the place. In a way he does. Away from the plant, he goes all out to be 'one of the boys'. He loves booze, broads and bordellos. He seems to think he's the prettiest thing in town. The company president, Victor Harper, treats him like royalty. I don't know why. Harper's either afraid of Levy's power or afraid of him personally. Big Mike likes to dig up dirt in people's backgrounds and use what he finds as blackmail. I'm not saying that's the case with Harper, but who knows?"

As the weeks passed, I saw many areas for possible improvement in the plant. But like the changes in the chassis assembly line, most of my ideas cost money to implement and would cause temporary disruption in the assembly process. With priority on the new model start-up, my suggestions were getting nowhere.

On the positive side, Benny and I were becoming good friends as well as compatible workmates. Benny said many complimentary things about my work to his supervisor, Roy Branson, Vice President of Engineering. I remembered Mr. Branson from his article about the new '47 model that Mary Burgdorf had given me to read the second day I was in town. When I finally met him, he was impressed that I could quote from the article.

Benny and I stopped off at the "Little Brown Jug Tavern" about once a week and drank a few Hoosier or Drewry Beers before going home. I was worried there might eventually be trouble since the "Jug" was a popular hangout for regular hourly workers almost all union members. But it was a big place with a varied clientele and was near the plant. Benny told me that he was never popular with the union due to the nature of his job, so it was best that we keep to ourselves in the Jug. Sometimes one of the fellows who knew Benny would walk by and make some snide remark, but there were no physical threats against either of us.

After a few weeks, Benny invited me to come home with him for supper. That's when I met his pretty wife, Susie and seven-year-old daughter, Tess. I envied Benny and his wonderful family. His wife was about my age and very friendly. Benny was twelve years older than Susie. Tess was a cute little kid. But strangely, I found myself watching Susie. Watching her graceful movements, Geschmeidig—"lithe" came to mind as she walked between the kitchen and setting the table for our dinner. She was attractive from every angle. Years of marriage and motherhood had not erased her natural beauty. Compared to his wife, Benny seemed so ordinary. I had to wonder what she and Benny had seen in each other to get them to marry, and I wondered what kept them together now. Tess, of course, tradition, convenience…and then it was time to be seated.

After three months on the job, Benny put me in for a raise. I was thrilled. This was my chance to buy a used car, something I wanted to do since my first day at Studebaker. I felt helpless having to walk everywhere. I couldn't even ask Mary Burgdorf for a date without a car. Before the raise, I had barely enough money to pay Mrs. Kirchall room and board, pay for clothes and personal expenses and still have enough to have a few beers with Benny from time to time. I had started to save for a car, but at the rate it was going before the raise, it would have taken years. The nearest Studebaker dealership was Sherman-Schaus-Freeman. It was within walking distance of the plant.

Like the falling leaves, the early autumn sun turned a bright orange and fell toward the western horizon. After my shift was over, I ran toward the dealership hoping to have enough light to look at the used cars. A thin elderly man in a pinstriped suit greeted me as I walked through the showroom door. His sickening-sweet cologne almost took my breath away.

Sounding like the man on the BBC, he said, "Good afternoon, sir. Are you here to see the new '47s?"

"No, I see them all day every day. I work at Studebaker. I'm here to look at used cars."

"I see. In what price range, sir?"

"Oh, about $200, I guess." His pasted-on smile disappeared. His thin caterpillar mustache twisted as if it wanted to escape his upper lip.

"Well, sir, to get a vehicle that will give you the reliable service you deserve, you may want to invest a bit more that that."

"No, that's all I can afford. Do you have anything in that price range?"

"Just a moment, sir." The skinny old man prissed over to the receptionist and whispered something to her. He then tucked his hands behind him, bounced on his toes and looked at the ceiling. Soon a young man in greasy coveralls emerged from the shop wiping his hands on a shop cloth. "This is Roger. He'll show you what we have under $500." I thought I would save my breath and not remind the salesman that I said $200. Roger led me to the back row of the used car lot where a sad line of jalopies waited for the next fool to arrive.

"How much for this old A Model Ford?" I asked.

"$300," Roger replied.

"How about this rusty old '39 Stude coupe with the bald tires?"

"$300."

"Could you start it up for me?"

"Yeah, lemme go get the keys." While he was gone, I gave the car a quick inspection. The body was rusty but the oil dipstick was fairly clean and the exhaust pipe had little soot in it. The odometer read 36,754. I doubted it was correct. That wasn't much mileage for eight years. Roger returned and after a bit of choking and coaxing got the old car running. I got in the drivers seat and drove it around the block. I had to pump the brake pedal to get it to stop. It smoked a little but it was all I could expect for the money.

"It runs alright," I said, "but this body is rusty beyond repair. I'll give you $190."

"Oh no. $250 is as low as we can go."

"$200 is my best offer." I walked away from the Stude and started looking at other cars. Roger disappeared without a word. I looked at all the other cars on the back row but the '39 coupe was what I wanted. I was not surprised when Roger reappeared.

"Thank you for your help Roger, but I'll look elsewhere. As I told the gentleman inside, $200 is all I can afford." Roger motioned toward the showroom.

"Come inside and we'll sign you up." When I got inside, the receptionist already had the paperwork almost completed.

"How much is your down payment?" she asked.

"Oh, I'm paying cash, I said." She looked disappointed. For the first time in my life, I owned an automobile. I drove to the nearest petrol station. After putting in a dollar's worth of fuel, I drove to Mrs. Kitchall's boarding house, a proud Studebaker owner. Before going to my room I went to the kitchen. I peeped in and saw Mrs. Kitchall smoothing an uncooked meatloaf like she was petting a puppy. Without turning around, she said, "Hi Van. How goes it?" What special power told her it was I without looking?

"Oh fine," I said. "May I use your telephone?"

"Sure Van. Gonna call your girlfriend?"

"Well, I don't really have a girlfriend, but I bought a car today and I figure that's one step toward getting a girlfriend." She laughed and pointed to the wall phone and returned to shaping her meatloaf.

"Number please." My vocal chords refused. "Number Please!"

"ATlantic3-2478," I choked out. The phone rang, once, twice.... My heart was beating fast.

"Hello, Burgdorf residence."

"Mrs. Burgdorf?"

"No, this is Mary. Would you like to speak to Mother?"

"Uh, no. You are the one I want to talk to. This is Van Hoffmann."

"Oh, hello, Van. How are you? We wondered what happened to you. Dad said you got a job at Studebaker and that you had moved into Mrs. Kitchall's boarding house."

"Yes, that's all true. I've been busy with the new job and trying to save some money. I finally saved enough to buy a used Studebaker." I took a deep breath and said, "Uh, I was wondering if you would like to go to the picture show with me Saturday night? The Big Sleep with Humphrey Bogart is playing at the LaSalle. I hear it's pretty good."

"I'd love to, Van, but I'll need to ask Dad. Hold on a minute." If I were a religious man, I would have been on my knees praying while she was gone. Finally, I heard the phone being picked up.

"This is George Burgdorf." Oh, no, I thought. Now what? "How are you, son. I would have thought we would have heard from you before now. Are you alright?"

"Oh, yes sir. I've just been working pretty hard and trying to save some money to buy a car. I finally bought one today."

"Good, good. So you want to date my little girl, do you?"

"Yes, sir, if it's alright with you."

"Well I think it will be alright if you bring her straight home after the movie."

"Yes, sir, I will." Soon Mary was back on the line and we talked for a few more minutes.

Our first date went well. After about an hour into the movie, I held her hand. She didn't squeeze but she didn't pull away either. I took that as a good sign, so I held her hand again on the way to the car. After a few more movies and dinners, Mary and I were becoming very comfortable with each other. I loved spending time with her and she seemed to like me too. Although we had kissed on the second date, it was just a peck. Mr. and Mrs. Burgdorf seemed to like me too. They even invited me to join them for another dinner at the Indiana Café. And best of all, the parents sat in the front seat and Mary and I sat in the back. On the way home, Mrs. Burdorf surprised me by asking if I was Catholic. Mr. Burgdorf gave her a disapproving look. I said that I was not active in any church but that I did believe in God. Things were quiet until we pulled into their driveway.

By the fifth date, things were much more passionate with Mary and me. As was our routine, we parked in the Burgdorf's driveway, agreeing that this was the best place to sit and talk. Her family could see that she was safely home long before she came inside. They could occasionally peek out the window and be assured nothing serious was taking place.

It was a cool evening that 20th of September. We didn't talk much after we parked. We mostly kissed and caressed each other. Although Mary was barely eighteen, she was skillful in the art of seduction. Our kisses became deep and sensuous. I was afraid things were getting out of hand. It was a cool outside, but the heat of our over-stimulated bodies soon fogged the windows of my old Studebaker. I wondered if Mr. Burgdorf could see it from his living room window. After almost an hour of passionate kisses, I was aroused beyond comfort. Knowing things should not go further, I suggested we stop and talk for a while. She agreed, and started talking non-stop. Her state of passion seemed to add boldness to her questions about my past life. I answered as honestly as I could while still hiding my true identity. I found myself lying more and more. When I finally walked her to the door, I wondered if I would be able to remember all the lies I had told. I felt I was digging a hole I might never crawl out of.

CHAPTER 5

The next few weeks seemed to fly by. My job at Studebaker was going as well as I could have hoped. Benny was a great boss and a good friend. It was comforting to have a friend in South Bend, but I wondered about my German friend, Karl Heinz. I was afraid to write to Karl, thinking my letter might be intercepted and my location reported to the authorities. But I missed Karl and was curious about his situation at White Sands. I hoped a letter from Van Hoffmann might not cause suspicion.

October 7, 1946

Dear Mr. Heinz,

My name is Van Hoffmann. I live in South Bend, Indiana. I work for the Studebaker Corporation. I was given your name as a possible "pen pal" and would like to hear from you. Please write to me at P.O. Box 711, South Bend 7, Indiana. I will look forward to hearing from you.

Your future friend,
Van Hoffmann

Two weeks later I received an answer to my letter.

October 21, 1946

Dear Hans,

I was very glad to get your letter asking me to be your "pen pal." Ha, ha. Since you get your mail at a post office box, I know that I can speak freely. I assume the Van Hoffmann name is one you took to throw the immigration authorities off your trail. I am curious how you got a job at Studebaker with no social security card.

When you left here, you caused quite a stir with Dr. von Braun and other high-ranking officials. I was questioned for hours but claimed no knowledge as to why you left. I did admit helping you get on our train at Bleicherode. I told the truth and said it was because you were my friend and you wanted to come to America. I was scolded for my misdeed, but not punished. Gate security was increased for a while. But things have died down now and work on the new rocket program is proceeding at a rapid pace. Many of us will soon be transferred to Huntsville, Alabama. I'll contact you when I have a new address.

    Your friend, Karl

When I walked in Monday morning, the Engineering secretary motioned for me to come to her desk.

"Van, Mr. Majors in Personnel called and wants you to call him right away. I'll get him for you." Without waiting for my reaction, she got Majors on the phone. "Hello, Mr. Majors? I have Van Hoffmann here." She handed the phone to me.

"Hoffmann? Why haven't I gotten the transcript from the University of Texas you were supposed to get for me?" I hesitated.

"Uh, Mr. Majors, I requested it sometime ago but never got an answer. My letter must have gotten lost."

"Well, I've waited long enough. I'll contact them myself."

"Yes, sir, maybe that would be best." What else could I say? Majors hung up leaving me to worry about what was to happen next.

The skies had been clear all week but about noon on Friday, the heavens opened and the rain poured down. I was working in the engine assembly area at the time. The old brick floor was damp. The smell of sewage burned through my nose. This was only one of many neglected maintenance problems at this hundred-year-old plant. After all wages were paid, I presumed not much was left for building maintenance. Having breathed that putrid air for a couple of hours, I was glad to hear the five o'clock bell ring. When I got back to the office to pick up my coat, Benny was sitting at his desk waiting for me.

"Hey buddy, want to lift a few before we head home tonight?"

"Sure, Benny. The Jug?"

"Yep. Coldest beer in South Bend. "Course a Hitler youth like yourself probably prefers his beer warm."

"Oh, Benny. Just because my name is Hoffmann and my grandparents were from Germany doesn't mean I'm a Nazi." Benny laughed. We ran through the rain to our cars. I got to the Jug before Benny and was lucky enough to find a parking place near the front door. Benny had to park in the back. The Jug was crowded. Loud voices and laughter took my mind off the low ceiling and thick smoke. The place was a dump but convenient to the plant. I saw several familiar faces. At one table there was a group of six that included Willie Wyatt and Jason Hughes, the Notre Dame student. I was surprised since I thought Willie didn't like Jason. Benny and I sat at the bar.

"I guess I better call the 'ball and chain' and tell her to keep my supper in the oven for a while. Order me a Hoosier, will you Van?" Although I had become accustomed to cold American beer, I left the two bottles untouched and warming on the bar while Benny was gone. I stared at my reflection in the mirror behind the bar. Hans Werner, you are a lucky man, I said to myself. You have a good job in the industry you love, a sweet young girlfriend who is as smart as she is beautiful. You have good health, and a great boss who is also a friend. But I was becoming increasingly worried about Benny's future. Lately, he seemed to have gotten more aggressive in his fight with the union. His latest project was to get rid of "group incentive" on the assembly line. This would lower the pay of almost all plant workers. I was surprised that upper management was even considering the change. They must have been desperate to bring wages in line with Detroit. If the change was implemented, a plant-wide strike was sure to occur. Nobody wanted that, not even the union, but the AFL-CIO Local #9 was not going to let this change go through without a bitter fight. Benny was on the phone longer than I expected. When he finally returned, he was smiling.

"Susie says two beers is my limit tonight. She wants me home in time to tuck Tess into bed. So here's to an early night!" We clinked bottles and took a swig. About an hour later, as we started out, Benny grabbed my arm and said, "Van, these beers are going straight through me. I better hit the rest room before I head home. See you Monday, buddy."

"Yeah, see you Monday." I cranked up the Champ and headed for Mrs. Kitchall's boarding house. I was eager to get home and turn on my new short-wave radio. I had been able to pick up Germany the previous night. It felt good to hear my native tongue being spoken again and get the latest news about the Allied occupation. One piece of news was completely unexpected. It was reported that in late March of 1946, the one thousandth Volkswagen automobile had been produced at the Wolfsburg plant. Even though this was a comparatively small number, I had no idea the plant was still standing and producing automobiles. I wondered if I had made a mistake by coming to America. If I were still there, I would be working on the design and improvements to the Volkswagen automobile. I might even be Manager of Engineering. It had been my ambition to be a part of the "peoples' car" project since Hitler announced the concept at the auto show in 1936. It was something that Germany needed. Without affordable automobiles, no country can be a world power. But I was in America now and I liked my new life. Maybe my priorities were changing. At that point, I didn't know. About eleven o'clock, I turned off the radio and prepared for bed. There was a loud knock on my door.

"Van, there's an urgent call for you on my telephone!" Mrs. Kitchall shouted.

"I'll be right there....... Hello, this is Van Hoffmann."

"Van, this is Susie Goodall. Benny's not home yet. He said he was with you. This is not like him. I'm worried sick."

"I left him at the Jug three hours ago, Susie. We were walking out together and he stopped to use the restroom. That's the last time I saw him."

"Well, something must have happened. I'm calling the police."

I went to bed hoping nothing was wrong.

At five a.m., another pounding on my door jarred me awake. It sounded louder than thunder. The whole room vibrated. I knew it wasn't Mrs. Kitchall. I grabbed my robe and headed for the door. The pounding continued. "Alright, alright!" I shouted. I unlocked the door to face two officers in blue uniforms.

"Van Hoffmann?" "Yes."

"You'll need to get dressed and come downtown with us for questioning."

"Questioning about what?"

"Just get your clothes on, Hoffmann. We'll talk downtown."

CHAPTER 6

The police station was almost empty when we arrived. Piles of cigarette butts in dirty ashtrays made the place stink like a beer hall on Sunday morning. Without a word, the two officers led me to a small room with no windows and had me sit in a straight wooden chair in front of a green metal table. The chair was cold and hard. The peeling paint on the dirty walls may have once been white but was now a dreary color I couldn't identify.

"Stay here, Hoffmann. Detective Arbitt will be along shortly to ask you a few questions. Come knock on the door if you need anything. We'll be near by." I wondered what was going on. Had my true identity been discovered? I could hear muffled voices through the door. I waited and waited. My throat was dry. Maybe I could get some water. The door opened and a short bald man with a large parrot-like nose waddled in. His face wore an angry frown. His loosened tie was stained and his rumpled suit had seen better days. He flopped behind the green table and lit a cigarette.

"Van Hoffmann?"

"Yes."

"Do you work for Studebaker?"

"Yes I do, why do you ask?"

"I'll ask the questions, Boy. What time did you get off work yesterday?"

"Five o'clock."

"Did you go straight home?"

"No. My boss, Benny Goodall and I stopped off at the Little Brown Jug Tavern for a couple of beers. Is something wrong?"

"Did you leave the bar together?"

"Yes, uh, well, not really."

"You either did or you didn't," Arbitt barked. "Which is it?"

"We started out together, but he went back to use the restroom."

"Did you wait for him?"

"No, I left and went home. Has something happened to Benny?"

"You tell me, Mr. Hoffmann. You were the last person to see him."

"What do you mean by that?"

"Don't play dumb, Hoffmann. Mr. Goodall was found dead this morning."

"Benny's dead? Oh God, no. How did it happen?"

"We were hoping you could help us answer that question."

"Well, I can't. He was inside the Jug when I last saw him. Have you called his wife?"

"Mr. Hoffmann, how many beers did you have?"

"I had two."

"And Mr. Goodall, how many did he have?"

"He had two also. Why would anyone want to hurt Benny?"

"That's what we intend to find out. I understand Benny Goodall was your supervisor. Is that correct?"

"Yes, that's true."

"How did you like working for Mr. Goodall?"

"He was an excellent boss."

"I asked, how did you like working for Mr. Goodall?"

"I thought I answered that. I liked it just fine."

"Mr. Hoffmann, your hostile attitude is not helping your case."

"My case? What case?"

"Hoffmann, as far as we know right now, you were the last person to see Mr. Goodall alive. So it is my job as chief detective for the city of South Bend and the county of St. Joseph to determine if you had anything to do with Mr. Goodall's death. By the way, Mr. Hoffmann, where are you from anyway. You talk like a kraut?"

"My family is of German decent. My grandparents speak fluent German."

"Which side were you on during the war?" I sat quietly and shook my head. From that point on, the questions became more and more hostile and insulting. It was obvious Mr. Arbitt was trying to get me to lose my composure. He was unsuccessful. After two hours of pointless questions and insinuations, Mr. Arbitt, without explanation, rose and walked out. The two officers in blue soon reappeared and took me home. They warned me not to leave town.

I immediately tried to call Susie Goodall. No one answered. I then drove back to the Jug to see if Benny's car was still there. It was, but was now surrounded by a white rope. Men in civilian clothes were dusting the car for fingerprints. One of those men was Detective Arbitt. When he saw me standing behind the rope, he walked over.

"Returning to the scene of the crime are we, Mr. Hoffmann?"

"Mr. Arbitt, as I told you a hundred times back at the station, I don't know anything about Benny's death. I came back here to find out where they took his body."

"It's at the City Morgue for an autopsy. It will be released to his family tomorrow. Is that old '39 Studebaker over there yours, Mr. Hoffmann?"

"Yes, why do you ask?"

"We'd like to take a look inside it, if you don't mind."

"I'm not a lawyer, but I doubt that you have that right."

"If you have nothing to hide, then there is nothing for you to worry about, is there? " Accepting his logic, I agreed to the search. In a few minutes, one of the plain-clothed men approached Arbitt and whispered something in his ear. Arbitt followed him to my car, opened the door and looked inside. The other man called to the photographer and motioned for him to come to my car. I walked over to see what the commotion was about. There on the floorboard behind the driver's seat was a wallet. After the photograph was taken, Arbitt took out his handkerchief and carefully picked up the wallet by one corner. Then, without touching it with his fingers, he opened it and read the driver's license name that showed through a little plastic window.

"Benjamin J. Goodall. Well boys, looks like we don't have to look very far to find the killer. Mr. Hoffmann, you're under arrest, suspicion of murder. Cuff him, boys!"

On the way back to the jail, my head was spinning with unanswered questions: Why would anyone want to kill Benny? How did his wallet get into my car? Before they put me in a cell, I was told I could make one phone call. I called the only one in South Bend that I could trust with such a serious situation. That person was George Burgdorf. I was aware that being arrested for murder would not help my standing with the Burgdorf family but I felt I had no choice. The story would likely be in Sunday's paper and on the radio. Mr. Burgdorf answered the phone when I called."

"What's up, Van?"

"I've been arrested on suspicion of murder of my boss, Benny Goodall. Someone planted his wallet in my car and the police found it there."

"Did they have a search warrant?"

"No, sir, but I gave them permission."

"Sounds to me like you need a good lawyer. I'll call my friend, Virgil Norman tonight. Are you in jail?"

"Yes, sir, I am."

"Alright, Van. Sit tight. We'll get you out on bail as soon as possible."

"Thank you, Mr. Burgdorf. Please explain my situation to Mary. I don't think I can talk to her right now."

True to his word, Mr. Burgdorf had me out of jail on Sunday afternoon. Not knowing what else to do, I went to work Monday morning as usual. As expected, there was an extensive story in the St. Joseph Gazette about Benny's murder. My name was mentioned as a suspect. Vice President Roy Branson was waiting in the engineering office when I arrived.

"Well, Hoffmann, I read about Benny's murder in the paper yesterday and came by to get your side of the story."

"Well, sir. Friday afternoon after work, Benny and I went to the Little Brown Jug Tavern for a couple of beers. After about an hour there, we left. Benny stopped off to use the restroom and I went straight home. That's the last I saw of Benny. Sometime that night or the next morning, someone planted Benny's wallet behind the front seat of my car. The police searched my car and found the wallet. I spent one night in jail and my friend George Burgdorf arranged for my bail. That's all I know except that Benny Goodall was a good friend and a great boss. He's the last person in the world I wanted to see dead."

"Alright, Hoffmann, continue your work as usual. Do you have a good lawyer?"

"Yes, sir, I think so. Mr. Burgdorf arranged for Virgil Norman to represent me."

"Oh, good. He's the best. Good luck, Hoffmann. By the way, I want you to continue with Benny's project to eliminate group incentives."

All eyes were on me as I walked through the plant that morning. I went directly to the chassis assembly area. This is the area that Benny had wanted to use as a test bed for the elimination of group incentives. The first familiar face I saw was Willie Wyatt. Willie was still assembling brake shoes. When he saw me he quickly looked back at his work. I thought that unusual. Willie almost always found some way to show his displeasure when I was around.

"Good morning, Willie. The job getting any easier?"

"No, not really," he said. "What are my chances of getting back on piecework?"

"I don't know, Willie. I don't make those assignments."

"Oh, I thought you did." I walked away but stayed in the area almost an hour. During that time, I watched Willie out of the corner of my eye. He seemed to be doing the same with me. It occurred to me that Willie was less combative, almost civil in our short conversation. I wondered why. Not only was he now getting lower pay than when he was doing grille assembly, but with the possibility of group incentive pay being eliminated, he stood to have his pay cut even further.

At lunchtime, I called Mr. Norman to see if there was any news on my case. He said that the police told him that there were no fingerprints on the wallet found in my car. There was thirty-three dollars in the wallet. Norman said that these facts weakened the case against me. Without a motive, he said the prosecution would probably not go forward with the case. The word "motive" dominated my thoughts all afternoon. What was the killer's motive? Whoever killed Benny wanted to blame it on me. I wondered why.

When I returned to the office at five o'clock there was a note on my desk telling me to call Benny's wife, Susie Goodall. I used the office phone. Susie's phone rang twice and then she answered. She was crying.

"Oh, Van. What am I going to do? Benny's mother lives in California and can't get here for four days. I've never been very close to my neighbors and I don't feel comfortable asking them for favors. Tess and I are here alone. I'm sorry but I just can't stop crying. I'm so upset, I'm afraid I'm not being a very good mother. You know like fixing good meals and getting Tess off to school on time. Without Benny, I'm just going crazy. I feel so lost. I don't think I can go on."

"Try to hold on, Susie. I know it's hard. Is there anything I can do to help?"

"Well, I hate to ask you this, Van, but since you were Benny's best friend, could you come over tonight? I'm afraid of being alone." She started crying again. I couldn't turn her down.

"Sure, Susie. Let me run by the boarding house and then I'll be right over. Can I pick up some burgers on the way?"

"You're a sweetheart, Van. Please hurry."

When I arrived, Susie was waiting at the door. She hugged me and started crying again. Tess ran over and hugged me too. We three stood like that for a long time. I felt uncomfortable when Susie held on to me. Finally, she stepped back and dabbed at her eyes with a damp tissue.

"Oh, Van, I'm being such a baby. Tess is holding up better than I am."

"It's alright, Susie. I'm sure it is of no consolation to you now, but everyone says the pain will lessen with time."

"I hope so. Van, you don't know how much it means to me for you to be here tonight." She rested her hand on my shoulder. "Oh, by the way, the police called today. Benny's body has been transferred from the city morgue to the Fowler Funeral Home. Would you go with me to make the arrangements tomorrow?"

"Sure, Susie. Whatever you want. Why don't we eat these burgers while they're still warm?" I wasn't planning to stay the night, but Susie kept crying and begged me to. I slept on her lumpy couch.

I was at work as usual the next day. I took off a few hours to help Susie with the arrangements for Benny's funeral. She didn't want to drive, so I picked her up and took her to the funeral home. I helped her pick out a casket. The funeral home director said we could have visitation the next day if we wished. Susie said she would wait until Bennie's mother arrived.

"Who killed my son?" were the first words out of Mrs. Goodall's mouth when we picked her up at the train station. No one said anything for a long time.

Finally, I said, "We don't know. The police are working on it."

She turned to Susie and asked, "Who is this guy, Susie?"

"This is Van Hoffmann. He was Bennie's best friend." Mrs. Goodall looked deep into my eyes without comment. I wondered what she was thinking. Very little else was said as we drove to the funeral home to see Bennie and greet his co-workers and neighbors. It was eerie seeing Benny laid out like that. When I looked at him, it was as though he was someone I didn't know.

When I dropped Susie, Tess and Mrs. Goodall off after the funeral, I said, "Let me know if there's anything else I can do." Susie kissed my cheek and ran into the house. Mrs. Goodall stood in the doorway holding Tess' hand and said nothing. Tess waved. I called later that evening to check on them.

After a few minutes of conversation, Susie said, "Van, I can't possibly thank you enough for helping me during this whole ordeal. You were like the Rock of Gibraltar. I don't think I could have made it without you."

CHAPTER 7

"Hello, Mary? This is Van."

"Van Hoffmann, I'm very upset with you. Why haven't I heard from you? According to the newspaper, you're a murder suspect. You haven't even called to explain. I've been worried sick."

"I'm really sorry, Mary. I guess I didn't know what to say while everything was still up in the air. But with your father's help and Virgil Norman's, the charges against me have been dropped. They didn't have enough evidence to continue."

"Well, I knew you weren't guilty but you could have at least called or come by and let me know what was going on."

"Yes, I suppose I could have, but between work and trying to help Benny Goodall's widow with her grief, I haven't had much time. Mrs. Goodall is having a really hard time accepting Benny's death." There was a long pause.

"How have you been helping her?"

"Well, with the funeral arrangements and things like that."

"Is that all?"

"I took food over the first night and I drove her around when she asked me to. She's very depressed, Mary. She cries much of the time. So I try to cheer her up. After all, Benny Goodall was a very good friend."

"Have you stayed overnight?" I hesitated and started to lie then decided against it.

"Yes, but don't jump to conclusions. It was strictly platonic. And it was just that one night."

"Oh, Van, how could you? Don't you know how people talk? Are you taking advantage of a poor grieving widow?"

"Mary, how could you think such a thing? Dammit, I slept on the couch, if you must know."

In an anger filled voice she shouted, "I don't care where you slept. You didn't have to stay overnight, that's for sure. And you could have called me unless you were thinking of something else. I think you've made a big, big, big mistake!" The phone went dead. When I called back, Mr. Burgdorf answered.

"Mr. Burgdorf, I'm afraid Mary is upset with me because I've been helping Benny Goodall's wife. I know I should have kept Mary informed, but I guess I was distracted."

"Well, whatever you said has upset her greatly. After she hung up, she ran to her room crying. And Van, I'll be honest with you, when Mary is upset, so am I. So I suggest you not call back until this thing blows over. Goodbye, Van."

"But, but," I said into a dead phone.

I starred at my ceiling wondering how I could have gotten myself into all this trouble. My false identity was likely to be revealed as soon as the University of Texas responded to Hamilton Major's request for Van Hoffmann's transcript. Detective Arbitt had made it clear he was not convinced I was innocent in the Benny Goodall murder. He would surely continue to try to dig up something to tie me to the murder. And to add to all my troubles, it's likely I have lost my sweet young girlfriend and the support of her father. This Sunday afternoon was turning out to be as dark and cold as the blowing rain that was pelting my windowpane. I hid my face in my pillow wishing for a miracle to turn my life around.

By now I could tell the knock on my door was Mrs. Kitchall's knock.

"Van, phone call for you. Better hurry. Sounds like a lady with romance on her mind," she said with a chuckle.

"Oh yes, I'll bet," I shouted back at the door. As I walked down the dimly lit hallway, I wondered if Mary had gotten over being mad at me. "Hello, this is Van."

"Hi, Van. This is Susie. I got Benny's mother off this morning and Tess and I are here alone again. I wondered if you had any plans for dinner tonight. You've been so kind looking after me when I was at my lowest; I thought it's time I fixed a nice dinner for you. I've got a meat loaf already in the oven. Scalloped potatoes and mushroom gravy should hold you until you dig into my special apple strudel. How does that all sound?"

"It sounds wonderful, Susie. You sure you're up for all that?"

"Definitely! I'm in a cooking mood and I can't think of anyone in the world I'd rather share it with than you. Can you come over?"

I laughed. "Sure, sounds good."

Susie met me at the door looking radiant and smiling widely. She was obviously a couple of glasses of wine ahead of me. That's okay, I thought, whatever it takes to help get her over her loss. She kissed me on the cheek. She smelled delicious. The whole house smelled delicious.

"I've missed you, Van. I'm glad you're here. Would you like something to drink?"

"Sure, why not?" I said. Susie was wearing a cream-colored dress cut low in the front so that her cleavage begged to be released. As she turned and headed for the kitchen, I couldn't keep my eyes off her firm rounded derrière. I felt more than a little guilty. My friend, Benny was barely cold in his grave and here I was lusting after his widow. I tried to forget about her body but her frequent visits to the kitchen kept refreshing my memory. Coming or going she fed my hungry eyes. I visualized burying my face between her two full breasts and pressing them to my cheeks until I couldn't breath. Then I'd ever so slowly kiss my way up, up to her neck and chin, finally kissing her lips. Hans Werner, you're a randy, obscene bastard, I thought. My lurid thoughts proved that I had no conscience. I wondered what Mary would think if she knew what was going through my mind.

"Where is Tess tonight?" I said hoping to get my mind off Susie's body.

"Oh, I fed her early. She went to her room to do her homework. She may be asleep by now. The meat loaf is not quite ready Van. How about another glass of wine?"

"Sure, thanks." My inhibitions were quickly disappearing and yet I was having another glass of wine. I knew she was vulnerable: newly widowed and now, full of wine, but somehow I didn't care. Susie tuned the radio to a station that was playing dance music. *"You must remember this; a kiss is still a kiss. A sigh is still a sigh."*

"Wanna dance?" she said. Does a starving man want food I said to myself?

"Yeah, I guess," I replied. "Susie, do you realize this is the first time I have danced since college? I'm not sure I remember how." And so we danced, slow and close.

"I'd rather dance with you than Gene Kelley," she said. "You're a wonderful dancer, Van." I thought about what she said. The wine must have given me a special ability because I never was a good dancer before. The next song was by the Ink Spots. *"I don't want to set the world on fire, I just want to start a flame in you heart."* As we danced, I wondered if this was the woman for me instead of Mary Burgdorf. When the song ended, we stopped dancing but continued to hold each other close. She looked up at me, smiled a dreamy little smile, eyes half closed. Her lips begged to be kissed. And so our lips met, open and wet. We devoured each other. She kissed me as if she never, ever wanted to let me go. At that moment, I was torn. Why was I thinking about Mary?

"I'm crazy about you, Van," she said. "It's not just because I've lost my husband and I'm lonely. I knew there was something special between us the first time we met." We kissed again. She took my hand and put it to her lips and then led me to her bedroom. We finally ate a slightly overcooked but still delicious dinner at 1 a.m.

CHAPTER 8

Susie and I went out a few times; mostly dinners with Tess and then multiple rounds of unbridled passion back at home. It was working for both of us. At Susie's suggestion, I moved a few of my belongings over to her house and started enjoying all the joys of a new relationship with a wonderfully sensuous woman. Thoughts of Mary gradually faded when Susie and I were in each other's arms. But I was troubled by her frequent mood swings. One minute she was a passionate lover and the next she was a sobbing heartbroken widow. Sometimes she was giving and understanding and then she'd be extremely possessive and belligerent. I also began to worry about the gossip that my staying overnight would surely generate. I hoped Mary wouldn't find out, but in truth, I figured I had already lost her.

It seemed that every good thing that was happening was offset by one not so good. In the good column, I received a large pay raise and a promotion to Supervisor of Industrial Engineering, (Benny's old job) at Studebaker. In the not so good column, I got a call from Virgil Norman saying he was no longer representing me in the Benny Goodall murder case. He said his bill would be forthcoming. George Burgdorf had withdrawn his support. The good and the bad just kept coming. Ham Majors of personnel called and said he received my transcript from the University of Texas and everything was in order just as I had said. The next day, Detective Arbitt called and wanted me to come in for more questioning.

When I arrived at the police station, I was directed to that same drab windowless room painted a color without a name. This time, Arbitt didn't keep me waiting. He walked in wearing that same rumpled suit and stained tie as before. But this time, he was smiling.

"I heard Virgil Norman has dropped you. Do you have another lawyer?"

"No, I don't. Do I need one?"

"That's your decision. But I'll tell you this, Hoffmann, you're our one and only suspect in Benny Goodall's murder. I knew, if I was patient, you'd finally screw up and give me what I needed to nail you. Sooner or later, you bums always do."

"What are you talking about, Arbitt?"

"Well, here's the story, Hoffmann. Since you wiped your fingerprints off Goodall's wallet, I didn't have enough evidence to proceed with the case without a motive. Now I have two motives. You killed Benny Goodall to get his job and to get his wife. Do you admit that you have been promoted into your boss's old job?"

"Yes, but I'd never murder anyone for a job promotion."

"Isn't it true that you are now living with Susie Goodall, Benny Goodall's widow?

"Living there, no. I've spent the night at her house a few times, but we only developed a relationship after Benny's death." Arbitt slapped the table with his open hand. I was startled at the frightening bang.

"Well, Romeo," he shouted, "You must be the world's greatest lover to pull that one off. Hell, you were in the sack with Goodall's wife and the mother of his child before he was even cold in the grave, probably sooner. Yeah, we've got you this time. No question about it. We've got a murdered body, you at the scene of the crime and now we have two motives. Smells a lot like first degree to me." Arbitt sat quiet for a few moments and then said, "I'll tell you what, Hoffmann. You can save yourself a lot of years in prison if you'll go ahead and admit that on the spur of the moment, without premeditation, you killed Benny Goodall. Although you don't deserve it, we'll try to get you a second-degree murder charge and with early parole you should be out in five or six years. What do you say?"

"Look, Mr. Arbitt, I didn't kill Benny Goodall. You want a motive for his murder? I'll give you a motive. How about the union Local #9 at Studebaker wanted Benny eliminated because he was about to get rid of group incentive pay?"

"The union killed Goodall? Oh, brother, that's a good one. You'll have to do better than that, Hoffmann." Arbitt sat and stared at me for a good minute and then said, "OK. I've had enough of you. You can get out of here for now, but don't even think about leaving town. We're watching your every move. You try to leave and we'll put you under the jail!"

It was obvious that Detective Arbitt's mind was made up. I was the killer. Case closed. Well, I wasn't the killer, but to get out from under the dark cloud of suspicion, it looked like I would have to find the real killer myself. I had no idea where to start. Certainly, I would get nowhere asking questions of or trying to befriend union members such as Willie Wyatt or "Big Mike" Levy. George Burgdorf would know what to do, but at the moment, he was very angry with me for hurting his daughter. I hoped he hadn't found out that I had moved in with the murdered man's wife. But I was desperate so I decided to take a chance and call Mr. Burgdorf. Knowing that Mary's job at the library started at nine o'clock, I called at nine-ten hoping to catch her father still at home. George Burgdorf answered.

"Mr. Burdorf, this is Van Hoffmann. I know you asked me not to call but I wondered if it is at all possible that I could meet you somewhere and try to explain what has happened?"

"Well, let me tell you something, boy. I know what has happened. You have broken my little girl's heart and if I ever see your 'Heinie' face again I'll do my damnedess to break your neck."

"I know I'd probably deserve any punishment I got, sir. I'll admit I treated Mary badly, but I never lied to her."

"You never lied? You're lying now, you Nazi son of a bitch. I never was fully convinced you were who you said you were, so after you hurt Mary; I hired a private detective to look into your past. The first thing he found out was that you have been spending the night with your dead boss' wife. Then, it was easy enough to trace you back to the Hoffmann family in Ft. Worth, Texas and how you stole their dead son's identity. By piecing together police reports and Greyhound Bus schedules, my man was able to trace you all the way back to White Sands, New Mexico, and von Braun's rocket scientists. That information cost me a pretty penny but it was worth it." I was speechless and shocked at how much he knew. I wondered if he was going to turn me in. He continued to berate me.

"I now know that you are a fugitive, an illegal alien by the name of Hans Werner. The only reason you are not on a boat headed back to Germany right this minute is because Mary begged me not to turn you in. Unfortunately, for some unknown reason, she still cares about what happens to you. God knows why. So, Werner, let me make myself crystal clear. Don't ever bother this family again. And if I can convince my daughter, I'll still get you deported, assuming you can wiggle out of the Benny Goodall murder charge. So goodbye, Herr Werner, and good riddance!"

I sat by the phone stunned. I had been discovered and by a very powerful and well-respected South Bend citizen. What would I do now?

* * * * * * * * * *

I now had four time-study technicians and three Industrial Engineers under my direction. Without much experience in supervision, just keeping ahead of my subordinates was a full time job. Work responsibilities along with the time spent with Susie and Tess gave me little time for creative thought and no time at all for work on a small car or my zinc-air battery idea.

It was a sunny Friday afternoon as I finished up my reports and looked forward to a quiet evening with Susie and Tess. I picked up my lunch pail and started for the door. Roy Branson, Vice President of Engineering, stopped me in the hall.

"Van, we need to have a long discussion about several subjects, but I don't think here at the plant is a good venue. There are too many eyes and ears just waiting to get rumors going. I want you to come over to my house tomorrow about ten o'clock? I know Saturday is your day off but if it weren't important, I wouldn't ask." He gave me directions.

"I'll see you tomorrow at ten," I said. Well, that killed the plans that Susie and I had for a picnic out at Worster Lake. I knew she would be disappointed and would probably cry when I told her. But my boss told me to meet him and I considered that important. I couldn't say no. Susie did cry when I told her and refused to make love that night.

The next morning, she was a little nicer. She even loaned me Benny's car to go see Mr. Branson. She asked me to check out why the inside courtesy light was not working when the driver's door was open. The problem was easily fixed. I removed a broken toothpick wedged beside the on/off button on the door jam. I wondered why the police had missed it in their search of the car. It helped explain why Benny's murderer was not seen that tragic night. Although I felt strange driving the car Benny was killed in, it was a much nicer and newer car than my old '39 Champ. Benny had bought one of the first new 1947 Studebaker Commander Regal Starlight coupes with the futuristic "coming or going" look. The car was maroon with lots of chrome and a wrap-around rear window. It was shiny and beautiful. I saw several new '47 Studebakers as I cruised through Mr. Branson's upscale neighborhood. I pulled into his circular driveway and parked in one of the six spaces surrounded by a well-manicured lawn and perfectly trimmed hedges. Branson met me at the door.

"Come in, Van. Welcome! Again, I apologize for taking up your Saturday but when you hear what I want to discuss, I think you'll understand why we need extended, uninterrupted time to talk. Come into my library and make yourself comfortable. Coffee will be served shortly." Floor to ceiling bookshelves filled two of the four mahogany paneled walls of this spacious room. Awards and other mementos along with richly bound volumes on various engineering and management subjects filled the shelves. I wished I could spend the day just perusing his fine collection. After we got settled and started sipping our coffee, Branson spoke.

"Van, we have a long and hard journey ahead if the Studebaker Corporation is to be saved. Our costs are the highest in the automobile business. Benny told me that you believe the high wages and the poor work ethic of the plant workers at Studebaker is the biggest reason for our high costs. Do you still feel that way?"

"Yes, sir, I do. I'm more convinced of it every day. I don't want to minimize our need for more modern equipment, but high labor costs is unquestionably our biggest problem. Ford and General Motors have ten times greater volume to absorb their labor costs. By rights, our costs should be much, much lower just to stay competitive."

"Van, as you may know, Benny and I had started to formulate a plan to bring union wages in line with Detroit and at the same time deal with the belligerent attitude of many of our workers. But Benny's death changed all that. My theory is that when word got out that we planned to reduce wages by eliminating group incentives, Benny was killed. I believe there is a connection, especially when the murderer or murderers tried to frame you by placing Benny's wallet in your car. With Benny gone, I decided to bring you into the loop as my partner on this cost reduction project. I realize you are still the number one suspect in Benny's murder, but you had no motive and the union did. What the unionists don't realize is they are killing the whole Studebaker Corporation and the future of thousands of workers. We can't let that happen. Are you with me so far?"

"Yes, sir, Mr. Branson."

Branson glanced at his notes and wrote something. He then looked up and said,

"Alright, good! By the way, call me Roy. Now if you are going to help me solve our problems at Studebaker, we've got to get you out from under this suspicion of murder thing. My friends at the police department tell me they were not going to pursue the case against you until you got promoted and moved in with Benny's wife. Now they think you had a motive, maybe two. I think the first thing you must do is must move back to the place you lived before?"

"To tell the truth, Roy, I've thought about it. I certainly realize living with Benny's widow looks bad. Let me think about that one. By the way, when you were talking to your friend in the police department, did he say how Benny was killed?"

"Oh yes. It is believed he was struck from behind with a blunt object, maybe a blackjack, and then choked to death. He had a bruise on his left temple and a red line around his neck indicating a belt or strap of some sort was used to choke him. I'm surprised that wasn't in the papers."

"So, that's how it happened. The police wouldn't tell me."

"All right, another subject. The German city of Wolfsburg has been attempting to produce a small simple car they are calling the Volkswagen. This project started under Hitler before the war. Wolfsburg, Germany is in the British sector of occupation and therefore it is at their discretion to decide what to do about the bombed out plant and its workers. At present, they are slowly making cars just to keep the workers busy. They have made about one thousand so far. The British officer in charge has offered the company to several British and European automotive manufacturers but no one seems to want it. They have now started offering it to U.S. car companies. We are one of the first. We now have one of their cars out at the Proving Ground for testing. I'd like your opinion of the car and a recommendation on what Studebaker should do, if anything, with the Volkswagen." Roy reached into a nearby desk drawer and pulled out an 8x10 black and white photograph of the car. I couldn't believe what I just seen and heard.

"If we like the design concept and Studebaker wants to be involved," I said, "would we run the plant there and export or would we manufacture the car here?"

"Certainly, we would manufacture in Germany first and then when the operation is running smoothly we might make an American version here. It all depends on whether the car is any good and if there is a market for a small air-cooled, rear-engine car like the Volkswagen."

"Let me say this, Roy, I am extremely interested. I have followed the VW concept from the beginning and definitely would like to be involved."

"Excellent! I suggest you go out to the Proving Ground tomorrow. Since tomorrow is Sunday, you'll have total access to the car and the test track. I'll call Ed Reynolds and tell him to unlock the garage and let you in.

"O.K. Next subject. Van, I have had extensive conversations with our president, Victor Harper. Although he is frightened at the thought of upsetting the union and possibly causing a strike, he admits the company will eventually fail unless we get our costs down. He has tentatively given me permission to eliminate the group incentive system on the chassis line. But if the union calls a strike, and they probably will, I know Harper will give in and we'll have to go back to the old system. Do you have any ideas?"

I sat quietly for a few moments and then said, "Suppose we transfer the present chassis line workers to piecework incentive jobs or other 'group incentive' assembly line jobs and quietly replace them on the chassis line with new and/or non-union workers. That way the old trouble makers might let us implement the new system without realizing its long-term implications. Also, we could work out problems on a limited basis without having the agitators sabotage our efforts. At least, we'll have a foot in the door."

"That's a good idea, Van. Getting enough workers as you described may be difficult since most present workers belong to the union. But I think your idea could work. See, that kind of thinking is why I wanted you as my partner in our goal of saving Studebaker."

We continued to talk the rest of the morning and on through lunch. An attractive young Negro maid in a starched blue and white uniform served our lunch consisting of chicken-salad sandwiches and a fruit cup. After sitting our trays down, she closed the door behind her. We saw no more of her until later when she cracked the door and asked if we needed anything.

"No, thanks, Rose," Roy said. "We'll be through in here in a little while. Then you can go home."

"Has Rose been with you long," I asked.

"About a year. She only works part-time for me. Since my wife died last year, I needed someone to come by for a few hours every day or two to help with cooking and housework. Rose used to be a Studebaker factory worker but got pregnant and wanted a part-time job so she could take care of her baby. She's not married and the father hasn't taken responsibility, I felt sorry for her and gave her a job as my housekeeper."

On the way back to Susie's house, I thought of how to tell her about tomorrow. I dreaded facing her. She was reading a magazine when I walked in.

"Hi, Susie. How was your day so far?"

"Shitty, thanks to you. Tess and I were really looking forward to that picnic today. Have you had lunch?"

"Yeah, I ate at Roy's house."

"Oh, so it's Roy now. What happened to Mr. Branson? Benny never called him Roy."

"He asked me to call him Roy. Is that a problem?"

"Oh, no. No problem. Are you in a bad mood, Van?"

"I was in a great mood until you told me your day was shitty thanks to me." Susie looked at me with rage in her eyes.

"How could you be so uncaring after all I've been through?" she whined. I followed her to the kitchen. She had two plates with sandwiches covered with wax paper on the dinette table. She picked them up and pitched them in the sink.

"Well, Mr. Big Shot executive, you think you can break away from the job long enough to take me and Tess on that promised picnic tomorrow?"

"I'm sorry Susie, but I've got to go out to the Proving Ground tomorrow. The British have sent us a new Volkswagen to test."

"Well, I'll be damn. I think you love that job more than you love me. Do you deny it?" I didn't answer. She started to cry and pulled at her hair. "I hate Studebaker," she screamed. "It killed my husband and now it's killing us." She cried even louder and ran into the bedroom. I heard the lock click. It occurred to me to go try to make peace, but then I decided, why bother?

CHAPTER 9

I left without waking Susie. As I walked toward my old '39, I glanced to the west. The clouds rose up from the flat Indiana horizon like a huge black blanket. Oh no, I thought. If it rains, it will interfere with my evaluation of the VW on the test track. But I couldn't let a little rain spoil the day. The excitement I felt as I drove to the Studebaker Proving Ground was almost orgasmic. My little '39 buzzed along Western Avenue like an ME 262. Its tires sang a song against the smooth pavement. I was sailing along at seventy miles an hour. The old Stude had never gone that fast before, at least not since I owned it. Bugs splattered my clean windshield but I didn't mind. A sprinkle of rain then dotted the glass. I turned on the wipers but I was going too fast for them to work. Studebaker should abandon vacuum-powered wipers, I thought, and go with electrics. Even buzzing along at seventy with no wipers didn't bother me. Did I care? No! I was smiling from sheer joy. My greatest ambition in life was to help develop the Volkswagen concept and it appeared I might finally have the chance. I wheeled my car between the entrance gate's stone posts topped by giant castings of the Studebaker wheel. I felt destiny had brought me to a great milestone of my life. The rain stopped and the clouds parted long enough for the sun to shine on the world's largest living sign. On the hill to my right, tall pine trees spelled out the word "Studebaker." I knew at that point I was at a special place and time in automotive history. I savored the moment.

The uniformed guard waved me through and pointed toward the garage. He obviously had been told that I was coming. That made me feel important. I parked my car and walked up to the office entrance. The door opened just as I reached for the knob. A handsome young man in a tan shop coat greeted me. Even though it was Sunday and I knew it was probably his day off, the gentleman wore a tie and his hair was neatly combed. His horn-rimmed glasses gave him a look of intelligence.

He smiled and said, "Mr. Hoffmann?"

"Yes. I'm Van Hoffmann."

"I'm E.T. Reynolds. Mr. Branson called yesterday and said you would be out this morning to evaluate the Volkswagen automobile the British sent from Germany. Would you please come this way?" Our footsteps echoed off the cavernous enclosure. The heavy smell of petroleum was like perfume to me. In the far corner of the garage I recognized the familiar beetle shape under a canvas tarpaulin. I could hardly wait to see what was underneath. Reynolds grabbed one corner and I another. We carefully peeled it back. There it was, just as I remembered. The car appeared to be little changed from Ferdinand Porsche's original design, the same car I saw at the Berlin auto show ten years earlier. The little car was dull black and dusty, but in my eyes it was shinny and beautiful. I felt reunited with an old friend.

"It's gassed up and ready to go, Mr. Hoffmann. Here is the key. I'll be here in the office if you need anything."

"Danker schon, uh, I mean thank you." Reynolds nodded and walked away. I slowly looked the car over. Every detail of the body construction was as I remembered. It appeared, however, that some parts were hand-made and not the best workmanship. Careful examination revealed several changes that would be necessary for it to be acceptable in the American market. Before I even drove the car I knew the mechanical brakes needed to be replaced with hydraulics. A pull cable to replace the bonnet handle would give security to its contents. A larger windscreen and back glass would improve visibility. I suspected Americans would want chrome trim and electric turn signals instead of those "idiot sticks" that flipped out from the B post. Fortunately, none of these improvements would increase the manufacturing costs significantly. I circled the car impatiently. I was more than ready to drive the Volkswagen. I guessed it would drive like a Kubelwagen and it did.

Having gotten accustomed to American cars, I was surprised how loud the engine was. Maybe a better muffler and some soundproofing would minimize that annoying 'sewing machine-like' hum. After a few turns around the test track, the car's interior grew quite warm, even with the windows down. I figured proper venting might solve that problem. Several other needed improvements for the interior were obvious: door on glove box, start with the key rather than a button, an accelerator pedal rather than a roller and a sun visor on the passenger side. The steering was very quick. The rear end came loose when I turned too sharply. But the car was fun to drive. After a few more rounds, I felt a pain in my lower back. I wanted to adjust my seatback angle, but there was no adjustment. I turned off the main track and drove the VW over the washboard road a few times. I realized I was at the end of my endurance. I had been driving for over two hours. Had it not been for my back pain, I would have been happy to drive the little bug until it was out of petrol. I headed back to the garage and drove toward a door that opened just as I approached. I got out and stretched before taking a final look at the car. I noticed the wheels and tires seemed too big. They looked out of proportion. Maybe 16-inch wheels were needed on some rough roads in Europe, but in this country, 15-inch had become the standard. Mr. Reynolds approached.

"How did it go, Mr. Hoffmann?"

"Oh, it went fine," I replied. "By the way, since you'll probably be seeing a lot more of me in the future please call me, Van."

"Very good, Van. Call me Ed. Do you want us to run any further tests before you make your report?"

"Yes, please. Just run your standard series, you know gas mileage, zero-60 acceleration, brake horsepower, hp at max rpm, braking distance 60 to zero, the standard stuff."

"Alright," he said with a smile. "We'll get right on it."

As I drove my '39 back to town, my head was spinning with thoughts of improving the VW. I wanted to throw myself headlong into the development. I realized that doing so would drastically reduce my time with Susie and Tess. What exactly were my obligations to Susie at this point anyway? I considered this only briefly. I was hungry for the opportunity that had befallen me. I realized a car was taking precedence over a woman's love or was it just lust? I knew what I had to do. I stopped by Mrs. Kitchall's boarding house to pay the rent. I'd kept up the pretense of living there despite the fact that I had been staying at Susie's almost every night for the past fortnight. Now all I had to do was tell Susie my decision.

It was already getting dark and had started to rain again when I pulled into her driveway. Time had passed so quickly. She met me at the door.

"I was getting worried about you, Babe. I'm glad you're home."

"Oh, Susie, it was so exciting testing the Volkswagen. I've made a list of improvements to be made so the car will be acceptable in the American market."

"Come sit down and tell me all about it." We sat together on her sofa. I could smell inviting aromas from the kitchen. Tess was nowhere in sight.

"Well, first, I have something else to tell you. This project along with my other responsibilities at Studebaker means I'm going to have to work many long hours including weekends to get everything done. That has forced me to make some hard choices. I really want to do these projects for Studebaker but then if I do, it's going to be a constant source of friction between us." As soon as the words left my mouth, I realized how curt and flimsy they sounded. But I couldn't take them back. I hoped she'd appreciate how much this opportunity meant to me. Couldn't she read it in my face?

"Oh, Van. I know we can work it out somehow," she said. "I realize I've been too possessive lately. I'll try harder. I don't want to lose you."

"Susie, this decision has been really hard. But I've decided we shouldn't be together so much anymore." She frowned. I was afraid she might cry.

"What do you mean?" she asked.

"Mrs. Kirchall still has my room. So starting tomorrow, I guess I'll spend my nights there for awhile."

"Your mind was made up even before you talked to me about it, wasn't it? Wasn't it?"

"Yes, I suppose so, but I have wanted to be involved with the VW project since it was announced ten years ago." Susie looked puzzled.

"You were a school boy in Texas ten years ago. Wasn't the Volkswagen Hitler's idea?"

"Yes, but it was a good idea. Please try to understand."

"Oh, I understand all right. I understand I've lost the two loves of my life, both in less than five weeks. Why wait until tomorrow, Van? Why don't you just get your shit and leave right now?" she shouted. I stood quietly for a moment trying to carefully choose the right words for my reply.

"Good idea," I said.

CHAPTER 10

Back at the boarding house, I lay on my bed and stared at a river and its tributaries formed by the cracks in my ceiling. I wanted to sleep, but couldn't. I felt guilty about leaving Susie. I wondered how I could I make it up to her without moving back in? But thinking above my waist, I had real regrets that I had been so open about seeing her. This was, after all, a town where futures are made or lost by what important people think of you.

Benny's killer was still a mystery. The police seem to have no suspects other than me. Finding the real murderer would accomplish two objectives. First, I would no longer be under suspicion and second, Susie would surely appreciate my efforts. The fact that Benny was found dead in his car and was choked to death would make one think the killer was hiding in the back floorboard. If Benny had been accosted in the parking lot, he might have fought the aggressor off. I didn't think the killer would have taken that chance. So I figured the murderer was already in Benny's car when he opened the door. He might have seen the killer but the parking lot was dark and the interior light switch had been disabled. Another thing occurred to me. That was a new car and Benny was extremely proud of it. I was almost certain he wouldn't have left it unlocked in a dark lot behind a beer tavern. The murderer might have lifted the door lock knob with a coat hanger inserted above the window glass. But this would have taken time and skill. Since there was no sign of a forced break in, I figured the murderer likely had a key. To have a duplicate key made, without Benny's knowledge, it would be necessary to have the car's serial number and access to the key codes. That information would only be available to authorized personnel in the Studebaker Employees Sales Department. I needed to find out who those authorized personnel might be.

First thing Monday morning, I called Roy Branson. "Roy, this is Van. I tested the Volkswagen yesterday and although it needs a number of minor improvements, I think its potential is unlimited. I wanted to tell you that before I made a formal report which will take a couple of days."

"OK fine, Van. Anything else?"

"Yes, sir. One quick request. Since you own a new '47 Studebaker, would you request an additional set of keys from the Employees Sales Department and find out the name of the person who takes care of your request?"

"Could I ask why?"

"I'll tell you later," I replied. "Trust me, it's important."

When I returned from lunch, there was a sealed white envelope on the center of my desk marked, "Van Hoffmann-Confidential!" The note inside was from Roy.

> *Van: The lady that has the files on employee car sales also makes the replacement keys. She is an evening student at Notre Dame by the name of Sarah Hughes. When I went by to pick up the keys, I noticed she didn't seem to have much to do. She must know somebody upstairs......Roy.*

I thought about what Roy had discovered. It didn't make sense. A young college student can make spare keys for any new car sold to an employee. I wondered if her files were locked at night. After work I walked over to the Administration Building. That old building looked like something from another century. That's because it was. The wall directory said her office was Room 213. Although it was only 5:45, the building was almost empty. I tried the door. Locked. Walking back down the hall, it hit me! Sarah Hughes, Notre Dame student, easy job, knows somebody. Jason Hughes, piecework incentive job, Notre Dame student, knows somebody. Are those two kids related?

The next morning as soon as I had given my engineers and technicians their assignments for the day, I headed for the chassis line. Willie Wyatt was still assembling brakes. And there was Jason Hughes, installing the rear wiring harness. I walked over to Willie's station first.

"Good morning, Willie. How are you this fine day?"

"Still hoping to get a piecework job. You sure you can't help me with that? You're a big wheel now, ain't you?"

"Well, I did get a promotion, but I still have nothing to do with personnel assignments."

"I hear you and Roy Branson are pretty thick these days. I'll bet he could get me a better job if he wanted to."

"Maybe he could, but it's not my place to ask him."

"Aw, come on Van, don't be a horse's ass."

"Be nice, Willie," I said with a smile. I then walked over to Jason's station.

"Good morning Jason, how's school?"

"Oh, hello, Mr. Hoffmann. School's OK. I graduate in three weeks and then it's goodbye South Bend."

"Where's home for you?"

"New York City."

"You got family back there?"

"Just my parents."

"No sisters or brothers?"

"I have a sister."

"In New York?"

"No, she's in college."

"Oh yeah, where?" I asked.

"Look, Mr. Hoffmann, I hate to be rude, but I can't chat with you and keep up with my job, sorry." I nodded and stepped back from the line.

Two things struck me as strange about my encounters with Willie and Jason. First Willie seemed friendlier. Even when he called me a 'horse's ass', it was said in a joking way. Also, he seemed to know more about my relationship with Roy Branson than I would have expected. And Jason's reluctance to talk about his sister seemed odd. He had one of the easier jobs on the line and had no trouble keeping up yet he broke off the conversation when I asked where his sister went to college. From that encounter I felt sure that Sarah Hughes must be Jason's sister. So what? Was this fact connected to Benny's murder in some way?

On an impulse, after work, I stopped by the Jug to have a beer. This was the first time since Benny's murder that I had set foot in the place. Blue smoke hung low in the air. The jukebox pumped out Betty Hutton's *"Doctor, Lawyer or Injun Chief."* At the corner table Willie Wyatt, Jason Hughes and several of their buddies were laughing and talking loudly. I waved and then headed for the bar. I ordered a Hoosier and wondered why I was there. Soon, Al Dexter took over the jukebox duties and twanged out a song that had everyone in the bar except me singing. *"Lay that pistol down, Babe, lay that pistol down. Pistol packin' mama, lay that pistol down."* In a few minutes, Willie walked up behind me and slapped me on the back.

"What chew doin' in this here workin' man's bar, Mr. Big Shot? Did the Widow Goodall pitch your ass out or sumpin'?" It was apparent from Willie's slurred speech and his beer and bourbon breath he was well on his way to being drunk. Should I consider this a problem or an opportunity?

"Hey Willie, what's going on with you and your friends?" I said, ignoring the Widow Goodall slur.

"Oh nothin' mush," he answered. Me and the boys just tossin' down a few boilermakers to pass the time. Wanna join' us?"

"Oh, no thanks. I can't stay long. I see Jason sitting over there with you. Are you two friends now?"

Willie leaned in close as if telling me a deep dark secret. "Oh, I jez keep Jason around sos I can keep an eye on him. You wouldn't know by lookin', but that there college boy's got a few screws loose."

"What makes you say that Willie?"

"I'm not at liberdy to say. Jez take my word for it. That boy's crazy as a goddamn bed bug. Let's jez leave it at that. Sure you won't join us?"

"No thanks. I'll see you at the plant tomorrow." I finished my beer and left. As I opened the door of my old '39, I wondered if I should have taken Willie up on his offer to join him and his friends. I knew I would be stepping into a potentially volatile situation that could go a variety of ways. I hesitated, scratched my head, checked behind my front seat, cranked up the Stude and headed to the boarding house.

The Next Morning
Hamilton Major's Personnel Office

Back in Germany, it was common for buildings that are a hundred years old or older to be in daily use. But in America almost everything, with the exception of Studebaker buildings, seemed newer. The Studebaker Personnel office seemed especially ancient and drab. Even the front door had a raspy unoiled sound as I opened it. Inside, the rotund Hamilton Majors sat in his broken down wooden swivel chair. It was hard to tell where the chair stopped and Ham started. I guessed he would someday die right there in that old chair.

"Good morning, Hamilton. I stopped by this morning to ask about the possibility of hiring a Notre Dame student to help me on a research project. I am aware we sometimes use college students in the plant, but wondered if they are ever used for office jobs?"

"Yes, Van, sometimes. What did you have in mind?"

"Well, maybe a chemistry or physics major to do storage battery research for me."

"We've never hired any students to do technical work before but I don't know why we couldn't. It would take a vice president's signature to get it authorized though."

"Did Sarah Hughes in Employee Sales have a vice president sign off on hiring her?"

"Sarah Hughes, Sarah Hughes, oh yeah, I remember her. She had better than a VP signature. As I remember, she had Mr. Victor Harper's signature."

"Why would our president be interested in some college student," I asked?

"Hey, don't ask me. By the way, Van, I like you and want to give you some good advice. You'll last a lot longer around here if you don't ask too many questions, especially about those fellows up on the top floor. I learned that a long time ago. That's why I'm still here."

"OK. Thanks, Hamilton. I will get back to you later."

As soon as I got back to my office, the department secretary handed me a message saying Roy Branson wanted to see me right away. I hurried to his office.

"Oh Van, thanks for coming over so quickly. I know you're a busy guy so I'll make this short and to the point. I talked to Victor Harper and told him you were very enthusiastic about the small German car, the Volkswagen, and that you were working on a detailed report of your findings and recommendations. He said not to bother. Harper said if the French and British don't want it, we shouldn't either. Besides, he said, we don't have the money or personnel to develop a car for a market that doesn't exist."

"That's crazy," I said. "Hell, he hasn't even seen the car. I doubt he's even seen a photograph. You know what I think. I think "Big Mike" Levy has convinced Mr. Harper that we shouldn't be involved in any project that doesn't directly benefit the local union. Of course, it would benefit the union if we ever made the car in South Bend but they can't think that far ahead. Damn, damn, damn!"

"Take it easy, Van. I know you're disappointed but there is nothing we can do about it. Harper has already ordered the car be returned to Germany." I stomped out of Roy's office. This news changed everything. Studebaker had the opportunity of a lifetime dumped right in its lap and the president wouldn't even consider it. Between the union and Victor Harper, I didn't see much hope for the company.

After I cooled off a bit, I made a decision. I would keep quiet about the Volkswagen decision and spend my energy trying to solve the Benny Goodall murder. And then I would go to Detroit and see if minds there were more open to a small inexpensive car. If unsuccessful in Detroit, then I'd somehow try to get back to Wolfsburg to work for Volkswagen. But I couldn't go anywhere until I found Benny's killer.

After lunch I walked over to the Administration Building. I climbed the stairs and entered Room 213. The office was empty except for a young girl who had two open books and a notebook spread before her.

"Pardon me, Miss Hughes, my name is Van Hoffmann from the Engineering Department. As you may have heard, I am a suspect in the murder of Mr. Benny Goodall." She looked up, put her hand to her mouth. With eyes like saucers, she struggled to talk.

"Uh, um,....why are you telling me this?" she asked. She was obviously shaken by my abrupt manner.

"I know that you made a spare set of keys for Mr. Goodall's car a few days before his murder."

"Oh, no. You are mistaken. You can check my records."

"I suspected you might deny it and of course you would not have recorded it. But you and your brother will be in deep trouble once the police know the truth. So I suggest you not play games with me. Now I doubt either of you knew that the duplicate keys would be involved in a murder, but nevertheless you could be considered accessories to the crime when the police find out about your involvement. I won't go to the police with this information if you can convince Jason to tell me who put him up to getting those keys made. Tell him to call me tonight at ATlantic 2-4321 at exactly 9 p.m. Write it down. That's AT2-4321 at 9 o'clock. Good day, Miss Hughes." I turned and left, hoping my bluff had worked. In truth, I had no proof that spare keys were involved in the murder. It was only a theory. If I guessed wrong about the spare keys, there was no harm done.

"On my way home that afternoon I stopped by the Indiana Army-Navy Surplus store on Michigan Avenue. It was a big warehouse type building with rows and rows of olive-drab green mess tables loaded with surplus WWII equipment. The huge room smelled like the inside of an army tent. I had been there several times before looking at all the military gadgets for sale. I remembered from a previous trip seeing a wire-recording machine. It had two spools of wire on top, was painted olive drab and was made by the Armour Company. Luckily, they still had it. Twenty dollars and twenty minutes later I was at the boarding house testing it with Mrs. Kirchall's telephone. It worked. The phone was located on her kitchen wall. I informed Mrs. Kirchall that I was expecting an important call at 9 p.m. She said I could have privacy at the phone at that time. I was as nervous as I'd ever been when at nine the phone rang.

"Mr. Hoffmann, this is Jason Hughes. My sister told me you came by today and accused her of making a spare set of keys for Mr. Goodall's new Studebaker. I don't know where you got your information, but it's simply not true."

"Yes, it's true, Jason. But if you want to deny it, I'll give this information to the police and let them determine its validity. You can expect you and your sister to be called in for questioning tomorrow." There was a long pause.

"Can't we work this out some way other than involving the police. I'm almost ready to graduate and I really don't want to get involved."

"You're already involved Jason, only the police don't yet know it. If you'll tell me who put you up to this, I promise not to go to the police."

"I'm gonna have to think about that before I answer."

"No, I must know your answer now or I'm on the way downtown as soon as I hang up this phone."

"OK, OK. Somebody gave me money for those keys. I thought they were just going to steal the car, not murder Mr. Goodall."

"Who gave you the money and how much was it?"

"I can't say. He'll hurt me."

"How much money did he give you, Jason, how much? You can tell me or tell the police, take your choice."

"Uh, two hundred dollars."

"Did you split it with your sister?"

"No. She knew nothing about the $200. Please, just keep her out of this. I asked her to make the keys as a favor and not to tell anyone. She didn't ask why."

"Who gave you the $200, Jason?" There was no answer. "Was it Willie Wyatt?" Still no answer. "It was Willie wasn't it? Tell me Jason, don't you take the rap for that bum."

"O.K. Willie gave me the money, but I know he didn't kill Mr. Goodall."

"How do you know that?"

"Because he and I were in the Jug until late that night and Willie never went outside. When we left, the police were already there."

"You mean to tell me Willie was drinking beer until the wee hours and never left the table?"

"Oh sure, he went to the men's room a couple of times, but I'm pretty sure he never went outside."

"Did the police question you and Willie?"

"Only briefly. We didn't know anything except that you and Mr. Goodall left together early in the evening."

"Alright, Jason. Your secret is safe for the time being. But if you alert Willie, I'm going to the police. Understand?"

"I understand."

My gamble had paid off. I now knew my theory about the duplicate keys was correct. But if Willie didn't go outside, he must have telephoned someone to tell him that Benny and I were there. I figured that someone, who already had the keys to Benny's car, drove to or near the tavern, unlocked Benny's car, disabled his interior light and then hid behind the seat until Benny came out. He likely locked the car from the inside so as not to arouse suspicion. If all that were true, the big question was, who was the person Willie called?

First thing the following morning, I headed for the chassis line. Jason and Willie were at their stations working. When Jason saw me he looked away. Willie looked up and nodded when he saw me. I walked to his station and handed him a note and then walked away. The note said: *Come to Mrs. Kitchall's boarding house at 6 p.m. this afternoon. I have a recording of a phone conversation that implicates you in the Benny Goodall murder.*

At six o'clock, there was a knock on my door.

"Come in, Willie, and sit down. I think you'll be interested in this recording I made last night." Willie sat down without a word but his face was drawn and pale. After the recording finished, Willie sat speechless. I pretended to turn the recorder off but instead hit the record button.

"Willie, when you gave those keys to the killer, did you know what he was up to?"

"Look Hoffmann, I don't know anything about the murder. Jason in full of shit on that recording. I told you that guy was nuts."

"I don't think so Willie, and I don't think the police will think so either. Now either tell me who you gave those keys to or I'll take this recording spool to the police."

"First off, recording someone on the phone without their knowledge, what kind of shit is that?"

"It's legal, Willie. The police will be glad to get it."

"Let me tell you something Mr. Smart Ass, unless you want to end up like Benny, I suggest you forget about this whole damn thing including that recording. In fact, let me have that spool!" Willie got up and made a move toward the recorder.

I stepped in the way and said, "Don't try anything Willie, I've made a copy of the conversation with Jason and also had a trusted friend listen to it. So just sit back down before you get in more trouble than you are already are in." Willie stood his ground. I slapped the table and shouted, "Who gave you the $200?"

"I ain't saying no more! But I will tell you one thing. If I'd a knowd Benny was gonna get killed, well, I just thought they'd steal his car."

"Who, Benny, who?"

"I ain't saying, but I will say this, you better watch your back, Hoffmann!" Willie stormed out and slammed the door. My heart was pounding and I felt lightheaded. But I was a little closer to finding Benny's killer than I was. To be on the safe side, I gave the spool with Jason and Willie's voices on it to Mrs. Kirchall to hide in her apartment. The more I thought about the information I had, the more I knew I needed to share it with someone I trusted.

As soon as I got to work the next morning, which was Friday, I called Roy Branson. "Roy, I wondered if you plan be home tomorrow? I've got some news about Benny's murder that I can't talk about here at the plant."

"Yes, I'll be home. Come over about ten, like last time and we'll discuss whatever you want to talk about."

"Fine, see you then." I figured I better get my new information to Roy quickly. Maybe he could advise me on how to handle Willie's threats and what future steps could be taken to find the killer.

CHAPTER 11

My '39 "rust bucket" looked completely out of place in Roy Branson's upscale neighborhood. The car left a trail of smoke as it rattled along the way. I pulled into Roy's driveway and parked where my clunker couldn't be seen from the street. There was no response to the doorbell. I waited and waited. First I knocked softly and then hard. Still nothing. This was confusing. It was exactly ten a.m. and Roy Branson was a stickler for punctuality. Finally, I tried the door. It was unlocked. I cautiously looked inside.

"Roy! Hey Roy!" I shouted. No answer. I guessed Rose wasn't working today. I looked around. The house seemed empty. I was aware of a strange smoky odor. I shivered, I didn't know why. I felt I was somehow intruding into forbidden territory. I crept through the hall calling, "Roy! Roy!" I looked in every room. The door to the library was closed. After knocking and getting no answer, I opened the door and stuck my head inside. "Roy! Ro." Oh, my God! I froze. Roy was sprawled face down on the floor. Blood puddled on the rug beside him. I stood frozen. I didn't know what to do. I started to reach for the phone to call the police when I heard wailing sirens. Within seconds, police cars were in the driveway. I felt faint. Within seconds, four or five blue-clad men with pistols drawn were around me. One young officer checked Roy's pulse.

"No pulse sir, but he's still warm.

"What is your name, boy?" an older officer asked with a voice as raspy as a rusty gate hinge.

"Van Hoffmann."

"Did you kill this man?"

"Me? No, no. He's my boss at Studebaker. I was supposed to meet him here at 10 o'clock. When I walked in just a couple of minutes ago, this is the way I found him."

"Looks like he was shot in the back, Sir. See this small entrance hole?" the young officer said pointing to the bloody stain below Roy's left shoulder blade. "Oh wait, here's another entrance hole at the base of his skull. Both shots were up close. See the powder burns on his shirt?"

"Frisk Hoffmann and then call Detective Arbitt and tell him to get over here right away," the lieutenant ordered. "Tell him to bring the fingerprint guy and a photographer. Don't you guys touch anything in the room." The lieutenant slipped on thin cotton gloves and began to look around the room. After checking shelves and behind books he started opening drawers. He carefully opened the top drawer of a nearby desk. The lieutenant took a pencil from his pocket and dug into the drawer. He lifted a revolver by its trigger guard. The captain cocked his head as he examined all surfaces of the pistol. "This is a military type, 38-caliber Smith and Wesson, Model 10 with a four-inch barrel," he said to another officer taking notes. The crusty old captain smelled the open end of the barrel then slid the pistol back into the open drawer. "It's been fired recently too," He shouted. "Okay, boys, book Mr. Hoffmann on suspicion of murder and take him downtown."

* * * * * * * * * *

Like the condition of my life, the cell was cold and dreary. My thin mattress smelled of unwashed bodies. Paint on the walls and ceiling was peeled like sunburned skin. The urine smell from the dingy toilet wafted through the little concrete room and refused my attempts to ignore it. How could things get any worse? After only twenty-seven years, my life seemed over.

At six p.m., an overweight kid brought me my supper. It was served on an army-type compartmented tray. Both the macaroni and cheese and the baloney sandwich were cold. I nibbled around the edges. I wasn't very hungry. A few minutes later, Detective Arbitt showed up. We talked through the bars.

"Well, Hoffmann, looks like you really screwed up royally this time. Did you get yourself another lawyer after Virg Norman dumped you?"

"No, didn't think I needed one."

"Believe me, you do! I'm not even gonna bother to question you tonight, unless you wanna confess and get this thing over with," he said.

"I didn't kill Mr. Branson. I was set up again."

"Yeah, right. Okay, I'll get the boys to let you out to make one phone call. See you Monday, Hoffmann." Arbitt left without another word. He was right about one thing; I needed a lawyer. And I knew I needed a good one, not some disinterested young Public Defender. I knew a very good one, but I wondered if he would consider representing me again? I called Virgil Norman. A kid answered and said his dad wasn't home. I left a message for Mr. Norman to contact me at the St. Joseph County jail.

Sunday was one of the worst days of my life. I didn't see anyone except the fat kid who brought my meals. There was no one to turn to except my own unfortunate self. Each minute seemed like an hour. Finally, finally, the day and night passed. It occurred to me that good days fly by; bad days creep. Monday morning after breakfast, a guard unlocked my cell, put me in handcuffs and led me to a visiting booth where Mr. Norman was waiting. His face was a welcome sight. I was instructed to sit and keep my hands below the counter as Norman and I talked through the heavy wire screen.

"I brought you a copy of yesterday's St. Joseph Herald so you could see what you're up against, Van." In bold one-inch high type, the headline read: "Studebaker Executive Murdered." The caption below read: 'Engineer, Van Hoffmann Arrested.' "I'll leave the paper here. After I got your message last night, I called George Burgdorf to ask him how he felt about me representing you again. He said I could do what I wanted but he would have no part in helping. When I asked why, he said it was a personal matter. Van, I'll be honest with you. I could go either way on this. I doubt you can pay my normal fee and I wouldn't have considered representing you except I smell something fishy about this whole business. You standing over the dead body as the police arrive doesn't make sense. If you were the killer, wouldn't you have tried to flee before the police got there?"

"Mr. Norman, to be honest, the police were there before I even had a chance to think."

Norman continued. "That makes me wonder. Who called the police and how did they get there so quickly? I suspect that Branson knew and trusted whomever shot him, otherwise the killer probably wouldn't have been able to get in the house undetected and get close enough to shoot him in the back." Norman massaged his temples and then said, "Remembering that you're still under suspicion in the Benny Goodall murder, you may be considered a flight risk, so I'm not sure I can get you out on bail." We continued to talk for another half hour. Finally, he agreed to represent me and said I could pay him in installments.

Back in the cell, I racked my brain to make some sense of this whole mess. By the police showing up just after I arrived made me wonder if the killer wasn't trying to accomplish two objectives; get rid of Roy Branson and get rid of me by making me look like the murderer. That sort of double play could also have been the strategy when Benny Goodall's wallet was found in my car.

Using that theory, whoever did this must have known about my ten o'clock appointment with Branson. Unless Roy's phone at Studebaker was tapped, the only ones to know I was coming over was his secretary or his maid, Rose. This is assuming he planned to have her there to serve us coffee and lunch like before. If she were there for our meeting, she would have discovered the body or heard the shots. Unless? A guard appeared interrupting my train of thought.

"You got another visitor, Hoffmann." He unlocked the cell, slipped on the cuffs and led me back to the visitor's window. I was stunned to see Susie.

"Susie, my God. You are the last person I expected to see. I figured you would never speak to me again."

"I know you didn't commit that murder, Babe. You are a kind, gentle person. You'd never kill anyone, not Benny, not Mr. Branson, not anyone."

"You mean you're not mad at me?"

"Oh, I was hurt when you moved out but now since you're in so much trouble, I figured you needed a friend."

"Well, that's about the nicest thing anyone has ever said to me!" We sat for a few moments without speaking. Finally, I said, "Let me ask you something, Susie. Did Benny ever go over to Roy Branson's house?"

"Sure, a few times over the years. Why do you ask?"

"Did he ever mention Branson's maid, Rose?"

"Yes. He said Rose was an attractive Negro girl who had a young baby."

"Did Benny know who the father of the baby was?" She smiled and looked down.

"Oh, he said some of the guys thought 'Big Mike' Levy might be the father but no one knew for sure. Someone said that Levy and this colored girl had been seen together a couple of years back. But it was just idle gossip according to Benny. But it's interesting that Benny was told the baby is light skinned."

"Do you have any idea what prompted Roy Branson to hire Rose?"

"All Benny ever said was that she was a factory worker and when she started showing, she knew she would have to quit her job. Benny said she put a notice on the bulletin board with a sad story about needing a part time job so she could feed her baby. I guess Mr. Branson saw it, felt sorry for her and hired her as his part-time maid and housekeeper."

"Oh, so that's how it happened?" We continued talking until the guard returned and said our time was up. I thanked her for coming. She blew me a kiss and left.

The next few weeks in that stinking cell made me long for the freedom I had taken for granted up to that time. Knowing I was being held for a crime I had nothing to do with made it all the more frustrating. Although Mr. Norman had used his considerable influence and legal knowledge, he was unable to get me out on bail. He said the court ruled I was considered a "flight risk." Fortunately, Mr. Norman, by using some of his city hall contacts was able to get the trial scheduled quickly.

Chapter 12

St. Joseph County Criminal Court

Newspaper photographers' flashbulbs popped and temporarily blinded me as I was led up the steps to the old courthouse. With a guard on each arm and still in handcuffs, I wondered what the Burgdorfs would think when they saw my picture in the paper. This being my first look inside an American courtroom, I was naturally curious. The high ceiling echoed as people talked loudly trying to be heard. What surprised me most was the curiosity of those seated or standing inside. People starred as if I were from another world. My handcuffs were removed when we were seated. I looked at the jurors who were mostly middle-age men. Although Mr. Norman had prepared me for any eventuality, he continued to fill me in on the general situation. As an example, he said that jury selection was slow but had proceeded without major problems. This high profile case seemed to be of great interest, so avoidance of jury duty was rare. The biggest problem was finding jurors who didn't know that I had previously been charged in the Benny Goodall murder. He also told me that several of the jurors were either present or retired union members. This was not a good sign since I knew I was not popular with the union. Mr. Norman said this was unavoidable in a factory town like South Bend.

The courtroom was packed on that first day of testimony. Norman pointed out a large man who had entered the rear of the courtroom. It was union president, Michael Levy. I had never met Levy and was surprised that he came to my trial. I supposed he was curious. Big Mike was a great slab of a man, muscular built, tan, handsome, and confident. His dark hair was well oiled and combed into a ducktail. His eyelashes were long and heavy, almost feminine. He wore an expensive looking dark blue pinstriped suit and his black patent leather shoes glistened. He smiled and was continually shaking hands with people who approached him. His friendliness was strangely appealing. He seemed instantly likeable. He even signed a couple of autographs.

The court was called to order and everyone stood as Judge William Ransom took his place. After my 'not guilty' plea, prosecuting attorney general, Jerry Goldsmith made his opening statement. He pulled at his suspenders as he took command of the courtroom. It was obvious he was very experienced and felt at ease in presenting his case against me. He pointed out that I was a very smart but overly ambitious person and had a strong motive to eliminate my boss to get his prestigious and high-paying job. The fact that I was standing over the dead body and had hidden the murder weapon in a nearby desk drawer was evidence enough to prove that I pulled the trigger. Goldsmith even insinuated that my German heritage had something to do with my aggressive, unethical nature. His words were well chosen and persuasive. Then Virgil Norman got up and made his equally impressive opening statement. Norman was a big man with a waistline that hinted of countless nights of wining and dining. He unbuttoned the jacket of his perfect-fitting suit as he paced the floor. A golden chain restrained his bright red tie. Looking each juror in the eye, he pointed out that I was a mild mannered person with no criminal record not even a traffic ticket. (The Benny Goodall affair was not mentioned). He summarized by pointing out that I didn't try to escape from the murder scene as the real killer had done. I felt lucky to have him defending me. Goldsmith called his first witness, Police Lieutenant Bill Cugart.

Jerry Goldsmith's first question was, "Lieutenant Cugart, how did you find out that there was trouble at Mr. Roy Branson's home?"

Bill Cugart in his deep raspy voice answered, "Our dispatcher received an anonymous call. The caller said she heard two shots that seemed to have come from Mr. Branson's house. The dispatcher then alerted me concerning the call. Me and four other officers in two squad cars headed for the scene."

"Where was the call made from?

Cugart replied, "Our dispatcher traced the call to a phone booth near Mr. Branson's house."

"Did the dispatcher give any other details?"

"Yes. His report said that a female caller told him that she was driving through the neighborhood when she heard what sounded like two shots. When asked to give her name, she said she didn't want to get involved and hung up the phone."

"What day and time did the call come in?

The lieutenant glanced at his notes and then replied, "October 14, 1946 at 9:57 a.m."

"I see. And what time did you arrive at the murder scene?"

Cugart answered, "10:04 a.m."

"Wow! That's pretty fast, lieutenant."

Cugart smiled. "When there's trouble in South Bend, me and the boys don't mess around." Laughter rattled through the courtroom.

The judge shook his head. "Order! Counselor, let's stick to the subject."

"Yes sir. When you and the other officers entered the Branson home, what did you find?"

"We found Roy Branson lying on his face in a pool of blood. The defendant, Van Hoffmann was standing over him. Branson had been shot two times from the rear."

"How do you know that, lieutenant?

"Because entrance wounds look different from exit wounds. Besides there were powder burns on the back of Branson's shirt. That indicates close range.

"Was Mr. Hoffmann holding a gun?

"No, but what we believe to be the murder weapon was in a nearby drawer. It had recently been fired. It was a 38-caliber Smith and Wesson Model 10 with a four-inch barrel."

"Were there prints on the pistol and also did you trace the serial number?"

"There were no prints of any kind on the weapon. There was also no way to trace the weapon since the serial number had been removed."

Goldsmith turned, toward the judge. "That's all for now, your honor."

Judge Ransom spoke to my attorney. "Cross examine, Mr. Norman?"

"Thank you, your honor. Lieutenant Cugart. When you drove to the murder scene, did you have the windows of the squad car down?"

Cugart laughed. "Heck no, it was cold that day."

"When you arrived at the crime scene, what was the defendant doing?"

Cugart shrugged and said, "He wasn't doing anything. He was just standing there like he was in a trance."

"From the time the shots were fired, let's say about 9:45 to 9:50, to the time you arrived 10: 04, or about 15 minutes, the defendant just stood there and didn't try to escape? Doesn't that seem strange to you, lieutenant?"

Goldsmith rose with his hand raised. "Objection! The question calls for an expert opinion from the witness."

"Sustained." The judge thought for a moment and then added, "Whether or not it seems strange that the defendant stood over the body for 15 minutes, Mr. Norman, is for the jury to decide, not Lieutenant Cugart."

Virgil Norman continued. "Lieutenant Cugart, have you ever in your long career witnessed a criminal remaining at a crime scene longer than he had to?"

"Yes I have. But it was always when the guilty party wanted to give himself up."

"I understand. Then I must ask you, did Mr. Hoffmann admit to killing Roy Branson?"

"No, he did not."

"Lieutenant Cugart, did you see a car parked in front of Mr. Branson's house when you arrived?"

"No, sir, not at first, but when I reached the front door, I turned and saw an old Studebaker coupe sort of hidden behind a large bush. It was Mr. Hoffmann's car."

"I see. Was the car in one of Mr. Branson's regular parking spaces?"

Cugart smiled. "I don't know. I didn't pay a lot of attention to where the grass stopped and the gravel started." He looked to the audience for approval. Again, the crowd chuckled.

"You have been very helpful, lieutenant. No further questions, your honor." As my life hung in the balance, it appeared to me that Lieutenant Cugart was just having fun.

The judge then said, "Call your next witness, Mr. Goldsmith."

"I call Jeff Richards, police dispatcher. Mr. Richards, did you receive a call at 9:57 on October 14, 1946?"

"Yes, sir, I did."

"Mr. Richards, based on your years of experience, would you say the caller was a man or a woman?

"Definitely, a woman, sir."

"Again, based on your experience, would you say she sounded excited?"

"Yes sir, quite excited."

"No further questions, your honor." Judge Ransom as if timing each witness, glanced at his watch.

"Cross-examine, Mr. Norman?"

"Thank you, your honor. Mr. Richards, based on your years of experience, would you say the woman caller was young or old?"

Goldsmith shouted, "Objection. Counselor is asking for an opinion, besides I fail to see how the woman's age is relevant."

"Overruled. The dispatcher's opinion is acceptable, but I suggest Mr. Norman gets to the point soon, if he has one. Answer the question, Mr. Richards."

"She sounded young, but not a child."

"Again, based on your experience, would you say the caller was black or white?"

"Objection! The question calls for a conclusion on the part of the witness. Your honor, would it be too much to ask Mr. Norman to refrain from these irrelevant questions?"

"The objection is sustained."

"No further questions, your honor." The judge looked at the ceiling. He seemed disinterested. "Mr.Goldsmith, call your next witness."

"I'd like to call Mr. Boris Carville, county coroner." Using a cane to steady himself, Carville waddled to the witness stand. He glanced left and right as if expecting an ambush. His lab coat seemed inappropriate for the courtroom.

"Mr. Carville, did you examine the dead body of Roy Branson?"

"Yes I did, but I didn't do a full autopsy."

"Well, what did you do?"

"Since neither of the two bullets exited the body, I made incisions only large enough to remove them."

"A 38-caliber bullet will in most cases go completely through the body. Why not in this case?"

"They were hollow points. They spread or flatten as soon as they hit any significant resistance."

"Mr. Carville, in your opinion, why did the shooter choose this type of ammunition?"

"Well, I don't know. I don't read minds but I will say that hollow points have greater 'knock down' power, they tear up the body more."

"Were the two slugs that you removed fired from the Smith and Wesson 38 that Lieutenant Cugart found in the nearby desk?"

"Come on, Jerry. You know the ballistic guys do that matching work."

Judge Ransom interrupted. "Mr. Carville, you should know we don't refer to people by their first names in this courtroom. Now answer the question. Did the bullets match the gun?"

"The ballistics guys said they did, but to ask me is hearsay. You lawyer types should know that." Goldsmith shook his head and smiled, "No further questions of this witness."

"Mr. Norman, would you like to cross examine?"

"No, your honor." The witness slowly left the courtroom grumbling something inaudible. The only words I could pick up were, "Waste of time."

"Mr. Goldsmith, call your next witness."

"I have no other witnesses at this time." Things were quiet for a few moments. Had the judge forgotten what he should do next?

"Mr. Norman, do you have another witness?"

"Your honor, I'd like to call Miss Rose Baxter." Miss Baxter was escorted into the courtroom and was sworn in. She was wringing her hands and appeared nervous. "Miss Baxter, what was your relationship with the deceased Mr. Roy Branson?"

Rose squirmed and spoke in a barely audible voice. "I worked for him part time as a maid."

"How did you get to work on those days you worked for Mr. Branson?"

"I took the bus from near my apartment and walked three blocks from the bus stop to his house.

"Did you ever work for Mr. Branson on a day that the defendant, Mr. Van Hoffmann was there at the house?"

"Yes sir, a couple of times."

"Did you work for Mr. Branson on Saturday, October 14, 1946?"

"No sir, I didn't." I wondered why Mr. Norman had called Rose Baxter. I was soon to find out.

" Your honor, I'd like to enter as evidence, Roy Branson's desk calendar for the month of October 1946 and point out the notation in Mr. Branson's handwriting on the day of Saturday the 14th. Let me read it to the jury and Miss Baxter. Quote; '10 a.m.- Van Hoffmann at my house. Rose to come over at 9'." Norman showed the calendar to Judge Ransom and prosecuting attorney, Jerry Goldsmith. Goldsmith seemed to know about the calendar and only glanced at it. It was admitted as evidence. Rose wiggled in her chair. Norman continued. "Miss Baxter, you testified you didn't work that day. Did Mr. Branson ask you to work?"

"Well, er, yes sir, he did ask me, but my baby was sick, so I couldn't."

"Oh, I'm sorry. Did you take your baby to see a doctor?"

"No sir, it was just a cold."

"Who normally takes care of your baby when you are working?"

"Er, Thelma, a neighbor in my building."

"Did you ask her to baby-sit that Saturday, October the 14th?"

"No, sir. She weren't home."

"How about your baby's father, was he available?"

"No, sir, he weren't neither."

"What is the father's name?"

Goldsmith jumped to his feet and shouted, "Objection, the father's name is irrelevant to this case!"

Judge Ransom agreed, "Sustained."

Virgil Norman took off his suit jacket and pulled his pants up over his potbelly. He walked slowly toward Rose never taking his eyes off of her. Rose looked down, then from side to side but not in Mr. Norman's direction. "Miss Rose Baxter, I want to remind you that you are under oath. Here is my question: On the morning of Saturday, October 14th, did you leave your apartment for any reason?" Rose hesitated and glanced up at Mr. Goldsmith. There was a period of silence.

Judge Ransom intervened. "The witness is directed to answer the question."

"Yes, sir, I left for just a short time."

"Who stayed with your baby?"

"My neighbor, Thelma."

"Miss Baxter, I thought you said she wasn't home. You realize I may call Mrs. Thelma Johns as a witness. Tell me, Miss Baxter, exactly what time did you leave your apartment?"

"I'm not sure, about 8:30, I guess." The white of Rose's eyes was visible around her pupils. Norman moved toward her.

"What time did you return home?"

"Oh, I don't know, around ten, maybe." Norman loosened his tie and spoke loudly, "Where did you go?"

"Er, er. To the grocery store." Norman rolled his left cuff up two turns. "Which one? What is the name of the store you went to?"

" I don't remember."

"You didn't go to the grocery store did you, Rose Baxter? You went to Mr. Branson's house didn't you? Didn't you? (Rose hid her face and started to cry)

"I don't remember. I'm scared. Do I have to keep answering them questions, Mr. Judge?"

"Well, yes. But you can take your time." Norman continued to speak loudly.

"I'll ask you again. Did you go to Mr. Branson's house that morning of October 14th?"

"Yes, but I didn't kill him!"

"Well, if you didn't kill him, who did?"

"I don't know."

"You saw the dead body didn't you?"

"Yes, sir. But I didn't kill him."

"Were you still there when Mr. Hoffmann arrived?"

"No sir."

"Mr. Branson was already dead when you left wasn't he, Miss Baxter?"

"Yes, sir. I found him dead when I got there."

"Miss Baxter, did you make the call to the police?"

"What call?"

"You know very well what call. The call saying you heard shots from Mr. Branson's house." Goldsmith jumped up.

"Objection! Your honor, counselor is badgering the witness. He is frightening her. I had advised her before the trial of her rights under the 5th amendment."

The judge admonished Goldsmith. "Well in that case, it's not necessary for you to do it again. Mr. Norman, you may continue."

"How did you get from Mr. Branson's house to the pay phone? Did Mike pick you up? Answer, yes or no, Miss Baxter. Did Mike Levy pick you up near Mr. Branson's house and drop you off to make the call to the police, yes or no?"

"I don't remember." By this time Rose was sobbing heavily. I felt sorry for her. Mr. Norman continued to bore in.

"Did he then pick you up and take you home?"

"I don't remember."

"Your honor, Miss Baxter has testified that the defendant had not arrived before she left and that Roy Branson was dead when she arrived. Therefore, there is not a shred of evidence that Mr. Van Hoffmann had anything to do with the murder." I watched helplessly as the judge summoned Mr. Goldsmith and Mr. Norman to approach the bench. He then directed that the jury leave the room. I couldn't hear what was being said. All I saw was a lot of finger pointing and arm waving. The discussion must have gone on for fifteen minutes. There was a low hum in the courtroom as people (me included) wondered what was going on. As Mr. Norman turned to face me he was smiling. I knew that the news was good.

Judge Ransom said in a very loud voice the two sweetest words I had ever heard, "Case dismissed." Looking a bit irritated, prosecuting attorney, Jerry Goldsmith, walked over to our table. He ignored me and shook hands with Mr. Norman.

He then turned to me and said, "Don't think you're off the hook, Hoffman. We're still coming after you on the Goodall murder." He turned and walked away.

Chapter 13

My first day of freedom was wonderful but confused. I went to my room at Mrs. Kitchall's boarding house, locked the door and went to bed. I didn't know what else to do. I wondered if I still had a job at Studebaker. Since it was Saturday, I had two days to decide what my next move was to be. Mr. Norman advised me to "lay low" for a few days. After what Mr. Goldsmith said to me after the trial, I'll admit, I was quite worried. I believed that union leadership was capable of doing just about anything to maintain power and protect the high wages at Studebaker. I guessed getting rid of me was still high on their list. So who knows what information they might supply to Goldsmith?

I had suspected all along that Mike Levy might have been involved in Benny Goodall's murder. If he was Benny's killer, I figured he was smart enough to have an alibi for his whereabouts on the night of Benny's death. I didn't think he would claim to be at a public place. That would require too many witnesses. A single reliable witness would be safer. Perhaps a girlfriend. It was widely known that Big Mike had many girlfriends. Who would know who they were, I wondered? Willie Wyatt, maybe? I still had that wire recording that would implicate him and Jason Hughes in getting the duplicate key to Benny's car made. And Willie gave those keys to someone, probably the killer. I decided to approach him again.

On Monday morning I walked out to the chassis line to talk to Willie. When I arrived, he was still assembling brakes. I walked up to him, leaned down and spoke in his ear.

"Willie, can you meet me this afternoon after work? We need to talk again. I still have the recording implicating you in getting the duplicate key made for Benny's car. But I've kept my word and haven't turned it over to the police and won't if you'll help me find Benny's killer." He shook his head and frowned.

"Hoffmann, I wish you would just leave me alone. Just being seen talking to you could get my legs broken. I'll meet you in the railroad waiting room at six if you promise not to talk to me any more here at the plant. OK?"

"OK. You got a deal. See you at six." I looked for Jason, but he was nowhere to be seen. I asked the foreman where he was and was told he graduated from Notre Dame and had gone back home to New York. A piece of the puzzle had now disappeared.

Willie showed up at six as requested. Except for ticket clerks, the place was empty. Willie started the conversation.

"Hoffmann, let me set you straight on something. You have pushed me to the limit. I ain't gonna take any more shit from you. You better back off or else."

"Look Willie, you've got to realize where I'm coming from. I've been set up as the murderer of two different men. Through the skill of my lawyer, Rose Baxter testified in court that I couldn't have shot Roy Branson. But I'm still a suspect in the Benny Goodall murder. Only you know who you gave that duplicate set of keys to and who gave you the $200 to have them made. I suspect it was Mike Levy but without your help, I can't prove it. Now is a perfect time to bring that bastard down from his lofty throne. Will you help me?"

"Not only no, but hell no! You must think I'm crazy. If I put the finger on Big Mike, my life wouldn't be worth a plug nickel."

"Let's look at it another way, Willie. If you help bring a murderer to justice, your part in the crime will likely be forgiven since you had no idea the keys were part of a murder scheme. You'd be a hero rather than a villain."

"Listen, Hoffmann, the union and most of this town love Big Mike and if I ever did or said anything against him, I would be hated. Even if Mike was out of the picture, there's plenty more guys to take his place."

"Quit thinking about the union, Willie, and think about what could happen to you if you are convicted of being an accessory to murder. You could go to prison for many years."

"Yeah, maybe. But who's gonna tell the cops about my involvement with the duplicate keys if you're not around?"

"Are you threatening me again, Willie?"

"Yeah, I guess I am. You turn that recording over to the police and get me in trouble and you're a dead man!"

"I figured that might be your response. But getting me out of the way won't keep the information away from the police. That recording not only includes Jason's telephone conversation implicating you but I also recorded your threats when you were in my room last time. It's all safely locked away with instructions to be turned over to the police if anything happens to me. So you see, Willie, my continuing good health is your best defense."

"Van Hoffmann, you're a sneaky son of a bitch. I agreed to meet you at the station 'cause I figured you couldn't record me here."

"O.K. Willie, let's cut to the main question. Did Mike Levy give you $200 to get a spare set of keys made for Benny Goodall's car or not? Yes or no." Willie rubbed his forehead. The decision to answer or not answer was obviously more than his brain could handle at that point. He was aware of his choices.

"I need some time to think it over, Hoffmann."

"I'll give you two days and then I'm going to the police. If something happens to me in the meantime, the police will still get the recording plus a letter from me saying that you threatened me if the recordings were given to them. Two days, Willie. Two days!" Without another word, Willie turned and stormed out.

I knew Mr. Norman would advise me not to, but I took the opportunity to make an unannounced visit at Rose Baxter's apartment. After my knock, she cracked the door about two inches. I could smell cabbage or something equally as odorous wafting through the narrow door opening.

"Hello, Rose. I'm sure you remember me, Van Hoffmann."

"What do you want, Mr. Hoffmeyer?"

"It's Hoffmann. I just want to talk to you. You see I suspect Mike Levy was Benny Goodall's killer. Also, I'm pretty sure he's the one that got you involved in Mr. Branson's murder. If we can get him put away for good, he can't hurt you any more."

"Look here, Mr. Hoff, whatever. I'm in enough trouble already. My lawyer told me that I can't talk to nobody about my case."

"Yes, I understand. But I'm not talking about your case. I'm talking about the Benny Goodall murder. May I come in for a few minutes?"

"Naw, sir. I don't think so."

"I guess you know, Big Mike has many girlfriends. You were not his only one. Do you know who he's seeing now?"

"Listen, I'm gonna have to ask you to leave. You're just gonna get me in more trouble."

"What's her name, Rose? Her name is all I need." Rose slammed the door hard. I heard the lock click.

From behind the door I heard her shout, "Go find that whore, Bessie Henderson!"

Bessie Henderson, Humm. I wondered if she would talk to me. First, I had to figure out where she lived. The phone directory had no listing for Bessie or B. Henderson. There was a number of Hendersons, however. I called them all. When a man answered, I'd hang up. If a woman answered, I'd say, "Bessie?" When I called the Milton Henderson residence, I got the response I was hoping for.

"Bessie?"

"Yes."

"This is Beauty Works Florist. I have a dozen red roses to deliver to you but we spilled water on the card and can't make out the address."

"Roses, huh? Who are they from?"

"I don't know. The man paid cash and didn't leave his name. Wait a moment and let me look at the card. It says 'Dear Bess. Do you still love me? M. L.' That's all it says. I need an address to deliver them." The phone was silent for almost a minute.

Then she said, "954 Huron, Apartment # 21."

I got in my '39 and headed for the apartment building on Huron Street. I had no idea what I would say or do when I got there.

My knock was quickly answered. The door opened revealing a young woman wearing tight yellow slacks and a flower print halter tied at her waist. Her flame-red lipstick was liberally applied. She wore too much perfume. But beneath her cheapness I saw an attractive, well-endowed young woman. I was amazed that she smiled and welcomed me inside.

"If you're the flower delivery guy, where are the poses?" I didn't answer. "Who are you, anyway?" She closed the door and locked it as soon as I stepped inside.

"I'm Van Hoffmann. I made up the story about the flowers just for a chance to talk to you."

"Well, here I am. So talk."

"As you may have read in the papers, Miss Henderson, I'm under suspicion for the murder of a Studebaker executive named Benny Goodall. Someone tried to frame me by placing Mr. Goodall's wallet in my car. The only way I can clear my name is by finding the real killer. I suspect that Mike Levy may have had something to do with the murder and since you are or were a girlfriend of Big Mike's, I thought, well, I hoped you might shed some light on the possibility that he was involved."

"Hoffmann, you got a lot of nerve coming here like this and accusing Mike. I knew there was something fishy about that dozen roses bullshit, so I called Mike to come over here to protect me. Mike!" From the next room the big bruiser wearing a wide smile appeared.

"Well Hoffmann, Bess is right, you've got more balls than brains. You obviously don't know who you're fuckin' with here. So let me fill you in. Mike Levy runs this town, the cops, the Studebaker plant, the mayor, the whole kitten caboodle. The only reason you're walkin' around free today is because Virgil Norman got you off and I didn't choose to stop it. And now you come here and think my sweetheart will turn on me. Bessie loves me too much for anything like that, don't you, Baby?" She smiled and nodded.

"Well, I know one of your sweethearts that may turn on you," I said. "Her name is Rose Baxter."

"That nigger is full of shit. Besides, she never was no girlfriend of mine. I got higher standards. She'll get hers one of these days just like you will, you fuckin' Kraut." Levy stood silent for a few moments and then smiled showing a set of perfect white teeth. "I know it may surprise you, but I'm in a good mood today so I'm gonna let you off easy. Here's the deal. I'll leave you alone if you'll do the same for me." Not knowing what might happen to me if I didn't agree, I reluctantly said OK.

"Now you're using your head, Hoffmann. Let's shake on it." He walked over and extended his right hand. I shook it. He didn't let go. His mighty grip was crushing. Then like a flash of lightning, he jerked me toward him as his left fist slammed squarely into my nose. It felt like my whole head exploded. I knew my nose was broken without feeling or looking. He finally released my right hand and pushed me against the door.

"Hoffmann, that little love tap is just a sample of what you're gonna get if you don't back off. Now get your Boche ass out of here and if I ever hear from you again, I'll break every bone in your fuckin' body!" Bessie opened the door and Big Mike pushed me into the hall. The door slammed shut.

I knew I needed medical help right away. I stood there bleeding all down the front of my shirt. My mind was so addled from the pain of the blow that I couldn't think clearly enough to decide what to do next. I instinctively grabbed my nose to try to stop the bleeding. When I did, a lightning pain made me scream like a cat whose tail just got stomped. It hurt worse than when Mike punched me. Somehow I made it back to my car and to a hospital emergency room. The Novocain eased the pain as the ER doctor realigned the broken cartilage so that my nose was back to its approximate original location.

On the surface, it would appear that my visit to see Bessie Henderson was a complete failure. I walked away with a broken nose, a threat against my life and little else. The only useful thing was finding out that Big Mike and Bessie were on good terms. Therefore, if Mike was involved in Benny Goodall's murder, Bessie might be his alibi. It was a long shot theory but all I had to go on at this point.

Mrs. Kitchall met me in the hall as I staggered to my room.

"Oh, my God, Van. What on earth happened to you?"

"I got in a fight. Well, it wasn't much of a fight. There was only one punch from a fist the size of a cannonball and as you can see, it came from the other guy."

"You poor boy. Is there anything I can do to help?"

"Yes there is. Do you have any film in your Kodak Brownie?"

"Yeah, I think so. You want me to take your picture?"

"Yes and could you witness a statement I plan to make?"

"Sure, Van, just a minute." Mrs. Kirchall returned with the camera and we stepped back outside to catch the fading light of the late afternoon sun. She took shots from various angles making sure my bloody shirt showed. Back inside, I wrote a longhand statement recounting in detail my visit to Bessie Henderson's apartment and the unfortunate encounter with Big Mike Levy. Mrs. Kirchall witnessed my signature. I asked her to turn the document over to police along with the wire recordings of Jason Hughes and Willie Wyatt if anything happened to me.

I knew when I returned to work, I would be bombarded with questions about the large bandage on my nose and the black circles surrounding my eyes. After much deliberation, I decided to tell the truth. I knew that I might be putting myself in harm's way by revealing Big Mike Levy as the one who broke my nose, but I felt exposing him was worth the risk.

CHAPTER 14

Our department secretary's voice quivered. Even over the intercom, I could tell something was wrong. "Van, Mr. Victor Harper wants to see you in his office right away. What should I tell his secretary?"

I pressed the talk key. "Tell her, I'm on my way." I sat for a moment stunned by this request. The president and chairman of the board wants to talk to me? I had never even met the man and had only seen him at a distance. I walked over to the administration building expecting to be fired because of the Mike Levy incident. I had told everyone who asked that Big Mike was the one who broke my nose. When asked why, I said that I thought he was involved in the murder of Benny Goodall and I told him so. I figured Mr. Harper probably heard about this and considered me a troublemaker and a disruption to his cozy relationship with the union boss.

A lone desk dominated Mr. Harper's outer office. The three chairs that sat against the wall were surely a half-century old. A large polished wooden sign with raised metal letters on the secretary's desk read; "Miss Rogers." Her face was stern and hostile with lips that appeared permanently taut. Her black hair was stretched tight and tied into a small bun behind her head. The heavy woolen suit she wore was from another era. She looked old enough to retire but I suspected no one would dare suggest it. Was it her or the office that gave off a kind of 'old people's' odor? She didn't look up as I approached her desk. I cleared my throat.

"Yes?" she asked without raising her head. It was if she was annoyed that I bothered her.

"I'm Van Hoffmann. Mr. Harper asked that I come to his office right away." She looked me up and down spending extra time checking the conspicuous bandage in the middle of my face. She sat for a moment, perhaps trying to decide if I was worthy to enter the president and board chairman's office. After an awkward wait, she told me to have a seat. I would have to wait until Mr. Harper was off the phone. I did as directed all the while wondering if he was really on the phone or was she simply showing her power. In a few minutes she rose and motioned me to follow her through the huge mahogany door. Harper's office looked like Mussolini's. A large wooden desk sat at the far end of the cavernous room. Harper looked somewhat insignificant behind it. The secretary led me to one of the overstuffed chairs in front of the overstuffed president. He didn't rise to greet me.

"Have a seat, Hoffmann. I'll get right to the point. Besides the newspaper articles, there are many rumors circulating about you. The latest is that you had a fist-fight with the president of our union. Is that rumor true?"

"Well, sir, it wasn't much of a fight. The only punch came from Mike Levy. That blow broke my nose."

"He must have had a good reason to hit you. As you should know, Mr. Levy is highly regarded in this company and this community. So your confrontation with him was ill advised. But more importantly, Mr. Hoffmann, you have been charged with the murder of two key engineering employees. Although Mr. Branson's housekeeper testified that Branson was dead before you arrived, the cloud of doubt still hangs over you in the Benny Goodall murder. Now, Hoffmann, it's just a matter of time before the national media pick up on these stories. When that happens, the reputation of the Studebaker Corporation is bound to be damaged. We can't let that happen. Tell me one good reason why I shouldn't fire you?"

"For one thing, sir, the engineering department is short handed now. They need me."

"That may well be, but we just can't have this kind of friction going on between our management people and the union." He sat silently with furrowed brow and stared at me. Finally, he said, " I may regret it, but I've decided to give you one more chance. But let me make myself crystal clear on one thing, the next problem you cause will be your last one here at Studebaker. And definitely, no more confrontations with the union or Mr. Levy, understood?"

"Sir, with all due respect, you must know that Mike Levy and his union are major detriments to Studebaker's forward progress. The high wages and poor work ethic at this plant are keeping us from being competitive with Detroit manufacturers. It's as simple as that. If we don't somehow get those wages down, we'll be out of business in a few years." Harper's face flushed. He jumped to his feet and pounded the top of his desk.

"Who the hell do you think you are, Hoffmann? You have the audacity to barge in here and tell the president of Studebaker how to run his company?"

"I'm sorry, sir. I care about this company and was only stating an opinion."

"Just keep your goddamn opinions to yourself. You can go now." Harper sat back down. I started toward the door.

I turned and said, "Sir, I have a suggestion that might solve many of the problems that apparently I have caused and at the same time open new opportunities for the company. I have noticed that all our efforts in engineering and design are based on current models or models only one or two years out. As you know, Ford, GM and Chrysler all have advanced development programs geared toward the longer-term future. If we believe in the future of Studebaker beyond the 1940s, shouldn't we be studying and experimenting with automotive concepts that fit those long-term goals?"

"We don't have the money for such luxuries, Hoffmann."

"What I propose, sir is a very small group that would work at the Proving Ground. Perhaps only three or four people to start with. After we have developed something that top management agrees has potential, we could then talk about expanding. If you think my suggestion has merit, I would like to manage the project. I would be away from any possible conflict with the union or Mike Levy and I could report directly to you." Harper rubbed his chin and looked at the ceiling.

"I'll have to admit I especially like the part about getting you away from the plant and the union without me having to fire you. What kind of projects do you envision, Hoffmann?"

"I see enormous potential in simplifying our chassis and body designs to eliminate costs and weight. Weight savings, that yield increased gas mileage, could come from many places. As an example, maybe engine blocks could be cast in one piece with the valves located above the pistons. I've been reading about a new overhead valve engine that GM is developing for Oldsmobile and Cadillac. If that development is successful, the weight and cost savings could be substantial. I envision a four-cylinder engine that might even be more powerful than a six-cylinder flat-head with the same displacement." Harper lifted a cigar from his humidor and clipped the end. He lit it and slowly blew smoke in my direction before he spoke.

"I'll think about it. In the meantime, Hoffmann, stay out of trouble. That's an order!"

I nodded and left without another word. On the way back to my office, I scratched my head and wondered how Mr. Harper could be so blind to the high wage problem. If he were not an intelligent man, he wouldn't have risen to the position he held. Yet, he was allowing the company to lose market share because of the union's hold on the company's purse strings. Yes, the union would probably strike if wages were lowered and the incentive program eliminated, but to me taking a strike was a necessary evil. And his outright rejection of the Volkswagen concept without an evaluation made no sense. But at least he seemed open to my forming a new long-term development group. He probably figured by keeping me on the payroll but away from the plant, he could avoid any negative publicity that I might cause.

CHAPTER 15

Days passed with no word from Mr. Harper. Things in the plant were getting worse. No one seemed to respect me any more. Union members often teased me. Comments like "Be glad it's just a broken nose, Hoffmann, next time, Mike'll probably break your fuckin' neck." You hear something often enough, you start to believe it. I wanted nothing more to do with Big Mike Levy.

March 3, 1948, Mr. Victor Harper called. His words were like food for a starving man.

"Alright Hoffman, I'm giving you approval to head up a long term development group to be headquartered at the Proving Ground. There are just a couple of ground rules before you start. First, say nothing to anyone about the new assignment. Just gather up your things and disappear. I want it to appear that you've resigned. And you'll only have one assistant to start with. His name is Jack Yearwood. He is a mechanic from our maintenance shop. He's not a union member. He'll show up at the Proving Ground garage at 8 a.m. tomorrow morning. Your salary and Yearwood's will remain the same. Your expense budget will be $1000 per month. Send your monthly report to the accounting department. I will contact you when I want a report on your activities. Any questions?"

"Thank you, sir. That all sounds good but I'll need more assistants and a larger expense budget to do the job."

"Sorry, Hoffmann. That's the best I can do. Take it or leave it."

"I'll take it!" That afternoon I put my drafting tools, triangles, slide rule, engineer's handbook and other supplies in a cardboard box and loaded them in the trunk of my Studebaker. I then went back inside, picked up my portable drafting board and about 50 sheets of drafting paper imprinted with the Studebaker logo and started for the door.

Jenny, our department secretary stopped me as I was walking out, "What's going on, Mr. Hoffmann, are you leaving Studebaker?"

"All I can say is I've enjoyed my time here in the engineering department but I'm won't be a part of it after today."

The fourth of March was an overcast day. The northwest wind blowing off Lake Michigan was strong and cold. The heater in my '39 worked but heated the car very slowly. The problem was the rusty floorboard and doors with ragged rubber seals that let in too much outside air. The guard waved me through the Proving Ground gate. As I drove between the giant stone posts, I glanced to my right and again marveled at the name "Studebaker" spelled out in tall pine trees. I felt that same warm excited feeling I did the day I tested the Volkswagen. I parked at the garage and was greeted by Ed Reynolds.

"Good morning, Mr. Hoffmann, nice to see you again."

"Thank you, Ed. Since I'll be working here for the foreseeable future, please call me Van. Has Jack Yearwood arrived?"

"Yes, he's over in the shop checking out our welding and engine diagnostic equipment. By the way, you may use any of our equipment if the need arises."

"I appreciate that. We'll do our best to stay out of your way and not interfere with your vehicle testing programs."

I walked over to the shop just as Yearwood came out. He was a tall rawboned fellow in his late 50s. His face was wrinkled and speckled with age spots. A burned down cigarette with a long ash dangled from his mouth. "Jack Yearwood? I'm Van Hoffman." Yearwood stuck out a dry calloused hand, which I shook. "Mr. Yearwood, let's go over to this table and have a little chat. May I call you Jack?"

"Sure and since I'm about twice your age, may I call you Van?"

We both smiled and I nodded.

"Tell me about yourself and how long you've been with the company, Jack?"

"Twenty-eight years. I started on the line back in 1920 assembling wagon wheels. We stopped making wagons when they brought the car manufacturing from Detroit to South Bend. In the next few years I worked in every department from punch press to engine casting. When the union started pestering me to join and I refused, I spent a couple of years in new model development. Then when Raymond Loewy's bunch came in '37, they put me in the maintenance department. At first, the department was non-union, but soon they signed up everybody but me. I've been under constant pressure ever since. I refused to join. I guess that's why they sent me out here to work with you."

"If you don't mind me asking, Jack, what do you have against the union?"

"Oh, I've nothing against collective bargaining. But when the union gets too strong and starts dragging the company down, that's when I draw the line. And that's exactly what has happened at Studebaker since way before the war."

"Well, Jack, I agree completely with your philosophy. As you have probably heard, I recently had a little "dust up" with Big Mike Levy, president of the union."

"Yeah, I heard. By the way, the murder of those two executives that were trying to eliminate incentive pay seems to have just gotten swept under the rug. Something's rotten in Denmark if you ask me."

"Yes and since someone tried to frame me on both murders, I would have to agree. But that whole business can be very distracting. I suggest we just forget about the union for a while and think about the long-term future of car design. You and I are going to develop a low cost car that will assure Studebaker's future, union or no union. Jack, that is our goal." Jack nodded.

We sat at that green metal table all morning defining our objectives and outlining the work to be done. I was impressed with Jack's knowledge in so many areas of automotive manufacturing technology. Not only did he have exceptional hands-on skills, he seemed to possess an unusually keen insight into the whole business. We agreed that as soon as the pent-up demand for new cars was met, competition between American manufacturers would become more aggressive. This would surely lead to price-cutting, something Studebaker could not do and survive. I suggested that in lieu of wage reductions, our only chance to save the company was to develop a simple low-cost vehicle that almost any family could afford. There was nothing like it on the market. Others had recognized this unmet need, but no U.S. company had successfully filled it. American Bantam had come out with a tiny car in 1939. But it was just too small and antique looking. They ceased production in '41 and never started back up. The Crosley Company introduced another "toy" car, last year. But again, it was entirely too small. It would be dangerous to drive something like that on the open highway. Jack and I agreed our design needed to be a real car, just the right size, perhaps a 95- to 100-inch wheelbase, with room for four adults. It had to be simple and easy to manufacture. What we were discussing was a modern Model T or "people's car." I mentioned the Volkswagen concept and told Jack about testing the prototype a few months earlier. I failed to mention that I was intimately familiar with every aspect of its design from its 94.5-inch wheelbase to its 36-horsepower rear-mounted, air-cooled engine. In time, he would surely detect the VW influence in my designs. I told Jack that I thought Ferdinand Porsche's original body shape was a good starting point. But those individual fenders added costs. The "beetle-like" body silhouette would certainly cut through the wind, but a new "slab side" design would be cheaper, add more passenger room and would look more modern. I sketched out an overall shape on a piece of typing paper and showed it to Jack.

We first needed to decide on the engine. Would it be air-cooled or have a radiator? Would it be in the front or rear of the car? Studebaker's expertise was with water-cooled front engine automobiles. Realistically, this had to be given priority. The more radical our design, the harder it would be to sell top management. Besides, rear-mounted, air-cooled engines in the past had been problematic, even the VW's. Water-cooled engines have the big advantage of a simple effective heater. That is something Americans expect.

Although I didn't tell Jack, back when I was a time-study man, I had worked on my zinc-air battery concept at night. I had used a motorcycle battery case to contain the potassium hydroxide slurry with its organic component. The 6-volt output seemed adequate to crank a small starter, so I decided to try the battery in our prototype.

I knew we couldn't use the present Studebaker flat-head six. It was too big and heavy for the car I envisioned. I thought a lightweight four-cylinder overhead valve engine with a displacement of about 1.5 liters would do the job.

Jack and I spent the next few days in the Studebaker library pouring over engine design and development literature. (SAE) Society of Automotive Engineers papers on engines with the camshaft inside the cylinder block and valves operated by pushrods were of special interest to us. We found that valve-in-head engines had been around since the late 20s but were expensive and noisy. Over the years, improvements had made them more practical. We noticed that most of the recent authors of articles about overhead valve (OHV) engines were GM engineers. Automotive News mentioned that GM might introduce a V-8 version overhead valve engine in the '49 Olds or Cadillac. After reviewing the prior art, Jack and I made numerous sketches and drawings before we settled on a design approach we hoped to prototype. Since Jack was an excellent welder, we decided to fabricate the prototype engine block from steel rather than trying to go through all the steps of casting. We would use Studebaker pistons with shortened rods. Other stock parts such as the crankshaft, main bearings, valves, etc. could also be used if modified.

The next few weeks were very busy. I worked ten to twelve hours a day at the Proving Ground garage and then took my drawing board home and worked several more hours. Susie called a couple of times, but I suppose she gave up on me when I told her the kind of hours I was working. I admit I was completely obsessed with the car. I often thought about Mary but my car design always seem to crowd out any thoughts of trying to get back together with her. Besides, Mr. Burgdorf had threatened bodily harm if I bothered her again. So I decided for the time being to concentrate on the car.

CHAPTER 16

B etween Jack's salary, buying steel plates, and welding supplies, my $1000 budget for the first month was soon gone. I knew it would be impossible to purchase the parts necessary to build our prototype car even if we got most of our parts from Studebaker. Transfers between departments were not free. I hesitated to appeal to Mr. Harper. He had made it clear that when he wanted to hear from me, he would let me know. If I made waves, he might rethink the whole project. What to do?

The garage was a beehive of activity most days. Studebaker and competitor vehicles roared in and out at all hours. Jack and I kept to our little corner, trying to stay out of the way. Sometimes the noise was so loud I couldn't think. Exhaust smoke got pretty thick at times. But I knew better than to complain. Occasionally, Ed Reynolds came by to chat. I welcomed his visits. He was always congenial. On one such visit he came up with a gem of an idea.

"How's the small car project going, Van?" he said.

"Oh, it's going OK, I guess. My biggest problem is money for supplies and parts."

"Oh yeah? What do you need?"

"Since we plan to use as many parts from the Studebaker parts bin, if we had a '47 or a '48 Champion sedan we could disassemble for parts, that would be ideal." Ed paced back and forth.

"Does the Champ have to be new?"

"Well, no. New would be better, but not required."

"When we get through testing them here at the track, they're far from new!" he said with a chuckle. "Tell you what, Van. I have a two-door Champ that we put about forty thousand on before one of our drivers flipped it on a high-speed turn last week. The frame is bent and the body is pretty banged up. Also, it probably needs a ring job. We were just gonna scrap it. But it's yours if you want it."

"I'll take it, sight unseen."

Ed soon had the car dragged into our little work area. Jack and I jumped on the car like two hyenas at a kill. We disassembled it, cataloging the parts we planned to use and scrapping the others. After we stripped it down to the frame, Jack pulled the engine and set it aside for parts. The 112-inch wheelbase was too long for our purposes, so I marked where a 12-inch section of the frame should be removed. As it turned out, the slight twist caused by the wreck was not a problem once the two halves were welded back together. Jack did a beautiful job on shortening the frame, the drive shaft and other ancillary parts like brake and fuel lines. We planned to use the existing petrol tank and most of the exhaust system. Even though I was working harder than anytime I could remember, I was having the most fun of my life.

The drafting techniques I learned in Germany were not much different from those used in America. For the parts of my drawings Jack didn't understand, I was always there to interpret. Since the new four-cylinder engine was such a crucial part of our new design, I worked closely with Jack hoping to speed things along. I was optimistic about our progress on the engine design and fabrication until Jack brought me back to earth. He pulled up a chair beside my drafting table and lit a cigarette. He took a long pull, blew it out and turned to me.

"Van, you're a smart fellow and you work very hard. I admire that in you. But let's face it; neither of us knows enough about engines, especially over-head-valve engines to design one. I think we are wasting our time with the design we are working on." I sat frozen. I respected Jack's opinion but his words were unexpected. Even though his comment hurt my pride, deep inside I guessed he might be right. We needed an expert to help us.

"Who's the best engine design engineer in the company, Jack?"

"Don't ask me. It's been ten years since I worked at the foundry. Ed Reynolds probably can help you."

I found Ed in his office hard at work. When I asked him, Ed said a man named Fred Ruskin at the engine block foundry knew more about engines than anyone else in the company. I decided to give Mr. Ruskin a call and see if he would help me.

A gruff voice barked, "Yeah?"

"Mr. Ruskin, this is Van Hoffmann out at the Proving Ground. Mr. Victor Harper has assigned me the project of doing long-range development on future automotive designs. I am working on a new four-cylinder overhead valve engine design but I am not sure I'm headed in the right direction. I was wondering if you could take a look at my drawings?"

"Hoffmann, you say? Van Hoffmann? Aren't you the guy that got into a fist fight with Big Mike Levy."

"Well, it wasn't much of a fight. I insinuated that he might have been involved in the Benny Goodall murder. That's when he broke my nose."

"I don't know, Hoffmann. The last thing I want is a problem with the union."

"There's no risk, sir. I could come to your office. I wouldn't take much of your time."

"No. I don't want you coming here. By the way, why a four cylinder? We don't even make a car small enough to be powered by a four."

"What I'm working on is a light weight, 100-inch wheelbase sedan to sell to the lower middle class family or as a second car for any family."

"Who told you to work on something like that? Every U.S. company that has tried to fill that nitch has failed. The Willis Americar, the American Bantam and the Crosley have all flopped. What makes you think you can do better?"

"Well sir, there were problems with each of the cars you mentioned. The Bantam and the Crosley were just too small. I figure you've got to seat four adults comfortably and have a car that is big enough to be safe on the highway. The Americar was a good size but the design was old-fashioned and most important, 1940 was not the time to introduce such a car. In the early to middle '50s, I think the public will be ready for a small inexpensive car that gets good gas mileage."

"Well Hoffmann, you seem to have done your homework. I live out on Quince Road so coming to the Proving Ground is not that far out of my way. Tell you what, I'll see you tomorrow after work and take a look at your design.

True to his word, Fred Ruskin came by the next day. He walked into the garage like he owned the place. He was a short stocky man with a round belly. His belt rode low in front. Although he waddled like a penguin, he seemed very sure of himself to the point of arrogance.

I was in a discussion with Jack when Ruskin approached "Where's this boy genius that's designing a new engine?" he shouted.

"Mr. Ruskin?"

"Last time I checked," he quipped. "You Hoffmann?" Without waiting for an answer he continued. "Who's that old bastard you got helping you, Hoffmann? I thought we'd gotten rid of Jack Yearwood years ago."

"You two know each other?" I asked.

"'Fraid so. This old codger worked in the casting department about ten years ago. I didn't think he could get any uglier, but I guess I was wrong." Ruskin and Jack shook hands and patted each other on the back. "OK, Hoffmann, let's see what you've got." I spread out the engine assembly blueprint and weighted the corners with pistons. Ruskin leaned over the drawing and studied it carefully for a good ten minutes. He then straightened up, shook his head and smiled.

"You're way over your head trying to design a push-rod engine, Sonny. GM with some of the best engineers in the world has been working on a practical overhead valve motor for years and those boys are still at it. It ain't that simple. I see several problems already with your design. Your connecting rods need to be shorter which means the bottom of the pistons must be cupped in order to clear the crankshaft. And your rocker arms are too spindly. They'd fly apart the first time you cranked it up. And that's only a couple of the problems. Frankly, you're not even close to having a workable design. Besides, if you are developing a four-cylinder, the weight and power advantages of an OHV are not that much over a flat head. Just do a four-cylinder version of our old 'stove-bolt' six. That should be relatively simple. You can use the same pistons and rods if you want to. You'll have to shorten the camshaft and the crank. And you can probably get away with just three mains. Scale down the starter, generator and cooling system. OK? Well, that's it in a nutshell. Gotta go. Mama gets testy if I'm late for supper. Keep this guy straight, Jack. Don't let him bite off more than he can chew." Ruskin turned and was gone.

Jack and I sat and looked at each other for a few moments until finally Jack spoke. "You know, Van, Fred may not be the most diplomatic guy in the world, but frankly, I think he's right on the money about our engine design."

"Yeah maybe, but from all I have read, the OHV engine promises to be lighter and more powerful than a flat head. It's the wave of the future. Ten years from now flat heads will be obsolete."

"Well, my crystal ball is broken," Jack said, "but I'll tell you one thing, if we are going to have a four cylinder manufactured by Studebaker in the foreseeable future, we best take Fred's advice."

"Damn, Jack. This really hurts. It sets us back weeks. We've got so much time invested. I don't want to give up now."

"Well, you're the boss, but I think we'd should do what Fred suggested and scale down our present six."

"I hate to admit failure. I hate it worse than anything."

"It's not failure Van, it's just an adjustment, a change of direction." And so that very day, we scraped the new engine design and I started working on a four cylinder based on the old Studebaker six. Ed Reynolds was able to furnish a set of drawings of the six, so I didn't have to start from scratch. Jack had already started working without any drawings.

At quitting time, with Jack gone, I sat exhausted. I hadn't realized how tired I was until I was alone and the garage was quiet. I didn't take my work home that night. Except for the rattles of my car, I drove home in silence. I had worked so hard on the new engine and now it all seemed wasted. I walked into my room, lit only by a few rays of defused twilight and looked around. Everything seemed old. The chest of drawers painted brown, the roll-top desk with the roll-top missing, even my bed with its sagging springs portrayed an image of failure. I knew I didn't belong here. I thought about my boyhood home in Magdeburg. Instead of waiting for those four walls to close in, I decided to treat myself to dinner and a movie. It seemed like a very long time since I had done anything except work, sleep and try to stay out of jail. My '39 found its way to a familiar old restaurant.

As I sat alone in the elegant surroundings of the Indiana Café, my thoughts drifted back to that night when George Burgdorf invited me to join his family there for dinner. Mary looked beautiful that first night. As our relationship grew, I imagined I'd spend my life with her. I was so foolish. I let it all slip away. I neglected Mary for a brief affair with Susie Goodall. I hoped I might run into the Burgdorfs at the restaurant that night. I knew it was one of their favorite places. It didn't happen.

I didn't know what was showing at the LaSalle. I took my chances. It was *13 Rue Madeleine* starring James Cagney. It was a spy film set in early World War II. We all know who won the war and the winners always have the privilege of writing the history. Like every other American war film I'd seen, the Germans were very evil. The movie didn't cheer me up. Later that night, I lay in bed thinking about Mary, then Susie and then about my father. He was always the voice of reason in our little family back in Germany. Now after almost two years in America, I felt very alone. No family, no friends, not even an identity I could call my own. George Burgdorf was my surrogate father for a while. Now it was Jack Yearwood. Crusty old Jack, so unrefined, so uncouth, so uneducated in the traditional sense and yet his wisdom and advice might save the project and my future at Studebaker.

Chapter 17

While Jack built a four-cylinder version of the standard Studebaker six, I sketched a body for our small economy car. After making a one-tenth-scale side-view drawing, I blew it up to full size and glued it on a couple of sheets of plywood that I had joined at the edge. I took a jigsaw and cut out the silhouette including the wheel openings and propped it up beside our frame. The shape was awkward. This made me realize how limited my styling skills were. When I told Jack how frustrated I was he said I just needed to "get laid." I didn't agree. What I needed was body styling expertise.

Ed Reynolds told me that Raymond Loewy's stylists who designed all Studebaker cars and trucks were some of the best designers in the business. He also told me that they worked in great secrecy. Only top Studebaker executives were allowed access to their work area. That left me out. Since I didn't have the budget to hire a designer, there was only one course left. I would have to keep trying until my body design was attractive. After making many sketches, I finally came up with a side-view silhouette that I thought reasonably attractive. The passenger compartment, hood and trunk looked very much like Porsche's Volkswagen shape. But the headlights were vertical and inset or "frenched" and there were no separate front and rear fenders. The windshield and back glass were larger, slightly curved and slanted more than the old VW. Even though this was progress, I still wasn't satisfied.

Every night I read everything I could find on car styling. The Studebaker library was limited. I was told that the St. Joseph County Public Library had a better selection of books on automotive body design. Should I go to the library to see what they have and risk seeing Mary? I knew if I didn't see her, I'd be disappointed. I finally decided. I'll go!"

The uneasiness I felt when entering the library made my heart pound. I felt light headed. I wondered if Mary would even speak to me. I opened the library door and looked inside. She sat at her desk, talking to a patron. She didn't see me come in. Staying out of sight, I waited for an opportune moment to make my presence known. Finally, the person she was talking to left and I cautiously approached. When she saw me, her beautiful smile changed to a look of surprise.

"Hello, Mary. Remember me?"

"Oh, Van. I'm shocked. What are you doing here?"

"My excuse is I'm looking for books on automotive styling. The real reason is to see you. I know we can't talk here. Could we go somewhere nearby at lunch time?"

"I don't think so. I'm still very upset with you and my father feels the same. I don't think I can believe anything you tell me, anymore."

"Mary, I know my relationship with Susie Goodall was ill advised, but that's completely over now and I promise nothing like that will ever happen again."

"Well, Van or Hans or whatever your name is, it's too late for us. I'm dating someone else now. We'll probably get married."

"Oh, I didn't know. I wish you the best. You're a wonderful girl and I envy the lucky man."

"Well, now that we have that settled, it's my job to help you find what you are looking for. Automotive styling, you say?" I followed her to the shelf where the automotive books were. Her familiar fragrance reminded me of our many pleasant hours together. It reinforced my conclusion that I was an idiot for letting her get away. She picked two books from the shelf and handed them to me is if I were a stranger. I thanked her and sat at a table out of sight of her desk. Knowing Mary was nearby, I found it impossible to concentrate on the books. I figured I'd have to check them out and study them at home. I walked up to Mary's desk.

"Excuse me, Mary. I'd like to check these books out, but I don't have a library card." She handed me a slip of paper.

"Just write your name and address here and I'll issue you a card. Are you still using the Van Hoffmann name?"

"Yes, I have to. I would probably be sent back to Germany if I used my real name. I wish you could understand why I did what I did. I wanted so much to work in the automotive industry and not being a citizen, well, I took a dead man's identity."

"The identity thing was bad enough, but when you told me your relationship with Susie Goodall was platonic, that was the last straw."

"It was platonic at the time I told you that. It was later that it became more. It was wrong, very wrong, Mary. I know that now."

"I'm afraid it's too late, Hans. As I told you before, there's someone else in my life now."

"Please don't hate me, Mary. I still care for you."

"Here's your card and your books. If you are sincere in your feelings for me, that is unfortunate. Because, it's over!" Mary rose and walked away.

I stood like a zombie. I tried to absorb her harsh words. Although I had done nothing to mend the relationship, somehow I foolishly felt or hoped it would work out in the end. I was wrong. All I had now to give my life meaning was the car. That incomplete, inanimate assembly of steel, glass and rubber was my new family, my friend, my everything!

As I drove back to the Proving Ground, I made a decision. I would forget about Mary and Susie and any other female until the car was finished. That wouldn't be much of a change. For all practical purposes, I was already putting most my energy and attention to the prototype car. But from now on, it would be 100%.

When I walked into the garage, I didn't see Jack. I looked for Ed Reynolds to ask him if he knew where Jack was. Ed was nowhere to be seen either. That was strange. I heard noise from the engine testing room. When I looked inside I saw Jack, Ed and several technicians gathered around the dynamometer next to the engine test stand.

"What's going on?" I shouted.

Ed turned to face me. "Van, come over here. This is amazing! Your little four-cylinder has got all the power of a six. And listen to that baby purr. In all my years, I've never seen anything like it. Jack just brought it in, mounted it on the stand, timed it and cranked it up using your zinc-air battery. It ran perfectly the first time, much better than anyone would expect. What magic dust did you and Jack sprinkle to get this little rascal to perform like that? It's unbelievable!"

"I'm not quite sure, Ed. We used the pistons from the Champion. Since the old engine needed a ring job and the cylinder walls were scored, Jack bored it out a few thousandths and used oversize rings, but the displacement is still only about 120 cubes, still much less than a six."

"Well, I don't know what you guys did, but you've got a winner here. Why don't you let me mount it in one of our Champ bodies and test it on the track?"

"Oh, no, no. When you're through testing here, I want it mounted on our shortened lightweight frame. We'll just have to figure a way to build our special body quickly."

Ed still bubbling with enthusiasm said, "I'm really impressed with that engine, Van. I've checked and double-checked the tests. That little four is revolutionary. What you and Jack have accomplished is, I can't find a better word, except 'extraordinary'." I wasn't sure I understood why the engine was so efficient. I suspected the battery had something to do with its power. But now, I had to figure out how to quickly fabricate the new body.

The next step was to make cross-sectional templates every ten inches using the centerline of the front wheel as zero. I defined the body shape through a series of cross sections both front to back and side-to-side. Transferring those shapes into sheet metal was another matter. I planned to use the cowl and doors from the wrecked Champion but had no idea how to shape the remaining body sheet metal. But now I felt invigorated. The outstanding success of our engine and my decision to clear my mind of any thoughts of Mary or Susie made me feel more confident, more intelligent and more focused. There was something magical happening. I couldn't explain it, but I knew it was real. Could it be my zinc-air battery contributed to more efficient combustion? Maybe. We'd figure that out later. But first we had to build a body.

Within hours, I conceived of a way to quickly make body panels. I envisioned 10" wide aluminum sheets bent and attached to a grid of wooden ribs cut to the body contours that I had previously established. There was one potential obstacle. The aluminum panels had to be joined and the seams finished. I crossed my fingers and approached Jack.

"Jack, do you know how to edge weld .040" thick aluminum sheets?"

"Is a pig's ass pork?" he answered with a smile.

"I'll take that as a 'yes'. Suppose we build a wooden grid similar to what you fellows did for clay bucks over in the styling studio, but make the outer contours accurate to the finished body shape. We then will attach the aluminum sheets to the wooden grid and to each other. Does that make sense?"

"Sure does. I hear that's what Ghia over in Italy is doing on some one-off jobs."

"How could we finish the joints so they are smooth enough to prime and paint?"

"You're in luck, Herr Hoffmann. Jack Yearwood also happens to be an expert lead man."

"Lead is heavy, Jack. We've got to keep the car light or it won't perform well."

Jack smiled. "When I get through with the welding and grinding, there won't be much lead left."

"Excellent, let's get started," I said.

As I cut out the ribs and attached them to the frame, Jack followed with shaped aluminum panels. He truly was a skilled welder and very fast. It was all I could do to stay ahead of him. I worked late every afternoon just to have enough for Jack to do the next day. In ten days, he had our car in the paint booth. The finished body was more than I hoped for. We installed the old Champ front seat so the car could be driven. Even in red-oxide primer, she looked great! I named her Freda.

"Well, Van, here's the keys to Freda, the freedom machine," Jack said. "I checked with Ed and he said the track was open this afternoon. She's gassed up and ready to go. I think you should have the privilege to be the first to drive her."

"Thank you, Jack. I want you to know, this is the biggest day of my life and you deserve much of the credit for making it happen. I have confidence that Freda will make us both very proud."

"Good luck, my friend. Drive carefully!"

I timed the acceleration as I took my first lap around the big oval track. Zero to sixty in ten seconds. Excellent for a four! I continued to accelerate. Sixty, sixty-five, seventy. At eighty, Freda was winding at only about 2400 rpm thanks to the Studebaker overdrive. Even with its short wheelbase, she was stable on sharp turns and there was no hint of the rear end breaking loose. I drove the car almost the entire afternoon over every part of the test track including the steep grade and the washboard road. I was not disappointed in any aspect of her performance.

By the time I returned to the garage, Freda was filthy. Jack stood in the doorway holding a set of binoculars.

"I've been watching you, boy. You and that little buggy gave that old test track quite a workout. I'm glad I only primed the body and didn't paint the finished coat. I would have to do it over again."

I jumped out of Freda, almost too excited to speak. "Jack, she performs like a dream. I've got to get Ed to document everything so I can take it to Mr. Harper right away."

The next three days were hectic. As I worked on my report to Victor Harper, Jack painted Freda a shiny battleship gray, the only auto paint he could find in the garage. Ed Reynolds was kind enough to take a series of photographs for me to include along with my report.

On the last page of my report I wrote:

In summary, Mr. Harper, the following specifications (all verified by Ed Reynolds) prove the superiority of this vehicle:
Wheelbase... 100"
Capacity... 4 adults with normal head and legroom.
Engine... 4 cylinder-(a smaller version of our standard flathead 6)
Displacement... 120 cu."
Cooling System... Standard front-mounted radiator. (Willys Jeep radiator used on prototype.)
Exhaust System... Most components from Champ. (Glass-packed muffler is used to increase power and cut costs and give the car a sporty sound.)
Drive train... Studebaker 3-speed, w/ overdrive and shortened driveshaft.
Body... Special aerodynamic shape. Uses standard Champion sedan cowl and doors. Prototype body constructed using .040 aluminum sheet formed over wooden grid. Estimated weight of steel-bodied vehicle, 2100 lbs.

Performance.0 to 60... 10 seconds
Fuel efficiency... 38 mpg highway

    As you can see, the performance of the prototype is outstanding. Of particular interest are the acceleration and the fuel efficiency. Manufacturing costs are yet to be determined. But even if the car is made in our existing plant with its high labor costs, the costs should be considerably less than any vehicle we now manufacture. I welcome future evaluation by whomever you suggest.
Van Hoffmann
Manager of Advanced Vehicle Development
Studebaker Proving Ground

I personally delivered the report to Mr. Harper's office so as not to be delayed by the inter-office mail. The next week waiting for a reply was agonizing. Jack and I used the time to fit window glass and make special lightweight seats.

After a week of no reply from Harper's office, I called to find out what was going on. His secretary answered.

"Miss Rogers. This is Van Hoffmann out at the Proving Ground. I left a report of a new vehicle development program at your office a week ago and I wondered if Mr. Harper has seen it."

"Mr. Harper is a very busy man. Your report will have to wait its turn in his priorities."

"I understand, but this report is of extreme importance. The future of Studebaker may depend on what action Mr. Harper takes after he reads it."

"The future of Studebaker depends on almost every action of our president. Good day, sir."

I stood looking at the handset. I screamed, "Arschloch." (asshole) Luckily, no one was around to hear my outburst. I was sure Harper had not seen the report and maybe would not see it in the foreseeable future. In my opinion, that bitchy old woman was assuming way too much power. I couldn't stand still while the most exciting new vehicle to come along in years was sidetracked by an aging secretary who likely had problems only a team of psychiatrists could solve.

I called Miss Rogers back.

"Miss Rogers, this is Van Hoffmann again. I would like to schedule a meeting with Mr. Harper at his earliest convenience."

"Oh, I'm afraid that's impossible. If he wants to see you, he'll initiate a meeting. It may be awhile. The board of directors is in this week. I'll tell Mr. Harper you called. Goodbye." I couldn't remember ever being this angry. I knew that the real problem was Victor Harper, not his secretary. She was simply an extension of his own arrogant, self-important attitude. I realized that if this project were ever to get off the ground, it would take drastic action.

CHAPTER 18

Two days passed and still no word from Mr. Harper. How was I going to get his attention? Then it hit me. Wouldn't it be great if I could present the car to the whole board? To have any chance at all, I needed to find out the Board of Directors' schedule for the week. But I couldn't just burst into the boardroom unannounced and make my case. I rubbed my temples, searching for an answer. At some point in the week, the board will surely play golf. I knew Miss Rogers would not tell me when or where, so I asked Ed Reynolds the name of the most exclusive course in South Bend. He said it was the Morris Park Golf and Country Club. I called them.

"Pro Shop? This is Van Hoffmann, Mr. Victor Harper's assistant. I want to double check his tee time and the number of slots you have allotted to him and the Studebaker Board."

"Let me see, Mr. Hoffmann. Here we are. They are scheduled for three foursomes starting at 10 a.m."

"And the day?"

"Tomorrow, of course. Is there some problem? Miss Rogers has already checked these arrangements."

"No, no, no problem. Thank you." I hung up.

By this time, I was driving Freda almost exclusively. My '39 had been parked at the Proving Ground garage for several days. I loved driving that little prototype car. The low rumble escaping from her tailpipe reminded me of the big Mercedes and Porsches I admired as a boy. Even though Freda had only four cylinders, the glass-packed muffler made her little engine sound strong and powerful. I learned Freda's limits on the test track and felt I was now an expert driver behind her steering wheel. My plan to get Harper's attention was risky. It might get me fired. But I couldn't sit still and not bring this opportunity out in the open. As part of the plan, I took two large sheets of poster board and boldly painted on each, "1951 Studebaker Economy Car."

I didn't drive to the Proving Ground that next morning. I ate a leisurely breakfast and then headed out McKinley Street to the Morris Park Country Club. The tree-lined neighborhood reeked of class and wealth. Freda looked out of place but on we persevered. I drove around the country club parking lot until I saw the pro shop. I looked for a place to park where Freda wouldn't be seen by the golfers parking nearby. Walking down to the first tee, I was surprised at how well kept the course was. The grass was smooth and green and still a bit damp from yesterday's rain. At 9:35, I made my way back to watch for Mr. Harper and the board. At 9:40 three shiny black chauffer-driven Studebaker Land Cruisers arrived. Mr. Harper and three other men got out of the first car. To my surprise, Mike Levy was in the group. After the three cars unloaded, the board and Big Mike entered the pro shop. At 10:05 the first foursome, Vic Harper, Levy and two other men were starting to tee off. I waited until the third group was on the first green before I made my move. Using masking tape, I affixed the cardboard signs, one on each door and positioned myself behind Freda's steering wheel. I took a deep breath, started her up and proceeded toward the first green as fast as I could go and still be in control. When I passed the green, I was going 53 miles per hour. The four startled board members stopped their putting to watch this unusual sight. On I drove, passing the second green at about the same speed. The golfers pointed and shouted. I made two sliding circles around the number three green. On the second pass I noticed deep ruts Freda was making. Sliding to a stop, I jumped out and ran over to the shocked foursome.

"How do you like our new economy car prototype, Mr. Harper? Harper stood with his mouth open, apparently too shocked to speak.

He finally regained his composure and shouted, "Hoffmann, are you out of your mind? What in the hell are you doing?"

Mike Levy stepped forward and spoke to Mr. Harper. "Want me to take this kraut to the police for you? He's obviously broken a number of laws."

"No, you just stay here with him and I'll send a caddy back to call the police." Harper hesitated. "No wait, we don't want this in the papers. Hoffman, get this vehicle back to the Proving Ground at once. Be in my office at 9 a.m. in the morning. That's an order."

"I'll be there, sir. But you didn't tell me how you liked the car."

"You impertinent ass. You better get going before I turn Mike loose on you." I certainly didn't want that to happen so I jumped in Freda and peeled out in the direction of the #2 green. Figuring I couldn't get in any more trouble than I was already in, I drove even faster on my trip back to the parking lot. As I passed the board members waiting on greens two and one, several men waved. I thought that strange. I waved back. As I approached the pro shop, I saw several people watching from the parking lot. Unfortunately, one of them was a uniformed police officer. He motioned for me to come to him. I was so excited, I didn't think. I just kept going. Freda jumped the curb and headed for the open road. The policeman blew his whistle. Too late, I was on my way back to the Proving Ground.

I pulled Freda inside the garage. I killed the engine and patted her dash. "You did a great job today, dear girl. I'm really proud of you." Her horn honked. "You got a short in your wiring, Freda?" I asked.

Jack walked over. "You talking to that car again? Hey, what's this sign? '1951 Studebaker Economy Car.' What the hell you been up to, boy?"

"Jack, you won't believe what I just did. I drove Freda all over three holes of the Morris Park Golf Course at over 50 miles per hour. I shocked the shit out of our board of directors!"

"Oh my, God. You're not serious. What possessed you to pull such a crazy stunt as that?"

"I figured it was the only way I was ever going to get Mr. Harper's attention. Oh, he was mad as hell and will probably fire me, but I did get his attention."

I got rid of the two signs and asked Jack to throw a tarp over Freda. I expected the police to show up at any moment. They didn't come. I drove my '39 back to the boarding house that afternoon. I was surprised the police were not there waiting. I didn't sleep much that night. I was too excited. The next morning I drove to Mr. Harper's office for our 9 a.m. meeting. Miss Rogers was at her usual place looking as unpleasant as ever.

"Good morning, Miss Rogers. How are you this lovely day?" She looked at a remote spot on the ceiling.

"Sit down, Hoffmann! Mr. Harper isn't in yet." I sat quietly thumbing through an old copy of Automotive News. Finally, Harper walked in. He walked past me without making eye contact and stopped at Miss Roger's desk. She handed him a stack of papers and he disappeared into his office without a word. After about fifteen minutes, Miss Rogers' phone rang. After a series of "Yes, sirs," the bitter old woman looked my way and pointed toward Mr. Harper's door. I walked in to find him pacing back and forth behind his desk. I stood perfectly still, waiting for something to happen. Mr. Harper looked at me with squinted eyes. He started to talk then coughed as if choking on something.

He cleared his throat and barked, "Hoffman, in all my years, I have never before been associated with anyone as difficult to deal with as you. That stunt you pulled yesterday really showed me what kind of person you are. By all rights you should be an unemployed jailbird right now. That would have been my choice, but two of my board members think we should evaluate your silly-looking little car. I don't agree, but as a courtesy to them, I have asked our new Vice President of Engineering, Bob Nitske, to cost the car and evaluate its potential. Mr. Nitske will be your new boss starting tomorrow. Any questions?"

"Yes, sir. Could you ask our sales and marketing people to also evaluate the car's potential?" Harper's face was flushed. Veins on his forehead were visible.

"Dammit, Hoffmann. Is there no end to your audacity? I'm beyond sick of your 'know-it-all' attitude. I'll decide those kinds of questions!" Mr. Harper reached in his back pocket and pulled out a handkerchief. He wiped his forehead and continued. "The only reason you weren't arrested is that I assured the club president that Studebaker would take care of the damages if the incident were kept out of the papers. I convinced him that the stunt was planned." Harper held on to the edge of his desk. He again wiped his face and said, "Hoffmann, I never, ever want to see your face again. Now get your ass out of here before I change my mind and fire you." I left without another word. As I walked past Miss Rogers, I smiled and gave her a snappy salute. She raised her shoulders, closed her eyes tightly and shook as if she had a chill.

I went back to the garage and sat at my drawing board. What was I supposed to do? Was it my responsibility to contact my new boss for instructions? My questions were answered when I arrived at the garage the next morning. A tall well-dressed man was leaning inside Freda's hood. I walked over and stood silently waiting for him to notice me.

After about a minute, I cleared my throat and asked, "Mr. Nitske?" The man quickly straightened and bumped his head on Freda's hood. The middle-aged gentleman rubbed the back of his salt and pepper gray hair, finally looking my way. "Are you Van Hoffmann?" I nodded and stuck out my hand. He shook it firmly and said, "Pleased to meet you, my boy. I've only been with the company a couple of weeks and yet I've heard more about you than anyone else except maybe Mike Levy. You're becoming quite the topic of conversation. That stunt you pulled at the Morris Park Golf Course day before yesterday was really something. You're now a hero at the water cooler. But Victor Harper tells me you are a difficult employee and a challenge to supervise."

"Sir, when the superior performance of this prototype vehicle was repeatedly ignored, I felt drastic action was justified. If that's being difficult to supervise, I plead guilty."

"Well, Mr. Harper also cited other problems like your fight with Mike Levy."

"Did Mr. Harper tell you that I was framed as the murderer of your predecessor, Roy Branson? I suspected Mike Levy was somehow involved in the murder and I told him so. That's when he broke my nose." Nitske smiled and shook his head.

"Well, I'll say this for you Hoffmann, you're quite a character. But as far as I'm concerned, you are starting in my department with a clean slate. But one more crazy stunt and out you go. From now on, you and I are going to concern ourselves entirely with the prototype car and not past problems. Have you given the car a working name?"

I smiled and replied, "I call her Freda, and my assistant, Jack Yearwood calls her the Freedom Car. Have you met Jack?"

"Yes, I have. We had a long talk. Seems like a talented guy. Freedom, Freedom. I like that name. Of course, if the car is ever produced, the marketing guys and the ad agency will probably have other ideas. Okay, let's get started."

Mr. Nitske and I sat and had a detailed discussion about every aspect of Freda's design and construction. Neither he nor I could explain her outstanding performance in both acceleration and gas mileage. The weight of the car and the strength of a 220 c.i.d. four cylinder would predictably yield lower numbers, but Freda was not predictable. Nitske vowed not to lose those outstanding numbers with "design improvements." I was happy to hear him say that.

Within a week, Nitske moved a team of four engineers out to the Proving Ground garage. He said he wanted me available but if I'd like to work on another unrelated project, it would be okay with him. I got the hint and told him about the zinc-air battery that was in the prototype car. I admitted that I knew little about its capabilities and how to control its output. I asked for an assistant with a background in physics or chemistry. Nitske said he would see what he could do. In the meantime, he allowed Jack to help me with the battery program.

In the next few weeks, the team of engineers analyzed every nut and bolt of Freda's engine, drive train, chassis and body. It was difficult to accept these strangers making decisions on Freda's production design without consulting me. But I kept telling myself that what they were doing was necessary if the car was ever to be put in production.

Chapter 19

8 p.m., January 3, 1949

As I walked the deserted streets near my boarding house, I marveled at the heavy snowflakes hurrying to the ground. Only dim lights from nearby homes lit the way. The cold wet snow clung to my face. I breathed deeply feeling the chilly air clearing my lungs and my brain. I wondered why I was out in that weather when I didn't have to be. I could be in my warm room reading or listening to German music on my short wave radio, but no. I chose to be alone out in the frigid night, shivering and thinking. The night reminded me of the night I slipped away from the plant at Wolfsburg. But some things were very different. At least I wasn't soaking wet and freezing. But my ambition was still the same as then. And with recent developments, my goal of helping design a "people's car" had a real chance of becoming a reality. Bob Nitske was having Freda repainted for the upcoming Chicago Auto Show. This was to be Chicago's first major postwar show. Although he did not suggest I go as a company representative, Chicago was close and I could go on a weekend like anyone else as long as I paid my own way. I smiled at the thought of Freda and her new coat of sky blue paint and all those thousands of people admiring her aerodynamic shape. On I walked. Snow was several inches deep and the temperature was below freezing. The northwest wind off Lake Michigan cut through my thick coat.

Getting the '39 started every morning took considerable preparation. I parked as close to the boarding house as I could. That way the wind wasn't so strong and I could reach the engine with a drop cord and a 60-watt bulb that I laid on her engine block. Mrs. Kitchall gave me an old blanket that I draped over the hood to hold in some of the warmth. But my worn out starter was dragging and my battery had seen its best days. So, starting the old Stude was painfully slow. It would cost me thirty-four dollars to get a new starter and since I was still making payments to my lawyer, I couldn't spare the money. If only Freda were available, I wouldn't have to worry. Even in the coldest weather, her zinc-air battery cranked like she was in the tropics. I couldn't yet prove it, but I suspected the battery was a big factor in Freda's outstanding performance. As an added benefit, the battery was smaller and twenty pounds lighter than the old lead plate type. Since it didn't need recharging, it required no generator. But Mr. Nitske said he suspected the battery would probably have to be replaced once a year. Nitski said he thought the basic idea was good, but that other top executives he had talked to felt Studebaker owners wouldn't accept having the annual battery change requirement.

The month of January was quiet. The 1949 Studebaker models had been introduced with little fanfare. They were face-lifted '48s that were face-lifted '47s. It was the third year of the same design. Other manufacturers had come out with all new models. I saw ads in magazines and an occasional new car on the street. But South Bend was a Studebaker town and few other makes traveled its streets.

A week before the show opened, Freda was loaded on a car carrier with several standard 1949 Studebaker models. I missed Freda's gray color, but I had to admit, she also looked great in blue. Hell, she'd look good in any color. Jack and I stood in the garage doorway. I shouted goodbye. Freda's horn honked.

"Did you hear that, Jack? That's the second time that's happened. I checked the wiring and couldn't find anything wrong. Very strange."

"Yeah, strange indeed," Jack said with a smile." I wonder if it has anything to do with that little zinc-air battery of yours?"

Since I knew my boss would be in Chicago and wouldn't drop by the garage, I went all week without shaving. With my long blond hair and scraggly beard, I looked more like a street bum than an engineer. But I had a plan. I took off early Friday and went shopping. At Woolworth, I bought a pair of horn-rimed glasses with clear lenses, a package of temporary brown hair dye and a dark brown eyebrow pencil. At Sears-Roebuck, I bought a pair of overalls and a plaid cap with earflaps. After supper, I went to my room and prepared for my trip to Chicago. I dyed my hair and stubby beard; I dressed in my farmer's outfit, and put on my hat and glasses. Looking in the mirror, I was startled by the stranger in my room. I went into the hall and knocked on Mrs. Kirchall's door. She opened it and looked me up and down.

"Can I help you, sir?"

"Yes, Madam," I said in my best mid-western voice. "I wondered if you have a room to rent. I hear that German fellow is not working out."

"Where did you hear that?" she said. I took off my cap and glasses and spoke in my natural voice.

"He told me himself." Her eyes widened as her face erupted into a big smile.

"Van Hoffmann, you rascal. What are you made up for? Going to a costume party?"

"No, I'm going to the Chicago Auto Show tomorrow dressed as a farmer. If you didn't recognize me, I don't think Studebaker people will either."

"Why don't you want to be recognized?"

"I want to listen in on conversations without revealing my identity. That way, maybe I can get a true picture of what people think of my prototype car."

"I'm sure you can get lost in the crowd," she said. "There'll be lots of hayseeds just like you looking at the cars."

Wearing my full disguise, I caught the 6:35 a.m. bus to Chicago. I realized that this was the first time I had been on a bus since I arrived in South Bend three years earlier. The two-hour trip gave me ample time to plan my day. A short three-block walk from the Greyhound station took me over to Halsted Avenue where I caught a local bus to the International Amphitheatre on 43rd Street. Once inside, I resisted the temptation to linger among the beautiful new cars of other manufacturers and headed directly for Studebaker. Attendants in dark blue jackets and golden Studebaker nameplates circulated among the cars, talking to people and answering questions. The vehicle attracting the biggest crowd was Freda. I blended in and listened to some of the discussions.

"What's this thing supposed to be? It looks like a big bug," a middle-aged man said.

"It's a new design of an economical car. It will get 38 miles for every gallon of gas it uses. Would that interest you?" the attendant replied.

"Well, yeah, I guess. How much will it cost?"

"We don't know that yet, sir, but probably less than our Champion 2-door."

"When's it coming out?"

"We're just judging interest here at the show. The decision to produce the car hasn't been made." I worked my way nearer Freda until I got the attendant's attention.

"Who would want a car like this?" I asked.

"Anyone who is interested in saving money and maybe a family that needs a second car. The reaction to the car so far has been very good!

Obviously, it's not for everyone, but those who have stopped to ask questions seemed impressed," he answered. That was good news to me. I decided to look at the other cars and check back on Freda periodically during the day.

My next stop was the Cadillac area. If there is life after death, this was surely one section of heaven. The new '49 was even more beautiful than the '48 which was "all new" that year. Especially lovely was the fast-back Sedanette. That rear fender with its gorgeous front curve was perfectly accentuated with small fins at the top of the rear edge. Best of all, the '49 Caddy had a new 331c.i.d. overhead valve engine. A spokesman said the engine was much smaller and lighter than the previous one, yet more powerful. I was now certain OHV engines were destined to obsolete the old flat heads in just a few years.

Chevrolet, Plymouth and Ford all had new bodies for the 1949 model year. Only the Ford's was outstanding in design. If the rumor I heard was true, two Studebaker designers designed this car. As the story goes, Bob Bourke who was manager of Raymond Loewy's studio was forced to terminate one of his designers, a young fellow named Dick Caleal. Caleal contacted George Walker, a design consultant for Ford, about a job. The deal was if Dick came back in two weeks with a quarter-scale model that Walker liked, he'd give him a job. Wanting to help the poor fellow, Bob Bourke and fellow designer Bob Koto built a clay model on Caleal's kitchen table. Dick took the model to Walker who showed it to Ford executives. That 'kitchen table' model evolved into the new 1949 Ford design. Not surprisingly, George Walker got credit for the design.

I visited Chrysler, DeSoto, Dodge, Lincoln, Mercury, Pontiac, and Oldsmobile. All had new bodies for 1949 but none showed much imagination and were bulbous and painfully bland. Nash, Packard and Hudson had bodies that resembled inverted bathtubs. Crosley's little car was shown, but like previous models it was just too small for the open road. And I heard the car had engine and brake problems. The only car that I thought might be competition for Freda was a prototype that Kaiser-Frazier showed. They called it the "Henry J". It was reasonably attractive, had a 100" wheelbase and was powered by the "Go Devil" 4-cylinder engine from the Willys Jeep. They planned to introduce it sometime in the next year.

When I got back to the Studebaker area, a large crowd was gathered around Freda. Just in front of me I recognized Victor Harper and Mike Levy. I inched closer and listened.

Big Mike spoke in Harper's ear. "You know, Vic, if we put that little car into production, we'll lose money on every one we make."

"Why do you say that, Mikie?"

"Well, it's gonna take the same amount of labor as any other car, yet you'll have to sell it for less money. Even if it sells well, we'll be knocked off in a short time." Harper nodded and then turned toward Levy.

"Well, the problem is, I have a couple of board members who think there is a market for a small economical car like that and I can't convince them otherwise."

"Just tell them you've talked to the president of the union and he's against it and hinted at a strike."

"Come on, Mikie. Don't talk like that. Why are you so against the car?"

"Well for one thing, that Kraut that designed it. He's anti-union from the word 'go'. We need to find a way to get rid of that little shithead and producing his car will only make him stronger."

"Yeah, he's a real pain alright. I would have fired him long ago except he might cause us more trouble as an ex-employee. You know, spilling his guts to the papers. I think he knows more than he lets on." Both men stood silently for a few moments and then Harper said, "Hey, I have an idea. Why don't you and I drive this little car back to South Bend tomorrow? Then we can give personal testimony to all its shortcomings. You to the union and me to the board." As I listened to Levy and Harper, I distinctly heard a noise from the platform where Freda sat. It sounded like a groan. Big Mike turned his head and cupped his ear. As he did, he looked directly at me. He turned back toward Freda for a moment and then looked at me again. He nudged Mr. Harper. I disappeared into the crowd.

The bus ride back to South Bend gave me time to think. How could the prejudices of the union boss and the company president be overcome? And then my thoughts turned to Big Mike and Mr. Harper driving Freda back to South Bend. I didn't like the idea, but there was nothing I could do.

It was very late when the Greyhound pulled into the station in South Bend. This had been a long day. After coaxing my '39 to start, I made my way home. I decided to wait until tomorrow to wash my hair, shave and try to look like my old self.

It was almost noon when I finally greeted Sunday morning. I stayed in my room until I had gotten rid of all traces of my disguise. The hair color didn't completely wash out but all things considered, I looked much like myself again. I enjoyed the free day but looked forward to going back to work on Monday. As was my normal routine, after Sunday night supper, I return to my room and turned on the radio to a local station to hear the news. After the weather report and a couple of minutes about the Fighting Irish of Notre Dame, the announcer stopped mid sentence.

"Just in! A terrible automobile accident that occurred on Highway 20 near Michigan City this afternoon has claimed the life of Studebaker president and board chairman, Victor Harper. From reports just received, Harper and Union local #9 president, Michael Levy were the only occupants of the car. They were driving a prototype vehicle that had been on display at the Chicago Auto Show. Levy was thought to be driving. His passenger Victor Harper was dead when the Indiana State Police arrived. Levy is in critical condition in the St. Joseph County Hospital. First on the scene was Studebaker Vice President of Engineering, Bob Nitske, and Board Vice Chairman, Ray Hobson. Nitske said they were following the prototype car to make sure nothing went wrong. According to Nitske, for no apparent reason, the car veered off the main road and over an embankment, resulting in the death of Harper and Levy's injuries. We will have more details as they come in. Now back to our regular program."

A million thoughts ran through my mind. I knew that Freda was in perfect mechanical condition. What could have gone wrong? Would the car be blamed for the wreck? How bad was the damage? Since Michigan City was only 36 miles away, I considered going out to find Freda, but figured the car was probably impounded in a lot somewhere and I wouldn't be able to see her. Maybe the car was towed back to South Bend. Not knowing what else to do, I went to bed. I tossed and turned most of the night.

When I arrived at the garage Monday morning, no one was working. Everyone was standing around talking about the tragic accident. I joined Jack, Ed Reynolds and a couple of the engineers.

Ed who also worked for Niske said that he got a call late last night that he was to thoroughly inspect the prototype car for mechanical failures. He said that the inspection was to be done in a secure location. The prototype car would arrive at the garage that morning.

At ten o'clock when Freda was hauled in, Bob Nitske was riding in the cab of the wrecker. He got out and while the driver unloaded Freda, he gathered us around for a briefing.

"Gentlemen, we have a very serious situation on our hands. I have been instructed by board vice chairman, Ray Hobson to restrict the inspection and evaluation of the prototype to Ed Reynolds, Jack Yearwood and myself. A member of the state police will also be present around the clock until my report has been submitted to Mr. Hobson. All other personnel will return to the Engineering Building downtown and work at that location until further notice. Are the any questions?"

I asked, "May I take a look at the car before I leave?"

"I'm afraid not, Van. I have my orders. Everyone has to leave now." As I passed by Freda on the way out, I couldn't help noticing how little she was damaged. A couple of side windows were cracked and the top was dented and scratched, yet it was reported that she rolled over several times.

"Good luck, Freda," I said as I passed. Her horn honked causing everyone in the garage to freeze.

Chapter 20

I felt lost at the engineering office. Nitske gave me no assignments so I wandered around looking for something to do. In the plant I received jeers and slurs, such as, "Hey Kraut, I hear your toy car hurt Big Mike. You'll get yours soon enough, you son of a bitch!" I decided being on the plant floor was not a good idea. As I headed back to the office, I passed the chassis line. There was Willie Wyatt assembling brakes. He yelled at me.

"Hey, Hoffmann. Get over here. I've got a few choice words for you." Not wanting to show weakness, I walked over to his station. Willie shouted loudly so all workers in the area could hear. "Your shitty little car put Big Mike in the hospital and the whole union is damned mad. Your car is a killer!" I chose my words carefully.

"There was nothing wrong with that car, Willie. My guess is the wreck was caused by the driver."

"Bull shit. Mike is a great driver." I moved closer to Willie and leaned down to whisper in his ear.

"Willie, I know what you're doing. Make a big show so everybody thinks you're mad. I know better. There's no reason for you to continue to hide the fact that Levy was the one who gave you the $200 dollars for the extra keys to Benny Goodall's car. He can't hurt you now. He may be out for a long time. You know as well as I that Big Mike killed Benny. I said I wouldn't turn the recording of you admitting to getting money for the keys over to the police, but things have changed. We need to talk."

"Okay, but I got to think this thing through," he said in a low tone. Then he shouted, "Now get your ass out of here before I hit you with a brake shoe!" Several workers applauded. I hurried away.

Not being able to go to the Proving Ground to see what was happening to Freda was driving me crazy. My curiosity was getting the best of me so I called Jack Yearwood at home.

"Jack. How's the evaluation coming?"

"We're done as far as I know. I've been instructed to keep quiet on the results until the official report is released."

"Come on, Jack. You can tell me. After all, I'm the designer." There was a long pause.

"Oh, OK. I suppose you have some rights. Here it in a nutshell. We couldn't find anything wrong with the car. Now if you breathe a word of what I just said, you've lost a good friend."

"OK, Jack. Not a word. Thanks."

The next two days were pure misery. Because of the jeers and insults I had received when I walked through the plant, I stayed in the engineering office. But I had nothing to do. The other engineers ignored me. I didn't even have a desk of my own. I sat in a folding chair in a back corner of the main drafting room and read all day. Three years of hard work had come to this. Finally, Bob Nitske called the whole department together for an announcement.

"I'm sure you all have been anxiously awaiting a report on the cause of the wreck that killed our president and board chairman, Mr. Victor Harper and injured our union president Mr. Michael Levy. Newspapers have gone into some detail about the circumstances surrounding the tragic accident and for the most part, they were accurate. The biggest question remained however; did the car have defects that might have caused the accident? Did a tie-rod come loose, did the brakes fail or was it some other mechanical failure?' Careful examination by an unbiased engineering team found no mechanical defect in the vehicle. Even so, for a number of reasons that I won't go into today, the board of directors has unanimously decided that the prototype vehicle is to be destroyed and all future work on the small car concept is to be suspended. I will be contacting each of you who have been involved in the project with your new assignments in the next few days. That is all for now. Please return to your workstations."

I was so stunned I could hardly move. They were going to scrap Freda. My whole world was crumbling. I ran out of the office, jumped into my '39 and drove as fast as I could to the Proving Ground. The guard at the gate stopped me and pointed to a slip of paper mounted on a clipboard.

"Mr. Hoffmann, I've been instructed to let only the people listed on this paper into the grounds and your name doesn't appear. I'm sorry, sir."

"You know me, Frank. I've been working out here for months."

"I'll lose my job if I let you in. I'm sorry."

"Get Ed Reynolds on the phone, he'll get me in."

"It won't matter what he says. My instructions come from Mr. Nitske."

I drove back to the office and tried to find Nitske. We ran into each other in the hall. It turned out he was looking for me, also.

"Oh, Van, there you are. Let's find somewhere quiet where we can talk." We ducked into an empty office. His gaze frightened me. He seemed to read my thoughts. "First off, you have every right to be upset. I know how much of yourself you put into that car and now it's to be destroyed. "Upset is not an adequate word, Mr. Nitske. More important than my personal disappointment, it seems so unwise to destroy a car with so much promise and you, yourself said that car was not the cause of the wreck."

"It was not up to me, Van. But I must admit the board had some good points in making the decision they did. No matter what the engineering findings were, the union and others will always blame the car since to do otherwise would naturally place the blame on the driver. In fact, the union has said it would strike if we don't destroy the car. Although there have been many wildcats, this would be the first formal strike in Studebaker's 100-year history. The first shift is already forming a picket line." I interrupted.

"Oh, so that's it? The union has spoken. We certainly can't place any blame for the accident on the great Mike Levy, can we?" I pounded the wall behind me with the ball of my fist.

"Take it easy, son. The decision is made. There's nothing you or I can do about it." I felt desperate.

"Can I purchase the car?"

"No. That's not possible."

"Why can't I buy it?"

"Liability. We've already got a huge problem with Mr. Harper's family. We simply can't allow the car to be in private hands."

"So what's to happen to me? Do I still have a job?"

"Starting tomorrow, you will be a junior time-study engineer. Your pay will be reduced accordingly."

"That's the job I started with three years ago. And I can't work in the plant anymore. They hate me out there."

"Sorry, Van. That's the best I can do." With that news, I knew I couldn't stay at Studebaker much longer. I now had two objectives; leave in an honorable way and somehow save Freda.

I needed good advice from someone I could trust. I made an appointment with Virg Norman. I had only one more payment left to make for his work defending me in the Roy Branson case. On my way to his office, an idea hit me. I had gotten a letter from Karl a few days earlier inviting me to visit him at his new location in Huntsville, Alabama. Maybe I should take him up on his offer. I pulled the letter from the glove compartment of my car and read it again.

March 14, 1949

Dear Hans,

I bet you are surprised to hear from me. I'm sorry that it has been so long between letters but as I told you earlier, I'd wait until my transfer to Huntsville, Alabama before I wrote again. Dr. Von Braun and many of his scientists and engineers are in the process of making the transfer. The work continues to be exciting but highly pressurized. By that I mean our goal is to be able to develop a rocket capable of launching an orbiting satellite within the next five years. It is believed the Soviets have the same goal.

We are all treated exceedingly well here and are becoming quite Americanized. We expect to be granted our citizenship in the near future. Are you still posing as the cowboy engineer, Van Hoffmann? I heard on the news that the Studebaker president got killed in a car wreck. Did you have anything to do with that? Ha, ha.

After three years, you should be getting a vacation. Why don't you come to Huntsville and visit your old Berlin Institute roommate? It would be great to see you again and trade stories. Write to me soon.

Your faithful friend, Karl

I drove on to see Virgil Norman. His office looked the same as when I last visited only, like Mr. Norman, a little older. He welcomed me into his conference room. His pleasant secretary served coffee and cookies on expensive-looking china. We sank into huge leather chairs. I started the conversation.

"First, here is my final payment on the money I owe. I'd probably be in jail today if it weren't for you." A slight grin softened his stern face.

"Glad to help, Van. I believed in you."

"Next, sir, I have some things to discuss which are confidential. I've been told that lawyers are sworn not to reveal what a client tells them. Is that true?"

"Yes, that's essentially true. What do you want to tell me?"

"Well, I've been living a lie for three years. My real name is Hans Werner. Near the end of the war, I left Germany and entered this country as a scientist with Dr. Werner Von Braun. My ambition was to be an automotive designer so I left White Sands, New Mexico, assumed a dead man's identity and got a job here at Studebaker."

Mr. Norman raised his eyebrows and said, "That's quite a story, young man. I suspected something about you didn't ring true."

I continued. "Except for being framed in two murders, things have gone well at Studebaker and I was able to develop a new compact-economy car concept out at the Proving Ground. The car's performance was terrific and so it was shown at the recent Chicago Automobile Show. That's the vehicle Victor Harper was killed in and Mike Levy injured."

"Yes, I know. Now I have something to tell you but you can't repeat it. OK?" I nodded. He continued. "After your car proved mechanically sound, some things didn't add up in my mind. So, I did a little checking on my own. Using my contacts with the state, I requested a copy of the official accident report. The state police report showed a few details the newspapers didn't print. First, Victor Harper's neck was broken and was killed instantly. Mike Levy survived but may be paralyzed from the waist down. When they pulled Levy from the car, his trousers were around his knees. In accidents like this, it's not unusual for shoes to fly off, but not a belt unbuckled, pants unzipped and pulled to the knees. Levy was in the driver's seat." I sat speechless for a few moments while I considered the possibilities.

Then I said, " I'm really surprised. Mr. Harper had a wife and three grown children." Norman held his hand up is if to stop me.

"Well, we don't know for sure what happened but at least we have a possible reason why the car suddenly drove off an embankment. Even though that information could have been made public, with respect for the surviving families, I doubt it will ever be reported. Shall we change the subject? Was there anything else you wanted to discuss?"

"Yes sir. Studebaker is planning to destroy my prototype car to avoid a union strike. I have been demoted and I'm hated in the plant. There's simply no reason for me to remain in South Bend. I looked for an open door at Studebaker and there is none. So, I've decided to leave. I want to start a new life using my real name. But without Van Hoffmann's social security card, I won't be able to get a decent job anywhere. What can I do?" Norman starred out the window for a few seconds.

"Okay, Hans. Here's what you do. First, give two weeks notice at Studebaker. Ask your boss for a letter of recommendation. In whatever state you end up, you could request an official name change to Hans Werner. Once the change is granted, they'll issue you a new social security card with the same number as the one you have now."

"That sounds too easy, Mr. Norman, do you think that will work?"

He laughed and said, "Maybe. But there's no guarantee. And, by the way, the threatened strike at Studebaker is to avoid the elimination of piecework incentive pay. The injuries to the union boss and the death of the company president are just an excuse."

"How do you know that, Mr. Norman?" I asked. He took a slow sip of coffee before replying.

"I really can't reveal my sources, Hans. Just take my word for it." I left the office knowing I had been given good advice.

The next day, I turned in my resignation as Norman suggested. Nitske said it was expected. After a few days he handed me a letter of recommendation. After telling Ms. Kitchall I was leaving, I wrote a letter to Karl saying I was taking him up on his offer to come to Huntsville for a visit. I didn't think my '39 could make the trip but I knew a car that could.

CHAPTER 21

"Hello, Jack? This is Van. Sorry to bother you at home, but I have a question. Have they destroyed Freda yet?"

"Yeah, sorta. We did what they usually do to old prototypes and wrecks. You know that big wooded area in the middle of the test track. Well, I drove your car down there and parked it among a bunch of wrecks. I did as I was told and cut the gas line to drain the tank. Sometimes they cut old prototypes in two at the "B" post, but I didn't see the point, so I didn't."

"Jack, I just can't let her sit there and rot. How can I get her out of there?"

"I'd like to help you buddy, but I'm back in maintenance now. Besides, I'd lose my job if I helped you steal that car. It belongs to Studebaker you know."

"Yes, I understand. Thanks anyway, Jack." So confident that I could somehow free Freda from her awful fate, I placed an ad in the South Bend Tribune and the St. Joseph Gazette to sell my 1939 Studebaker. The price of $100 assured a quick sale. I had a buyer within a week. After driving the car, the buyer agreed to pick it up at a designated spot on Willow Road just a block off Western Avenue at 9 a.m. on Saturday a week from the day we made the deal. I then signed over the title to him. With only $100 involved and him in possession of the title, I suppose he trusted the car would be where I said it would be on Saturday.

In hindsight, I wondered if I had made a mistake putting so much of myself into the development of that prototype car. I had completely neglected any life outside of that garage and what had it gotten me? I felt neglected and lonely. On a whim, I called Susie Goodall to tell her goodbye. I was surprised when she invited me over for a "going-away" present.

Friday night, I told Mrs. Kitchall that I would be leaving at 3 a.m. I didn't sleep very much that night. At two, I put my bare feet on the cold wooden floor. After dressing, I loaded my few belongings in the '39. I started it up for what I hoped would be the last time and made my way out Western Avenue toward the Proving Ground. The high stonewall on the left told me that Willow Road was just ahead on the right. I turned onto Willow and immediately found the previously agreed-on lane where I parked the car. After retrieving the one-gallon can of petrol and one-foot length of rubber hose from the trunk, I headed back toward the highway. It was still dark. Only a half moon in an overcast sky gave me any light at all. Was it the cold damp air that made me shiver or was it fear? There was no traffic on Western. I climbed the stone wall that surrounds the grounds. As I dropped to the ground, I felt a sharp pain in my left ankle. Oh no, I sprained it. I could barely walk. How was I going to push Freda's clutch in? I limped on toward the test track, a gallon gas can in one hand, hose in the other. The ground was rough and hazardous. I stumbled several times but kept going even though every step was painful. Walking past the dark garage and onto the test track, I could barely see the wooded area ahead where Jack said he parked Freda. My ankle pain and the excitement of the unknown were twin distractions from my goal. Breathing hard from the long walk, I wanted to sit down and rub my ankle but I kept moving. What if I couldn't find Freda? Even if I did, would she start? And the biggest challenge was how to get out the front gate. On weekdays, the guard was supposed to open it at 6a.m., but this was Saturday, so I wasn't sure. If anything went wrong, I didn't think I could make it back to my '39 on foot.

By this time, the pre-dawn light was enough for me to see the general outline of some of the wrecks. That clump of trees held a wealth of information. Discarded car designer dreams were piled unceremoniously awaiting Mother Nature's inevitable claim. Sport cars with no tops, deteriorated seats and missing floorboards, station wagons with dented fenders and rotted wood sides and rusty truck pieces all begged for my attention. I wished I had more time and more light but I had to find Freda. When I saw her, I forgot all the other vehicles.

"There you are girl. I missed you. Don't worry, we're back together again and we'll be back on the road soon." I patted her hood. Her horn honked. "No, Freda. Be quiet. We don't want to be discovered." I walked around her. None of the tires were flat. Fortunately, I brought a penlight with me. Otherwise, trying to repair the gas line underneath the car in the dark would have been nearly impossible. After pouring in one gallon of petrol in her tank and a bit to prime her carb, she started right up. As quietly as possible, I drove back toward the gate and hid the car behind some trees nearby. Pain from my ankle shot up my leg. I tried to concentrate on the task at hand. The gate was closed. The night was overcast and still. I waited. Surely there was a night watchman somewhere around but I didn't see him. About six a.m., a light came on in the garage office. In a few minutes, an overweight fellow with a cigarette in one hand and a cup in the other emerged from the building. It looked as if he was headed in my direction. He came within 30 meters of where I was parked but didn't see me. I guessed he was still half asleep. The light in the guard shack came on and then the guard unlocked the front gate. After pushing it open, the pudgy little man returned to the guardhouse. He sat drinking his coffee and smoking.

The time had come. I pressed the accelerator pedal. Freda sped toward the gate. The guard ran to block the way by waving his hands in front of him. Freda's horn blasted louder than ever before. At the last second the guard jumped to safety and Freda and I shot through the gate and slid into a left turn headed west toward Chicago. I flipped on the headlights. Without looking, I was sure the guard was on the phone calling the police. On we traveled, forty, fifty, sixty miles per hour. On my left I could see the grounds' stonewall flashing by. Now out of sight of the guardhouse, I slowed and made a quick right turn into Timothy Road. After a couple more turns, I was back on Willow and alongside my old '39. A quick switch of the already loosened license plate from the '39 to Freda and after retrieval of my belongings, we were on our way south. I hoped the police would look for me west of town. Since it was just a little after six a.m., the South Bend streets were almost deserted. Every stop was painful since I had to depress the clutch with my left foot. I stopped for a petrol fill-up and a Snickers bar in Lakeville a few miles south of town. Getting out of St. Joseph County was my first priority.

On I drove, hour after hour, staying on Highway 31 all the way to Indianapolis, Louisville, Nashville and further south. I was careful not to exceed the speed limit. I did not want to get stopped in a car with no title or registration papers. It was a long and tiring drive but Freda ran smoothly all the way. At the Alabama state line, I got off on State Road 53 for the last 22 miles into Huntsville.

The sun was setting as I wheeled into town. I stopped at a phone booth and called Karl to get directions. He was surprised I had made such good time. With hands on hips, Karl stood in the middle of his apartment's parking lot waiting for me. He was still as handsome as ever. The only change in three years was his speech, which sounded more American than before. He patted me on the back and helped me take my things inside. My left leg was throbbing. Once in his kitchen, he thrust a Sterling Beer into my hand. It was only slightly cool and tasted wonderful. In a few minutes, I had another. Even though I was very tired, we talked for a long time bringing each other up on what had happened in our lives in the past three years. Karl seemed confident about his future. He had already gotten several promotions and American citizenship was right around the corner. He loved America. Even though he had been in Huntsville only a few weeks, he already had a new girlfriend. He compared German and southern American girls and said southern girls were prettier, more passionate and easier to get along with than the frauleins he had dated.

"How about your love life, Hans?"

"Lately, it's been pretty much non-existent, Karl. I dated a young girl for a while but that relationship fell apart when she found out that I had sex with the widow of my murdered boss."

"Oh, Hans. How do you get yourself into these situations?" Without waiting for an answer, he said, "So what's next for you, my friend?" I looked at the floor trying to come up with an answer. "Well?" he asked.

"I have no idea, Karl. I have no job, no prospects, very little money, I'm driving a stolen car and walking around in a dead man's shoes."

"Oh, don't worry, my friend, you'll bounce back. Hey, I'm eager to see that prototype car you designed. It's too late and dark tonight, but we'll check it out after breakfast in the morning. Since it'll be Sunday, what do you say we sleep late?"

"That would be great, I really need some rest. I've been up 22 hours." Although Karl's one-bedroom apartment was small, it was comfortable and his foldout sofa bed was as comfortable as the bed I had in South Bend. I felt safe and contented and slept soundly.

Karl woke me Sunday morning with a cup of fresh-brewed coffee and a German breakfast of cheese, cold cuts, a hard-boiled egg and hard bread. I felt like I was back in the old country. After breakfast we went out to look at Freda. It was a pleasant sunny day with a cloudless sky. When I commented on how nice the weather was for March, Karl said it was typical for Alabama.

As we approached Freda, I said, "Karl, I must warn you, this is no ordinary car. She has special powers." He rolled his eyes. "I'm serious. On a number of occasions when something has pleased her, she's honked her horn. If something displeases her, she may make a groaning noise or worse."

"Are you crazy, Hans? You don't believe that kind of stuff do you?"

"I know it's very unlike me to be superstitious or believe in the supernatural, but there's been too many instances that prove to me this car is more than just steel and rubber. She has a heart." I walked over and put my hand on her hood. "Freda, Baby. You're a great car and I love you." Her horn honked. Karl's mouth dropped open.

"Son of a ...How did you do that, Hans?"

"I didn't do anything but give Freda a compliment."

"Aw, man, you're spookin' me out. There must be some rational explanation."

"Well, here's one possibility. Do you remember me telling you about adding fast-mutating microbes to the zinc-air battery's electrolyte? Well, that may have something to do with the car's ability to respond to outside stimuli. It seems as time goes by, the car gains power and dare I say, intelligence."

Karl stood rigid for a moment and then said, "If that's the explanation for the car's actions, what you've created is revolutionary."

CHAPTER 22

After I gave him a ride in my special car, Karl showed me his new 1949 Nash. I thought he would have chosen a smaller car. To me, it was awkward looking. But its "inverted bathtub" styling didn't seem to bother Karl.

"Hey, Hans, look at this!" He pulled on a lever beside the passenger seat. Like magic, it flopped into the horizontal.

I smiled and said, "You randy bastard. You bought this car because the front seat folds into a bed." He smiled and did a grinding motion with his hips. Even though I didn't care for the styling, I'll admit, the car was roomy and comfortable. He took me on a tour of the city pointing out sites of interest such as the huge Redstone Arsenal where he worked. We stopped and toured the Huntsville Depot. It was built in 1860 to house the Memphis and Charleston Railroad Co. eastern division headquarters. The building was now a passenger depot. The structure was interesting but not very old compared to European standards. A 1926 Ford Model TT truck was on display. Karl had to pull me away so we could continue our tour of the city. I was impressed seeing Main Street lined with beautiful antebellum mansions built by wealthy cotton farmers. Cotton farms still dominated the outskirts of Huntsville. A million tiny white shreds lined the road for miles. When I asked why Huntsville was picked as the new home of the space program, Karl said it was the work of Alabama senator, John Sparkman.

I took an immediate liking to the city. Everything was so green and the people were friendly. With no other good options, I decided to try to get a job and stay around for a while. I stayed with Karl for a couple of days while I searched the want ads. He didn't complain, but I knew I was cutting into his social life and I needed to find my own place as soon as possible.

Luckily, Redstone Arsenal was looking for engineers so I filled out an application for employment. My credentials as Van Hoffmann and my letter of recommendation from Studebaker got me hired. My German accent didn't hurt. I decided my vow to use my real name would have to wait. I hoped Redstone wouldn't contact Mr. Nitske at Studebaker as he would surely tell them I was a car thief. Worse, Studebaker would know my whereabouts. With Karl's help I found an inexpensive one-bedroom apartment near the arsenal. Those first few days on the job were stressful wondering whether or not my problems at Studebaker would be revealed.

The work was design of equipment for the assembly of rocket parts. The pay was good and the surroundings pleasant. My immediate supervisor was a young engineer named Adolf Muller. He was one of the original engineers who came to America with von Braun. It was all I could do to keep from telling him that I too came over on the Queen Mary and for a time was with his group at White Sands. He said I looked very familiar. So did he and many others in our department.

Adolf was about thirty-five, very bright and dedicated to his job. He was an ideal supervisor. He gave me my assignments and let do the job without interference. He seemed happy with the quantity and quality of my work. He said good engineers were scarce in that part of the country and was glad I decided to come south.

Since I didn't own Freda and had no title, registering her in Alabama was impossible. The only answer was to buy another car. I really hadn't worked long enough to accumulate the down payment on a new car and besides, I loved Freda and didn't think I could bring myself to part with her. But I knew that eventually, I would have to.

Since no civilian automobiles were made during the war, most pre-war cars were worn out but new cars were now available. Having visited the Chicago Auto Show and having read every car magazine I could get my hands on, I decided the car for me was a new Henry J made by the Kaiser-Frazer Corporation. It was the most like Freda of any car on the market in 1950. Both cars had 100" wheelbases and four cylinder engines.

Madison County Motors was the Kaiser-Frazer dealer in the Huntsville area. I parked Freda in the far corner of my apartment parking lot and Karl and I went down to Madison Motors in his car to see what kind of a deal I could get on a Henry J. The man, who turned out to be my salesman, was very different from the gentleman who sold me my '39 Champ back in South Bend. This one was in his mid-thirties, wore a plaid sport coat and yellow pants. Last time I saw anyone dressed like that was on the Morris Park Golf Course. He met us in the parking lot and introduced himself even before I was out the door of Karl's Nash.

"Howdy fellows, I'm 'Slick' Simmons. You boys here to trade in that there Nash?"

"No, I'm here to see what kind of a deal I can get on a new Henry J," I said.

"Henry J, huh? You're in luck, my friend. We just got our first one in yestiddy. We ain't even cleaned her up yet, but I'll garrendamntee ya that baby's fer sale."

"Well, Mr. Simmons, how much is it and can I buy it on time?" I asked.

"From the way y'all talk, I'll bet you boys work out at the arsenal. Am I right?"

"You're a smart man, mister. Just started a few weeks back."

"Well, if'n you got a job out there, I ain't worried 'bout gittin' my money. We'll tote your note right here at good old Madison Motors. Two hundred down and you're in the driver's seat." He grabbed me by the arm and led me inside. "Let's go take a look at that new Henry J, boys. She's a beaut, dark blue paint and genu-wine no-stain seat covers. She's got little fins in the back just like a baby Cadillac. And I'm told she gets 40 miles to a gallon out on the road."

"Well, you've been told wrong, my friend," I said. "Motor Trend said it gets 24.9 mpg on the average."

"True, true, but I was talkin' 'bout drivin' from Monteagle to Chattanooga. It's downhill all the way, you know." He gave out with a big belly laugh and slapped me on the back. After examining the car and driving it around the block, I ended up paying the list price of $1299 but the two hundred down was the thing that closed the deal. After signing the papers, I drove back to my apartment building as proud as could be. I polished her all afternoon and drove her to work Monday morning. I wondered what I was going to do about Freda.

CHAPTER 23

I longed to be myself and not Van Hoffmann. I was sick of the deception. Again, I considered the idea of having an official name change to Hans Werner but decided against it since I was an employee of Redstone Arsenal and a number of employees there might recognize the name. Besides, what was the point? It just seemed too risky.

I always tried to park my new Henry J away from other cars if possible. Although I had owned her for several weeks, she was yet to have a single scratch. That night after work, I parked in a corner of my apartment's parking lot near Freda but away from other cars. I gave the car a final dusting, a little pat and headed for bed.

The next morning when I came out to go to work, I was shocked and saddened at what I saw. Someone had crashed into the side of my beautiful Henry J, caving in the left door and quarter panel. I stood there not knowing what to do. Some drunk must have rammed into my car and then drove away. I figured it might be someone who lived in the complex so I began searching for a car with blue paint on its bumper. After finding no blue paint traces on any car, I headed back to call the police and my insurance company. And then it hit me. I had checked every car but one. I hesitantly approached Freda. I somehow felt guilty even thinking the unthinkable. But the evidence was irrefutable. Blue paint was smeared all over her bumper. I couldn't have been angrier.

"Damn you!" I screamed and then I kicked her front fender. Freda groaned and lunged at me. "I thought we cared about each other. How could you do such a thing? I had no idea you were capable of jealousy! I get another car and you try to ruin it. Why?" She groaned again. "You pull a stunt like this again and you're headed for the scrap heap." I knew in my heart that I could never destroy Freda, I loved her too much, but I couldn't let her get away with what she did. That night I chained her rear axle to a tree until I could cool off and decide what to do.

After I told Karl what had happened, he was finally convinced Freda had special powers. He advised me to get rid of the car. But how? I hated to see all the work that had gone into Freda wasted. Technically, the car was the property of Studebaker. I hoped the hysteria caused by the accident near Michigan City had died down by now and a more sensible evaluation of Freda's great potential could take place. For her own good, I decided to return Freda to South Bend.

I left Huntsville late Friday afternoon after work and drove all night. Freda ran well. We arrived in South Bend early Saturday morning. I drove directly to the Engineering office and parked Freda at the front door. I left the keys in the glove box. I then made my way to the Greyhound Bus Station and purchased a ticket to Nashville, Tennessee. I took a Trailways bus from Nashville to Huntsville. During the long hours back and forth to South Bend, I had plenty of time to reevaluate my life. My new life in Huntsville was very pleasant. I had a good paying job and a promising future at Redstone. My friend Karl and I were getting along well and had a lot of fun together. I looked forward to our Friday night poker parties. In short, I saw a very good life ahead for Van Hoffmann. But I was not Van Hoffmann, rocket engineer. I was Hans Werner, automotive engineer.

With my first anniversary at Redstone Arsenal approaching, I started planning for the two weeks vacation I would be entitled to. I missed Germany. I missed the automobile business. The real me wanted to visit Wolfsburg, my mother and sister's graves and, of course, the Volkswagen plant. I heard they were turning out cars in substantial numbers these days. I didn't see how that was possible in the plant that was in ruins when I left five years earlier. Where did they get the money to rebuild, I wondered? Fortunately, Wolfsburg fell just inside the British zone so free enterprise could still exist. Maybe that was the answer. My curiosity was getting the best of me. After applying for a passport, I sat and worried that there might be some problem because of my stolen identity. I was pleasantly surprised when the passport arrived. Now I could plan a trip back to Germany.

With Trans World Airlines flying to Europe with the beautiful new 4-engine Lockheed Constellations, it was possible to go to Germany, spend a week there and return to America all in a two-week period.

CHAPTER 24

The flights to London and then to Hannover were exciting. I figured if I had my life to live over again, I might want to get into aeronautical engineering. But it was too late for that. I was thirty years old and dedicated to automotive engineering. From Hannover it was a short train ride to Wolfsburg. At the train station, I rented a bicycle, strapped my backpack on the luggage carrier and peddled out toward the plant. The weather was sunny and cool, simply delightful. Ah, my Fatherland! The country I thought was doomed when I left was struggling back. I hoped Germany might again be a world power. I smiled and felt at peace. I was home! I wondered if leaving Germany might have been a mistake. On I pedaled. Along the way, I was impressed at how busy everyone was. The roads were clean and paved. If it hadn't been for a few bombed out buildings, there was little evidence there had ever been a war. As I neared the plant entrance, I noticed a small cottage that looked very familiar. Was that the place I stayed the night I escaped from the VW plant? Maybe so. I pedaled up to the door and knocked. No answer. I knocked again, this time harder. The door squeaked and opened a few centimeters. An elderly man with long white hair and beard showed his face in the crack. I could never forget that face.

"What do you want, young man?" he said. His accent took me back five years. I loved the sound of my native tongue. I hoped my German was not too rusty.

"I guess you don't remember me," I said, "but five years ago, through your kindness, I was saved from the freezing cold. I was soaking wet from the canal at the Volkswagen plant and you let me dry out and spend the night in front of your fireplace. You even gave me some food the next morning. You are a very kind man and I want to thank you from the bottom of my heart."

"Yes, I remember you now. Did you make it to Nordhausen?"

"Yes, I did. You have a good memory, sir."

"That is about the only thing I've got left that still works. Old age has caught up with me."

"I would like to do something for you to repay for your help that night so long ago," I said.

"Oh, that's not necessary. I may not be around much longer anyway. With the Soviet sector so near; you never know when they will try to gain more land. I'd just as soon die as be under their control."

"How close are they anyway?"

"Well, Wolfsburg is just barely inside the British zone although we don't see the British much anymore. Nordhausen is inside the Soviet zone." All of a sudden, his face tightened and he let out a slight groan. "I'm sorry, son, but my old legs are about to give out." I could see the old man was shaking badly and needed to sit, so I thanked him again and was on my way.

As I neared the canal which borders the VW plant, a flood of old memories came rushing back. Although the weather that spring day was nothing like the miserable cold of the night when I escaped, I still felt a chill as I rode up to the bridge. A guard stepped out to greet me.

"May I help you, sir?"

"Yes, my name is Hans Werner," I said. "I worked at this plant during the war and I now live in America. Are there tours available for visitors?"

"Only by special arrangements, sir. I'm sorry."

"Oh." I lowered my head in disappointment. My curiosity as to how the plant had changed and how the cars were now being assembled made me want to tour the plant, but how? Figuring I was well beyond punishment for leaving without permission, I thought of my old boss, Otto. "Do you have an employee here named, Otto Haniel?" I asked.

The guard thumbed through a think catalogue and finally said, "Yes, here he is. He is foreman in the fuel tank assembly section." I smiled. How ironic. That was where I discovered the fuel sabotage scheme.

"Could you give him a call for me?"

"I'm not sure he is working this shift, but I'll try." In a few moments the guard handed the phone to me.

"This is Otto Haniel. To whom am I speaking?"

"Hans Werner." There was a long silence.

"Where are you Hans?"

"I'm at the main gate." Again a period of quiet.

"Stay there. I'll be right out." The line went dead. It occurred to me that by the tone of his voice Otto might still be holding a grudge. Should I just turn and leave. My curiosity was too great to abandon my only chance to see the plant. Soon, Otto appeared from one of the factory buildings. As he waddled in my direction, old negative feelings invaded my mind.

Otto had gained weight but still wore those same glasses on the end of his bulbous nose. As he approached, I extended my hand. He walked up to me and stood for an instant as if considering whether or not to accept it. Finally, he gave me a weak shake.

"Hans Werner. It's been a long time. Where have you been?"

"I went to America with Dr. Werner von Braun's rocket scientists."

"Interesting. Hans, my shift will be over in about an hour. If you can wait around, you can come home with me this afternoon and we can discuss what has transpired in the last five years."

"I'd like that."

"I'll meet you here in one hour." Without another word, Otto turned and walked back into the plant. I spent the next hour riding my bicycle along the canal, admiring the rebuilt plant. I'd forgotten how long it was. Maybe they added on because it looked to be a mile long. It was hard to believe so much progress had been made in only five years. Again, I wondered where the money came from for the rebuild. As promised, in one hour, Otto was at the main gate along with hundreds of others whose shift just ended. As it turned out, we were within walking distance of Otto's home. Being a long-term employee must have given him priority when the new apartment houses were built.

Otto's wife met us at the door. She was a stout woman built like an oil drum. I had never met her before but she looked just as I imagined. Otto introduced us and ordered her to bring beers. She quickly returned carrying two large ceramic steins with foam streaming down the sides. After we had settled into two tattered overstuffed chairs, Otto turned to me.

"Hans, I never thought I'd see you again. Why did you leave us at a time when you were so desperately needed?"

"Well, Otto, I knew we were close to being overrun by the enemy and I had a chance to join my college roommate who was one of Dr. Werner von Braun's rocket engineers. I caught up with him in Bleicherode and he got me into his group. I spent the last five years in America. It's a wonderful country with endless opportunities."

"So is your native Germany." I shifted in my chair trying to think how to respond.

"If you're trying to make me feel guilty, it's not working, Otto."

"Feel however you please. You were not the only one to abandon our cause. There were only a few of us who stayed to save the plant when nearly all the workers and many supervisors disappeared. And you know something, Hans, we kept things going even when there was little food, few supplies and only British officers as customers for our cars. We hung

151

on. Little by little, we started working our way back. Often managers had to trade Volkswagens to farmers for food for our workers. The British had no interest in running the plant and gave us little help. They tried to sell or give the plant away to numerous European and American manufacturers but there were no takers. The only offer was from the Russians. Realizing they only wanted more land, the British declined the offer."

I interrupted. "I was working at Studebaker in 1948 and evaluated one of your early models. Unfortunately, top management there saw no future in the car."

Otto smiled. "It's lucky for us the stupidity was so widespread. The British finally gave up and turned over ownership and management to us Germans. That's all we needed. And, by God, we're starting to make a success of the operation."

"You must be very proud, Otto. I'd give anything to see what has been accomplished." Otto finished his beer, waved to his wife for a refill and then lit a cigar before he responded.

"The only way that I can think of to get you in is for me to recommend you as a new employee. That way, showing you around the plant will be authorized."

"Oh no, I have a job in America. I'm just here for a visit."

"It would not be a commitment. All you have to do is fill out an application and then we'll go for a tour." I sat for a moment before I realized Otto was right. This was likely my only chance to see the factory."

"I'll do it," I said. "Thanks for the opportunity."

After we ate, the conversation took a more serious turn. Otto's tongue loosened after a couple more beers. "Right after you left, there was more sabotage," he said. "The SS came back and threatened to kill me if I didn't solve the problems. What was I going to do, shoot every worker on the line? All that saved me was the advancing Americans. I had to hide out for a few days because the workers were running wild, destroying everything in their path. I feared for my life. Some supervisors were tortured and murdered by the workers. And they say we Nazis were brutal. There was complete chaos at the plant for a few days. The American foot soldiers finally restored order after they were told American children lived in Wolfsburg. It wasn't true, but the story saved us from the wrath of the workers. The American ground troops were surprised the town even existed. It was not on their maps even though their airplanes had bombed us three times. A few of us went back to the factory to try to pick up the pieces. I remember walking in stagnant, ankle-deep water; afraid what was left of the roof might collapse. We sure could have used your expertise in getting the machinery running again."

"Why did you need me?" I asked.

"Das Werk lobt den Meister," he replied. (the work proves the craftsman) I was surprised he recognized my work was valuable. "Hans, I remember you were able to solve several very serious cases of sabotage before you left."

"Thank you for remembering, Otto." After those compliments, I began to look at Otto in a different light. I didn't want to admit it, but he was starting to get to me. Although Otto didn't suggest it, I realized if I had stayed and helped rebuild, I would probably now be Vice-president of Engineering.

"Who's running the operation now, Otto?"

"A couple of years ago, a former Opel executive named Heinz Nordhoff was given the presidency. The British then disappeared. When Nordhoff came in, employee turnover was 100% per year; we had no dealers, no salesmen-nothing and worst of all, no cash or credit. But little by little Nordhoff helped us on the road to recovery."

"Is there any chance I might meet this man, Heinz Nordhoff?"

"There's a chance, but he's a busy man. We'll see tomorrow." Otto offered to let me sleep on his couch and I quickly accepted since I had made no hotel arrangements for the night.

Just before I drifted off, I recalled the events of the day. I was amazed how much Otto had changed. He now seemed to want to help me even though I left him in a precarious position five years earlier. The old Otto would have held a grudge and would have wanted revenge. The new Otto seemed different. Had the war changed him or was he acting?

I could hardly contain my excitement the next morning as we walked through the plant gate. We went directly to the employment office. Otto helped me fill out an application. While I was working on the application, he called his foreman to make sure all was well in the fuel tank assembly section. We then started on a plant tour. The floors were clean, walls painted and machines spitting out parts in a most efficient way. Starting at the end of the assembly line, I clocked shinny new Volkswagens being driven away at the rate of about one every ten to fifteen minutes. This was painfully slow by American standards but the cars looked and sounded great. I was sure the rate would increase. Very little was the same from five years earlier. The bunker where we took shelter during the bombing was gone as was my old office.

"Otto, you people have done wonders with this factory. But I wonder why the assembly line is running so slow."

"That's because of lack of parts or supplies somewhere along the line.

We're still limited by having enough capital to pay the workers and buy supplies too. But things are getting better as time passes. It took us over two years to make our first one thousand cars. Now we're up to about fifty thousand a year. I'm told we could sell ten times that many if we could make them."

As we toured each department, I found myself drinking in the process and wishing I was part of it. As we walked down a long hall, two well-dressed men approached.

"That's Heinz Nordhoff and his Engineering manager coming toward us, Hans. Maybe you can meet him. Herr Nordhoff, sir!" Otto shouted.

"Yes, Haniel, what is it?"

"Sir, I'd like you to meet a friend of mine, Hans Werner. He is visiting from America. He worked here as a design engineer during the war and has been in the U.S. working for Studebaker since then." Nordhoff smiled and shook my hand and introduced me to his Engineering Vice President, Fritz Voss.

"Studebaker?" Nordhoff asked.

"Yes, sir. In fact, I was the one who evaluated the Volkswagen prototype you sent to us. I gave it high marks, but top management had no interest in pursuing the project. I even developed a similar small-car prototype using mostly Studebaker parts. It tested well and was shown at the Chicago auto show, but never was put into production."

"Yes, I saw that car. It looked very good. Of course, as you may be aware, we here at VW decided to stick to Dr. Porsche's original body design and make technical improvements rather than have yearly body changes like American manufacturers."

"I think that is wise, sir. I left Studebaker a year ago because we disagreed on that and a number of other issues, in particular the way they let the labor union dominate their decisions."

"We have to a large extent avoided that problem here, Herr Werner. We share our financial situation with our workers and they seem to understand that we all have the same objective. By the way, Werner, where are you working now?"

"I am employed by Dr. von Braun's rocket development group at the Redstone Arsenal in Huntsville, Alabama."

"Well, good luck. If you ever decide to come back to your native country, we might have a place for you. We're always looking for good experienced automotive engineers." After meeting Herr Nordhoff, I saw him as one of the reasons VW was making such great progress.

"Well, Hans, what do you think of our president?" Otto asked.

"I am very impressed."

"You should be. He essentially offered you a job. Why don't you take him up on it?"

"I'll have to admit, I'm tempted, but I have obligations in America." After our tour, Otto made arrangements for me to spend a couple of nights in a Wolfsburg hotel. This free time gave me an opportunity to see how the city had grown and to visit my mother's and sister's graves.

As I rode my rented bicycle from the hotel out to the old Wolfsburg Forest Cemetery, dark clouds gathered overhead. The graveyard was on a slight rise surrounded by thick woodland. A light sprinkle cooled my face. It looked like I might get caught in a rainstorm. Since I had come this far, I decided to keep pedaling. By the time I found the cemetery's caretaker shack, raindrops dampened my shirt.

"You picked a bad day for a bicycle ride, son," the old man said. I smiled and nodded. The caretaker's tattered clothes and leathery skin told me he did more than sit in his hut. If anyone's appearance ever suited his job, his did. He was stooped and wrinkled from years in the sun.

"I'm here to find the graves of my mother, Freda Werner and my sister, Eva Werner. Can you help me?"

"I don't know," he said. "When did they die?"

"It was the day of the last enemy air raid, August 5, 1944." The old man fingered through a well-worn notebook, occasionally stopping to scratch his tobacco-stained chin whiskers. He wrinkled his brow and shook his head. I feared the worst.

"Things were confused after the bombs fell," he said. "I am not sure, ...wait, here's the deaths from the August 5th raid." A calloused finger ran over the yellowed page. "Freda and Eva Werner, section ten, plot #42 and 43. You'd never find it. I'll show you where it is." He hobbled to the corner of the shack and retrieved a tattered black umbrella. When he opened it, two of the ribs were collapsed. What was left was much too small to share. Since the rain was pouring, I was getting drenched. When we reached the location, the only grave markings in this area were tiny concrete posts that were flush with the ground. Brushing the wet grass away, I found one marked 42 and next to it, one marked 43.

"I'll leave you here, sonny. I think I'll go back where it's dry." He hobbled away leaving me with my thoughts. The dark sky only added to my loneliness. Although soaked and chilled, I stood for several minutes remembering the wonderful woman who nursed me as an infant, guided me as I grew and most importantly, gave me a sense of purpose in life.

When my father was away searching for work, she was always there for Eva and me. When Father was called to the army, she took care of us and when he was killed she was there to provide comfort and stability. I realized how much I loved and missed her. And in the next grave, sweet little Eva who had only just begun to live when her life was snuffed out by that awful war. While standing there, I realized that I was the only person in the world that would ever visit these graves and when I was gone, their memories would be lost forever. Before I left Germany five years ago, I had planned to someday take their bodies back to our hometown of Magdeburg for a proper burial and dignified gravestones. I knew that was not possible now. Magdeburg was inside the Russian zone and I lived in America. The least I could do was to arrange for gravestones here in the Wolfsburg Cemetery. But I had neither the time nor the money on this trip. Someday, I thought. The clouds overhead seemed even darker: a fitting backdrop for my dark emotions. I left the cemetery sad but glad I had made the trip. Rain and tears wet my face as I splashed through the puddles headed back to my hotel.

When I picked up my key, there was a message in my box.

Hans Werner,

Fritz Voss, Engineering Vice President called me today to request that you come by for an interview tomorrow. There is no obligation to do so but I think you may be able to learn more about our company by speaking to him. He will expect you at 9 AM. The main gate guard will give you a visitor's badge and direct you to Herr Voss's office. Call me before going back to America. Otto Haniel

Even though I knew that I would go back to America, I was flattered that Volkswagen was interested in me. I decided that I had nothing to lose so at 8:45 the next morning I was at the main gate pinning on my visitor's badge. Herr Voss was a middle-age man with blond hair and slim muscular body. I am sure when he was younger, he would have made a good model for Hitler Youth publicity photos. The interview was pleasant but very formal and business-like. He started by telling me a bit about his own career. He said he worked with Heinz Nordhoff at Opel. He then told me of the wonderful progress that had been made at Volkswagen during the past two years. But more importantly, he revealed some of their ambitious plans for the future. He abruptly changed the subject catching me off guard. I guessed that was his intention.

"What design changes to the current Volkswagen automobile would need to be made for the vehicle to become successful in America?"

I hesitated, gathering my thoughts before answering. "Well, sir," I said, "Although I can suggest a number of technical improvements, there are also cultural barriers and lifestyle differences that must be overcome before the VW will be acceptable to Americans."

"And what might they be?" he asked.

"In the U.S., petrol is inexpensive and readily available. So kilometers per liter is not top priority. Also, most Americans would consider the Volkswagen too small. I own a Henry J made by Kaiser-Frazer, which is only slightly larger than the VW, but it's not a big seller. Very small cars have never sold well in America. To be successful, I think you must advertise the car's high quality and maintenance-free performance. Maybe, in time, Americans will see the benefits of an economical, well-made small car."

"That's interesting," he said as he cocked his head, rubbed his chin and stared at some non-existent object in space. "What technical improvements would you suggest?"

"First and most important, hydraulic brakes."

"Oh yes, definitely!" he said. "We are already making that change this year. What else."

"It's a small thing, but you need two taillights. Also, put the turn signal handle on the steering column. And those 16" wheels are out of date in America. Use fifteens. And last but not least, ventilation of the interior must be improved."

"Thank you, Herr Werner. How would you like to work on those improvements yourself?" I sat speechless. Without waiting for my reply, he continued. "If we can agree on salary and we find nothing in your record to disqualify you, I'm offering you a job. May I assume you are still a German citizen?"

"Yes, I am still a citizen. But, I have obligations in America and must return." Voss seemed surprised.

"Just in case you change your mind, I will have my secretary type up a letter of intent with our salary offer. It will be good for 60 days." I left the office, called Otto to thank him for his hospitality and then pedaled my bicycle to the Wolfsburg train station.

CHAPTER 25

I jumped as the big Lockheed Constellation touched down at New York's Idlewild Airport. I forgot it was natural for the tires to squeal when they hit the pavement. When my feet touched the tarmac, a strange uncomfortable feeling came over me. I headed for U.S. Customs. Somehow, I knew I didn't belong in America. I was a fraud, not really an American, not really anybody. Van Hoffman was a dead man. I wanted the world to know I was Hans Werner. But first, I had to get through customs as Van Hoffmann. I had never been superstitious, but this Friday the 13th might change my mind. The customs agent seemed to take much more time evaluating my passport than others who were ahead of me. I must admit I had a bad feeling about the attitude of that agent. Maybe it was because he looked exactly like the propaganda photographs of Jews that I saw in Germany when I was a teenager. He looked evil.

"Where did you go in Europe, Mr. Hoffmann?" he asked.

"I landed in London, flew to Hamburg and then traveled by train to Wolfsburg, Germany."

"Why Wolfsburg?"

"That's the home of the Volkswagen factory. I'm a automotive engineer."

"Did you have business there?"

"No, just visiting a friend who works there."

"Are you a United States citizen?"

"Yes, I am."

"And where is your home?"

"Huntsville, Alabama."

"Where were you born, Mr. Hoffmann?"

"Ft. Worth, Texas." The agent looked at me suspiciously for what seemed a long time. "Where did you get that German accent?" Although irritated by his intrusive questions, I maintained my composure and told the same lies I had told so many times before. He finally stamped my passport and waved me through. I wanted to run but settled for a fast walk to baggage claim.

* * * * * * * * *

I arrived back in Huntsville late Saturday. This gave me a chance to rest. I was scheduled to go back to work at Redstone the following Monday. As soon as I reached my drafting table Monday morning, my supervisor, Adolf Muller walked up.

"Hey, Van. How was the vacation? Did you leave town?"

"Yes, I went to Germany."

"Germany! Lucky you. You'll have to tell me all about it sometime, but right now we've been given a new rush-schedule on the R-43 launch platform. We're all going to have to burn some midnight oil to be finished on time. It's that important." I was going to come clean with Adolf about my name. But I felt guilty doing it when I was so needed on the R-43 project. Besides, I could use the overtime money. Adolf gave me my instructions and I got right to work.

Karl cancelled our regular Friday night poker game/beer party so that he and I could talk. It was to be just the two of us that week. He wanted to hear all about my trip and I wanted to talk to him about my decision to drop the Van Hoffmann name. He met me at his door and thrust a Sterling Beer in my hand.

"Welcome back, you old Nazi," he said playfully.

"I'll have to admit, Karl, being back in Germany felt very natural to me. I was Hans Werner. I was myself. Karl, I'm really sick of living a lie. While I was gone, I decided to go back to my real name and stop lying about being Van Hoffmann."

"That is big news," he said. "But I hope you realize it will probably cost you your job at Redstone. It may even get you deported. Have you considered that?"

"Yes, I have. But if that happens, Volkswagen has offered me a job as a design engineer." Karl's mouth dropped open.

"No shit! Have you informed your boss at Redstone?"

"No, I didn't say I was going to take the VW job. I've decided to help out on the R-43 platform project for a while. They need me and with the overtime, I'll be able to save some money. But my mind is made up. I'm going back to being Hans Werner as soon as possible." That night I realized how much I would miss Karl's friendship if I moved back to Germany.

CHAPTER 26

I wondered whether Freda was scrapped again or re-evaluated. How could I find out? The only people in South Bend that I could talk to openly were Mrs. Kitchall, Susie Goodall and my attorney, Virgil Norman. I decided to send an airmail letter to Mr. Norman. I could have called but it would have been more expensive and besides, I could choose my words more carefully in a letter.

Dear Mr. Norman,

It's been over a year since I left Studebaker and South Bend. My curiosity prompted me to write this letter hoping you could fill me in on the latest news at Studebaker. As you may be aware, I left town in the prototype car that I developed. I drove it to Huntsville, Alabama where I now live and work. Several weeks later, I returned the car to the Engineering Building at Studebaker. Do you know what happened to it?

Has there been any progress in determining the murderer of Benny Goodall or Roy Branson? Am I still a suspect? As I told you earlier, I believe Mike Levy was involved in both murders. Any relevant news will be appreciated.

Sincerely, Hans Werner
(known in South Bend as Van Hoffmann)

I chose to have a post office box when I first moved to Huntsville. Like in South Bend, it gave me complete privacy. Anyone writing to me only needed my box number. That made any name or no name acceptable. Ten days after sending the letter to Mr. Norman, I retrieved this letter from my post office box:

Dear Hans,

I received your letter and was happy you are apparently staying out of trouble. When your prototype car showed up in front of the Studebaker Engineering Building, it caused quite a stir. The St. Joseph Gazette sent reporters to cover the story. It made the front page. When a mechanic tried to start the car, he was severely shocked when he turned the key. He was sent to the hospital. A wrecker was sent to haul the car back to the Proving Ground, but all four brake shoes were stuck and could not be freed. A trailer was then sent and the car was dragged onto its bed. As the driver started to leave, billows of black smoke escaped through the grille opening. The driver took the fire extinguisher from his cab but when he opened the car's hood, there was no fire or any apparent reason for the smoke. When he got back in his cab, the smoke started again. The driver unhooked his trailer and drove away. It was four days and several more unexplained problems before the car was finally returned to the Proving Ground. The newspaper called it the "car that wouldn't die."

It is my understanding that police detectives are still working on the Goodall and Branson murders. Your disappearance did not help your standing in either case. Chief detective Arbitt has let it be known that he still thinks you were involved in both murders even though there was not enough evidence to press charges. He has issued a warrant for your arrest for car theft. They found evidence that the car was taken across state lines. That makes, it a federal offense.

I hope this answers your questions.
Best of luck to you,
Virgil Norman

I thought if I returned Freda, it would not be stealing. I guess I was wrong. I worried that eventually I might be found and arrested. But Freda's antics made me smile when I read Mr. Norman's letter.

It was already a month since Mr. Voss made the job offer at Volkswagen. I needed to make up my mind soon; was I to go or stay in America? This was the biggest decision of my life. I was leaning toward going back to Germany, but I would have to quit my job at Redstone, just when they needed me most. Also, I didn't have enough money saved to buy a plane ticket and other expenses associated with moving to Germany. I decided to write a letter to Mr. Voss of Volkswagen and explain my dilemma.

About ten days after sending the letter, I received a certified check for $500 and a contract that I was to sign and return before cashing the check. The die was cast; I was going home to Germany. I gave my employer notice saying I had another offer; I didn't say where. I also failed to mention my real name. Since my car loan was yet to be paid off, I netted only $125 from its sale. I shipped my few belongings to Otto Haniel's home figuring I would arrive before the shipment. The hardest part of leaving was saying goodbye to Karl. He had been such a good friend all those years. I wondered if I would ever see him again.

CHAPTER 27

The sky over New York City was overcast. Black clouds were outlined with a purplish border. An occasional flash of lightning in the east made me wonder if my flight might be delayed. I hoped I wouldn't have to spend another day as Van Hoffmann. Idlewild Airport was crowded with people scurrying around never making eye contact. As I approached the TWA International counter my stomach churned, like I was about to appear on stage before thousands. The attendant gave me a boarding pass and directed me to the waiting area. I was glad to be leaving New York.

My plane ticket got me as far as Hannover but I was still over ninety kilometers from Wolfsburg. I took a bus from Hanover to Wolfsburg. The coach pulled into the Wolfsburg station, two kilometers away from the factory and Otto's apartment. I called Otto's home but there was no answer. The hour was late and the winter night was closing in. My only option was to spend the night in the bus station. At least it was warm but there was no place to lie down. Noise and light prevented any real rest that long night.

As the first light of dawn slipped through an eastern window, I again tried to call Otto. Still no answer. What to do? I dug a sweater out of my backpack, pulled my cap low over my ears and walked out into the cold morning air. A light sleet stung my face. I turned up the collar on my pea coat and leaned into the strong north wind as I made my way toward the Volkswagen plant and Otto's apartment. In Huntsville, this kind of weather would be unusual. I trudged along wondering if I made the right decision giving up my job, my best friend, my car and warm weather. It was too late to worry about it now. Finally, the huge and beautiful VW factory showed itself through the mist. Had I been a religious person, I suspected the walls around heaven would look much the same. My cold body forgot its misery for the moment. I even felt a fullness and warmth knowing I would soon be a part of the great Volkswagen organization. It was a lifelong dream of helping develop a small "people's car" was coming true. Since I needed a bath, a shave and a change of clothes, I decided to walk over to Otto's place before calling Mr. Voss. A knock on Otto's door went unanswered for several minutes. Finally, Otto's barrel-shaped wife appeared. She wore a sack-like dress with no belt. She appeared to have gained weight since I last saw her. Her round face was hard to look at. I don't think she recognized me at first. From that point on, I spoke in my native tongue.

"Good day, Frau Haniel. Do you remember me, Hans Werner?" She looked puzzled and didn't answer. "Is Otto home?"

"No, he's working today," she said.

"May I come in and get warm? I walked from the bus station and I'm chilled to the bone."

"Otto told me to not let unannounced people in."

"I tried to call this morning but there was no answer. May I use your telephone to call Otto?"

"You stay here, I'll call him," she said. In a few minutes she returned and motioned for me to come inside. "Otto is on the line," she said. I told Otto I was here but had yet found a place to stay. He said to put his wife back on the phone. She spoke in hushed tones. After hanging up she turned to me. "Otto says to give you a meal and a place to rest and he would be home in four hours."

"Oh, that's wonderful. May I make one more call?"

"If it's local," she said. I nodded.

"Mr. Voss, this is Has Werner. I'm finally here in Wolfsburg."

"Oh yes, Werner. When can you start?"

"I can start tomorrow."

"Tomorrow is fine. Your supervisor will be Wilhelm Kittel, Manager of Interior Systems. When you arrive, tell the guard to call Kittel and he will come sign you in. Glad you're here, Werner. We are looking forward to working with you."

"Thank you, sir."

When Otto got home that afternoon, he gave me a weak handshake and diverted his eyes from mine.

"Have you called Mr. Voss yet?"

"Yes, I start tomorrow. Unfortunately, I have no place to stay." Otto paced back and forth rubbing his chin as if in deep thought. He whispered something to his wife and then turned to me.

"Hans, you can stay here tonight, but you must find a place of your own tomorrow. You should have made arrangements before you arrived." Otto was right.

"I'm very sorry, Otto. I feel terrible imposing on you like this." I lowered my head.

"Well, someday I'll need a big favor and I'll expect you to come through for me."

"Your kindness will definitely be repaid," I said.

I never did find out what Otto's wife's name was. He always referred to her as "Frau." She seemed more like a housekeeper than a wife. I guess my time in America had influenced my feelings about the treatment of women. After a supper of sautéed pork chops and sweet and sour red cabbage, Otto said he was in the mood for some music. I was surprised he chose a recording of the *Concerto in E minor* for violin by Mendelssohn followed by Bach's *Minuet in G major*. I had no idea Otto had such lofty tastes in music. Then he put on Lale Andersen's record of *Lili Marleen*, a German Army favorite. After he turned off the music, for some reason the discussion turned to life in the late thirties.

"You know, Hans, those days were the greatest in the history of Germany. There was great hope and progress. Everyone had a job and national pride was never higher. Today, if we openly talk about progress made under Hitler's reign, you are looked upon as a traitor. The Nazi government is simply not mentioned any more. So I suggest at Volkswagen you avoid the subject if possible."

"That won't be a problem with me, Otto. Although I agreed with many of Hitler's plans, some I did not."

"Really?" Otto asked. "What didn't you agree with?"

"Well, for one thing, land acquisition by force. Another was his extreme hatred and harsh treatment of Jews." Veins in Otto's neck seemed to expand as if some internal pressure was trying to escape. He rose to his feet, sucked in his large belly, pushed his spectacles up on his red bulbous nose and banged his fist on a table.

"The stinking Jews were taking over the country before Hitler stopped them. Surely, you knew that, Werner. They controlled the banks and were friends with the communists and the unions. They foreclosed on my sister's house and put her family out on the street. Jews were ruining our country. Hitler was right to put his foot down. They had to be stopped!" Although there was an element of truth in what he said, being his guest, I felt it was inappropriate to respond to his outburst, so I sat quietly. Otto continued. "And we were right to invade Austria, Czechoslovakia and Poland. Germany's very survival depended on it." I couldn't let that comment pass.

"What did those countries have to do with Germany's survival?"

"Don't talk like a fool, Hans. We were only taking back what was stolen from us at the end of the World War I."

"Poland?"

"We needed the farmland and natural resources as well as the peasant labor Poland provided. Hitler's biggest mistake was trusting Stalin as an ally. If we had won the war, today Hitler would be Europe's greatest hero." I decided to say no more although I knew it was Hitler that double-crossed Stalin, not the other way around. My host was becoming too excited. I wouldn't have been surprised to hear a "Heil Hitler" come out of Otto's mouth at any moment.

"How about some more music," I suggested. Otto's wife went to the record player and selected an album. Otto took it from her and smiled.

"Frau has selected the Hansel and Gretel Overture, Hans. I suppose, some people will always be children." He put the record on, lit a cigar and slumped into a large overstuffed chair to listen. I sat quietly with my eyes closed. The sweet music played as I tried to sort out my conflicting thoughts about Otto. I could not dismiss the fact that he had helped me get the job with VW. Yet his love for the old Nazi days bothered me. I remember how brutal he was with the prisoners during the last days of the war. At the time, I thought it was self-preservation rather than dedication to Hitler's cause. Maybe I was wrong.

It had been a long tiring day. I dozed and finally fell asleep on the couch. I don't even remember Otto and Frau turning out the lights and going to bed.

Chapter 28

Wilhelm Kittel met me at the guardhouse. He was a tall, clean-cut young man and I emphasize the word "young." He looked as if he should still be in school. He wore an expensive-looking dark suit and a red tie. His leather overcoat reminded me of those worn by high-ranking Nazi officers during the war. I felt a bit shabby in my old war surplus U. S. Navy pea coat. Since I was now passed thirty, I realized for the first time in my life, someone younger than I would be my boss. After spending the necessary time filling out forms in the personnel office, Herr Kittel took me to the engineering office. The office was a large open room with perhaps forty drawing boards in four extremely straight lines. Everyone looked busy. No one looked up as we walked by. Except for the German discipline and order, I recognized nothing from five years earlier. Kittel showed me my workstation where I left my coat and gloves. Then we went to his office. It was nothing more than four two meter tall partitions hooked together.

"Have a seat, Werner. We need to get to know each other. Herr Voss tells me that you have been living in America for the last five years and that you worked four of those years at the Studebaker Corporation."

"Yes, sir, that is true. I started there as a time-study engineer and ended up developing a small, low-cost prototype car much like your Volkswagen."

"Interesting. So what happened to your prototype?"

"We showed it at the 1949 Chicago Auto Show. Feedback was excellent. Unfortunately, the company president and the president of the union drove the car back to South Bend and were involved in a tragic accident. Although damage to the car was minimal, the project was cancelled. That's when I left the company. I went to Huntsville, Alabama and got a job at the Redstone Arsenal working on rocket launch platforms."

"That's a fascinating story. So you went to America in 1945, is that correct?"

"Yes, that's right. The war was just winding down when I left the plant here in Wolfsburg."

"Why did you leave and how did you get to America?" he asked. I wondered if I might get in trouble on the first hour of my first day if I told the truth. But I was through lying. I had enough of that in America. But still I felt uneasy and nervous. I hoped it didn't show.

"Before I answer your question," I said, "let me give you a bit of background. Since I was a student at the Berlin Technical Institute from 1936 to 1939, my passion has been automotive design. Specifically, I wanted to be a part of the Volkswagen team here in Wolfsburg. My father was killed on the eastern front leaving my mother and sister for me to support. I was lucky enough to meet Dr. Porsche's son, Ferry and got a job here in 1940. I moved my family from our home in Magdeburg and started work. Unfortunately, the expanding war necessitated that I stop work on the VW automobile and help design and build the Kubelwagen. My mother and sister were killed in the air raid of August 1944." Kittel frowned and shook his head. I wondered if it was sympathy for me or hatred of the enemy. I paused to let that part of my story sink in. "As the American army approached in April of '45, Hitler sent word that we were to destroy the plant. I was not going to be a part of that, so I left and joined my college roommate in Bleicherode. He was a member of Dr. Werner Von Braun's rocket scientists who went there to escape the advancing Russians. My friend was able to pass me off as one of his group. Days later, we were captured by the Americans and were soon on our way to the United States." Kittel sat with his mouth open as if about to speak, but no words came out. He looked down, rubbed his forehead and then his eyes found mine.

Finally, he asked, "How did you convince your supervisors in America that you were a rocket scientist? That is a very specialized field."

"Well, I am an engineer, so I knew the basics. Also, I claimed to speak only German which limited my communication with the Americans."

"That's an incredible story, Hans. But one thing still puzzles me. How did you get away from von Braun's group? Weren't you all prisoners of the Americans?"

"Yes, technically, but our captors were very good to us and gave us considerable freedom. We even got paid for our work. I simply left and took a bus to South Bend, Indiana."

"That sounds too easy. You were not an American. How did you get a job at Studebaker without citizenship or references?" I wondered how much detail I should go into. I decided on a shortened version of the story.

"I had to assume a false identity. Also, I was able to befriend a well-known South Bend businessman who vouched for me."

"Well, Hans, I'll say this for you, if you as ingenious in your job here as you were in the saga you just related to me, you'll have a long and productive career. But let me add this. If you are as dishonest here as your story suggests you were in America, your career will be very short." I felt properly warned.

"Don't worry about that, Herr Kittel. I'm through lying. Besides, the truth is much easier to remember." We both laughed.

Then he said, "Call me Will, Hans. Almost everyone else does. Herr Voss mentioned several improvements you had suggested that would help make our VW more acceptable in the American market. Among the suggestions was better ventilation for the interior and putting the turn signal lever on the steering column. Is there anything else in the interior you would suggest?"

"Yes, but good ventilation and the turn signal should come first in my opinion."

"All right. Your first assignment will be to reengineer the turn signal system. The work should include detail drawings, a wiring diagram, a three-dimensional working prototype and a comprehensive report as to the need for the change, cost considerations and the expected improvement in customer satisfaction. I don't want opinions; I want solid facts to back up your assumptions. Understood?"

"Yes, sir." The morning had gone quickly. I was getting hungry. Those cold cuts at Otto's place were inadequate for more than a couple of hours. Luckily, Will had the same urge.

He glanced at his watch and then said, "What do you say we go to the cafeteria and get some food?" As I walked down the cafeteria line, I loaded my tray anticipating this might also be my evening meal. "Free food for employees is quite a benefit," I said. "I haven't seen that in America."

"It started right after the war, Hans. By necessity, our wages were low and many of our workers didn't have money for food. Our managers went out looking for supplies and customers for our cars and in some cases traded cars for food. Using this method, we were able to give our workers one good meal a day. I suspect that's how we retained many of our best employees."

"Will, I hate to bring this up but I have no place to stay tonight. "

" I'll call the VW Guest House where you can stay for a couple of days. I'll give you the rest of the day off today to find permanent housing. I suggest the apartments across the canal."

"Thank you, Will. "

* * * * * * * * *

I walked over to the apartment complex office and inquired as to the availability of a one-room apartment. They told me there was a two-month waiting period. I was put on a waiting list. Since the complex was sponsored by VW, I could have moved in without paying an advance. That was no conciliation since there were no rooms available. I wondered if I could extend my stay at the guesthouse. I walked around aimlessly wondering what to do. The streets were quiet. The crackle of the icy snow covered ground beneath my feet was the only sound. Soon I realized I was near the cottage of the old man who had given me shelter that cold night five years ago. Although I saw him on my visit two months earlier, I decided to go by again and see if he needed anything. I still wanted to find a way to repay him for his kindness.

I knocked on his door. Once, then harder.

A weak voice from inside said, "Who is there?"

"It is Hans, the chap that you helped five years ago and the one who visited two months ago." It was quiet for several seconds.

"What do you want? I'm not dressed for company."

"I don't care how you are dressed. I just want to see you and help you if I can." Another long pause and then the door cracked opened. The old man looked thinner and more aged than he did just two months earlier. It was obvious that he hadn't bathed or shaved in days.

"I would invite you in, son, but my fire went out and I'm not able to get it going again."

"Maybe I can help if you'll allow me." I looked inside at the cold dark room. One flickering candle was the only light. "Is there any coal in your scuttle?"

"No," he said. "There's a small pile out back but I'm too weak to get it." It was obvious that this old gentleman would not long survive without help.

"Let me get your fire going for you." I took the scuttle and a small shovel from beside the fireplace and walked toward the back door. The house was in shambles. Empty cans and dirty pans and dishes were scattered about. The smell of his chamber pot was strong. I emptied the pot in the outhouse behind the cottage and then scooped the pot half full of wet snow. I had to scratch around a bit to find his small coal pile. After getting the fire restarted, we both sat close by and warmed up.

"In all this time, sir, I never told you my name. It is Hans Werner." I detected a slight smile on his worn wrinkled face.

"My name is Waldo Rosenblum." I sat quietly, wondering how he survived the war. He seemed to read my thoughts. "Yes, I'm Jewish," he said. "After Hitler's reign, there are very few of us left."

"Do you have any family Herr Rosenblum?"

"No, they're all gone. In 1940, my wife and two sons were taken to Hannover to work in a factory there."

"What ever happened to your family?" I asked.

"I really don't know but I do know that all other Jewish people taken from this area never returned."

"I'm so sorry." I reached over and patted his bony knee. "How did you escape?"

"If I had been in a city or town, I suspect I would be dead now. Living out here, they somehow missed me. Even the Nazis let some slip by, I suppose. All Jews were required to register and were soon assembled in the ghettos of major cities. I simply didn't sign up. My wife and sons did and were taken away."

"How have you survived these last few years?"

"During the war I used a false non-Jewish sounding name. After the war, I had some money hidden, but with high inflation, it soon ran out. I worked a small garden behind this house and some neighbors gave me food. But they're all gone now. Times are hard. I'm 79 years old. My health is poor, so I've accepted that my time on earth is nearly up."

"Don't talk like that. I just started my job at Volkswagen today. Soon, I'll have some money. I'll help you, Herr Rosenblum."

"You are very kind. Please call me, Wally. That's what my wife use to call me."

"All right," I said. "You call me, Hans." He nodded and sat quietly. "I'm going to have to leave you now, Wally. I told him I would come by tomorrow afternoon with some food and make sure his fire was still burning. He thanked me and extended his cold, wrinkled hand for me to shake. I considered it an honor to do so.

* * * * * * * * *

After a warm, soaking bath at the VW Guest House, I dressed, carefully tied my tie and went in for my first full day of work. It involved meeting co-workers and learning where to go and who to see to get things done. The atmosphere was very different from Studebaker. Everyone at Volkswagen seemed to have the same objectives, survival and growth. Those that I met were courteous but not overly friendly. After I left the office, I thought about Wally and his miserable situation. I found a local market and I picked up a half-kilo each of dried kidney beans and rice and also a large onion. I decided to cook a recipe often served in Huntsville, red beans and rice. When I arrived, I found Wally wrapped in a blanket in his rocking chair pulled close to a dying fire. His tousled thin white hair obviously hadn't been combed all day. I stirred the little fire and added a lump of coal. I found an old cast-iron pot on a shelf, added water and beans and set it on our now blazing fire.

"Well, Wally, we have well over an hour to wait before I can even add the rice and onions, so what shall we talk about?"

"Oh, I don't know. Tell me about your new job," he said.

"There's not much to tell after one day. I'll be working on an electric turn signal to be mounted on the car's steering column."

"Turn signal? I thought drivers stuck their arm out the window when they wanted to turn." I laughed and nodded. Wally continued. "You know something, Hans. I never learned to drive a car. When I was younger, only the wealthy had automobiles. Living way out here, we didn't even see cars until they built the Volkswagen plant. This area was all open country with just a few villages scattered here and there. The nearest village was Fallersleben." Wally coughed. He seemed to have trouble breathing. Finally, after another series of coughs, he continued. "The new village across from the Volkswagen plant was named Wolfsburg. They got that name from the 14th century castle, Schloss Wolfsburg that belonged to Count Werner von der Schulenburg. The Nazis took 5000 acres from him for the plant and town." He smiled. "Most of the land was swamp and infested by mosquitoes. Of course, it has been built up tremendously since then." The next hour went by quickly as I sat and listened to this intelligent but feeble old man tell his life story. When he talked of his wife and children his eyes filled with tears. And I must admit mine did too. I hoped that I could somehow help to relieve some of the loneliness and sadness of his present situation. But from his demeanor and actions, I feared his life would soon be over unless his health improved.

I found two bowls and washed them in water that I pumped from his well. Although he had never eaten the red beans and rice combination before, he seemed to appreciate the fact that it was hot and came to him without effort.

After eating his fill he said, "Dunker schoen, Hans. I'll have this again tomorrow. Where are you staying tonight?"

"I'm at the Volkswagen Guest House. I have to move out tomorrow though. Two days is the limit for new employees. Unfortunately, there's a waiting list for the company apartments. So I'm not sure where I'll be staying tomorrow night." We sat silently for a few moments before Wally spoke.

"You could stay here. I have a spare room that's now just used for storage."

"Wally, that's very generous of you but I couldn't impose on you like that."

"We'll, we could call it a business arrangement. You fix me a meal every night and I'll give you a place to live." I knew if I took Wally up on his offer, I would be doing more that just fixing one meal a day. But I felt an obligation to the old man and besides I had no other options, so I agreed.

* * * * * * * * * *

What surprised me most about my fellow workers was how capable they all seemed to be. I always got sensible, logical answers to my questions. I made progress on my turn-signal project during the first two weeks, but nothing spectacular. Of greater significance was the receipt of my first paycheck. I went shopping for groceries for Wally and me. What a joy it was to finally buy sausages, eggs, cheese, smoked fish, bread, cabbage and a variety of canned goods. Wally met me at the front door. Knowing it was my payday, he was dressed, had shaved off his scraggly beard and his hair was combed, all ready for the celebration that I promised.

"Good evening, my young friend," he said. "What have you in those bags?"

"Clear a place on the table and I'll show you!" Moving quickly with the help of his cane, the feeble old man showed agility I had not seen before. "You are looking spry this evening, Herr Rosenblum. It appears you have been busy today. Even the fire is blazing. Where did you get the coal? I thought you were out."

"Oh, that's wood I collected from the yard and along the roadway."

"I am proud of you, Wally. It must have taken you all day."

"Ya. I'm slow but determined. I even scrubbed the dirt off my rusty old body in honor of your first paycheck."

"Well, I couldn't be happier," I said. "Before I start preparing tonight's meal of Bratwursts, sauerkraut and potato dumplings, I have a surprise for you." I reached into one of the sacks and withdrew a bottle of WieBer Riesling wine. I got the idea a few days earlier when I was cleaning out a cupboard and found two dusty old wine glasses. I retrieved the now clean glasses and poured each glass half full. Wally sat speechless. Finally, his brow furred, he covered his eyes and began to sob. I was stunned. What had I done wrong?

"I'm sorry, Wally. I thought the wine might make you happy. Forgive me." His bony body shook as he attempted to control his tears. Finally, he was able to talk.

"Oh, Hans. The problem is that I'm a sentimental old fool. Seems the older I get the harder it is for me to control my emotions. The last time I drank from these glasses was eleven years ago. My wife and I sat at this very table and toasted our love with a bottle of Riesling. I hope you understand these memories of mine are an odd mixture of sorrow and joy."

"I'm sorry. I didn't know. I'll put the wine away and get started on our meal." Wally gently touched my arm as I reached for the bottle.

"You'll do nothing of the kind, young man. We'll have a glass together, if you will allow me at least one toast to my dear Miriam."

"I'd be honored," I said before the lump in my throat prevented further comment. Candlelight flickered through the golden liquid as he raised his glass high and looked toward heaven.

"To you, Miriam my love," he said.

"To Miriam," I whispered as I touched my glass to his.

CHAPTER 29

Even though the work at Volkswagen was interesting, I must admit my greatest pleasure came from seeing the improvement in Wally's health and working on improving our living conditions. Each night we discussed our progress on the house and planned future work. Of course, I did most of the heavy cleaning and repair work but surprisingly Wally was able to do some inside painting and minor cleaning. He seemed to take a greater interest in his hygiene and his surroundings with each passing day.

As the weather moderated, we discussed what outside projects were needed. The list included painting, window washing and grass cutting. Also, he mentioned a garden. I admitted I knew nothing about gardening. Wally said he would teach me. I had no idea how much physical work would be involved. And since Wally was unable to do anything more than supervise, I soon found myself digging and planting on a grand scale. I knew that our garden would help on the food bill. But after working at the plant all day and then coming home to work a couple of hours in the garden before fixing our evening meal, I often fell in bed exhausted. I realized that taking care of Wally and improving the house was drawing my attention away from improving the Volkswagen. Strangely, I didn't want to change a thing. Wally realized how hard I was working to keep everything going.

"Hans," he said, "If we could figure out someway that I didn't have to bend down and cook in our fireplace, I think I could fix some of our meals. Miriam and I had a cast-iron stove at one time but they took it for scrap metal during the war." I thought about what he said and then replied.

"You know what would improve our lives more than anything else, Wally, is electricity. As you know, there's a power line running in front of the house. As soon as I save enough money, I plan to buy some wire and fixtures for the house and then get us hooked up to the power line. We could get a hot plate, and then you could help with the cooking. What do you think of that?"

"Electricity? Waldo Rosenblum with electricity? I'm too old to learn to live with electricity."

"Well, I'm not," I said. "I miss it. It gives good light and much, much more. We could even get an electric pump for the well. That would bring water right inside the house and you know what that means."

"No, what?" he asked.

"Indoor plumbing, a flush toilet. Wouldn't that be wonderful?"

"I don't know, Hans. How could we ever afford all of that?"

"There's an American expression; 'where there's a will, there's a way'," I said. "And somehow, we'll find that way!" He shook his head and smiled. It occurred to me that Wally had used the word "we" in talking about finances. Were we now a team?

With the turn signal project finished and turned over to the draftsmen, I was ready for another assignment. I hoped it would be more important than the last one. Will Kittel called me into his office to discuss what that assignment might be.

"Hans, you did well on the turn signal project. It was on time and within budget. Your next project is based on input from a large number of customers who smoke. They have complained that there's no place to lay their cigarettes while driving or a place to put them out when finished smoking. We need to install ashtrays for both front and rear passengers."

"Will, I was hoping to work on something a bit more important than ash trays. If we are ever going to sell VWs in America, we need a stronger engine, 15" tires and larger brake shoes and a host of other improvements. Have you heard about the new tubeless tire development?"

"Yes, I have. But don't forget, Hans, this is the Interior Design Engineering Department. Those projects don't fall under my jurisdiction. Besides, the ash tray project is important."

"Maybe so, but it's so simple. I'm capable of more."

"In that case, the project should go very fast." I could see I was getting nowhere and decided to take on the assignment without further argument.

"All right, Will. I'll get started right away. I'll need the research file for background." I left the office disappointed.

On my way to lunch, I noticed a new posting on the bulletin board:

Family Day Celebration
May 4, 1951
As a token of appreciation to our employees and
to celebrate the manufacture of our 200,000th
Volkswagen automobile, employees and their families
are invited to tour our plant and enjoy a picnic and
music under a large tent to be set up in our parking lot.
Shuttle busses will run from the VW Apartments and
from the Wolfsburg town center to the main gate.
Festivities begin at 10 am.

That sounds like fun, I thought. There's only one problem, that's Wally's 80th birthday. I couldn't leave him alone on his birthday, and he certainly is not able to walk from home to the factory and then tour on foot. On the other hand, he hadn't been out of that yard in months. It would be good for him to be around people again. I wondered if the company would provide a wheelchair for the disabled.

The Company Nurse said she would have a wheelchair available at the gate for Wally but it would be against company policy to let it be taken off the premises. How to get Wally from home to the plant was now the problem, assuming he wanted to go.

That night I told him about the celebration and asked if he was interested. I mentioned the wheelchair at the gate.

"I'm not sure I can walk from here to the plant, Hans. I'd like to go with you, but I don't think I'm able."

"Well, it will be your birthday and a very special one at that. It's your decision, but it would mean a lot to me if you decide to go. You're the only family I have. You must know by now that I love you like a father. If you want to go, we'll find a way."

"Hans, now that you have said that, I've something that I need to say to you. Because of you, I now have a reason to live. You've given me hope and companionship. If I am like your father, then you are like my son. When I die, I want you to have this house and land. You've put so much of yourself into this place; it should be yours when I'm gone. All I ask is a decent burial."

"That won't be for a long while, Wally. I expect at least ten more good years out of you, unless, of course, some jealous husband shoots you first." Wally didn't smile.

"I'm serious about willing the house to you, Hans. If you'll get a will drawn up, I'll sign it."

"No, I couldn't do that," I said.

"I've got no one else, Hans. You want the state to take it?"

"No, I guess not." I considered his logic. "All right," I said, "If that's what you want, I'll do it."

The spring weather with its warmer temperatures and longer days gave Wally and me a chance to be outside more. With the open house celebration only two weeks away, I suggested we take a walk every afternoon before the evening meal. He agreed. For the first few days we went only 200 meters or so and at a very slow pace. He always let me know when it was time to turn around and returned home. Except for the day it rained, we walked every day, a bit farther and faster each time. On May 3rd, we made our turn for home in front of the main gate to the plant. Wally now had the confidence to join me for the open house celebration the next day.

I woke Wally with a steaming cup of coffee and a sweet roll on his birthday.

"Happy birthday Wally. Are you ready for our big day at Volkswagen?"

"Good morning, Hans. Yes, as soon as I get this old body moving, I hope I'll be able to walk to the factory and not hold you back too much."

"Don't worry about that, it's your birthday and you can set the pace of the day's activities." After a breakfast of smoked herring and dark bread we headed out into the cool spring morning. The air was sweet and clean, with no hint that there was a large industrial plant nearby. I watched Wally closely, intentionally slowing the pace to make sure he did not exert himself too soon. As promised, wheelchairs were at the gate. Never having used one before, Wally was apprehensive. I finally convinced him that all he had to do was ride. Off we went.

Although there were guides provided in the various departments, I gave Wally a running commentary as we progressed on our tour. We first went through some of the office areas. In engineering, I pointed out my drawing board and the small cubicle where my young boss worked. In the factory, we first toured the punch press area. The noise level was normally extremely loud in this area, but that day the presses were still.

As we approached the fuel tank assembly area, the guide there was speaking to a group of guests. It was Otto Haniel. He didn't notice us approach.

"Wally, you've heard me speak of Otto, who was my boss here during the war, well, he is that large fellow over there. He let me spend the night when I visited recently and also helped me get my job here at Volkswagen."

"Sounds like a fine man," Wally said.

"Yes, he has his good points." About this time, his audience moved on and we approached. Remembering Otto's feelings about Jews, I wondered if I should introduce Wally. I hoped for the best. Why should I hide my friend?

"Hello, Otto. How are you?"

"Hans Werner! I haven't heard from you in a long while. What have you been doing?"

"Oh, just working. Otto, this is my friend and landlord, Waldo Rosenblum. Today is his 80th birthday. Wally, this is Otto Haniel. He is foreman of this department." Otto nodded but didn't offer to shake Wally's hand.

"You say Herr Rosenblum here is your landlord?"

"Yes. In a way. I live at his house in exchange for certain tasks that I perform."

Wally spoke up. "He's being modest Herr Haniel. I'm a feeble old man and Hans takes care of many of my needs."

Otto frowned for a moment before asking, "How did you two meet?

I answered. "The night I escaped, um, left the factory six years ago, I got soaked from head to foot in the canal. I was freezing cold as I walked along the road. I saw Wally's house. He let me inside to warm up. He even gave me food the next morning."

Wally interrupted. "Hans is like a son to me now. He probably saved my life when he moved in."

"That's quite a story," Otto grunted. He turned away from Wally and starred at me with piercing eyes. "We figured you left through the canal, Hans. We found your briefcase stuffed with drawings the next day."

Wanting to change the subject, I said, "That was a long time ago. The war is over, Otto. Much has happened since then. By the way, I'm amazed at the progress made here in this factory." Otto shrugged his shoulders. Wally and I moved along to the next department. After our delicious luncheon, we lingered for a while to listen to the German band play old favorites. Wally was quiet. He leaned back and closed his eyes. I was worried that he might be fading, so I suggested we leave before the concert was over. He agreed. We turned the wheelchair in at the gate and started the one and a half kilometer walk back home. By the time we arrived, Wally was tugging on my arm, but we made it and he was proud of his accomplishment.

CHAPTER 30

Wally and I enjoyed the beautiful June weather. A feeling of joy was in the air. Our garden was coming along nicely. The corn was tall and green, the tomatoes were beginning to ripen and the beans were almost ready to gather. Our main problem was pumping water from the well for irrigation. What a tiring and time-consuming job that was. There was also much left to do around the house. But every improvement made life better for us. After running wire for lights in each of our four rooms, I contacted the Wolfsburg Power Company and made arrangements for a hook up. The inspector who came out said the installation was acceptable and we soon had electric lights. Wally was delighted, especially after I purchased a hot plate. He started cooking two or three evening meals a week. I could usually tell when Wally was cooking. I could smell his sausages and cabbages long before I reach the house. Other improvements such as the pump for the indoor plumbing would have to wait until I saved more money. I also had plans to get a telephone so Wally could call for help if needed.

At Wally's insistence, I had a solicitor draft a simple will and Wally signed it. Now if something happened to him, I would inherit his house and lot. I did not look forward to that day. I figured he would live many more years if his health continued to improve the way it had in recent months.

On a sunny Monday afternoon in late June, Wally met me at the gate. He didn't say hello; he just looked at the ground.

"It is unusual for you to meet me out here, Wally. What is the occasion?"

"Hans, I've been thinking."

"Oh, that's good to hear," I said.

"Don't make a joke, Hans. This is serious. I've gotten to know you very well in the past few months and I think I know what motivates you. I don't think it's growing a garden, or cooking and cleaning for some poor old man. I surely don't think house painting, washing windows or digging a cesspool is what you were put on this earth for. You're an automotive engineer and a good one. All you talked about in our early conversations was your ideas for improving the 'people's car.' Now, you hardly ever mention your work. That bothers me. I'm beginning to think that this house and my well being are too much of a distraction for you. I care about you too much to dissuade you from your dreams. Hans, I suggest you spend less time on this house and me and more time thinking about your career."

"What brought this on?"

"Nothing in particular. I just want you to be happy and fulfilled."

"I'm uh, happy. Fulfilled? I'm not sure what that means."

"Hans, you're a young man. You need to concentrate on your future. You need to think about getting married. How long has it been since you've been with a woman?" I looked down and didn't answer but admitted to myself it had been awhile. Wally kept pressing. It seemed he had prepared a speech and was determined to deliver all of it. "What do you say, Hans? More engineering and less gardening in the future?" I smiled and nodded.

"Wally, you are probably the most considerate man I've ever known. Who else but you would be so unselfish? But you must realize that you are my only family and it's very important to me that my family is well cared for." Wally was determined.

"To see you climbing in your profession would make me happier than having a toilet inside the house." I thought about what he said.

"Maybe you're right about my career, but you must realize that your happiness and my happiness are one and the same. But, I'll try to hit a better balance in the future. Now; if we're ever going to have an indoor toilet, I need to be digging on that cell-pool hole out back." Wally fixed the evening meal that night and I finished a rectangular hole that two coffins could fit in. I hoped Wally wouldn't fall in before I could get it covered with logs, tin roofing and dirt.

From that day on, I took Wally's advice and started concentrating on Volkswagen projects more. I completed the ashtray project ahead of schedule. I think my boss, Will Kittel finally realized that I was capable of more challenging projects and that I was not satisfied with the assignments I had been given thus far. I certainly made it no secret that ashtrays and turn signals did not excite me.

"Hans, I'd like to discuss your next assignment when you have a few minutes," Will said as he passed my drawing board late that early summer afternoon.

"How about now?" I asked.

"All right. There's been a lot of discussion at corporate level lately about building a market in America. Fritz Voss said that when you interviewed for this job, you suggested several things that would need to be done before we could have a chance in that huge market. Herr Voss and Herr Nordhoff think, based on your years in America and your time at Studebaker, your input might be valuable in determining what changes in our approach and possibly the car itself need to be made. Therefore, you will be invited to several high level discussions in the next few days and asked for your opinions on this very important opportunity for our company."

"That sounds great. I believe I can be of value to that objective." After Will left, I sat and thought about the upcoming meetings and made a few notes. I loved the idea of our great little car being sold in America. I couldn't wait to get home and tell Wally the good news.

I ran the 1500 meters to our little house. Wally was waiting at the front door with a glass of wine in his hand.

"Hello, Wally. You've started drinking a bit early today haven't you?"

"Don't be funny, young man. You know I seldom drink. This is for you."

"That's very thoughtful of you, but what's the occasion?"

"Nothing special. I'm just looking for ways to show how much I appreciate you and all you have done for me." I was stunned by that comment. It was unlike Wally to be so open with his feelings. In the past the most physical contact I ever had with him was a handshake. But that beautiful afternoon, I took his frail body in my arms and gave him a big hug.

"Wally, I have the most wonderful news. I've been asked to meet with executives at the top level of our company to discuss the American market, more specifically, how to sell VWs in large numbers over there." Wally's face beamed as if he personally was the beneficiary of the good news.

"Oh, Hans, what an opportunity for you. I couldn't be happier."

"Well, in that case, why don't you have a glass of wine with me?"

"Here, twist my arm," he said as he extended his bony left arm in my direction. We both laughed.

"You certainly are in a fine mood today, Wally. Explain yourself."

"I'm happy when you are happy, my son." I put my arm around the old man's shoulders as we walked inside. I found the second wine glass and poured some for my friend. We toasted our good fortune and discussed plans for the evening meal.

CHAPTER 31

As I was ushered into the office of Volkswagen's president, Heinz Nordhoff, my heart was beating so hard I feared it might show under my shirt. Fritz Voss, Vice President of Engineering and several other executives that I had not met were already assembled. I looked around the rather modest office. I expected mahogany paneling. Instead the walls were covered with wallpaper. Behind his cluttered desk was a credenza crowded with family photos and various awards. After the introductions, Herr Nordhoff quickly got down to business.

"Gentlemen, the United States of America is the largest market for automobiles in the world. Even though auto manufactures from numerous European countries have attempted to penetrate this huge market, their successes have been few. The preponderance of post war car sales in the U.S. has been by Ford, General Motors and the Chrysler Corporation. To a lesser degree, independents such as Nash, Studebaker, Hudson, Kaiser-Frazer and Packard have also found markets for their offerings. Our export program in other countries has been very successful, yet in American our total unit sales to date number less than one thousand. That is simply unacceptable!" He paused and looked at each man individually before continuing. "Our VW automobile is high quality, unique in design and engineering and is unlike anything the U.S. has to offer, yet, it hasn't sold well there. I will now open up the meeting to you learned gentlemen to tell me why." I sat quietly while a series of design solutions were suggested. Mostly, they had to do with making our VW bigger and more powerful like American cars. I knew this was not the answer. Herr Nordhoff squirmed in his seat and seemed a bit irritated. Finally, he interrupted.

"Gentlemen, gentlemen! Have I not already made it clear that the basic Porsche body design and engine are not to be changed?" No one replied. Things got very quiet, embarrassingly so. Everyone seemed to be studying the floor. Finally, I saw my chance to contribute. I gathered my courage. I then stood and directed my comments toward Herr Nordhoff.

"Having recently spent five years in America, may I suggest, sir, that the VW is not acceptable in America for a number of reasons." Nordhoff leaned forward and picked up his pencil. I continued. "First, the perception that the Volkswagen is a Nazi car or 'Hitler's baby' must be overcome." Eyes widened and mouths dropped. I thought I heard someone groan. I knew I had touched on a taboo subject. I wondered if some of the men present might have been officers in the German Army, maybe even SS. I knew that what I had said was true, so I pressed on. "Second, U.S. auto companies have convinced the car-buying public that bigger is better. The family automobile in America is to a large degree, a status symbol. Our VW and several other European cars are perceived as too small, not 'real' automobiles. Third, and perhaps most important, other importers have concentrated on sales. Parts and service have been secondary leaving the perspective buyer to worry that if he buys a foreign car, he may not be able to get it serviced. Parts imported into the U.S. for repairs have traditionally been slow to arrive and expensive often leaving the owner immobile and frustrated. If our approach to the market solves these three problems, I think our Volkswagen will be a big success." Nordhoff scratched his balding head and rubbed his chin before speaking.

"I can't disagree with your logic, Werner, but those are three very formidable obstacles. Let's take them one at a time and perhaps suggest a solution to each. Hitler's car, you say? Are Americans still holding a grudge six years after the war?"

"Yes, sir, I think so. Realize that Americans think almost everything that Hitler promoted turned out negative, even evil. I'm not here to debate whether or not Americans are justified in their perception. I'm simply stating the facts. But, on the positive side, Americans do recognize Germany's superior technology. We should reinforce that perception in our advertising of the VW and then back it up with the quality of our product. But I must add, Americans are constantly bombarded with exaggerated claims. I suggest that we stress the Volkswagen is an 'honest car'."

"All right. Point well taken. What about the 'bigger is better' perception? How can we change that without changing our VW body?"

"I don't think we can for everyone. But our car has many desirable features that American cars don't have. I think once those features are well known, it might become fashionable to be seen in a thrifty, well-made, easy to park vehicle that can take almost any kind of abuse or bad weather and still keep running. Our market segment need not be limited to low-income people." Nordhoff took notes as I spoke. Without warning, an older gentleman whom I hadn't met rose and spoke loudly.

"Werner, living in America, surely you must realize that time after time small cars have been introduced there. May I mention Austin, Crosley, Henry J, Nash Metropolitan and numerous European brands? What makes you think we will succeed when so many others have failed?" I knew the gentleman had forgotten the purpose of the meeting. I summoned my courage and shot back.

"Sir, it was my understanding from our president's opening statements that this meeting was to try to find ways to sell our Volkswagen in America not to justify our lack of success." Several men chuckled. The older gentleman cleared his throat and started to reply when Nordhoff interrupted.

"All right. All right! Enough of that." He turned back to me.

"You mentioned giving priority to service over sales. How can we do that with the limited number of dealers we have in America, many of them without VW trained service personnel?"

"That very well may be the case now, but in the future, I suggest all our dealerships should have good VW service departments and a complete complement of parts before they are allowed to sell our cars." Several of the executives shook their heads and frowned.

"That could be quite expensive and time consuming, Werner!" Nordhoff responded.

"Yes, sir, but the payoff could be tremendous. As you mentioned earlier, the U.S. is the world's largest market for automobiles." Nordhoff looked down at his notes and then back at me.

Then he said, "Thank you for your input, Herr Werner. You have given us several things to discuss. We may be calling on you again as our project progresses. You are excused." I walked back to the Engineering Office wondering what kind of impression I had made on President Nordhoff. Also, I feared I might have alienated the gentleman who made the comment about small cars in the U.S. Was I perceived as just a youngster with wild and impractical ideas or did the men there think I made good suggestions?

Several days later, I was again invited to the president's office. This time there was only Nordhoff and Fritz Voss there. After I was seated and given a cup of coffee in a fine china cup, Nordhoff spoke.

"Since our previous meeting, we on the executive staff have discussed your ideas and for the most part believe them to be sound. But if we set up service departments in America before we advertise the vehicle, as I said earlier, it will be quite costly and time consuming. That's not to say we won't take that approach if necessary, but teaming up with existing U.S.

dealers who already have service departments would be much faster and less expensive. We already know that the big three have no interest in our product so we have decided to contact the U.S. independents as possible partners. We'd like your help in that endeavor."

"Well, sir, I must point out that our choices are limited. Nash and Kaiser-Frazer already have their own small cars and therefore would probably not be interested in taking on our VW. Nash just came out with the 100" wheelbase Rambler and K-F has the 4-cylinder, 100" wheelbase Henry J. I owned a Henry J when I lived in Huntsville. It's a good little car but not a big seller. That leaves Studebaker, Packard and Hudson as possible partners. None of those three are in good financial condition and I know Studebaker once turned down a chance at the Volkswagen; for the wrong reasons I might add. Of course, we have a better car now than the one we evaluated three years ago. It's possible Studebaker could be more open to a joint venture today, especially since Nash and K-F are already selling small cars." Nordhoff sat quietly for a few moments rubbing his chin and then pointed his index finger in my direction.

"All right. Here's what I want you to do, Werner. Since you know the people at Studebaker, I want you to go over there and see what kind of arrangement can be made to sell and service our VW through their dealerships. I'll send someone else to Hudson and Packard. These will be preliminary meetings to judge interest. If one of the three companies looks promising, then a team will go over and finalize the deal. Incidentally, you are being transferred to the export department with a raise in pay and a bonus."

"Thank you, sir. I look forward to the new assignment." I was bursting with pride and joy as I left the meeting. I wondered how much the raise and bonus were going to be. I'd just have to wait and see. When I got back to the office, I made three phone calls. The first was to the telephone company authorizing a phone to be installed at the home of Waldo Rosenblum. Second was a call ordering an electric pump for Wally's well. And third was a call to a local plumber to install a toilet, sink and bathtub at our house. I then hurried home to tell Wally about my promotion. I decided to wait to tell him about my trip to America.

My head was in a whirl for the next few days as I assumed my new assignment in the Export Department. Although my transfer and promotion was now official, it was not widely known throughout the company until a small article in the company newspaper spread the news. Tucked in among a number of other personnel changes was this announcement:

Hans Werner, an engineer in the Interior Design Department has been transferred to the Export Department and promoted to Senior Design Engineer. Werner who worked for Volkswagen during the war, later spent six years in America where he was employed by the Studebaker Corporation in Indiana. Later, he was a member of Dr. Werner von Braun's rocket development group in Alabama.

When I got home that afternoon, I was surprised to find Wally talking on the phone.

After he hung up, I asked, "Who were you talking to, Wally?"

"Oh, I was just checking the exact time." He then smiled and said, "If you must know, I just wanted to talk to someone and didn't know anyone to call."

"You can call me at the office anytime you want to. You have my new number don't you?"

"Ya, but I know you are a busy man. You don't have time to chat with me."

"Of course I do. Anytime, Wally. Anytime."

"Big news, Hans. Today, I took my first urinerte in the new water closet and then, washed my hands in our new basin. It was all very nice but are you sure you can afford all these luxuries?"

"Wally, I told you I got a promotion. If you don't believe me, look at this article in the company newspaper." I unfolded the paper from my pocket and pointed to my announcement.

"You don't have to prove anything to me, Hans. I know you got a promotion, but all I'm saying is maybe you need to be more careful with your money. You never know what's going to happen. Remember the thirties. Those years were painful for many Germans. If it were not for Hitler's many public works programs and a growing military, there would have been tremendous unemployment. Unfortunately, Jewish people were left out of the new jobs. Many left the country. Those that didn't were rounded up and sent to concentration camps or to munitions factories. My wife and sons registered and were taken away. I somehow escaped notice."

"Well, Wally, let's try to forget the past. These are prosperous times and we should enjoy them. Have you thrown out that smelly old chamber pot yet?"

"No, but I'll put it away somewhere. I never throw anything away." Wally reminded me of my mother. She too was thrifty and never disposed of anything that could possibly be used later.

CHAPTER 32

I wrote a letter to Studebaker's President and Board Chairman with a copy to Bob Nitske, VP of Engineering. I used my real name with no mention of Van Hoffmann. I thought a little surprise might do them good. I looked forward to seeing old friends like Jack Yearwood, Ed Reynolds, Virgil Norman, and, of course, Susie Goodall. I hoped I would not see Big Mike Levy or Willie Wyatt.

In a few days, Bob Nitske answered my letter and welcomed me to Studebaker for preliminary talks. Our department secretary made all the arrangements for my trip to America. The TWA flight to New York was to be followed by an American Airlines flight to Midway Airport in Chicago. I was to pick up a VW demonstrator at Emporium Imports on State Street and drive the VW to South Bend. I still had my Van Hoffmann driver's license if I got stopped. I sent a telegram stating that I would be arriving in South Bend on September 4, 1951. I had our secretary book my stay at the LaSalle even though I could have chosen a better hotel. It seemed that everything was falling into place for the trip. The only thing that bothered me was Wally's welfare while I was away. I had put off telling him about my trip for fear it would upset him, perhaps even frighten him to be alone again for several weeks.

Finally, on August 20th, I decided to tell Wally of my plans. I walked home slowly that warm humid afternoon, choosing my words as I walked. Dark clouds gathered overhead and a light sprinkle of late summer rain wet my face. I picked up the pace hoping to get home before a downpour. I wondered if I was making too much of my anxiety about telling Wally of the upcoming trip. I turned into the yard just as a flash of lightening lit the western sky. Once on the front porch, I stopped to wipe the rain from my face. I took a deep breath and entered the front room. Although still early in the day, the gathering storm offered little light.

"Wally, I'm home!" No answer. "Wally," I shouted louder. "Wal...."
I froze. Wally was on his back on the floor. There was no movement.

"Oh, God, no!" I rushed over and felt his neck, hoping for a pulse. I couldn't find one. His skin was cool. When I tried to raise his head, I felt some resistance. I turned on the electric light and took a closer look. His eyes were slightly open and glazed. His mouth was open. I almost lost control. I was frantic. Again, I desperately tried to find a pulse. I noticed red scratch marks on his throat and multiple scratches and bruises on his face. The shock of seeing him that way almost took my breath away. Was it possible someone had murdered my dear friend? Who could be so cruel to want to hurt this poor helpless old man? And why, why? I laid my head against his chest still hoping for some sign of life. Nothing! What should I do now? I called the Wolfsburg Police Department. I didn't touch anything except the phone. I just sat with my head in my hands until the police arrived.

After the police made an extensive search of the house, they dusted for fingerprints and took photographs. One of the officers commented on the fact that no drawers or closet doors were opened. They then took Wally's body to the coroner for examination. I went with them to the police station for questioning.

The interrogation room was bare except for three straight chairs and a small table. The two interrogators were both large uniformed men. They reminded me of the SS men who questioned and threatened me six years earlier. The older of the two started the questions.

"Hans Werner, is that correct?"

"Yes."

"How long have you known the deceased, Waldo Rosenblum?"

"I first met him about six years ago."

"What were the circumstances surrounding your meeting?" I wondered why they needed that information, but I co-operated hoping it might somehow lead to Wally's killer. I searched my memory and answered.

"I was caught in a winter storm and he gave me shelter for the night."

"When did you next see him?"

"I left Germany and spent six years in America before coming back to work at the Volkswagen plant here in Wolfsburg. As soon as I could, I visited Wally to check on his welfare. We became friends. At his suggestion, I moved in with him. That was six months ago." Why all these questions? I thought. Couldn't they see I was upset?

"What time did you leave the plant today?"

"The regular time, 5 p.m."

"Can you confirm that time? Did others see you leave or did you sign out?"

"I'm not sure who saw me. I just started working in the Export Department recently. There's no sign out sheet there."

"All right. One of our men will check that out. It is my understanding that Herr Rosenblum's property is outside the Volkswagen ownership zone. Is that correct?"

"Yes, that is true."

"What property or valuables did Herr Rosenblum have other than his house and lot?"

"None that I know of."

"Did he have a will?"

"Yes."

"And who is the beneficiary?"

"I am."

"I see. And how long ago was it that he signed the will?"

"I don't know exactly, about ten days."

"Since there was no indication of a robbery when we investigated. Do you know of anyone, other than yourself, who would benefit from his demise?"

"No. Definitely not! He knew very few people and had no money hidden as far as I know. I can't imagine anyone wanting to hurt this poor old man."

"Well, it appears someone wanted to hurt him. But in absence of robbery, can you suggest a motive, Werner?"

"No, I can't."

"Well, that leaves you as the only one with a motive, doesn't it?"

"What are you getting at? I didn't kill Wally. He was my best friend. He was like a father to me. I couldn't hurt Wally. Besides, he had been dead for some time when I arrived home. His body was cold and starting to stiffen when I found him."

"We'll have to get the coroner's report to determine the time of death and when you left your office to determine the possibility of your involvement. You are not to leave the city until this matter is sorted out. You may go now."

The rain was now heavy and I was several kilometers from home. I went back in the station and requested a ride home. It was granted. As was all cars in Wolfsburg, I was taken home in a Volkswagen.

The house was ghostly quiet when I walked in. Thunder outside added to the frightening scene. As I sat in Wally's favorite chair, head in hands, I noticed a tiny red spot on the wooden floor. I jumped to my feet. With ammonia and scrub brush I attacked the spot as if it were the enemy.

Tears ran down my face as I scrubbed. But I couldn't scrub away the hurt. Who could have wanted to kill Wally? Who and why? It made no sense. Although Wally was a weak old man, the killer must have been someone with sufficient strength to hit him hard enough to overpower him down and choke him to death. There was no indication of forced entry. Wally never locked his door. And no drawers or cabinets were opened or anything else that would suggest a robbery. I wondered if he knew his killer. All my thoughts and emotions centered around Wally, until; I just remembered, I am supposed to go to America in less than two weeks. Yet the police said I couldn't leave the city until I was no longer a suspect. That could take months. I decided to try to see Herr Nordhoff the next morning. Maybe he could advise me.

I didn't sleep much that night. The house was as empty and dark as a deserted coal mine without Wally. I tossed and turned trying to figure out why this tragedy happened. Not one single clue entered my mind. The next morning, as usual, I got dressed and went to work. The first thing I did was stop by Nordhoff's office and made an appointment to see him. I hoped I could get to him before he read the morning paper. That was not to be. When I finally was escorted into his office at ten a.m., Norhoff held up the front-page story about the murder.

"What's this all about, Werner?"

"I wish I knew, sir. When I got home from work yesterday, I found Herr Rosenblum dead. I have no idea why it happened. Wally was just a poor eighty-year-old man."

"The paper says that you are suspected of being the killer."

"That's probably because Wally recently willed his house to me and the police have no other leads as to why this murder happened. I feel sure I'll be cleared as soon as the coroner establishes the time of death."

"Oh? Why is that important?"

"Well, sir, the body was cold when I found him. But until I'm cleared, I can't leave the city. As per your instructions, I'm supposed to be in America in less than two weeks."

"Yes, that is true. We'll see if we can expedite the investigation. I'll have my legal department interview others in 'Export' as to your departure time yesterday and turn this information over to the police."

"I think that will be valuable, sir, but the police told me they also will check with my fellow employees to determine the time I left the office."

"Our report will aid them in moving faster. I will mention in a cover letter, that it is important to Volkswagen's future that you make the trip to America as scheduled." Nordhoff then smiled and said, "I will ask that the police finish the investigation as quickly as possible. Our progress is vitally important to everyone in this town including the police. Without Volkswagen, Wolfsburg would not exist."

"Thank you, sir." I left the office a bit more optimistic than when I walked in.

* * * * * * * * * *

I made arrangements with the Wolfsburg Mortuary for a modest casket for Wally. I also arranged for a burial plot alongside my mother and sister's graves. Now except for my real father, my family was now all together. I was unable to find a rabbi to conduct a service. It appeared Wally was one of the last Jews in the Wolfsburg area. Except for personnel from the mortuary, I was the only person at the gravesite when the dirt was shoveled into Wally's grave. Now I had three gravestones that I vowed to get installed as soon as I could afford them.

It was a big relief when the police department called and informed me that I was no longer an active suspect in Wally's death. I couldn't believe how quickly the investigation went. Apparently, Herr Nordhoff's influence did expedite the coroner's report and their determination that I was still at the office when the death occurred. I was now free to make the trip to America as scheduled.

CHAPTER 33

My new German passport and a generous travel advance made the trip to America painless. In fact, the trip was just what I needed, a change of scenery and an objective that had nothing to do with Wally or our home. The flights and even the bus ride in Chicago were pleasant, even entertaining. Seeing the city, so busy and prosperous helped me understand why the United States was the strongest country in the world. Of course, it helped that no WWII battles were fought in any of its forty-eight states. I walked the short distance from the bus station over to States Street.

Emporium Imports was a prosperous-looking dealership. Huge glass windows and large potted plants accented the Mercedes, Porsches, and BMWs that took center stage in the showroom. A lonely little VW was parked off to the side. The dealership owner, Harvey Stone was expecting me. Mr. Stone was a native of Chicago and long-time car dealer. He was a middle-age man with well-oiled, jet-black hair combed straight back. He wore an expensive-looking tailored pinstriped suit with a burgundy silk pocket-handkerchief that matched his necktie. He radiated an air of confidence.

My first question after our initial greeting was, "How are the Volkswagens selling."

"They're not! I'm thinking of dropping them," he said. "Granted they don't take up much room, but they look out of place with the more expensive, high quality imports that I sell. Some customers even make jokes about the VW. I remember one man said it looked like a pregnant roller skate." I smiled and changed the subject.

"Do you have a service department, Mr. Stone?"

"No. I just sell 'um. I don't fix 'um." Mr. Stone was teaching me valuable lessons in how not to sell Volkswagens.

"Well, thank you very much," I said. "I guess I better be headed on over to South Bend. Do you have a VW for me to drive?"

"You can take this one here in the showroom. I doubt I'll miss a sale while you are gone. By the way, good luck at Studebaker. You'll need it." With that jolly send-off, I was on my way to South Bend.

I had been driving with my headlights on for about an hour when I saw the large lighted billboard at the South Bend city limits. In huge gold and blue letters it read, "Welcome to South Bend, Indiana, Home of the Fighting Irish of Notre Dame." Below the caption was a larger than life-size fullback stiff-arming some invisible opponent while running for yet another Notre Dame touchdown. Pulling into the LaSalle Hotel parking lot brought back a flood of memories. I asked for room 3A, the same one I slept in my first night in South Bend six years earlier. Since the hotel was almost empty, getting 3A was not a problem. I read for a few minutes and then starred at the cracked ceiling for a few more. It was hard to believe I was back in South Bend.

My appointment the next day was at 9 a.m. at the office of Studebaker Engineering Vice-president, Bob Nitske. When I walked into the office at 8:50, Mr. Nitske's secretary glanced at me over the top of her glasses. She then frowned and looked away like she was puzzled. The lady looked vaguely familiar but I couldn't place her. To me, she looked somehow out of place, a little too flashy to be an engineering secretary. She had long platinum-blond hair tied in a ponytail and wore a tight red dress that showed off her figure. I introduced myself as Hans Werner and handed her my business card. She studied it and then asked me to take a seat. She went back to her typing but occasionally I caught her glancing in my direction.

Finally, she said, "Mr. Werner, are you aware that you have an identical twin?"

"No, I have no brothers," I answered.

"Well, a couple of years ago, we had a young engineer named Van Hoffmann who looks exactly like you."

"What ever happened to him," I asked.

"I don't know. He gave his two-weeks notice and was gone. Didn't give a forwarding address." I smiled and nodded. She punched her intercom announcing my arrival. I heard a voice that said send him in. She then stood and slowly walked across the room. Damn, what a great body that woman has, I said to myself. Get your mind on your mission, Hans. She opened Mr. Nitske's door and motioned for me to enter that familiar old office of the Engineering V.P. The office looked the same as when Roy Branson occupied it. I realized it was larger than that of Volkswagen's president. Nitske stood to welcome me.

"Welcome to Studebaker, Mr. Werner." Nitske's eyes widened. "Hey! Wait a minute. What's going on here? Is this some sort of a joke? You're Van Hoffmann."

"I was Van Hoffmann, Mr. Nitske, at least I pretended to be, but my real name is now and always has been, Hans Werner. I was educated in Berlin and worked at Volkswagen during the war. Studebaker gave me a chance to continue working as an automotive engineer, but I couldn't do it using my German identity. It's all very complicated so I'll spare you the details. However, my true name and title are on my business card. I hope my past employment here won't be a factor in our discussions." I continued to stand waiting to be offered a seat.

Nitske looked at my card and shook his head as if he were trying to find the right words. The room was quiet until he leaned against his desk and loudly exclaimed, "You left under rather unfavorable terms, Werner. I don't see how that can be forgotten! Even though you gave two weeks notice before you left, let's not forget you stole a prototype vehicle from the Proving Ground."

"Yes, but I returned it. Besides, it had been scrapped when I took it."

"So we thought. But that does not excuse the theft. That was one very strange car you and Jack Yearwood developed."

"It was a very good car. I know you were directed to abandon the project, but I think the Studebaker board made a grave mistake. But fortunately, Volkswagen is offering a similar small car for your dealerships that will fill the same nitch that I was attempting to fill with my 4-cylinder prototype. As you know, both Kaiser-Frazer's Henry J and Nash's Rambler are already on the market. But it's not too late for Studebaker to jump in with a small economical car before the big three come to their senses. In short, I'm here to ask Studebaker to take a look at our latest, improved Volkswagen. I have one parked outside."

"Didn't we evaluate a VW several years ago?"

"Yes, Ed Reynolds and I did the study. You probably have our favorable report in your files somewhere. Then president, Victor Harper killed the idea after being urged to do so by Mike Levy."

"How would you know that?" Nitske countered.

"I overheard them talking at the Chicago Auto Show."

"Oh, come on, Werner. How can I believe anything you say?"

"I suggest you ask Mr. Levy his opinion of Studebaker producing a small car. I can predict a negative answer especially since I developed the small-car prototype he and Mr. Harper had a wreck in."

"For God's sake, Werner. That sounds positively paranoid."

"Yes, I suppose it does. But it was no secret that Mike Levy didn't care for me. Remember, he broke my nose when I accused him of being involved in the Goodall and Branson murders." Nitske rolled his eyes.

It was obvious he was not buying any of my reasoning. But I continued. "In any case, that was then. This is now. Mr. Harper is deceased and the pent-up demand for any new post-war car is coming to an end. Many marketing analysts believe the time will soon be here when there will be a large market for a small, well-made, economical car. We believe our latest Volkswagen is such a car."

"Are you suggesting Studebaker re-badge the VW and sell it in our dealerships?"

"No. We're suggesting it be sold as a Volkswagen in your dealerships. If such an arrangement could be agreed on, we would ask that your service personnel be trained by VW and that adequate parts be available at each dealership location."

"I'll be honest, Werner. At first blush, the whole scheme seems a bit unworkable. And your credibility doesn't help your case." Nitske rubbed his chin. "I suppose there's nothing to be lost by taking another look at the car. I'll see if Ed Reynolds can get on it right away. How long do you plan to be in town?"

"As long as it takes."

"All right. I'll get Ed on the phone. Do you mind waiting in the outer office while I call him?" I excused myself and closed the door behind me. The pretty secretary looked up and smiled.

"Miss Petty, I would like to apologize for playing a game on you a few minutes ago. I have no twin. I am, or was, Van Hoffmann. As I just explained to Mr. Nitske, my taking on a false identity was necessary to get a job here. By the way, is Mike Levy still the union boss at Studebaker?"

"He sure is. He was out for several months after that car accident a couple of years ago."

"Is he alright now? I asked.

"Yes, he's getting better every day! How long will you be in town, Mr. Werner?"

"Assuming Ed Reynolds can test the Volkswagen I brought, I estimate a week."

"And where are you staying, in case we need to contact you?"

"The LaSalle," I answered. At that moment, Mr. Nitske appeared at the door.

"Well, Werner, you're in luck. If you'll take the VW out to the Proving Ground this afternoon, Ed Reynolds can get started on the testing in the morning."

"Excellent," I said. "I look forward to seeing my old friend, Ed again."

"As soon as I get Reynolds' report, we'll talk again." I left the office aware that I was on my own for the next few days. It would have been common courtesy and normal protocol for Nitske to invite me to dinner but he extended no such invitation. I wasn't surprised.

The early autumn weather in South Bend was delightful. A clear, blue, sky was a perfect setting for the drive to the Proving Ground. I rolled the windows down and let the cool Indiana breeze blow through. The rush of the wind blended with the hum of the VW engine making a soothing sound. The modest houses and small farms along Western Avenue had changed little since I left. Up ahead, the old familiar concrete posts topped with the Studebaker wheel still guarded the entrance to the Proving Ground. Seeing my VW swing into the entrance, the cigarette-smoking guard stepped out of his hut, clipboard in hand.

I handed him my card and said, "Hello Frank, how's it going?" He looked at me and then at my card.

"Mr. Reynolds is expecting you, uh, Mr. Werner." He waved me through. As I drove away, I looked in my rear-view-mirror and saw Frank standing in the middle of the drive scratching his head.

I could see through his office window that Ed Reynolds was deeply involved in some paperwork. I knocked on his door. He looked up and smiled when he saw my face. He hurried to greet me and gave me a firm handshake.

"Van, Hans, whatever the hell your name is, welcome! Mr. Nitske explained it all to me on the phone, but I'm still in shock to see you again."

"You're a good man, Ed. If everyone at Studebaker was like you, this company would last another hundred years."

"Thanks, Van. I'm sorry, Hans. Do you have the VW outside?"

"Yes, I do. It's gassed up and ready to go. By the way, what ever happened to Freda after I brought her back to South Bend?"

"Freda, Freda? Oh, I remember that's what you called the small-car prototype? That's the most bizarre story ever. The car refused to be driven or hauled. The papers had a field day with the story. They called it 'the car that wouldn't die.' When they finally hauled the car out here, we were instructed to take a torch and cut it completely into two separate pieces."

"Where are the two halves?"

"Out in that clump of trees in the middle of the test track."

"Any chance I could take a look while it's still light?"

"You're not planning to steal it again are you?" he said with a chuckle.

"No, I promise I'll be good if you'll just let me just take a look at Freda for old times sake."

"I don't know, Hans. I know you and Jack put your heart and soul into that prototype." Ed hesitated then said, "But you know the rules about non-employees unsupervised on the property. I guess I could go with you but I've got a lot to do back here, so I guess I could bend the rules this one time."

"Thanks Ed. You mentioned Jack. How is Jack anyway?" I asked. "I heard they sent him back to maintenance."

"That's right. I guess he's still there. I haven't talked to him lately. By the way, how are you getting around while I'm testing the VW?"

"Oh, I don't know. I guess I could rent a car if I can somehow get back downtown or to the airport."

"That won't be necessary. I have a new '51 Commander Coupe we just finished testing. It has the new overhead valve V8 engine. You can borrow that for a few days." Ed pointed to the vehicle parked in the corner of the shop. "You haven't started drinking have you?"

"Ed, you know me better than that." I looked at the car's sleek body and felt honored to be able to drive it. "I'll be careful with the Stude," I said. "I love that 'bullet-nose' design. It's a great looking car. Who designed it, anyway?"

"A talented young fellow named Bob Bourke. He works for Raymond Loewy."

"It really is futuristic looking," I said, "like an airplane. I know I'll enjoy driving it. But first I'm going to walk out and take a look at Freda." I was pleased but a little surprised that Ed didn't object to me looking at the car. I left the shop before he could change his mind. The test track was quiet. Only the chirping of a sassy blue jay broke the silence. I wondered if I was making a mistake seeing Freda in her sad two-piece condition. I was almost certain it would be depressing but my curiosity was strong. As I approach the clump of trees where all the old obsolete prototypes were strewn, Freda's rear section caught my eye. As Ed had warned me, the car was completely severed at the 'B' post. It was evident that top management never wanted to see that car again. After some searching, I found Freda's front section on the far side of the other wrecks. I had an odd feeling as I approached, like I was being watched. I looked around. There was no one in sight. "Hello, Freda," I called out. Her horn honked. I almost fainted. Obviously, the battery and wires to the horn were still intact. I opened the hood. The little zinc-air battery was still there. Strangely, the rest of the car was filthy, but the battery looked almost new. I figured the organic component was still evolving. I knew I had to have that battery. Using a piece of flat metal

I found laying nearby, I was able to pry the terminals loose and remove the battery. Now what? I hated to steal it, but I knew Ed wouldn't let me take it? I hid it behind my back until I was near the shop and then hid it in some bushes. Being only a little larger than an army canteen, it was easy to carry and hide. I knew that if I got caught with the battery, I might be arrested and the whole project would be cancelled. But my decision was easy; I had to have that battery. Luckily, Ed wasn't looking out the window and didn't see me hide Freda's heart. I walked inside.

"Well, Ed, you were right," I said. "That prototype will never be a complete automobile again. It was such a good car. Do you remember conducting the tests just after Jack and I finished building her?"

"Sure do! The results were fantastic, completely unexpected."

"Yet top management killed the project," I said.

"Yeah, I was just as disappointed as you," Ed added.

"The VW you'll be testing tomorrow is almost as good. Hopefully, Studebaker will be more open-minded this time." Ed handed me the keys to the '51 Regal Coupe. I thanked him and walked outside to where the car was parked. If I drove to where I hid Freda's battery, it would be obvious something was going on if Ed happened to be watching. I had an idea. I got out and walked back inside.

"Ed, I know this sounds a little strange, but since the Stude has the new V-8 engine, what's the chances of me taking her for a spin around the test track?"

"Hans, you rascal. You know non-employees are not allowed on the track. It's a liability issue."

"Oh, come on Ed. The track is empty and I'll be careful."

"I'm taking a chance by even letting you have this car to drive in the first place."

"You know how much I appreciate that. Please Ed, for old times sake."

"Old times sake won't save my job if something happens. I'll let you do it, but if there's trouble, you stole the car."

"Fair enough," I said. I left the shop in a run. Driving the big oval was a lot of fun. It reminded me of the day I tested Freda. The new 232 V-8 was fast and responsive, just like Freda was. After making a couple of laps, I pulled the car next to where I hid the battery. I raised the hood and pretended to be checking out the engine. After putting Freda's battery behind the seat, I closed the hood and drove to the gate. The guard waved me through and I headed east toward the city.

The sun was still high in the sky and the temperature was delightfully pleasant as I buzzed along Western Avenue. What were my choices for the rest of the day, hell, the rest of the week? I could call Susie Goodall to see if she would like to see me. I really would have rather talked to Mary. But the last time I saw her, she said she was getting married. Instead, of calling anyone, I stopped by a Western Auto Store and bought a small volt-ohm meter and a roll of #10 insulated copper wire. I had to know why Freda's battery stayed charged so long and how much power it still had? Zinc-air batteries were known to be very moisture sensitive and Freda had been outside in all kinds of weather for a year. It didn't make sense that the battery would have any power left after that length of time. Back at the hotel, I took the battery to my room and tested it using the meter and wire leads. The results amazed me. The voltage was still exactly six, but the amperage was off the scale. Was the meter wrong? One way to find out would be to boost the voltage with a transformer and see how much the amperage fell. I jumped into the Stude and drove back to the Western Auto store and bought an automotive coil and a coil to distributor wire. When the clerk asked me what make and model car the coil was for, I said it didn't matter. I got a strange look. Back in my room, I ran a wire from one terminal of the battery to the low-voltage side of the coil. Before I could connect the high voltage wire to the meter, a giant blue arc jumped from the stripped end of the wire and made a loud crackling noise as it traveled to a water pipe across the room. Soon, the pipe started to glow. Blue smoke filled the air. I quickly pulled the lead from the battery terminal. I didn't want to burn the hotel down. I had never seen this kind of power in such a small package. I sat in wide-eye amazement at what this device had become. I was now sure that the organic component had continued to evolve making the power potential tremendous. The battery had also developed the ability to selectively change electrical circuits and switch to ground as the need arose. This would explain why the wrecker driver got severely shocked when he grabbed Freda's door handle. But what about the horn blowing and even starting the engine and engaging gears as Freda had done down in Huntsville? With the power potential exhibited in that hotel room, jumping circuits to make various connections seemed possible. Therefore, the battery could make the car do almost anything that a human could. Would the battery's intelligence continue to evolve? If it did.....Oh, my, God, I thought. I may have created a monster.

While I sat considering the possibilities of the tremendous power of the little battery, my phone rang.

CHAPTER 34

"Is this Van Hoffmann?" the male voice asked.

"At one time it was. Who is this?"

"Never mind who this is. Just listen, Hoffmann. If you value your life, I suggest you get your Hitler car and your kraut ass out of South Bend before the sun comes up in the morning. Otherwise, you're history." I recognized the voice and somehow felt a surge of bravery.

"Well, well," I said. "If it isn't my old friend, Mike Levy. I heard you and Mr. Harper had a little car accident a couple of years ago."

"Yes, you son of a bitch. I was laid up for months. You'll pay dearly for that accident if you ain't gone by tomorrow morning."

"Tell me something, Mike. Why do you hate me so much?"

"You know Hoffmann, I don't have to answer your stupid-ass questions and you know something else, you're pushing me over the line. I may come over and snuff your ass tonight." My courage disappeared. I hesitated. Fear ate at my soul like a vulture.

I swallowed hard, trying to ignore my fear and then shouted, "Come ahead, you faggot. I'll meet you anywhere you choose."

"You're calling me a faggot? I can get more pussy in one week than you can in a lifetime, you jerk off." I continued.

"If you're not a queer, how come you let old man Harper give you a blow-job the night of the wreck?"

Levy screamed. "That's it! I'm on my way to beat your ass to a pulp right now!"

I heard a loud click. I knew Mike was mad, maybe out of control. His temper was his biggest weakness. But I also knew he wasn't stupid. He probably realized there must be a reason I was a lot braver than the last time I confronted him. He would know better than to come to my hotel room and possibly walk into a trap. But outside on the street, I might be in grave danger. I realized I probably had pushed Big Mike too far. I started to get very worried. I thought about the possibilities. I realized I was in big trouble. But that guy has gotten away with the murder of two good men and his union was killing a great old company. Somehow, he needed to be stopped.

I didn't leave the hotel that night. After a bowl of soup in the greasy little coffee shop, I asked the desk clerk if the maintenance man was still on duty. I was told he was never off-duty. I found him in a basement room where he lived. His door was open. It was a dark and dingy hole in the wall and smelled of stale tobacco with a hint of Lysol. A grubby-looking man wearing a tattered bathrobe sat in a rocking chair drinking a beer. He smoked a stubby cigar and was reading a paperback novel. The only light in the room was a single bulb on a cord that hung over his chair.

"Hello, my friend," I said. "I'm staying here in your hotel all week and I wonder if you could help me with something."

"What's wrong, bud, your toilet stopped up?"

"No, nothing like that. Do you by any chance have an off-on switch like you'd use on the main power panel for the hotel. You know, heavy duty to take a lot of amperage." He laughed and shook his balding head.

"I've been working here for twenty eight years and I've never heard that request before."

"I know it sounds strange," I said, "but I'm working on a little project in my room and if you have such a switch, I'd like to borrow it for a few days." He slowly rose from his rocker and went to the corner of his cave-like room where a large rusty toolbox sat. He opened it and poked around in inside for a few moments. He grumbled something I didn't understand and then tilted the box on its side emptying its contents on the concrete floor. An assortment of miscellaneous objects covering everything mechanical that one could imagine. Using his foot, he scrambled through the jumble of tools and parts and came up with a red-colored Square D palm switch, much like the safety switch used on a punch press.

"Don't know where the hell I got this switch. It's spring loaded and only works when it's held down."

"That's ideal! May I borrow it for a few days?"

"Hell, you can have it. My main control panel don't use Square Ds."

"Thanks, mister," I said. "And that half roll of friction tape there, could I have some of that?" He picked up the roll and tossed it to me.

"Take it. Now if there ain't nothin' else, I got to get back to my story. Sam Spade's about to get his ass throwed in the East River." I left without another word and went back to my lonely room to think.

It occurred to me that only three people even knew I was in town; Bob Nitske, his secretary, Miss Petty and Ed Reynolds. One of those three must have alerted Big Mike as to my whereabouts. I knew Ed Reynolds wouldn't have done it. First, I didn't tell him where I was staying and besides, he's a great guy, definitely not a union sympathizer. I couldn't imagine Bob Nitske was the culprit. He was Vice president of Engineering. It didn't make sense that he would be a friend of Levy's. That left Nitske's pretty secretary, Miss Petty. She had the ideal job to feed information to the union and she looked a lot like the type Levy would go for. She had blond hair; big tits and wore too much makeup. Now that I thought about it, she even dressed flashy, just Big Mike's kind of woman. But how did she get a job as Nitske's secretary, I wondered? I decided to pay her an unannounced visit the next morning.

Before I went to bed, I made a holder for my zinc-air battery and threaded my belt through it so I could carry the battery behind my back like an army canteen. I securely connected the stripped end of a two-foot length of wire to the battery's positive terminal. I connected the other end to one terminal of my new spring loaded palm switch mounted on the front of my belt. Then with a short lead, I connected to the other terminal of the switch to the low-voltage side of the coil. From the high-voltage side, I ran an insulated wire over my shoulder and down my right arm and into my right hand. I stripped only a quarter inch of the insulation off and then wrapped multiple layers of friction tape around the wire about an inch from the end. Not wanting to electrocute myself, I double-checked my circuit. Everything looked good so I pointed the bare end toward the water pipe and pressed the palm switch on my belt. The blue and purple arc that shot to the pipe was even stronger than before and the pipe started to glow in two seconds. I released the switch, let out a sigh of relief, undressed and went to bed.

CHAPTER 35

The next morning, after checking up and down the street, I drove to the engineering office and walked in unannounced. Miss Petty glanced up and gave me a smile.

"Good morning Mr., uh, Hoff, uh, Werner. What can we do for you?"

"Good morning, Miss Petty. Is Mr. Nitske in?" I asked.

"No, he's in a staff meeting. Could I help you with something?"

"I guess not. Well, maybe. Could I use your phone for a local call?"

"Sure. Just push that right-hand button on the base to get an outside line." She shoved the phone next to a chair beside her desk. When I sat down, her strong perfume made me cough.

"Yes, operator, give me Branson 4730." Susie answered on the first ring. "Well hello, Susie. Do you know who this is?" She immediately recognized my voice, but didn't seem very friendly. "How are you and Tess?" She said okay and then asked what I was doing these days and why I hadn't kept in touch as I had promised. "I can't go into that right now, Susie. I'm in South Bend on business and have a free night tonight. If you could get a babysetter for Tess, I'd like to take you out to dinner and maybe a picture show. I could explain everything to you then. How 'bout it? I really would like to see you." She reluctantly accepted my invitation and I said I could pick her up at 6:30. I slid the phone back across the desk. "Thank you Miss Petty. Tell Mr. Nitzke I'm sorry I missed him." She smiled and waved as I left the office. I walked down the hall and then stepped into a doorway and waited. Soon, I heard Nitske's outer door open. I suspected Miss Petty was checking to see if I was gone. After she closed the door, I walked back quietly and put my ear against it. I could hear Miss Petty on the phone but couldn't understand what she was saying.

After leaving the Engineering Office, I drove to the Studebaker Maintenance Building. Unlike the main factory, I knew I could get in without a pass. I spotted Jack Yearwood in the corner of the large open shop. His welding rod threw a fan of sparks a couple of meters from his work. I stood quietly until he paused and with a flip pivoted his helmet from his face to the top of his head.

"Well, I see you can still run a smooth straight bead, Old Man." Jack swung around when he heard my voice.

"I'll be damned! Van Hoffmann. I never thought I'd see your ugly mug again. What brings you back to South Bend?"

"I work for Volkswagen in Germany now. I'm here on business. Got a minute to talk?"

"Yeah, sure. Since I joined the union, I come and go pretty much as I damn well please."

"Did I hear you right? Jack Yearwood is a union member? Did they threaten to castrate you or something if you didn't join?"

"No, not quite. But I'm gettin' older, Van, and I just got tired of fightin' it. Things are much better for me now. I have friends and I don't feel isolated. Say, it's a pretty day, let's go outside to talk." I instinctively knew he didn't want to be seen talking to me. My battles with Big Mike were well known by most union members. Once outside we sat on an old well-worn car seat. Jack lit a cigarette and took a long pull.

"Still sucking on those coffin nails, huh?"

"Yeah. 'Fraid so. My wife says I smell like an ashtray. I guess it does sorta cut into my love life. But what tha hell, like I said, I ain't as young as I use to be so, it ain't no big deal anymore."

"Say Jack, have you heard any rumors about who might have killed Benny Goodall or Roy Branson?"

"Not really. Most union guys think the company is better off without them."

"Really? Why?"

"Both those guys were known to be anti-union." I marveled at Jack's candor.

"So, they deserved to die?" I asked.

"Whoa, Van. I didn't say that. All I'm saying is you won't find too many of my union brothers have any interest in tracking down the killer or killers."

"Jack, what changed your mind about the union?"

"Wise up, kid. There are two sides of every issue. I was a sucker for too many years." I was shocked at how Jack had changed.

"You're not the same guy I use to know, Jack. And for your information, I'm not the same man either. My real name is Hans Werner. Van Hoffmann's social security card got me a job here at Studebaker and kept me from being deported back to my native Germany." His mouth dropped open as the news soaked in. Without another word, I turned and walked back to my car. "To hell with Jack Yearwood," I said under my breath. I hoped never to see him again.

After having some lunch, I drove back to Mr. Norman's office. His secretary said she expected him momentarily. I took a seat and waited. I felt apprehensive about what could happen later on that day. I was sure Big Mike would not give up on his threat to "snuff" me, as he put it. This was one reason I wanted to talk to Mr. Norman. When he walked in he greeted me warmly and ushered me into his office.

"Well, Hans, I see Mike Levy hasn't caught up with you yet. I hope you've come to your senses and have forgotten about trying to somehow get him to confess to murder."

"I admit I've yet to come up with a plan."

Norman smiled and then said, "I told you last night, he has nothing to gain by admitting anything. You should just lay low until you leave town. That's my advice."

"Mr. Norman, you've always known what's best. I can't count the number of times you've gotten me out of trouble. But Big Mike has already threatened me, so unless I spend the rest of my trip in my hotel room, he'll probably be out to get me."

"Pick up a couple of good books, go to your room and lock the door. That way there's a chance you may survive for the rest of the week."

"That's good advice, but it's too late. I have a date tonight with Benny Goodall's widow and Big Mike probably knows about it by now. I called her on Bob Nitske's secretary's phone. I think Miss Petty in Bob Nitske's office is friends with Levy."

"Jesus, Hans, is there no end to it? That was really stupid. Why do you keep asking for trouble? Have you no judgment, boy?" Mr. Norman stood. I could tell he was angry. "Get your butt out of here or I'm sending you a big bill for my time."

"Thanks for listening, Mr. Norman." I left and went back to the hotel to get cleaned up for my date. After dressing, I put the zinc-air battery which I called Freda's heart, the automotive coil, palm switch and wire in a paper sack and headed for the Studebaker coupe. If anyone was watching me exit the hotel, I didn't see him. The weather continued to be mild enough to have the windows down. The evening breeze blowing through the car was so soothing that I almost forgot the great danger that might be waiting for me later that night. All I could think about was how much I missed Susie's fragrant body.

I pull into Susie's driveway as I had done many times before. Before I could knock, she opened the door. We just stood and looked at each other for a few moments. Finally, without touching me, she invited me inside. She looked the same except maybe a few pounds heavier. I liked the way she looked, more like German women, except her dress was a little tight. I leaned in to kiss her, but she turned away.

"Van, I'm not sure why you called me after all this time. I hope you don't expect to pick up where we left off two years ago."

"No, I don't. I know I should have stayed in touch, but my life has been a series of crisis. After I left South Bend, I moved to Huntsville where my college roommate lived. I worked there for a year before moving back to Germany. I now work for Volkswagen."

"What do you mean, moving back to Germany?"

"There's a lot about me that you don't know, Susie. I grew up in Germany, worked at the Volkswagen plant during the war. My real name is Hans Werner." Susie sat down quickly. I thought she might faint. "Maybe I should have told you the last night before I left South Bend, but since I was in the country illegally, I was afraid to. I hope you understand."

"Not really. I guess I read too much into our relationship. I thought we were more than just lovers. I guess I was wrong."

"I don't know what to say, Susie. Why did you agree to see me tonight?"

"Curious I guess."

"Well, I'm glad. How is Tess?"

"Oh, she's alright. Growing like a weed. Hey, Tess! Come in here," Susie shouted. The bedroom door opened and out bounded a girl I would not have recognized on the street. "You remember this man?" Susie asked.

"Sure, Mom. That's Uncle Van Hoffsomething."

"Well, Tess, you sure have grown since I saw you last," I said. She frowned and pulled a black pistol from behind her back.

"Why didn't you write to us?" she screamed as she raised the pistol toward my head. I couldn't believe what was happening. To my surprise, a blast of water wet my face.

Susie reacted. "Tess! Dammit! I told you if you shot anyone else, I was going to take that silly water pistol away from you. Now, give it to me." The defiant little girl put the gun behind her back.

"Oh, it's okay," I said as I wiped my face with my handkerchief.

"No, it's not okay!" Susie shouted. "Give me the gun Tess." I realized this family problem might ruin the whole evening.

"That's a very realistic looking toy pistol," I said. " Tell you what, Tess, I'll give you two dollars for it. What do you say?" Susie stepped in.

"You better take it, Tess. Otherwise, it's going in the garbage." The little girl seemed pleased.

"Here, it's yours," Tess said as she passed the pistol to me.

"Tess, why don't you go to your room so Van and I can talk." I gave Tess the two dollars I promised. Without a word she wheeled around and skipped her way out the door.

"I'm sorry about that whole scene, Van. Since her dad's been gone, she's gotten to be quite a handful. I couldn't get a setter tonight. She's thinks she's too old for a setter and as a result makes it miserable for anyone who stays with her when I'm gone. I guess we'll have to stay here this evening. I've got some beef-stew on the stove if you're hungry. Tess has already eaten."

"Oh, I'm not that hungry right now. Got anything to drink?"

* * * * * * * * * *

Except for the absence of any affection, the evening went smoothly. I did most of the talking. I confessed that my obsession with car design had put any relationship in my life in second place. I didn't hold anything back as I reviewed the past two years. I told her about my dear friend Wally Rosenblum and his tragic death. I also admitted that since losing Wally, I had no one in my life that I loved or loved me. It was like I was married to car design. In fact, I really wasn't involved in design in my present job. When I asked Susie about her life, she told me how lonely she was and that she realized she sometimes took it out on Tess. It was obvious to me that Tess needed a father figure. For a moment I wondered what a life with Susie and Tess might be like. But no, I had burned too many bridges. That life would be quite impossible now. I lived in Germany, was not an American citizen and Mike Levy was out to kill me, so a future with Susie was out of the question. Around eleven o'clock, I decided it was time to go.

As I stood to leave, I said, "I'll write to you, Susie."

"Don't bother," she replied. Those two words cut like a knife. Without another word, I walked outside. I put on my battery belt, ran the heavily insulated wire down my right arm and tucked the fully loaded water pistol in my belt. Before getting in the Studebaker, I looked up and down the streets and driveways nearby but didn't see anything suspicious. When I backed into the street, I noticed my brakes were a little spongy. Thinking there might be air in the lines, I figured I'd drop by the Proving Ground tomorrow and get someone to bleed them for me. At each cross street I had to pump the pedal a little more to slow down. At this point, I knew there was something more serious than air in the brake lines. I wondered if the car had been tampered with while in Susie's driveway. And then it happened. In my rear-view mirror I saw a car pulling closer. It had no headlights. I speeded up. So did the car that followed. With no brakes, I knew I was going much too fast, but felt I had no choice. If I could make it back to the hotel, I would probably be safe, but that was two miles away. As I topped a hill, the car following was almost on my rear bumper. I knew if I didn't slow down I might have a terrible wreck. After my brake pedal went completely to the floorboard. I pulled the emergency brake. It came all the way out and had no effect on my speed. I turned off the ignition and tried to shift into low gear. I was going too fast; the gears simply made a terrible grinding noise. I jammed the shifter into second. This time it worked, but slowed the car little. I glanced at the speedometer. Fifty! Oh, God! What could I do? I swerved from side to side, bumping the curb on each side of the street. I was nearing an intersection. I bumped hard over the right hand curb and plowed through some shrubs and a mailbox, finally coming to a stop. I tried to blow my horn to call for help, but the horn didn't work. In seconds, my car door was open and there stood Big Mike Levy.

"Get out of the car, asshole!" he shouted. I sat frozen. He grabbed me by the collar, pulled me out and drew back his fist to punch me. I quickly pulled the water pistol from my belt and pushed it into his gut.

"Let go of me or I'll blast you, Levy." He glanced down and released his hold.

"You don't have the guts to shoot me, you little sissy. Besides, in this town, you'd never get away with it."

I stepped back and said, "Oh yeah, well watch this." Levy's eyes widened. I squeezed the trigger several times and wet both his legs from his crouch to his shoes. In amazement, he looked down and started to laugh. He almost doubled up he was laughing so hard.

"Is that the best you got, you silly-ass kraut?" He stepped forward. His face then turned dead stern, his eyes filled with hate. "Now say your prayers, Werner. I'm going to take great pleasure in beating you to death with my two bare hands."

I stuck out my left hand and pointed my index finger at him and said, "Stay where you are or I'll shoot."

"With what? Your little water pistol?" I dropped the pistol. With my finger pointed toward his groin, I hit the palm switch on my belt just as he reached for me. A brilliant blue and purple arc jumped the two feet between us and hit him jumping between his left and right leg, then continuing to the ground. Smoke leaped from his pant legs. He screamed and fell over. I released the switch and watched him roll around in agony. The smell of burning flesh filled the air. I followed as he crawled back to the open door of his car. He struggled to climb in. Just as he did, I gave him another jolt. He screamed again, slammed the door and sped away. After he was out of sight, the smell lingered. I leaned against my car's front fender and vomited Susie's beef-stew. After picking up the water pistol, I started up the Stude and backed into the deserted street. I put the car in low gear and let the engine idle me back to the hotel at three miles an hour. For the couple of times I had to stop completely, I simply turned off the ignition.

I rose early the next morning, afraid to look outside. Was anyone waiting for me? How bad was the Studebaker damaged? I ate breakfast at the greasy little hotel coffee shop and then called Ed Reynolds.

"Ed, this is Hans Werner. I want to come out this morning and get one of your guys to check out the '51 Stude you loaned me. It has no brakes and as a result, I had a little fender-bender last night."

"Dammit, Hans. I told you to be careful....... Well, okay, bring it on in. We'll check it out."

"Thanks, Ed. You're a real pal."

"Yeah, yeah. This is what I get for loaning you a perfectly good car and getting a wreck in return."

"It's not that bad, Ed. What can I say after I say I'm sorry?"

"That's a good title for a song, Hans, but it won't fix the car." I hung up and thought to myself, Studebaker has some of the greatest guys in the world like Ed Reynolds and the late Benny Goodall and some of the sorriest characters like Big Mike Levy and the late Virgil Harper.

As I had to creep along, it took me over an hour to make the trip to the Proving Ground. In the process, I gathered numerous horn blasts and a variety of angry hand gestures. Ed put the car on his lift and immediately found the trouble. Lines to two of the wheel cylinders had been cut (probably with a bolt cutter) as well as the cable to the emergency brake clevis. Also, it appeared the wire to the horn relay had been clipped. The reason I had some brakes at first is it took several pumps to empty all the fluid out of the system.

"This car was sabotaged, Hans. Someone wanted you to have a wreck. Got any idea who?"

"Sure Ed, I know exactly who. Big Mike Levy."

"How do you know that?"

""Because when I finally got stopped, he jerked my car door open and started to beat me up."

"What happened then?"

"Well, I shot him with a water pistol and that's all I can tell you right now, except he left me alone and drove away." Ed frowned and shook his head and then a hint of a smile crossed his lips.

"Hans Werner, if I didn't know better, I would think you made this whole thing up. But it's too weird to be a lie. You gonna report all this to the police?"

"No, I guess not. I can't stay around for any legal action. Besides Levy is too smart not to have a good alibi all set up. I'm just going to write out a statement as to what happened and sign it before a witness. If anything else happens to me this week, maybe the statement can be used as evidence against Levy." Ed fixed the brakes and the horn and buffed out the scratches in the front fenders and sent me on my way.

As Mr. Norman had advised, I spent most of the next couple of days at the hotel. When I did go out, I strapped on my battery pack and was careful to watch for any car that `might be following. On Friday, Mr. Nitske called and said the testing of the VW was complete and I could pick up the car. He also said he had talked to the board and the board decided to pass on my proposal for Studebaker to sell Volkswagens. He said he would mail a more detailed letter as an official rejection of our offer. Although disappointed and sure their decision was a mistake, I was not surprised.

After returning the '51 Stude to the Proving Ground, I again apologized to Ed Reynolds for the damage.

"Don't worry, Hans," he said. "Wrecks at the Proving Ground on test cars are common. By the way, did you see this morning's paper? Big Mike Levy is in the hospital and has been since Wednesday night. The paper didn't give a cause, but mentioned he had severe burns on his legs. That must have been some lethal water pistol you shot him with."

"If you don't mind, Ed, let's just keep the water pistol story to ourselves. OK?" Ed rolled his eyes and didn't answer. I drove back to Chicago and returned the VW to Emporium Motors.

When I told Harvey Stone of my unsuccessful trip at Studebaker, he simply laughed and said, "What did you expect, Werner?"

I thought for a moment and then replied, "I guess I wasn't too surprised, but I still think that someday soon there will be a big market in America for the Volkswagen."

Stone shook his head and said, "Dream on, Werner, dream on."

CHAPTER 36

When I checked my suitcase at Chicago's Midway Airport, I doubt the agent that took it had any idea that one of the most powerful electrical power sources known to man was lurking inside that very ordinary-looking piece of Samsonite. After I got back home in Wolfsburg, I stored Freda's battery in Wally's room for safekeeping. I wondered if it was continuing to mutate and evolve. But I couldn't think about that. I had to prepare my explanation for my failure at Studebaker. I did not look forward to my meeting with Herr Nordhoff and the other top executives. I soon found out I was not alone in my inability to convince an American manufacturer to take on the Volkswagen automobile. The other VW representatives reported failures at Packard and Hudson as well. When asked for the reasons no U.S. companies were interested in selling our VW in their dealerships, the prevailing answer was it was too small and old-fashion looking for the American market. I believed those objections could be eliminated in time and suggested we start from scratch and develop freestanding Volkswagen dealerships in America to achieve maximum sales. That would be the only way the VW would be given top priority. I also suggested that conventional advertising would probably not be very effective in America. On the other hand, creative ads might generate a sort of cult-like desire for this unusual automobile. Herr Nordhoff said he would think about my ideas. Meanwhile, I was assigned clerical jobs in the Export Department. Not having design assignments was frustrating. On the plus side, I was making more money and that allowed me to save enough for three tombstones. But all was not well. The truth is, I dreaded going home each night. Everything in every room reminded me of Wally. The house was cold and lifeless without him. I missed him terribly. Except for Karl Heinz back in Huntsville, Wally had been my only friend. I had loved the old man like a father. Day after day, I continued to worry and wonder who killed him. It seemed there was as little progress in finding Wally's killer in Wolfsburg just as it was finding the killer of Benny Goodall and Roy Branson in South Bend. The murderers had all gone unpunished. I finally decided that if the Wolfsburg Police could not even come up with a single clue relating to Wally's murder, then it was up to me to try to track down his killer. But how? I took out a sheet of paper and started a list of possible motives and my reaction to each.

Robbery. Not likely since no drawers or cabinets were opened and it appeared nothing was stolen.

Revenge. Unless Wally had some hidden secret that he had kept from me, revenge seemed unlikely.

Anti-Semitism. Possible. Propaganda caused great hatred of Jews before and during the war, some older Germans might still hold a grudge.

Wanting to hurt me. Those who knew me knew how much I loved Wally and knew how much I would grieve at his death. But I had no enemies in Wolfsburg that I knew of.

I went to our front porch and sat in Wally rocking chair. I was hoping for inspiration. I looked for an open door but there was none. The voice of reason seemed to say finding Wally's killer was hopeless. But I felt I was the only hope of bringing Wally's murderer to justice. I starred at the paper before me. Improbable as they may seem, I knew I must consider all possibilities. Over and over, I read the list. Only two reasons for murdering Wally held any possibilities at all. "Anti-Semitism" and "Wanting to hurt me." Both motives grabbed my attention. Could it be one of these....... or maybe both? I searched my mind for anyone that could possibly have either of those motives. Only one person I knew fit either category. Otto Haniel. I knew he was a devoted follower of Hitler and hated Jews. He once told me that the Jewish bankers had foreclosed on his sister's house and put her family on the street without any recourse. I remembered him killing those two Polish workers, so I was sure he was capable of murder. And I knew he was upset with me for leaving the plant near the end of the war. This meant he had to personally deal with the SS without my help. But somehow there was a great inconsistency in considering Otto as the killer. He had been kind to me when I came to visit to the point of feeding me and letting me spend the night at his apartment. He even helped me get a job at Volkswagen. That didn't sound like someone who wanted to hurt me. Yet......this was my only suspect. Now what?

I called Otto's number. He picked up on the first ring. "Ja, this is Otto."
"Otto, this is Hans Werner. How are you?"

"Oh, I'm all right. How are you Hans?"

"Good. I hadn't seen you since the plant tour and I feel I owe you and your wife a meal at a nice restaurant. Are you free this Friday evening?"

"I think so. What do you have in mind?"

"How about the Wolfsburg Palace?"

"You sure you can afford it? That's an expensive place."

"Well, Otto, I've done pretty well at Volkswagen and gotten several raises besides, you were so nice to me when I first arrived in Wolfsburg, I feel I should do something nice for you and Frau. What do you say?"

"What can I say? I can't turn down a dinner at a place like the Palace."

"All right then, I'll pick you up in a taxi at 6:30 on Friday."

Otto seemed to be determined to get the most out of the invitation. He had drunk three steins of beer and two schnapps before the cheese course was served. In the far corner of the room a piano played excerpts from *Carmina Burana*. Otto stood and strolled to other tables hoping to get someone to join him in song. There were no takers this early in the evening. Frau sat quietly and nursed her first stein. Finally, Otto tramped back to the table singing loudly. Frau looked at him, frowned and put an index finger across her lips. Otto glared at her before drawing his right hand to his left shoulder as if he were planning to give her a slap. She drew back and raised her forearm across her face. Otto laughed and signaled for another stein. Knowing that Otto's tongue was now loosened, I attempted to guide the conversation to pre-war Germany and all the public works projects that Hitler had started.

"You know, my little friend," Otto said, "After Hitler came to power in 1933, the economic health of Germany quickly improved. Within two years, unemployment dropped to less than one million. Many citizens were put to work on such projects as the Autobahn and of course our great Wolfsburg factory. I enjoyed the best years of my life. I went from an out-of-work brick mason to a full-time job building the factory. Did you know I was on the crew that helped lay the cornerstone? It was a beautiful day in May of 1938. I was as close to Hitler as I am to you right now." Otto again stood, raised his glass and shouted, "Long live Volkswagen!" Several men at adjoining tables repeated Otto's toast and so did I. I pointed out to Otto that one dark-haired gentleman sitting alone had shaken his head and didn't join in the toast. Otto must have assumed he was Jewish.

"I thought we had purged all the stinking Jews from Wolfsburg," he said loudly.

"Well, you did your part," I added. Otto didn't take the bait.

"The bastards keep coming back," he said. "They're like cockroaches; when you think you've got them all, another one shows up." I was hoping Otto would say something even more incriminating before he got too drunk. When the huge check came, I wondered if this evening had been a good investment. I decided it was time to leave while Otto could still walk. In the taxi, Otto and Frau sat in the back seat of the VW and I in the front with the driver. I decided to push my luck.

As he sat with his head laid against Frau's shoulder, I leaned over the seat back and said, "Otto, what's the best way to kill a Jew?"

"Any way is a good way," he slurred. "Shoot 'em, choke 'um, gas 'um or my favorite, beat their face in with your bare hands." Then suddenly, he grabbed his mouth and shouted, "Stop the car, I've got to puke!" The driver complied. I jumped out and held the seat back while Otto leaned out the door opening. As he started to tumble, Frau grabbed him and pulled him back. Not all the vomit made it to the ground. It was disgusting. After letting Otto and Frau out, I asked the driver his name. I told him he might be asked to repeat what he had heard Otto say, in particular how he would kill Jews. The driver who had a cleanup job ahead readily gave me his name and address. He added that Otto would never be allowed in his taxi again. I had also gotten the name of our waiter at the Wolfsburg Palace who had heard Otto's comments about getting rid of Jews. The next day, I visited the police department.

The chief detective took down the information that I gave him including the names of the waiter at the Wolfsburg Palace and the taxi driver. I freely admitted that I had encouraged Otto to drink too much in hopes he would say something incriminating. I agreed that what he said was not specific to Waldo Rosenblum's murder, but pointed out that Otto's comments certainly suggested a hatred of Jews and a desire rid Germany of them. I also mentioned that Otto gets off from work at 3 pm every day giving him two hours before I get home. The detective asked if Otto even knew Wally. I said that they met during a family day at Volkswagen. The detective said he would need much more evidence before he could commence a serious investigation but he would put the information I submitted on file. Believing that the police were unlikely to uncover any incriminating evidence, I pondered my next move.

I had great confidence in Herr Nordhoff's ability to get things done, I considered going to him with my suspicions about Otto. I debated bothering him but finally decided to give it a try. On Monday morning I dropped by to make an appointment with Herr Nordhoff to discuss the murder of my landlord and friend, Waldo Rosenblum. Nordhoff was a busy man. It was two days before I got in to see him. His secretary escorted me into his office at the appointed time.

"Good morning, Herr Werner. What can I do for you?" Nordhoff said.

"Good morning, sir. First, I want to thank you for your help in getting me cleared of suspicion in the murder of my friend and landlord Waldo Rosenblum. I now have new information on the case. I've already been to the police and I wouldn't bother you with this matter except that I believe the murderer to be a long time Volkswagen employee." Nordhoff frowned and looked over his glasses.

"Be aware Werner, if the name you give me proves to be wrong, it will reflect on you for possibly damaging an innocent man's reputation." I swallowed hard before I answered.

"Yes, sir. I accept that."

"Alright, what's his name and why do you think he is the killer?"

"His name is Otto Haniel. He is a foreman in our punch press department. I worked under him during the war and I personally witnessed him murder two workers suspected of sabotage. Later, he was quite upset when I left Wolfsburg before the war was over leaving him with no technical assistance. Also, by leaving, I was disobeying Hitler's orders to destroy the plant. At dinner this past Friday evening, he expressed his hatred for Jews and described the best ways to kill them. I have no proof that he is my friend's murderer, but I feel relatively sure that he is. He had two motives; his extreme anti-Semitism and revenge for what he considered to be my traitorous behavior back in May of 1945."

Herr Nordhoff looked puzzled. "Werner, you've presented me with quite a problem. If it turns out you've got the wrong man, we've wasted our time and money and possibly incurred a nasty liability. On the other hand, if we do nothing, we may have a murderer on our payroll who could strike again. We do not discriminate in our hiring of people with Jewish ancestry so we have Jews here at Volkswagen who might be in danger. Finally, do not under any circumstances mention that you have talked to me about this man."

"Very good, sir."

Chapter 37

C ar design wasn't a part of my life during this period. At the
plant, my work was mostly clerical, evaluating the potential
of various export markets. Although not particularly challenging, the
job paid well and I learned that there was a big world out there just
waiting for the Volkswagen. Even though production increased almost
every month, it seemed almost all the developing countries wanted
the car faster than we could produce it. But sales in the U.S. were still
almost non-existent. I had made my recommendations on what to do
about America, but there had been no action. I was told the company
would need to greatly increase its production capacity before making
any serious effort in the U.S.

To fill my spare time, I worked on evaluating and, hopefully,
perfecting the zinc-air battery which I called "Freda's heart." Each time I
tested the power capacity of the battery, it seemed to be getting stronger.
But I had no way of knowing what level of intelligence dwelt within that
little bundle of energy. Without being connected to some system such as
an automobile's wiring harness, I was left to wonder what the battery was
capable of. As I sat in Wally's rocking chair in front of a roaring fire, a
thought came to me. I needed a car like Freda. I wondered if Freda's heart
might be strong enough to power a small car using a direct current motor.
There was no better vehicle to use as a test stand than what was now
affectionately called the Volkswagen "beetle." Since almost everyone
living in Wolfsburg worked for VW and could get an employee discount,
there was no need for a new car dealership. I thought of purchasing a
new VW from the factory but I still didn't have enough money saved for
even a good used one. I wondered if a slightly wrecked VW might fill my
needs. When a car finally reaches the end of its useful life, it usually heads
for a junkyard and that is where I headed.

It was an especially cold and windy December day when I boarded
the bus for downtown. I exited in front of the Wolfsburg Wrecking Yard.
The wrecked cars were fenced in and well hidden.

After running to the tiny office to get out of the blowing sleet, I took off my cap, brushed my wet coat and said, "Do you have any VWs that are not badly wrecked?"

A young man in greasy coveralls answered. "Didn't you read the sign above the door? This is a wrecking yard. All our cars are wrecks."

"Ja, I know," I said. "But I'm looking for a VW that doesn't even have an engine. Just a reasonably good body and not too much rust."

"Well, there are probably twenty or more old VWs out there that fit that description, but I'm not leaving this warm office to help you find your perfect car. Feel free to look around and if you see something you like, get the number off the windshield and I'll give you a price."

"Danker schon." The sleet stung my face and the cold air cut through my jacket as I walked between the cars. But I was in no hurry. I wanted to make sure I didn't miss the perfect car for my project. The random array of wrecked VWs appeared to be the gathering of giant multi-colored dung beetles. With open bonnets and the way they were jammed together, it looked as if some pairs might be preparing to mate. Many had been stripped of fenders. Others were missing the engine. Finally, I spotted what might end up being the next Freda. She was a faded yellow color, (obviously painted with a brush) had no fenders, bumpers or engine yet all the glass, interior and basic body looked good. Its number was 123. I ran back to the office.

"Number 123. Let me see," the man in greasy coveralls said. "My sheet here says the engine was scrapped but the body is good. I'll take 200 D- marks for it."

"Are you aware, sir, it has no fenders or bumpers? 200 seems too high. I'll give you 100 marks for it."

"150."

"I'll go to 110. Did I mention it had no fenders? You can look for yourself."

"I'm not going out there in this weather. I'll take you word for it. It's yours for 120 D-marks."

"I'll give you 120 if you'll drop it off at my house sometime in the next fortnight."

"If you live in Wolfsburg, you've bought yourself a VW."

I built a wooden frame against the back of my house over which I nailed a large sheet of tenting that I had picked up a local war surplus store. I pushed the VW within this enclosure. After buying two new 6-volt headlights, I swung them overhead and connected them to the battery I had brought from America. The lights burned strong and were more than adequate for night work. But it was simply too cold in that tent to work. As 1952 made its debut, I tried to figure how to heat the tent without using expensive coal-generated heat from the house. I could wait for spring, but I was much too excited to delay the project. I purchased a small battery charger (which is nothing more than a transformer and rectifier). The transformer steps the house voltage to six volts and the rectifier converts it from alternating to direct current. I figured if I connected Freda's heart to the battery side and ran the current backwards, I might have enough power to heat a length of heating coil. I strung about five meters of coiled nickel-cadmium wire between the wooden frameworks of the tent's roof. After connecting to the battery, the wire glowed red and put out enough radiant heat to keep me reasonably comfortable on the coldest night. Again, I was amazed at the seemingly endless power of Freda's heart.

Fortunately, all systems in the VW were in working order except the engine, which, of course, was missing. All I needed at that point was a giant DC motor and a large rheostat to control the voltage to the motor. Back to the war surplus store, I found a starter motor from a German King Tiger tank. After getting a local welding shop to make a frame to mount the motor, I connected it to the transmission. With a huge rheostat mounted on the instrument panel and a heavy high voltage insulated wire connected to Freda's heart, I was ready for my first test of the drive train. After jacking the car's rear tires off the ground, I advanced the rheostat from zero. The rear wheels spun slowly at first. What I didn't expect was their extreme speed as I advanced the rheostat. I was eager to test the new Freda on the road. But first I had to register the vehicle, get license plates, mount headlights and tail lights on the body and make sure everything was working properly.

The road test went well, although a few minor adjustments were necessary. This was to be expected. The motor gave off a strange whine like a large electric generator. Although the battery propelled the car at a respectable rate, it failed to demonstrate any of the human-like qualities of the first Freda. The horn did not blow when I said, "hello." It made no moves of its own accord. To me, this was good news. That meant I had developed a revolutionary power source with no unpleasant side effects. With no fenders, no gas tank, no exhaust and a lighter motor, my VW was very responsive. I soon started driving her to the plant, even though it was a short distance. Many people stared and pointed as I drove by. I was known as the man with the "naked bug." Weeks passed as I continued to test the prototype. During this time, I was deciding whether or not to show my amazing vehicle to my old boss, Fritz Voss, VW's Vice president of Engineering. My employment contract clearly stated that any automotive related invention that I made while employed by Volkswagen was the property of the company. But I couldn't just sit on the development. I figured the invention was useless unless it was utilized in a production vehicle.

Obtaining a German patent might be difficult since some of the technology was quite old. As early as 1937, my microbiology professor had suggested that fast mutating microbes might have practical applications. I adapted his idea to zinc-air batteries. The addition of a solution of potassium hydroxide to the battery was a necessary component for generating energy, but that had been well known in the field for several years. But the tremendous power capacity that my unit possessed and its ability to solve problems were due to the human-like organic component, which was my secret. If patented, Volkswagen would claim the patent. Did I want to give the idea away? I took my time deciding.

The new Freda became my only passion. Every afternoon I went out to my work tent to make small improvements and to measure the battery's current. It appeared that the new Freda's battery, like the one in South Bend, had somehow developed the ability to extract electrical energy from the air. Early zinc-air batteries had to be replaced over time and were sensitive to moisture. This latest version seemed to be getting stronger with the passage of time and moisture had no effect. Incredible! I knew there must be some scientific reason for this energy-creating device, but I couldn't explain what it was except that it was obvious the battery had problem solving intelligence.

With no one to talk to, I got in the habit of talking to Freda. She never answered or made any indication that she understood my German language. Maybe if I spoke English, I could get some sort of reaction.

"Hello Freda, " I said in English. Her horn honked. Apparently, the memory from the first Freda was still intact. It appeared the battery was still evolving, still getting smarter. It had adapted to the VW wiring harness and seemed ready for more complicated tasks. I hoped the undesirable qualities like jealousy and revenge would not evolve. I tried to think of ways that the new Freda could express her intelligence in a positive way. Perhaps a multiple note horn might please her. I remembered when I was back in Huntsville; some of the good ole southern boys had car horns that played the first line of the song *Dixie*. I wrote to Karl asking where one might obtain such a horn. In less than a fortnight, a package arrived from the J.C. Whitney Company of Chicago, Illinois containing a horn that played the first line of *Dixie*. My old college friend had come through. I installed the horn and hit the horn button. The notes of the old southern anthem whose first line is *Well I wish I wa-as in the land of cot-ton* came through loud and clear. From that day on, those twelve notes greeted me every day when I said "Hello Freda." The J.C. Whitney horn consisted of five separate horns with a sequencing device built into the circuit. I wondered if simply listening to a song containing the same five notes as the song Dixie could reprogram that device. I determined those note were C, D, E, F and G. In the key of C, I sang the first line of the song *As Time Goes By*: *"You must remember this, a kiss is still a kiss."*

I then said, "Freda, you must remember this." Immediately, she played the first line of the song. My heart pounded with excitement. My incredible invention had to be shared with the world. But how?

One would think that the potential of the new Freda would make me the happiest person in the world. I could be rich if I left Volkswagen and sold the idea to some other company. But if Volkswagen pursued the matter, they might be able to prove that the development was done during my time as a VW employee, which to an extent was true. If Volkswagen incorporated a similar battery in the beetle, they could quickly dominate the world automobile market. Naturally, I would be a hero. But who could foresee how far the battery would evolve. It might develop a personality and start doing bad things like the first Freda did. I was sick with worry not knowing what to do. After several sleepless nights, I decided that the simplest, most straightforward thing would be to give the idea to Volkswagen. They would then be responsible for any unseen or unpleasant things that might occur. But I admit, I was still worried about what might happen.

My appointment to show the new Freda to Herr Fritz Voss was 28 February 1952. I drove the modified VW to the Engineering Development Garage as directed. Voss looked suspiciously at the strange looking, fenderless faded yellow car.

"I must tell you, this vehicle is not very pretty," he said. "What have you here that's so special, Werner?"

"First, this vehicle which I call Freda is totally powered by an electric motor. The motor is a starter from a World War II Tiger tank." I lifted the bonnet over the engine compartment. "As you can see, the zinc-air battery that powers the car is very small. This battery is already over three years old and has never been recharged or replaced. And here's another amazing feature; powered by that big starter motor, the car easily outperforms our own 1131cc petrol-powered VW engine and appears to be getting more powerful with age. I'm aware this all sounds like a fairy tale so I am prepared to turn the vehicle over to you for testing." Voss shook his head in disbelief.

"Werner, if this is some sort of joke, you are in trouble for wasting our time. But if what your claim is true, the face of the automotive industry will be forever changed."

"You won't be disappointed, Herr Voss. One other thing I failed to mention. Maybe it has no practical value, but the car can recognize songs and play them back on command."

"I don't understand," Voss said.

"Alright, watch this," I said. *"You must remember this, a kiss is still a kiss."* Voss' eyes widened in disbelief as Freda, using her five-note horn, played the first two lines of *As Time Goes By*.

Voss smiled and asked, "Does she know any other songs?"

"Freda can remember any song as long as the melody contains only the notes C, D, E, F and G."

Herr Voss shook his head and said, "I feel like I just landed on another planet."

Voss asked me to sign a release form. I said I would think about it but knew I should delay and keep my options open. Even though I was leaning in that direction, I was still not certain I wanted to turn over complete control of the project to Volkswagen. I continued to worry about what could happen if the intelligence in Freda's heart took a wrong turn. But I saw no harm in leaving the car with Herr Voss and his staff to test. I was given a company VW to drive back and forth to work while Freda was under evaluation.

In just a few days, enough testing had been completed to verify my claims as to the car's performance. I was asked for details on the construction of the battery. I only revealed the zinc-air and potassium hydroxide components and their relative proportions. I kept the addition of the organic microbes a secret knowing the performance couldn't be duplicated without it. There were two reasons for my reluctance to reveal the total formula. First, I felt it was good job security and second, until further testing was conducted, I was afraid what might happen if the microbe mutations were to continue in vehicles owned by thousands maybe millions of individuals throughout the world. The results could be catastrophic.

Even though members of the testing team were asked not to talk about the results of their tests, the rumor mill was soon in full buzz throughout the whole VW organization. People would come up to me in the cafeteria and say things like, "I hear your car from Mars is powered by little green men." or "Are you really Einstein's son?" I even heard someone say, "I hear the battery in your car is smarter than most of our workers." I would just smile and not comment when someone said something like that. In a fairly short time, I had become quite a celebrity within the organization. It was not a role I was comfortable with.

While I was again driving Freda back and forth to work, engineers were trying to duplicate the power of the zinc-air battery. Outside consultants in battery technology were called in to learn how my original battery had so much power and intelligence and their version of the zinc-air battery did not. I was urged to reveal the secret but I continued to refuse. I was rapidly losing popularity in top management circles.

I walked into the conference room unaware that most of the company's top executives would be there. Within those mahogany-paneled walls an impressive collection of industrial royalty was already seated and waiting for my arrival. I suspected another meeting had already taken place.

Herr Nordhoff spoke first. "Please have a seat, Werner. We have gathered here today to sort out some uncertainties that seem to have bogged the electric car program down. It is no secret that your battery-powered prototype tested far superior to anything we have seen in our previous research. Yet we have not been able to duplicate those results on our own. We are now certain that you haven't told us everything we need to know and would like for you to explain the reason for your reluctance to do so."

I was shocked at the president's straightforward question and was admittedly unprepared to answer. I struggled to come up with an acceptable impromptu answer. "Well, sir, I will admit I haven't divulged every detail of my development. I'm reluctant to do so since there is so much uncertainty in the long-term development of the battery. And, I don't feel comfortable losing all control of the project."

"May I remind you, Herr Werner, that you signed a contract with this company when you were hired that states your development work after that date is the property of Volkswagen."

"Yes, sir, I am quite aware of the contract, but I developed the battery starting in 1944." Nordhoff glanced at his notes.

"According to my records, you were an employee of this company in 1944 and early 1945. Isn't that true?"

"Yes, that's true. But I only adapted the special battery to an automobile when I was in America."

"Are you saying Studebaker had a hand in your development?"

"Uh, I think I've said too much already, sir."

"Hold on, Werner. You're not getting away that easy." Nordhoff rose from his chair and started to pace back and forth. "You're a reasonable man, Werner. I think you are smart enough to recognize a good deal when you see one. Here is my proposition: Give us the information we need to complete the development and you will immediately be a well-respected, well-paid executive of the company with a very secure future. Otherwise, your career will be very limited."

"Sir, that sounds like a threat." I couldn't believe what I had just said to the company president. Nordhoff firmly placed both his hands on the table and looked in my direction. His piercing stare said volumes.

He took a deep breath and then said, "It's not a threat, it's a statement of fact, Werner. We should all be on the same team here at Volkswagen. If you remain confrontational, I suggest you will be making a grave personal error." Nordhoff sat down. He closed his notebook and leaned back in his chair. "All right, enough of that. Let's get down to basics here. Although you have shown a high level of technical skills in powering the test vehicle with a DC motor, we all realize that the secret of the vehicle's performance is the battery. Consulting scientists have told us that no zinc-air battery has ever come close to the power yours' exhibited. They also told us that under the microscope they found living organic material that they suspect is more than simple contamination, perhaps even the key to the power potential. Are you going to save the company a year's research by defining for us the source of those microbes?"

"No, sir. I don't think I am." Nordhoff frowned, jerked his head back and looked at the ceiling, then slowly lowered his head to look directly into my eyes.

"Very well, Werner. It appears you have made your choice. You are excused." I walked out fully aware that my future at Volkswagen would not be pleasant unless I showed them how to nurture the fast-mutating microbes. But until I knew more, I felt it was just too dangerous to trust others with control of the project.

Days turned into weeks, weeks into months. There was no word from Herr Voss concerning his progress on development of a zinc-air battery like the one in Freda. I continued in my job in the Export Department. Why didn't they fire me?

The weather in April of 1952 was lovely in Wolfsburg. I bought a bicycle that I rode to work on nice days. It saved wear and tear on Freda and gave me a chance to get some exercise. At 5:15 on the third Friday in April, I unlocked my bike from the stand and started the ten-minute ride home. In the distance, I heard sirens screaming. This was a bit unusual in Wolfsburg. If it weren't for sirens in New York or Chicago, one would wonder what was wrong, but Wolfsburg? As I neared home, black smoke curled into the sky near where I lived. I could smell the smoke in the air. I began to get worried that the fire might be at my house. Soon, my worst fears became reality. Two fire trucks; a police car and an ambulance were parked in my front yard. Firefighters with large hoses were busy dousing the flames. I threw my bike down and ran toward the house. Just as I passed the ambulance, I saw two men loading a covered stretcher.

"Was someone hurt?" I shouted.

"More than hurt," one of the men answered. "Who are you, anyway?"

"This my house. What happened?"

"This man was burned, but he may have died of a heart attack. It's hard to tell at this point. There was a partial can of petrol near where we found him."

At that moment a police officer walked up and said, "I'm sorry sir, but you'll have to step back into the street. This is a crime scene."

"This is my house. Who is this person on the stretcher?"

"We don't yet know. Maybe you can identify him. Pull the stretcher back out, men." Although the uncovered face was blackened and burned, there was no doubt whose face it was. "It is Herr Otto Haniel," I said.

My attention turned to my house. The front looked undamaged. Against police orders, I ran around to the back. Freda was nothing but a charred, twisted sheet metal wreck. The tires were burned up. The smell of burnt rubber was overpowering. I tried to open the bonnet over the engine and burned my hand. The back wall of the house was partially missing and was still smoldering. Water was everywhere. The fire chief approached.

"I know this is your house, sir, but it's too dangerous to be up this close. You'd better move back until things cool off and we've had a chance to examine the structural damage on this back wall."

"I'm an engineer. I'll take my chances."

"Sir, that is not your choice to make. You've been told to step back, that's an order. You must move away until we give you clearance." I figured I had better co-operate.

"All right. But before I go, could someone pry open the engine compartment on this burned VW for me. I need to check on something." The chief motioned for one of the firemen to approach. The man went to the truck and returned with an extrication tool and easily opened the bonnet. I looked inside and to my dismay I saw that the battery was gone. The large cables to the battery were melted leaving only scorched copper but the battery itself had just disappeared. Did it burn completely up; did it explode or vaporize? I had no idea what had happened to Freda's heart?

CHAPTER 38

The chief detective of the Wolfsburg Police Department now admitted that it was possible that Otto Haniel was Wally's murderer, but of course, the question was academic since Otto was now deceased. The Wolfsburg News reported the whole story including the possible motives and links to the Waldo Rosenblum murder. There was no need to discuss it with Herr Nordhoff now. I was not in good favor with him for not giving all the details on how to develop the superior zinc-air battery. I figured the least contact with him the better.

For the next two months, my spare time was spent rebuilding the back of my house and thinking about America. Even with the possibility of confrontations with Big Mike Levy, I longed to be back in South Bend, working for Studebaker. Of course, it was only a pipe dream since Studebaker had not expressed any interest in ever seeing my face again. I wondered why I dreamed about going back to America when less than three years ago I couldn't wait to take a job at Volkswagen. When looking back the answer was self-evident. It was my passion for automotive design. I had done very little design work while at Volkswagen. To make matters worse, I had lost my good friend Wally. And now even my non-design job was in jeopardy. I decided it wouldn't hurt to write a letter to the U. S. expressing my desire to return.

My attempts to get back into design at Volkswagen got nowhere. I was repeatedly told that if I would help their scientists develop another battery like the one that was in my prototype VW, I could call my own shots and work on any design project I wanted to, otherwise, I would remain in the Export Department. I realized what was going on. If they fired me, they would lose all hope to get the battery's secret. But I couldn't take on the responsibility associated with the very powerful but unpredictable battery that contained intelligent, living organisms. So I sat stuck in the Export Department.

Late one afternoon, I asked the Export Department secretary if I could use her typewriter after work to type a letter. She said "yes" but she would be happy to do it for me. I declined.

Mr. Robert K. Nitske
Vice President of Engineering
The Studebaker Corporation
South Bend, Indiana, U.S.A.

Dear Mr. Nitske,

Since I met with you in September 1951, I have continued working at the Volkswagen headquarters here in Wolfsburg, Germany. My duties have alternated between design engineering and the Export Department. Although the Volkswagen automobile has continued to be perfected and is highly popular in Germany and many other countries, I realize the consensus is that it's not right for the American market at this time. I believe that will change in the next few years, however. I am aware that if Studebaker ever decides to get into the small economy car market segment, you will probably want to manufacture in South Bend. I can understand the logic of that decision.

Following are a few points for your consideration:

The small Nash Rambler continues to sell well in America.

The "Big Three dominate all other market segments.

With the highly competitive nature of the U.S. automotive market, the small car segment is the only one left that is not dominated by Ford, Chrysler or G.M.

The technically successful prototype that I developed in late 1949 used mostly Studebaker parts.

Developing a vehicle using the existing Studebaker inner body from the cowl back to the trunk would require minimum new tooling.

I could provide valuable technology as the leader of a team to develop such a vehicle as described above.

I believe the window of opportunity to be successful in the small car segment in America will close in the next three to four years. Entering and dominating this market may be the key to Studebaker's survival. I have several weeks of vacation coming up in June and would be happy to come to South Bend to discuss the matter further if you'd like. Please let me know your thinking on this matter.

Sincerely,

Hans Werner

I knew offering my services to Studebaker was a long shot considering my history with the company and past negative decisions concerning the small car market. But knowing that Studebaker was losing ground made me hope they would see the logic of my proposal. I figured Nitske was a reasonable man and was high enough in the company to influence major decisions. Four weeks later, I received the following letter from Mr. Nitske.

April 1, 1953

Dear Mr. Werner,

I received your letter of March 3rd and must admit you presented some interesting points to consider. Although rehiring you at Studebaker seems fraught with problems, I certainly am willing to talk to you further about your small car ideas. Please let me know the exact dates you would plan to be in South Bend and I will try to adjust my calendar accordingly.

Sincerely,

Robert K. Nitske

I could hardly contain my excitement over having a chance to talk to Studebaker about my small car ideas. Although I was excited about traveling to America in June, on the whole, I was not happy with my life at this point. My job was boring, I had no projects that excited me, and I had no close friends, male or female. I was aware that my miserable situation was my own fault. Every day was the same routine. Get up, go to work, come home, open a bottle of beer, sit on my front porch (in Wally's rocking chair) and feel sorry for my self until I got hungry. I then would fix a sandwich or heat a can of soup. I never made any attempt to learn to be a good cook. Thoughts of things mechanical distracted my mind and took priority. I was beginning to realize that life was passing me by. I wanted something else. I felt empty and lonely. Car design seemed to be a thing of the past, at least at Volkswagen. The zinc-air battery was also behind me. Although I considered it a great invention, losing it in the fire helped solve the problem of whether or not to share the technology with Volkswagen. The only thing I had to look forward to was my trip to America. I made all the arrangements including plane reservations, rental car in Chicago and hotel room in South Bend. (The LaSalle, of course.)

CHAPTER 39

It was a cloudy afternoon in late May as I sat on the porch, sipping on a beer, rocking and thinking. As the dark clouds passed overhead, I heard thunder in the distance. As the storm moved closer, the wind cooled me and a misting of rain dampened my face. The thunder was getting closer by the minute. By this time, the occasional lightning flash that lit the sky was only a second or two before the sound of thunder shook the earth. I sat trying to decide whether or not to go inside when something unexpected happened. A jagged bolt of lightning struck in the wooded lot next to my house. The sound was tremendous. I almost jumped out of my chair. Then, just as suddenly, everything was quiet except for a strange whining sound like two cats making kittens. A metallic smell filled the air. I wondered if the lightning strike was the cause. And then I saw a blueish-purple smoke crawl from the edge of the woods. It almost looked liquid as it rolled in my direction. I got up to investigate the source. I crept carefully around the smoke and toward the noise. A few meters into the woods, I was stopped cold. I saw Freda's heart making that ghastly whining sound and spewing purple gas. I thought that battery was gone forever. I rushed over and tried to pick it up but burned my fingers. It was still hot from the lightning strike.

"Freda, what are you doing out here?" I shouted. The gas eruption and the noise ceased. Without touching, I examined the charred tin-plated casing. While waiting for her to cool, I tried to figure out how she got disconnected from my VW and ended up thirty meters away. I guessed Otto must have somehow found out that the outstanding performance of my prototype VW was mainly due to its battery. He probably disconnected it from its cables and dropped it into the woods planning to retrieve it after setting the fire. I figured the exploding petrol contributed to his death and Freda's heart lay undetected until a lightning bolt found it. Or maybe she found the lightning bolt. Should I just leave the battery in the woods, or bury her or give her a new home in another car? I walked back to the house. I would decide tomorrow.

I didn't sleep much that night. I had too many decisions to make. It seemed fruitless to try to put the battery out of my life. It was obvious the Freda's heart would not die easily. In almost all living organisms, survival is a high priority. Freda's heart had proven that she was a living thing that had evolved in such a way that was difficult to kill. Her ability to survive was likely directly linked to her uncanny intelligence.

One very important consideration in deciding what to do with the battery was my safety while in South Bend. I had not forgotten that the battery saved my life when Big Mike Levy accosted me two years earlier. I felt no guilt in putting Mike in a wheelchair, perhaps for the rest of his life. After all, he was planning to kill me. And I doubted his grudge was any less now than it was that night two years ago. He probably hated me even more since I was responsible for him being partially paralyzed. I was still tossing and turning as the early morning light began to creep through the southern window of my room. But the night was not wasted. I had decided to repackage the battery in an American army canteen. In combination with a cartridge belt and ammo pouch to hold the high voltage coil, I could protect myself without being conspicuous. I could even walk around in a short-sleeve shirt if I wanted to. People would think nothing of the canteen and belt. My main concern was whether or not the transfer of the zinc-potassium hydroxide slurry to an aluminum canteen would affect its power and intelligence. Also, I wondered if the canteen would hold all the material. Although the charred can was no larger than a motorcycle battery, an army canteen was even smaller, slightly less than a liter. What if I had some material left over? What would I do with it?

The next morning was Saturday so I had all day to carry out my plans for repackaging Freda's heart. I approached the wooded lot with caution. Although the storm had passed over, the sky was still dark and gloomy. I walked slowly and carefully looking from left to right until I finally spotted her. Strangely, when I picked up Freda's heart, it was still warm. That was a definite indication of life. I took her into the house and placed her in the kitchen sink. I then jumped on my bicycle and headed to the military surplus store. A blind man would know where he was when entering that store. Army canvas has a special smell. That was the first thing that hit me. The items were laid out on long tables that I assumed were once dining tables for army mess halls. I wondered why there were more American and British items than German in that store. I soon found the table with the canteens, mess kits and cartridge belts. The American canteens and belts were so inexpensive I decided to buy two sets. I hurried home, eager to repackage the contents of the battery.

When I entered the kitchen, the metallic smell, really more of a stink, was overpowering. It seemed to have gotten stronger since I left two hours earlier. The steel container was badly burned. Lightning had welded the cover shut. I knew I would have to cut it open to get to the contents. My metal saw easily cut through the tin-plated container. I choked and coughed at my first exposure to the battery' interior. I put my handkerchief over my mouth and nose and gazed in wonder at the greenish metallic color the slurry had taken on. In the past, the color had always been a dark shade of gray. I was extremely careful not to spill any of it into the sink. I was afraid of what might happen if some of the slurry somehow made its way into the canal. Using a small kitchen funnel, I carefully spooned the zinc-potassium hydroxide mixture into the small canteen neck opening. I hoped the aluminum body of the canteen would not cause some unexpected chemical reaction. I was glad I had bought two canteens. There was almost enough material to fill both. I ran the leads through the predrilled holes in a rubber stopper so one wire went to the bottom of the canteen and the other would be near the top. After capping each with the stopper for anode and cathode leads, I anxiously connected my volt-ohm meter to the wires. The voltage was still at exactly six, just as it was in South Bend, four years earlier. Amazing! Testing for amperage would need to be done with care. If the battery had continued to evolve as I suspected, or if the lightning strike had somehow increased its power, I might have a very lethal weapon on my hands. To be on the safe side, I sat up test rig in my side yard. I first drove a piece of water pipe into the ground and wrapped the stripped end of the negative lead to it. About two meters away, I drove a wooden stake into the ground and taped the positive lead to its top. I was then ready to make a series connection of the battery's positive lead through the coil. When I did, a mighty bolt of lightning shot to the iron pipe. The ground beneath my feet vibrated as if an earthquake was in progress. Within ten seconds the pipe turned red, then yellow before it melted into a puddle on the ground. I pulled the wire out of the coil and fell back on the ground trying to absorb what had just happened. I realized that Freda's heart was stronger than ever even though it was only half as large. Now what?

CHAPTER 40

On June 23, 1953, I boarded a TWA Lockheed Constellation for my flight to New York City. Once there, I took an American Airways flight to Chicago. I was almost as excited about this trip as I was about the discovery and repackaging of Freda's heart. The canteen, cartridge belt, coil and wires were safely packed away in my luggage. At Midway Airport, I went to the Hertz Rent-a Car counter to see if they had Studebakers. The answer was "no." Since General Motors owned Hertz, I had to settle for a Chevrolet. The drive over to South Bend was pleasant enough although I didn't pay much attention to the scenery I was passing. I was thinking of what I would say when I met with Mr. Nitski.

After a snack at the LaSalle Hotel coffee shop and a long soaking bath, I fell into bed and slept like I was dead. I was late getting up on Sunday morning. When I finally did, I felt refreshed. The day was clear and cool, a little unusual for Indiana in late June. I decided I would spend the day touring around town. My first stop was the Sherman, Schaus and Freeman Studebaker Dealership on the corner of Lafayette and South Street. Right there in the showroom window was the most beautiful automobile I had ever laid my eyes on. I had seen a picture but in the flesh that 1953 Starliner Coupe was nothing short of gorgeous. The body was painted a sort of coral reddish color and the top was light tan. Chrome trim was minimal and tastefully placed. The front hood sloped gracefully between twin grille openings each accented with a floating chrome-plated bar. The slab-sided body was smooth with no ornamentation except for a molded-in crease that flowed into the door and curved gracefully toward the rocker panel. The rear fenders rose into a slight fin, its topside accented with a polished stainless molding that flowed from the "C" post to the taillight. I couldn't help but imagine a scene where I would be cruising out Western Avenue with all four windows lowered, heading out to the Proving Ground. My fantasy was broken as the same elderly salesman I had met when I bought my '39 strolled over. I would swear that he was wearing the same pinstriped suit he had on four years earlier. His thin caterpillar-like mustache twitched as he spoke.

"Isn't she a beauty?" he said with a faux English accent.

"You mean the car? Yes, she is," I agreed. "Is it a Champ or a Commander?"

"This one is a Champion, sir. Would you prefer a Commander eight cylinder?"

"No, thanks, the Champ is fine. Could I see the engine compartment?"

"I'll have someone open the hood for you," he said as if it was either too heavy for him or beneath his dignity.

"Don't bother. I'll open it." The old salesman nodded and stood back with his hands clasped behind him as he bounced up and down on his toes. The old flathead six engine looked the same as the one that was in my '39. I hoped it had more power. "How much is this car?"

"It's $2125 as she stands but I'm sure you will want a radio and undercoating which will add slightly to the cost. If you have a trade-in, we'll give you a very liberal allowance for it."

"Oh, no, I'm just looking for now."

"I see. Well, take your time but you won't find a more beautiful car on the market today. That's European styling by Raymond Loewy you know."

"Yes, I know." I decided not to inform him that Bob Bourke did most of the actual design work. What would be the point? I opened the passenger door. The dash and interior metal trim was a sort of mousey gray color which didn't seem to fit with the rest of the car. When I tried to close the door, it was obvious that it didn't line up properly. I had to close it hard for it to catch. I looked at the salesman. He looked at the ceiling. I picked up a brochure and left.

With a clear sky, a pleasant temperature and a new Chevy at my disposal, I decided to drive by the homes of some special South Bend residents. In the phone directory there was no listing for Michael Levy. There was only one listing for a Petty. I figured that L. Petty might be Mr. Nitske's secretary. The listing of 212 Rockne Drive was near the Morris Park Golf and Country Club, which was in a very nice part of town. I had the local news station on the radio as I headed out LaSalle Avenue and onto McKinley Highway finally arriving at the golf club. I drove up to the clubhouse remembering my exciting adventure when I drove the first Freda past the golfing Studebaker Board of Directors. After leaving the golf course, I drove up Rockne Drive. I passed a number of well-kept middle-class homes. In the distance I saw a blond lady and a man using a cane slowly walking along the sidewalk. Without a doubt, it was Miss Petty and Mike Levy. They didn't notice me as I drove by. I made a U-turn at the next intersection and pulled to the side of the street and parked. I watched the couple for a while, wondering if Mr. Nitske knew that his secretary and the union boss were a couple. Soon they turned around and started walking back in my direction. They were less than a block away. Should I start the car and drive past them or should I sit still and let them walk by me? Although I waited too long to make my decision, I finally started the car and pulled away from the curb. As I passed the couple, Mike looked directly at me and said something to Miss Petty. I watched in my rear-view mirror as they stopped and watched me pulled out of sight. "Well," I said to myself, "looks like Big Mike is back on his feet again." On I drove with no particular destination in mind, at least not consciously. Soon I found myself driving by the Burgdorf residence. George Burgdorf was outside planting flowers along his front walk. I slowed down but didn't stop. I remembered his physical threats when he thought I had mistreated his daughter. As I circled the block, I thought back through the whole situation. Yes, I neglected Mary to comfort Susie but I thought Mary went a bit overboard in her jealousy. That aside, if I somehow was able to make my way back to South Bend to live, I thought it best to have an important man like George Burgdorf as a friend rather than an enemy. He looked up from his digging when I stopped in front of his house. I'll admit my heart was pounding when I got out of the car. He stood and looked at me for a few moments and then walked in my direction. He carried his hand spade as he approached. He seemed larger than I remembered. I stood still in front of the car and faced him.

"What in the hell do you think you're doing coming to my home like this? You've got a lot of nerve, Werner!"

"I've come to apologize, sir." Burgdorf frowned and rubbed his chin.

"OK, make it quick, boy."

"First, I'm very sorry I caused Mary any pain. That certainly was not my intension. I truly hope she has moved on with her life and is happy now. As far as my assuming the identity of a dead man from Texas, it was the only way I could think of to get into the automotive business here in America. It worked for a while but I was not happy with the constant deception and decided to go back to Germany and be Hans Werner once again. I would like to come back to South Bend someday and I hope you will forgive me for the grief I have caused your family. That's all I have to say for now, sir." Mr. Burgdorf stood motionless. I hoped he was rethinking his former position.

"Although your apology seems sincere enough, you have fooled me before and I won't let that happen again. So let's just say I'm not going to knock your block off like I once threatened, but don't expect a hand of friendship either."

"Fair enough, sir. If I do get back to South Bend, I plan on being a good citizen and a contributor to making this town a better place."

"Fancy words, Werner, but still just words. What makes you think there's a place for you in South Bend? If you expect to re-enter the work force at Studebaker, be forewarned, your chances aren't good. The company is going down hill fast. Sales are declining and from what I hear, big layoffs are on the way."

"Well, sir, you may be right but I do have an appointment with Bob Nitske tomorrow to discuss my ideas for a small economical vehicle similar to the one I developed three years ago."

"A new vehicle as you describe might help, but Studebaker's problems go much deeper. The company hasn't gotten a new defense contract in quite some time. But most important, the labor force at Studebaker is overpaid and underworked. Manufacturing costs are just too damn high. It's really that simple. There's little chance the union will willingly lower their wages."

"Yes, sir, I agree. I saw that years ago. Well, I'll leave you now. Thank you for listening." Burgdorf nodded and didn't say anything else. I drove away feeling I had done the right thing. On and on I drove, just thinking and driving; Mr. Burgdorf, Mary, Mike Levy, Miss Petty, Mr. Nitske, the '53 Studebaker and, oh, yes, Susie Goodall all moved in and out of my consciousness.

The afternoon sun had just dipped behind the western horizon as I pulled into the LaSalle Hotel parking lot. I had no plans for the evening but I didn't want to stay in my room and read. I called the Indiana Café to see if I needed a reservation for just one person. They said they could work me in. So after a quick bath and a shave, I put on a clean shirt and tie and headed over to 747 West Indiana Avenue "Where food, wine and service warms hearts." I was seated in the corner at a table for two. I ordered a glass of Chablis and let my taste buds prepare for a great American beefsteak. I love German food but the steaks in Germany never seem to come up to American standards. I sat nursing my wine when to my great surprise, George Burgdorf and his wife walked in. Even more shocking was the other member of their party, Mary. Mr. Burgdorf spotted me right away and nodded in my direction. I don't think Mrs. Burgdorf or Mary saw me. I sat quietly sipping my wine and wondering what Mary's situation was. I figured she would be married by now, not living with her parents.

Before my main course was served, Mr. Burgdorf rose and walked in my direction. He stopped at my table.

"Well Hans, we meet again. How did you know we would be here tonight?"

"I didn't. It's just a coincidence, sir. I had to eat somewhere. You don't have to acknowledge my presence to your family, especially if you think it might upset Mary. I don't think she has seen me yet."

"Well, she's a grown woman now and she's just getting over a nasty divorce, she may want to see you. I'll ask her."

"Oh, no, please," I said. "Maybe it's best we don't stir up old wounds."

"Why don't we let her decide?"

"When I stopped by your house today, my objective was to apologize to you. I had no idea Mary was there."

"I told Mary that you stopped by and she seemed interested in everything that was said. She doesn't seem to be holding a grudge." With that Burgdorf walked back to his table. He leaned forward and whispered to Mary. She turned and looked in my direction. She quickly turned back. Mr. Burgdorf looked at me and shrugged. It's just as well, I thought.

My entrée was delivered but I had trouble concentrating on the food. Every time I glanced in Mary's direction, a new memory of our time together entered my mind. In particular those passionate sessions in the front seat of my '39 coupe came into focus. I remembered how fogged up the windows got on those cool night in the Burgdorf's driveway. Sometimes, we would have to stop and lower the windows in order to cool off before things got out of hand. She would laugh when I couldn't walk her to the door right away because of an erection. A few minutes later, George Burgdorf again came to my table.

"Hans, Mary says she would like for you to join us for coffee. What do you say?" I nodded and walked over. Mrs. Burgdorf offered her hand and I shook it. Mary did the same. When I took her hand she smiled and placed her other hand on top of mine. I couldn't help but notice her eyes were dazzling like before.

"Hello, Hans," she said. "It's been a while. A lot has happened during the past few years. Dad told me you came by today to apologize. That was good of you. I just want you to know, at least from my standpoint, there are no hard feelings. OK?" I smiled in agreement. "How long do you plan to be in South Bend?"

"I'll be leaving tomorrow afternoon, but I hope someday to move back here." Oh, God. Why did I say that? Maybe her father had already told her of my plans. Oh, well. Too late. The next few minutes were filled with small talk about what I had been doing in Germany. All three seemed interested in my stories about my dear friend, Wally Rosenblum and about the evil Otto Haniel. Mary said she was still working at the library, and if I had time tomorrow, to come by and see her before I left town. There was no mention of her divorce. We all shook hands again and I returned to my hotel elated but confused. Those few minutes with Mary went way too well.

I tossed and turned unable to go to sleep. There were too many things on my mind. Mary coming back into my life was the last thing I expected. And most frustrating was the realization that she was no longer just an innocent girl. She was now a voluptuous, mature and beautiful young woman. But the schoolgirl sweetness of the Mary I once loved was still there, maybe even more so. I wondered why she was so nice to me. Was it maturity or was she on the rebound from her divorced husband?

When I awoke Monday morning, with my head was still in a whirl. I arrived at Mr. Nitske's mahogany-paneled office at the appointed hour of 9 a.m. A smiling Miss Petty greeted me. Although she looked terrific in her expensive-looking baby blue silk blouse and tailored navy-blue skirt, I noticed her blond hair needed a root touchup. She gave no indication that she had seen me the day before. Being Nitske's secretary she was probably aware that I was in town on Sunday. She ushered me into his office and then left us alone. Bob Nitske already had his jacket off and his tie loosened. It appeared from the mess on his desk, he was a very busy man or maybe just a bit disorganized.

"Have a seat, Hans. Would you like some coffee?"

"No thanks, but I do have a request. Could we meet in the library instead of here in your office?"

"Could I ask why?"

"I have some things I'd like to show you and there's not room on your desk."

"Oh, all right." He rose and as we walked out he spoke to Miss Petty. "We'll be in the library if you need me." She smiled and went back to her typing.

Except for ten thousand old mostly unread books and some ancient furniture, the library was empty. The room had a depressing feel about it, dark and cavernous. After we were seated at one of the large wooden tables, Mr. Nitske said, "What did you want to show me?"

"Before we get started discussing the small car potential, I have some news that may surprise you. Mr. Nitske, are you aware that your secretary and Mike Levy are a couple?"

"Oh, for Pete's sake! That's ridiculous. I'll have to admit, Werner, I can't think of a worse opening line for someone who is interested in getting a job at Studebaker."

"Hear me out, sir. When I was here two years ago, I used Miss Petty's office phone to make a date with someone and she told Mike Levy about it. I'm sure of it. And yesterday, I saw the two of them walking together in front of Miss Petty's home on Rockne Drive. Haven't you ever wondered how Miss Petty can afford such a nice home on a secretary's salary? The reason I wanted to meet away from your office today was a fear she may be able to hear our discussion. Your office may be bugged. Haven't you sometimes wondered how the union always knows what's going on in top management?"

"I don't believe a thing you're saying, Hans. It all sounds a bit paranoid if you ask me. But today, I've got a tight schedule and don't have time to debate the issue so I'll just let it slide. You came all this distance so, let's talk about the small car you and Jack Yearwood developed four years ago. First, to what do you attribute its superior performance?"

"A number of things. It had a well-tuned four-cylinder engine, a lightweight body, mechanicals that had been proven and improved over many years and a zinc-air battery."

"How could the battery contribute to its performance?"

"I'm not going to go into great detail, but it has to do with the compression of the air/fuel mixture resulting in more efficient combustion. Also, in the future, the battery will be strong enough to drive several components now driven by engine power. Such things as the fan, oil and water pumps are examples. That will mean more power goes to driving the wheels. The generator and the heavy lead-acid battery might be eliminated altogether making the car lighter and have better weight distribution. But to be perfectly honest, Mr. Nitski, to get all the engineering expertise required to duplicate the performance of that earlier prototype plus the potential innovations I mentioned, I'm afraid you'll have to hire me." Nitski smiled.

"You think you've got me by the balls, don't you? Have you forgotten Jack Yearwood and Ed Reynolds still work for us?"

"That's not going to help. First, I never revealed to Jack or Ed that the battery was important to the car's performance. And second, I hear that Jack is now a loyal union member and last time I checked, the union was against a small car project." Nitski still seemed irritated. I wondered why the Levy/Petty romance bothered him so much. He took out a cigarette and fumbled for his lighter.

"All right. Next question: How are the Volkswagens selling in Germany and in other countries?"

"Very, very well. We will hit 500,000 VWs produced sometime in the next couple of weeks. Over half of the cars on the road in Germany are VWs. The price is right and the quality and durability are excellent. Exports are also growing faster than the plant can supply. We could sell twice what we do now if we could produce them. We're coming to America as soon as we can supply the demand we have already."

"From what I understand, the VW doesn't sell over here. It is just too small for Americans. Also, the design looks like a late '30s car. Quality is not that great either."

"Quality now is as good as anything in the U.S., better than most. As an example, I was down at the local Studebaker dealer yesterday to look at the new '53s. Although they are beautiful, fit and finish are lacking. I couldn't even get the door to latch without slamming it."

"Yeah, we got a ways to go getting the quality up on the new model. But getting back to the VW. What makes you people think a little car like the VW will sell in America?"

"Like I said in my letter, the Nash Rambler is already doing pretty well over here and when my company jumps in with the VW, it's all over. Then it will be too late for Studebaker. Even the big three will be squeezed if they decide to make a small car. The timing now is perfect. Studebaker could grab a big chunk of this market if you move fast."

"I don't know, Hans. Maybe there is a big market for a little compact car, but how can we get into it without spending a lot of tooling money we don't have?"

"First, you hire me. I'll develop the small car on a shoestring. I'll use mostly Studebaker parts and my technical knowledge from Volkswagen to develop the perfect small car. What I have learned over there is invaluable. Volkswagen is the best in the world at low cost manufacturing of automobiles. If you don't know it now, you will eventually find out." Nitske shook his head and wrinkled his brow. He seemed distracted. Was he still thinking about his secretary?

For the next hour, we went back and forth debating the pros and cons of the small car market. We talked about economy, quality, and fun of driving, styling, and resale value. Finally, Mr. Nitske ended the meeting.

"You've raised some interesting points, Hans. I'll discuss this with the executive staff and get back to you if we decide to pursue the matter further. I'm sorry to have to break it off, but I'm already late for another meeting."

He extended his hand, I shook it and then he left without comment. As I passed his office on my way back to my car, Miss Petty called out to me.

"You're not leaving us are you, Mr. Werner?"

"Yes, gotta get back to Wolfsburg before the Soviets take over our plant."

Miss Petty's face went blank. I don't think she realized I was making a joke. I wondered if she would tell Big Mike that Volkswagen is soon to be run by Russians.

"Are you on your way to the airport?" she asked.

"Yes, if I don't hurry I'll miss my flight."

"You come back to see us, OK?"

"OK," I said. I jumped into the Chevy and headed out Wayne Street toward the St. Joseph County Library.

I walked in the door but didn't see Mary at the check out desk. When I inquired as to her whereabouts, I was informed that her office was near the stairs. Behind the glass door seated behind a desk was a lady that looked more like a Miss Indiana than a Head Librarian. I knocked and Mary looked up and smiled. She walked over to meet me and gave me a little hug and a kiss on the cheek.

"Well, hello, Hans. I was hoping you could drop by before you left. Can you stay and chat for a few minutes?"

"Sure. Hey! Looks like you got a promotion. Congratulations!"

"Yes. When old Mrs. Smithson retired, the board offered me the job and I took it. It's just more work without a lot more pay. But with the recent economic downturn here in South Bend, I feel lucky to have any job."

"Yeah, I read about it in a Fortune magazine I picked up in New York. Changing the subject, Mary, I feel really lucky to have run into you Saturday night at the Indiana Café. Gee, you sure look good."

"You too, Hans. How did your meeting at Studebaker go this morning?

"Pretty well, I think. Bob Nitske didn't offer me a job but he didn't close the door either. Unfortunately, I got off on the wrong foot by telling him that his secretary was the union boss' girl friend. He didn't believe me, but it's true. Mary, I was wondering, do you have any suggestions as to how I can keep up with Studebaker news while I'm back in Germany?"

"Well, the best way would be to subscribe to the *South Bend Tribune*. But I suspect that might be a bit expensive in Germany. Tell you what. Dad and I both read the paper every day. If anything significant about Studebaker is printed, I'll clip it out and send it to you by airmail. But I'll need your address."

"Oh, Mary. That would be wonderful. How could I ever thank you?"

"Oh, I'll think of something." Mary laughed. I probably blushed. She was flirting and I was eating it up."

"Want to go to lunch, Hans?" she asked.

"I'd love to but if I don't leave now, I may miss my flight in Chicago and then I'd miss my New York flight to London." I wrote out my German home address, kissed Mary on the cheek and hurried to my car. Mary was on my mind all the way to Chicago.

Chapter 41

After a couple of days resting up from my overseas flight and taking care of chores around my house, I returned to my job in the Export Department. The job continued to be routine paperwork concerning sales to other countries. Occasionally, my supervisor would ask if I had done any more work on the zinc-air battery concept. I always answered "no." That wasn't quite true. I performed standard volt/amp tests on both of the canteen batteries I had made using the slurry from the battery found after the lightning strike. I set up tests in Wally's room that had stood empty since his death. Although both batteries still put out a steady 6 volts, the power potential of each had diminished. I wondered if the aluminum had a detrimental effect on the zinc-air slurry. I also wondered if maybe the small closure restricted the air, which is the source of the battery's energy. If restricting the air slowed or stopped the mutation, perhaps the intelligence of the microorganisms could be controlled that way.

To eliminate the aluminum as a possible source of the problem, I purchased six half-liter glass jars like those used for canning. I divided the slurry from the two canteens equally into the six jars. Except for the test wires running into the top of each, I drilled increasing larger holes in five of the lids. One jar was left with no holes and no chance for air to enter. Every afternoon after work I logged in the voltage and amperage from each jar. After a few days it was obvious that the amount of air intake was critical. The optimum size of the vent hole was about the size of a pencil lead. Having no air intake decreased the power, as did too much air intake. It was sheer luck that I had packaged my first automotive battery (Freda's heart) in a motorcycle battery case. The vents in the fill-caps must have been the perfect size.

Once I had determined the optimum air intake hole size, the next question related to the amount of material in each battery. I emptied all the slurry together and then divided it into three jars. One jar was 1/3 full; one was 2/3 full and one completely full. All had equal size vent holes for air intake. After ten days of testing, I found a direct correlation between mass and power. Yes, size matters, at least in zinc-air batteries. Next, I needed to find some way to measure the battery's intelligence. In the case of the "Freda car" I had developed for Studebaker, the horn blowing was a surprise, as was the strange human-like antics the car exhibited in both South Bend and Huntsville. When I installed the same battery in the Volkswagen here in Germany, it was able to play simple songs on a five-note horn after receiving a vocal command. The power in that version eventually increased to the point that it could propel the VW vehicle thus eliminating the need for a gasoline engine.

After Otto destroyed the car, I became afraid of what might happen if I helped Volkswagen develop another similar battery. In the past, the battery had expressed its intelligence in a number of ways, the latest being to call attention to its location by spurting bluish, purple smoke after being struck by lightning. My experiment compared two identical ½ liter batteries. Assuming they would mutate at identical rates, I hooked one up to a portable record player and one to the battery input connection of a portable radio. The six-volt output worked well to power a small six-volt DC motor for the record player. Only a rectifier and a small transformer were required to power the radio. I kept the record player busy playing my favorite German records from the war years. I especially loved the record *Wie einst Lili Marleen*, songs of Lane Andersen. Since post war anti-Nazi sentiment ran high, it was surprising the record was still available. On the radio, the only German songs from the war years were dance music such as *Komm mit nach Madeira!* In addition to the entertainment value of listening to the music, I was attempting to determine if either of the batteries would gain intelligence from the music. Weeks passed and nothing happened. The music only played when I put a record on or tuned in a music station. There was a possibility the battery's intelligence had increased but the record player or radio was not a suitable outlet. I longed for the excitement that Freda's heart had always provided with her unpredictable antics.

Mary hadn't forgotten me. I received a letter from her that included a newspaper article about Packard's pending acquisition of Studebaker. Her letter ended, "Affectionately, Mary." I was glad to hear from her. I hoped the Studebaker acquisition would be successful. What I really hoped for was a letter from Bob Nitske. On 24 January 1954, I received what I was looking for.

January 20, 1954

Dear Hans,

I apologize for waiting so long to get back to you. But I had good reason to delay. First, there have been a number of heated discussions about whether or not Studebaker should make a small car to compete with the Nash Rambler, Henry J and your Volkswagen. At this point, it appears we will at least do the preliminary work to develop a small car prototype similar to the one you developed several years ago.

We are therefore extending an offer to you of a two-year contract with the Studebaker-Packard Corporation at an annual salary of $9,000. If you accept our offer, we will arrange for your immigration papers and hopefully eventual U.S. citizenship. Also your moving expenses will be paid. This offer will remain in effect for a period of thirty days.

It may interest you to know that I now have a new secretary, Mrs. Holden.

Please let me hear from you as soon as possible.
Sincerely, Robert Nitski,
Vice President of Engineering

I thought the decision to accept Nitske's offer would be an easy one. I drafted my reply letter several times, but wadded the paper each time. I kept finding fault with my language, knowing I must phrase the wording perfectly. I finally realized why I was having so much trouble. Did I really want to leave my homeland? I still loved Germany. I knew if I took the job at Studebaker, I might never return. I was born in Germany, got my education here; my mother, sister and my best friend Wally were buried here. I had a good paying job and a chance to be a hero at Volkswagen, if only, if only.........All I had to do was turn over Freda's secret to Volkswagen and I could return to design. But, I couldn't take the chance. Freda's heart was just too unpredictable. I turned in my two-week's notice at Volkswagen and put my house in the hands of a local realtor. I wrote four letters to America; one to Studebaker, one to Mrs. Kirchall (to see if she had a room), one to Karl in Huntsville, and one to Mary. I discontinued the battery experiments since nothing had happened in the six weeks the radio and record player had been connected. I carefully packed one battery in a well-padded carton in my luggage to be taken on the plane and packed the other in a special wooden box with my household items that were to be shipped.

Luckily, the house sold quickly. Places to live in Wolfsburg were in great demand due to Volkswagen's expanding business. Leaving the house felt like saying goodbye to Wally for the last time. Since I was not in good standing at Volkswagen, my leaving turned out to be a non-event. There was no going-away party or even a handshake from the company president. I visited the graves of Wally, my mother and sister, and then boarded a Lufthansa flight for London.

CHAPTER 42

There are number of bends in the St. Joseph River as it makes its way out of Indiana into Michigan. The twisting and turning river is the dividing line between the cities of South Bend and Mishawaka, Indiana. Like the river, my Greyhound bus turned sharply as it entered the smoky South Bend bus station. I realized this town might be the permanent home of Herr Hans Werner. That thought was a bit frightening but spending the rest of my life in Wolfsburg was equally scary. A young black porter dragged my suitcase from the under-the-bus luggage compartment.

"This here yo' bag, Boss?" he said.

"Ya. danke scheon! I replied. The porter stood with his mouth open waiting for an answer. I smiled and grabbed my bag. He held out his hand. I put a quarter in it and headed for the taxi stand. I was so tired from traveling that it was hard to tell reality from a dream. Was I really in America?

Mrs. Kitchall seemed glad to see me. She even invited me into her kitchen for a ham and cheese sandwich. That was just what I needed after the two days of travel eating nothing but airline food and candy bars. My old room looked just the same. When I collapsed on the bed and starred at the ceiling, that old river of cracks was even more prominent than I remembered. I let my gaze follow them to the wall. But it was hard to keep my eyes open. I did what my body told me to do. I fell asleep in my clothes.

Monday morning was filled with administrative tasks related to my employment at the Studebaker-Packard Corporation. Contracts had to be signed. A physical exam followed the signing of immigration papers. All this paperwork was required before my green card could be issued and I could legally work for an American company. Even though I had previously been a Studebaker employee under a different name, I was treated as if I were a different person. In a way, I was. I compared all this red tape to what was required when I went to work at Volkswagen. It was much simpler there, but of course I was already a German citizen.

Bob Nitske was more congenial than on my earlier visit. His new secretary looked a lot like my mother. When introduced to Mrs. Holden, I asked if she was a native of South Bend.

"Oh, yes," she said. "My grandfather worked for Studebaker as well as my father. I worked in the plant myself for thirteen years. A couple of years ago I took night classes to become a secretary and here I am working for the best boss in the world."

Bob Nitske smiled and said, "You didn't have to say that, Mrs. Holden, you already have the job." We all laughed. Nitske explained how much the company had changed in the last couple of years. "Hans, we now have a younger more aggressive board of directors that is more open to new ideas. Otherwise, I wouldn't have gotten permission to investigate the possibility of our company entering the small car market. With Packard soon to be a part of the corporation, we will have a solid presence in the luxury field, with Studebakers spanning the medium priced market and hopefully a new vehicle to compete in the small economy car field."

"Yes, sir, that all sounds good. Does the company have the resources to tool up for new designs?"

"Not really, Hans. And that's only half the problem. Our labor costs are still the highest in the automotive world and our union doesn't seem to be willing to lower wages without a fight."

"Is Mike Levy still the union boss?"

"Yes, he is. He was out for a few months with some sort of problem with his legs and was confined to a wheelchair for a while. But now he's back full-time and only has to use a cane to walk. But enough about that. Your problem is to develop a four-cylinder, 104" wheelbase car that uses as many existing Studebaker parts as possible. As before, I want you to do the work at the Proving Ground. Ed Reynolds and his men will assist you in building the prototype. I can probably get Jack Yearwood transferred out there if you'd like."

"No, no, I don't think Jack would fit into my plans this time. But Ed Reynolds and I worked well together before. I look forward to working with him again."

"Where are you staying, Hans and do you have transportation?"

"I'm staying at Mrs. Kitchall's boarding house on West Sample Street. And I plan to walk over to Sherman, Schaus and Freeman this afternoon and buy a new Studebaker."

"That's great. Be sure to ask for the employee's discount."

I left Bob Nitske's office elated at the way things were progressing. As I walked into the Studebaker dealership, the same elderly salesman with the caterpillar mustache greeted me.

"Good afternoon, sir. May I help you pick out a new Studebaker?"

"Well, I know what I want. It's just whether or not you have such a car and how much will it cost me." The old man wrinkled his brow. "I want a new 1953 or '54 Starliner Regal Commander Hardtop with Sandusky Beige top and Coral Red bottom. And the doors must open and close properly. Do you have the car I have described?"

"If we don't, we certainly can order it for you. Hold on and let me check our inventory." While he was thumbing through pages in a loose-leaf notebook, I walked over to the window to view the line of new cars parked in the side lot. I saw the car I was looking for immediately. The number 41 was painted on the windshield.

"Oh, sir," I called to the salesman. "If you will get the keys to number 41 for me I'd like to give it a turn around the block before we negotiate a price." It was obvious that I had upset his usual sequence with my request. Yet he had enough experience to know that to make a sale, momentum must not be interrupted.

"Number 81, you say?"

"No! 41!"

"Very good, sir. I'll have Roger bring the car around for you." The old gentleman leaned in and whispered to the secretary. She called Roger's name on a loudspeaker. Soon a young man in coveralls emerged from the shop wiping his hands on a pink shop cloth. I remembered this being the same fellow I bought my '39 from five years earlier. Roger walked over to a cabinet, opened the door revealing about fifty keys hanging on nails. He grabbed #41 and motioned for me to follow. As I followed Roger to the '53 Commander, it occurred to me that the elderly salesman in the pinstriped suit had added nothing to the impending transaction.

"What's the deal, Roger? Does that old salesman own this place or something?"

"You got it, Pal," Roger replied. The doors of the coupe fit well and the V-8 engine gave the car plenty of pep. I was driving my new car toward the St. Joseph County Library only 45 minutes after I had walked into the dealership.

I parked in front of the red brick building, looked toward heaven and said out loud, "Thank you, Wally. Your house has provided me with my dream car and a nice bankroll. But I'd give everything I own to have you back." Being unsure about whether or not there is a "hereafter" I still hoped Wally could hear me when I said, "Thank you Wally. But most of all thank you for the love and friendship you brought into my life."

I walked inside the big two-story library building expecting to see the prettiest girl in Indiana. I was not disappointed. Mary looked up from her work when I tapped on her office window. Her face beamed when she saw me. She rushed to the door to greet me.

"Come in and close the door," she said. I did as she requested.

"Did the job with Studebaker come through?"

· "Yes, I'm starting tomorrow. I'll be developing a small car prototype; similar to the one I developed several years ago. I'll be working out at the Proving Ground like before."

"That sounds great, Hans." Mary stepped away from the window and motioned me to join her. She then pulled me close to receive her kiss. The feel of her warm body, her sweet clean smell and the taste of her lips made seven years vanish in an instant. It was like I was once more in her parents' driveway in my old '39 Studebaker basking in the passion of her kiss. She released her embrace, stepped back and smiled. "Welcome back to South Bend!"

"Wow, Mary! With that kind of welcome, I wonder why I ever left," I said as I tried to catch my breath. I hesitated and then I said, "You once told me it was over between us and that you were in love with someone else. What happened?"

"Hans, I was married for a couple of years but it didn't work out. I'm not going to go into detail, but let's just say I was not ready to be a housewife and mother. Maybe being Head Librarian in a small midwestern town doesn't sound too exciting but I have big plans for making South Bend and St. Joseph County a literary center. I want to have children reading and writing stories even before they enter first grade. I want to establish branch libraries all over this county. Every one from eight to eighty should have easy access to great works of literature or reference material for whatever project that happens to interest them. And I want to make those books and reference materials easily available, maybe even delivered to their door." Mary took a deep breath. "Excuse me, Hans. I tend to dominate the conversation when I start talking about my dreams for St. Joseph County. You just got here and here I am telling you my life plans. I'm glad to see you, Hans," she said as she took both my hands in hers. "I apologize for coming on a little too strong when you first walked in, but the older I get, it seems the more impulsive I get."

"I couldn't be happier that you are glad to see me," I said. I'll admit I was a bit surprised. Her letters were friendly but that kiss she gave me made me think there was a chance we might become more than just friends. She must have read my thoughts.

"Hans, let's take one step at a time. All either of us have to go on is a memory of those days of love before Susie Goodall entered the picture. But now that we're on the subject, let me say this; when it comes to relationships, I insist on fidelity. That doesn't mean that I'm possessive. I just think a serious relationship should be monogamous. But it's way too early for us to be talking about commitment. You just got here. Do you think you'll have any time for a social life?"

"Like you, I have great ambitions and will probably be working some long hours for a while, but I hope we can squeeze in some time to see each other."

"I'd like that," she said. "Hans, I'm going to have to leave now. I have an appointment with the vice-mayor to discuss some funding issues. I'm sorry but I have to go."

"Oh, that's alright. I should have called you before I came today. Can I see you sometime this weekend?"

"Maybe. Call me." Mary grabbed her jacket and waved and smiled as she rushed past me. I stood outside her office door trying to make sense of what had just happened. The most beautiful girl in Indiana just kissed me and I liked it a lot.

South Bend's weather can run the gamut from bitter cold to blazing hot. But most days, there is a nice breeze off Lake Michigan. That Tuesday's drive out Western Avenue toward the Studebaker Proving Ground was one of those perfect spring days we look forward to all winter. I was feeling wonderful. I didn't have a care in the world. All four windows of my hardtop coupe were rolled down and both front fender vents were opened. The breeze was delightful. As the old stone fence surrounding the Proving Ground came into view, I felt peaceful and secure. Maybe, just maybe, I had finally found my permanent home here in South Bend. From my boyhood home in Magdeburg to my student days in Berlin to my jobs in Wolfsburg, South Bend and Huntsville, no place seemed quite right until now. Sure, I had spent several years in South Bend before but there was always trouble; the murders of Benny Goodall and Roy Branson and of course my fights with Big Mike Levy. My biggest problem during that time was I was not myself. I was a dead boy from Ft. Worth, Texas. But now, I was me and I had a great job and a chance to develop the car I'd always dreamed of. What could possibly go wrong? I wheeled into the front gate, still topped by the stone Studebaker wheels. I stopped beside the tattered old guard shack. The overweight guard looking just as tattered in his too small uniform stepped up to my open window.

"Hello, Frank," I said as he leaned down to see the one who knew his name. Frank seemed confused, like he was supposed to know me but couldn't put the face and the name together.

"What is your name and business, sir?"

"I'm Hans Werner. I'll be working here at the Proving Ground starting today. Didn't Mr. Nitske's office call and tell you I was coming?"

"Let me check."

As he stepped back into his hut, I called out, "I'll be in the shop with Ed Reynolds if there's a problem." I drove away as Frank stepped back out into the drive to breathe my dust and exhaust fumes. Guards don't like their power challenged but I felt too eager to get started to wait for Frank to give me permission to enter.

"Well, here I am again," I said to a smiling Ed Reynolds.

"Yeah, just like a bad nickel you keep turning up." Ed extended his hand. "I'm joking, Hans. It's good to see you, my friend. Welcome back."

"Thanks, Ed. If it weren't for people like you and Bob Nitske, I think Studebaker would have been out of business years ago."

"Oh, I wouldn't say that. There are a lot of good people working for Studebaker-Packard. Nitske tells me you're going to work on a small car like the one you developed several years ago. That right?"

"Sure is. Do you have some mechanics that can help me?"

"Yep! Nitske told me to give you all the assistance I can. Boy, news travels fast concerning your rejoining Studebaker. Someone called yesterday and asked to speak to Hans Werner. I was certainly surprised to hear your name. This was even before Bob Nitske called to say you would be here today. I asked for a name and number but the party hung up or maybe we were just cut off for some reason."

"Ed, you are a good soul. You seem to always give people the benefit of the doubt."

"Yes, I guess I do. Gets me in trouble sometimes." I spent the rest of the day meeting the mechanics and making preliminary sketches of the small car I planned to build. The 104" wheelbase and the four-cylinder engine were not negotiable. Since the design of the original Freda prototype was well received at the Chicago auto show and its aluminum body was probably in reasonably good shape, I figured I'd save time by using the old body. I requested that the two halves be brought in from the wooded area where they were dumped. Ed summoned a wrecker driver. I rode with him out to the wooded area in the center of the large oval test track.

The foliage had grown considerably since I last entered that clump of trees and bushes. I directed the driver to back as close as possible to the area I guessed the two halves of Freda would be. He stopped and killed the engine. He said he didn't want to back in further. He didn't want to puncture his tires. I knew there was little danger of that. My guess was he just didn't want to bother backing through the bushes. I got out and I picked my way through the foliage. The graveyard of old wrecks seemed to have taken on its own life. Nothing was as I remembered. Freda's two halves were nowhere to be seen. Prototypes that I hadn't seen before were nestled low in the grass and bushes as if to hide from intruders. Designers' forgotten dreams were turned over to the heavy hand of Mother Nature awaiting her undignified disposal. A pickup truck made using the front end of a sedan, an early postwar station wagon with wooden paneling rotting away and a more recent sleek 1950 bullet-nose front clip with no rear end all blocked my way as I searched for Freda. I looked back to see the driver sitting high on the fender of his wrecker smoking a cigarette. I slowly picked my way through the underbrush, hoping not to step on a snake. Finally, in a location I didn't remember, I spotted Freda's front end.

"Oh, Freda! There you are." I guess I expected her horn to blow but it didn't. Of course not, her battery was safely stowed in my room at Mrs. Kitchall's boarding house.

"You say something, mister?" the driver shouted.

"Yes, I found half the car I was looking for. You think your cable will reach this far?"

"Don't know, we'll see." He threw the winch in neutral and walked the cable and hook out to where I stood. "What ya wanna drag this old piece of a wreck back for?"

I was in no mood to discuss my long-term strategy with this ignoramus, so I just said, "You'll see, my friend. In time, you'll see." I started to loop the cable around the rear of the transmission.

"Whoa! Hold up there, mister. Put that hook down. That's union work."

"Union work? What the hell are you talking about?" I shouted.

"It's in the contract. Salaried personnel can't touch my equipment. You looking for a grievance or something?"

"I thought all Proving Ground employees were non-union."

"Not drivers. Besides, Ed Reynolds ain't my boss. Now you want me to drag this piece of shit back to the garage or not?"

"Okay, just do your job." The driver hooked up the cable and slowly strolled back to the wrecker to engage the winch. With flat tires,

Freda's front half wobbled and jumped, nearly flipping over a couple of times before it reached the wrecker. I walked behind, hoping the surly driver wouldn't damage Freda's body any more than the weather already had. Like a victim of the gallows, Freda spun and jerked as she was hoisted into the air.

"When you get back to the garage, ask Ed Reynolds where he wants the car to be placed," I said. "By the time you get back, I'll have found the other half."

"It's time for my break, pal, sos don't expect me back for another thirty or forty minutes." I cursed under my breath knowing if I complained it would slow things down further. I began my search for Freda's back half.

By the time both halves were safely inside the garage, it was five o'clock. The wrecker driver left without a word. That was fine with me. Ed Reynolds had assigned two mechanics to my project. For tomorrow's work, I directed them to remove the aluminum body and weld and reinforce the frame back together. With that understanding, we all left for home. I could have hung around and worked on the new prototype's design but I was eager to drive my new '53 Studebaker. Oh, how I loved that car. I felt fortunate. I knew it wouldn't have been possible without Wally's inheritance.

Back in my room, I dialed Mary. Even though she lived with her parents, she had her own number.

"Mary, I'm glad I caught you."

"Oh, Hans. How was your first day at work?"

"Alright, I guess. I had my original prototype car rescued from the scrap heap. I hope to use many of its parts on the new prototype. What's happening in the wonderful world of books?"

"I'm so excited, Hans. Good things are starting to happen. I suggested to the board today that we put a large ad in the newspaper with a clip out opinion survey to gage public interest in some of my ideas. They agreed but said the cost of the ad would have to be paid for by the library. We couldn't spare the money so I talked to the St. Joseph Gazette editor about printing the survey as a part of a feature story about expanding county library services. The editor went for the idea in a big way. He's even considering a front page article."

"That's great, Mary. I'm so proud of you. When is this going to happen?"

"I hope it will run in the next day or two. I'm leaving town on Saturday morning for a conference in Washington."

"Do you have plans for Friday night?" I asked.

"If you're asking me for a date, the answer is 'I'm available, except it'll have to be an early evening. My plane leaves at 6:15 the next morning."

"Okay. We'll just go to dinner and then I'll get you back home early."

"Fine. Pick me up at six-thirty?"

"Sure. 'Can't wait to see you, Mary. Did I mention I bought a new car?"

"No, you didn't! I guess I'll see it Friday. Bye, bye, Baby."

"See you Friday." She called me "Baby." Wow!

Funny how a clear mind lets one relax. As I snuggled into my bed, my thoughts turned to Mary and that kiss she gave me at the library. The taste of her lips aroused a passion in me that had long been dormant. And best of all there were new dimensions to her personality. I never realized how smart and ambitious she was. She was unlikely to be clingy and jealous of my time if she had major interests of her own. And on top of all of that, she was soooo good looking. I loved her long brown hair and soft blue eyes. I drifted off to sleep as I pictured Mary sitting close beside me as we sped down the highway in my beautiful new Starliner hardtop coupe.

I jumped out of bed the next morning with a smile on my face. Mrs. Kirtchall's American breakfast was tasty and the smell and taste of her coffee was better than I remembered. I didn't tarry over a second cup though. I was eager to get in my Studebaker and head to my new job. As I unlocked the door, my euphoria was shattered. The windshield was broken. A thousand chards of shattered glass covered the seat and floorboard. Although the safety glass had left the bulk of the windshield in its frame, there was a hole completely through on the driver's side. The visibility to the front was nearly impossible. My guess was a hammer did the dirty deed. It was obvious I still had enemies in South Bend. This was no random act. I looked around for some clue. No other cars in the lot were damaged. I thought of calling the police but decided it would be a waste of time. Besides, they would probably require that I get the windshield replaced before driving the car. I slowly drove to the Proving Ground peeping through the hole to avoid running into anyone. I wondered if Big Mike had anything to do with the vandalism. I knew he had a huge grudge against me, but I didn't think he would personally risk being seen and possibly linked to this childish prank. He was too smart for that. But still, who else knew I was back at Studebaker and wanted to discourage me from staying? Whoever did this would probably not end it with that one act. If Big Mike hired someone to break my windshield, who might it be? Willie Wyatt perhaps? As I turned into the gate of the grounds, Frank, the guard, stepped out to see who I was. He probably couldn't see my pass taped to the inside of the broken windshield.

"Morning, Mr. er, Hans. Got a busted windshield, huh? Better get that fixed."

"Thanks, Frank. I'll do that, first chance I get." Ed Reynolds' two assigned mechanics were already hard at work on the frame of the prototype car. Most of the aluminum body had been removed and sit aside. As I came over to say "Good morning," they were lining up the frame halves getting ready to weld them together. Ed spotted me and walked over.

"Hello, Hans. How are you today?"

"Not so good Ed. Someone broke out the windshield of my new Studebaker last night."

"Sorry to hear that. Do you think it was random or has someone got it in for you?"

"I'm not sure, but my guess is this is somehow related to my anti-union views."

"Yeah, maybe."

"Well, in my opinion, they have got to be reigned in soon or Studebaker will go out of business. Our union workers are the highest paid in the industry, while we are trying to compete with larger companies that have much greater volumes. That is not a formula for success."Ed looked at the floor.

"If you don't mind, I'd like to change the subject, Hans. Do you want me to order you another windshield?"

"Yes, I would appreciate that. But make sure it is charged to me personally rather than my project. Some people would like nothing better than to catch me charging a personal expense to the company."

"Okay, but at least, let my boys put it in for you." I pulled my car inside the garage and started to remove the broken glass and the polished stainless windshield trim myself. Ed grabbed my arm and said, "Hold on there Hans, don't try to remove the trim. You'll bend it for sure unless you remove the whole windshield and its rubber at the same time. Here, let me show you." I accepted his help and thanked him for saving me from ruining my bright work. After about an hour, the new windshield arrived and Ed's mechanics installed it in about ten minutes. I stood in awe at the ease it was accomplished. One man wrapped a heavy cord in the groove of the rubber molding, placed the bottom edge of the molding and the new windshield in the frame, pulled the string and the windshield fell perfectly into place. I could tell they had done this job many times before. I felt lucky to have these two on my team.

CHAPTER 43

Iknew I was asking for trouble when I pulled into the Little Brown Jug parking lot that afternoon. But some irresistible force drew me in. I guess I wanted to see if I would be recognized after all this time or maybe I thought I could pick up some useful bits of information. In any case, I felt like going in was worth the risk. The place hadn't changed a bit. Smoke hung beneath the ceiling like a dark cumulus cloud. Studebaker factory workers were yelling and singing just as I remembered. Only instead of singing *Pistol Packin' Mama* they were singing along with *Shake, Rattle and Roll*. I headed for the bar and ordered a Drewry. Glancing around, looking for a face I might recognize, I saw Willie Wyatt at the same time he saw me. He immediately looked away when our eyes met. It seemed strange to me. I bided my time at the bar figuring he would eventually be unable to resist the temptation to come speak to me. In about ten minutes, Willie walked over. He had gained a few pounds especially around the middle. His face was red and a little puffy. I could tell he was pretty drunk when he leaned close and said, "Well, I'll be damned, if the kraut ain't back in town. I thought you went to Germany years ago."

"You are correct, Willie. But Studebaker wanted me back."

"Well, I don't know what for. What 'cha workin' on, Van?"

"Willie, I'm surprised you don't know my real name. It's Hans Werner."

"Hans, what? What happened to Van Hoffmann?"

"He never existed."

"I don't understand," Willie said.

"Never mind. Buy you a beer?" Willie recoiled as if I had insulted him.

"I can buy my own goddamn beer, Adolf, or what ever to hell your name is."

"Be nice, Willie. If I were you, I'd stay on my good side. I still have that recording implicating you in the Benny Goodall murder. I could turn it over to the police and with your present attitude, maybe I will. Of course, if you'll tell the police who paid you the $200 for a duplicate set of keys to Benny's car, that recording will never see the light of day."

"Dammit all, I don't know why I came over here. You're still the same ass hole you always were. You'd better watch your back, pal. Bad stuff is gonna keep happening 'til you leave this here town." I didn't respond. Willie returned to his table of friends. I nursed my beer trying to determine if Willie had given me any new information. He hadn't said much of value except he did say that bad things would keep happening. How did he know anything had already happened? I finished my beer and started to leave. Willie stood up and rushed over. He stepped in between the door and me.

"Why don't you and me just step outside and get this thing over with?" he slurred.

"Are you suggesting we fight, Willie?"

"That's zackly what I'm 'gesting, kraut!"

"In your inebriated condition, it wouldn't be much of a fight," I said. "Besides, it wouldn't solve anything. You'd still be a stooge for Big Mike. I can't believe you are stupid enough to continue to do his dirty work for him." The veins in Willie's neck popped out. I could tell he wanted to respond but was too drunk to come up with a good retort. "Speaking of stupid, did you know you broke the windshield out of the wrong car last night? Did you think I was crazy enough to leave my new car in Mrs. Kitchall's parking lot? You screwed up, Willie. And you're about to screw up again. You'd better go back to your drunken friends before you get hurt."

"I ain't a screed of you, Van."

"Oh, Willie. It hasn't been two minutes since I told you my name was Hans and now you've already forgotten it. Are you stupid, drunk or both?" Willie's eyes widened, he grimaced and took a wild swing at me. I ducked and he lost his balance and fell across a table and onto the floor. His friends who were watching all stood up. Some were laughing but some seemed angry. They all headed in my direction. I didn't know if they intended to pick Willie up or to beat me up. I didn't wait to find out. My car threw gravel as I sped onto the main road. I quickly turned onto a side street and turned my lights off. I sat there for a couple of minutes. It appeared I wasn't being followed.

Chapter 44

Mary looked radiant and happy when she appeared at her front door Friday afternoon. In the presence of her mother and father she only gave me a kiss on the cheek. I hoped for more later. Dinner at the Indiana Café was very pleasant. Mary tactfully divided her conversation between questions about my years in Germany, my new job at Studebaker and her plans for library services in St. Joseph County. I loved being with her. She seemed to hold no animosity about my indiscretions years ago with Susie Goodall. I was amazed at the candor Mary expressed. This was a lady that knew what she wanted and seemed determined to get it. Since she had to get up very early the next morning, I took her straight home after dinner.

As we pulled into her driveway she scooted close to me and said, "Hans, you are the kind of man I've been looking for. You seem to be a person who has ambition and knows how to achieve his goals. Unless I've misjudged you completely, I think you prefer a woman who also wants to accomplish something in life. If you will promise to be true to me, I'll promise the same to you. I'm really looking forward to getting to know you a lot better." My passion rose as I considered the possibilities. As soon as I killed the engine, Mary wrapped her arms around me and kissed me long and deep. "When I get back from Washington, I'll call you," she said. "How would you like to spend next weekend in Chicago with me? Daddy has an apartment at the Palmer House we can use. It would be fun getting away for a couple of days, don't you think? We could tour the city, maybe see a play, and eat at the Stockyards. I know you like good steaks and theirs are the best in the world. What do you say?" I sat speechless for a moment, basking in my good fortune.

"Mary, that sounds wonderful, I can't wait." With another kiss she was out my car and into her house. She didn't even wait for me to walk her to the door. That was fortunate. I would have had to walk like Groucho Marx. If this wasn't love, it was a reasonable facsimile thereof I said to myself.

I went back to my room and turned my attention to the Studebaker Corporation. As difficult as it was to get Mary out of my mind, I realized I had to focus. I knew from my discussions with Bob Nitske that the company was in bad shape financially. Low sales and high labor costs were the primary reasons. With the impending purchase of Studebaker by the Packard Corporation, the situation wasn't likely to improve. Packard's sales had also slipped over the past few years and Packard was long overdue for a major body redesign. Introduction of my new small economy car and its associated tooling costs would make the cash deficit even worse. I could see no way either company could survive without a huge infusion of capital. That wasn't likely in view of declining sales and increasing losses. There seemed to be no easy answer so I went to bed. There was so much on my mind. I couldn't go to sleep wondering about my future at Studebaker. If the company started making drastic cuts, my project might be the first to go. Every idea I came up with to save the company seemed to have major flaws. Then, all of a sudden, I had a mental breakthrough. I jumped out of bed, turned on the light and started to write. Based on my experience, in no particular order, I listed the following truisms:

#1. The width of all full size cars whether low-priced or luxury is near the same.

#2. The length of vehicles in America is almost directly proportional to the cost.

#3. The prestige or "snob factor" is determined by the design, length of the car, appointments, engine size, quality and the vehicle's name.

#4. Most parts suppliers have lower wage rates than union plants like Studebaker and Packard.

#5. Most parts suppliers would be happy to combine components into sub-assemblies and ship them to Studebaker-Packard ready to install on the vehicle assembly line. This is the technique Henry J. Kaiser used in WWII to quickly assemble Liberty ships. The challenge is close coordination and "just-in-time" scheduling.

#6. If only the wheelbase length of the three lines was different, many component sub-assemblies could be the same for all three makes; Packard, Studebaker and the new compact car I am developing. As an example, the vehicle owner would not know or care that the wheels for all three lines were identical 15" diameter or that master cylinders and steering gears were the same for all three makes.

#7. I'd use a 104" wheelbase for the low-priced compact cars and perhaps later a sports car, 116" for the mid-priced Studebaker line and 121" for the luxury Packard line and Hawks.

#8. Common mounting holes would allow for shock absorbers, rocker arms, steering gears, etc. to be standardized for all three lines. Transmissions and differentials could be the same on Studebakers and Packards.

#9. Doors and some body panels could be used on two or in some cases all three lines. Naturally, engines, radiators, brakes, springs, etc. would be different based on the vehicle's size and weight.

#10. Vehicle identification would be mostly visual. As an example, the traditional ox-yoke grille shape of the late 1930s Packard would denote it as a luxury brand. Studebakers would look more like Buicks or Oldsmobiles. Except for being a more modern design with slab sides (no individual fenders), my economy car would look somewhat like a Volkswagen.

#11. Engines for all three lines would be overhead valve type using as many existing components as possible such as pistons and valves from the present 232cid V-8. The compact line would have four cylinders. The Studebaker line would have either a six cylinder or use the present 232cid V-8. The Packard would be a 289 cid V-8 version using the same block as the 232. Later increases in displacement could be accomplished without new engine castings.

By using outside vendors for much of the assembly of components and strict adherence to standardization of parts between lines, costs will be drastically reduced. Standardization will mean larger volume runs, lower costs and lower break-even numbers. I believe that taking a major strike to reduce labor costs would sink the company. The above plan is our only chance for survival.

I went over and over the above plan, looking for flaws. What would Bob Nitske think, I wondered? I turned out the light and went back to bed. But it was no use. I was too excited to go back to sleep. I thought of getting up again. After all, I had all day tomorrow to rest. My better judgment told me to stay in bed. I would need tomorrow to reevaluate the plan with a fresh, rested eye. Hopefully, I would be able to present it to Nitske on Monday.

After arriving at the Proving Ground and checking on the progress of my prototype vehicle, Monday morning, I called Bob Nitske's office. Luckily, I caught him as he was leaving for a meeting.

"Yes, Hans. What's up? Make it fast. I'm on my way to a board meeting."

"Bob, over the weekend, I came up with a plan that I think will save Studebaker-Packard from extinction, even without a reduction in union wages. I'd like to present it to you as soon as possible. I don't think we can afford to delay."

"Think you can guarantee world peace and end poverty in Africa at the same time?" he said with a chuckle.

"I'm serious, Bob. With our merger with Packard, this plan is essential to our survival!"

"Hans, I have a full schedule all this week. Can you send me a write-up of what you have in mind? I'll read it at home and let you know what I think."

"Yes, sure," I said. "All I have now is rough hand-written notes. Could your secretary type it up for me?"

"Yeah, okay, gotta go, Hans. Sorry." He hung up. I gathered my notes and drove to Nitske's office. After Mrs. Holden finished typing my plan, I read it over. There were no mistakes. She promised to hand it to Mr. Nitske the moment he walked back into the office.

The next couple of days were agonizing. There was no word from Nitske. What did the long wait mean? Finally, he called.

"Hans, I want you to come to my office right away. I'm having a meeting with all the members of my staff."

"What's up, Bob?"

"You'll find out. Just be here within the next 45 minutes." After telling my technicians where I was going, I bumped into Ed Reynolds on the way to my car.

"You headed for Nitske's meeting, Hans?"

"Yes, I am. Do you know what it's about?" I asked.

"Not really, but my guess is it has to do with re-organization. You can bet Packard is going to want to reduce staff by combining some jobs."

"I don't like the sound of that," I said. "You want to ride with me?"

As we drove into town, a sprinkle of rain dampened my new windshield. The dark clouds overhead made the Engineering Building look drab and unkept. Walking into the front door I wondered how many years it had been since the bricks were cleaned and the woodwork painted. Why was I worried about building maintenance when my job might be at stake? Ed and I must have been the last to arrive. Mrs. Holden shut Nitski's door.

"Thank you for hurrying over on such short notice, gentlemen. I am aware that I may have interrupted important projects for this 'spur-of-the-moment' meeting, but I will assure you it's necessary." I looked around Nitske's smoke-filled office and noticed solemn faces nodding in agreement. I guessed everyone was worried about his own job. Bob continued, "With Packard's purchase of Studebaker, we now have a new president, Mr. Vance Jamison. As you probably know, he's been Packard's president for the past five years. As a result of the purchase, there have been a number of reassignments and promotions. I've been promoted to Vice President of Product Engineering for the combined Studebaker-Packard Corporation. Manufacturing Engineering will be a part of the Production Department from now on. There are to be more changes announced later. Our Product Engineering group will be responsible for S-P product planning, product design and styling, product testing, component engineering and testing with dotted line responsibility for component procurement. Hans Werner and I will share the product planning function. Being the boss, I will hold veto power over all long-range decisions," Bob said flashing a big smile. Nervous obligatory chuckles followed. "Hans will also be responsible for product design and styling. Ed Reynolds will be in charge of all vehicle and component testing and Randall Owens of Packard will serve as Manager of Component Engineering." He continued to read other assignments and then said, "After this meeting, Mrs. Holden will pass out a table of organization for the total department so that we all know where everyone fits. We will not have reductions in engineering personnel right away, but as you new managers get to know your people, some reductions will probably be required. I will schedule meetings with each department manager as soon as possible. I know you have a lot of questions, but please hold them until your individual meeting. Most of you can expect to spend some long hours in the next few weeks. So don't be surprised if the schedule of department deadlines will require a bit of midnight oil. I assure you, our very survival as a corporation depends on what happens in the next year or two. We are depending on all of you to skillfully plan and execute a strategy that will cause our new company to survive and prosper. I wish you all the best. Before you leave, please check with Mrs. Holden for your meeting schedule." With those parting words, Bob Nitske rose, stuffed some papers in his briefcase and left a room full of anxious engineers. I was happy about my promotion. It was almost certain that my new idea for standardization and purchasing of sub-assemblies was accepted otherwise I would not have been given responsibility for overall corporate vehicle design. I picked up my copy of the table of organization and Nitski's schedule of meetings. On the meetings schedule sheet I saw the item that ruined all the good news. I was scheduled to meet with Nitski on Saturday afternoon at four o'clock. After all these years, I finally had the chance to spend the night with Mary. Best of all, it was her idea. Maybe I could ask Nitski to change the schedule. I walked over to Mrs. Holden's desk.

"Pardon me, Mrs. Holden. Is there any chance Mr. Nitski's meeting schedule can be moved around. I already have a commitment for this coming Saturday."

"I'm afraid not, Mr. Werner. Mr. Nitski specifically told me not to make any changes. He said he had reasons for the sequence and any changes would be counterproductive. I'm sorry." I nodded a "thank you" and walked away. I knew if I missed the Saturday meeting, my whole future might be affected. But what would I tell Mary? After I dropped off Ed, I was so distracted, I don't even remember driving home. I kept wondering how I was going to explain things to Mary. Minutes after I walked into my room, my telephone rang.

"Hi baby, I'm back." Mary's voice was animated. I was afraid my news would dampen her perky attitude so I procrastinated.

"How was your trip?"

"It was terrific. I picked up a ton of new ideas. I can't wait to tell you about it. How's the new job going?"

"Oh fine. I just got a promotion. I'm to be in charge of product design for the whole Studebaker-Packard Corporation. I turned in a plan to introduce new models without spending a lot of money the company doesn't have. I guess that's the reason I got the job."

"Wow! That's terrific, Hans. We've got a lot to celebrate this weekend. All I've been thinking about is finally getting to know you a lot better, everything about you. I get excited just thinking about it."

"Yes, me too. But I'm afraid I have some really bad news. I have to work this Saturday afternoon and won't be able to go to Chicago. I'm really sorry, Mary. I tried to get out of it but to no avail." The quiet of the next few moments seemed an eternity. Finally, Mary responded.

"I can't tell you how disappointed I am, Hans. I know how important your job is to you but that doesn't make it any easier for me." After another long pause, she said, "Maybe we'll both be free for some future weekend."

"Could I see you Sunday afternoon, Mary? I really do have some things I'd like to talk to you about." There was another pause. Then in a very soft voice she said,

"Call me when you get out of your meeting Saturday and we'll talk. I'm a little upset right now. I gotta go. Goodbye, Hans." I slowly placed the phone back into its cradle. Could this one incident be reason enough for a breakup? If so, the relationship probably wouldn't have lasted anyway. But I knew I was crazy about the girl! I couldn't let her get away. I hoped when I called Saturday, she wouldn't be so upset.

* * * * * * * * * *

My meeting with Nitski started promptly at four o'clock and lasted three uninterrupted hours. The reason for my promotion was my proposal for the three lines of vehicles using many standard Studebaker parts and letting outside vendors provide many ready-to-use sub-assemblies. He wanted to know everything about my plan. This was difficult since I had not yet thought though every aspect of the project. Fortunately, Nitski said my staff would be large enough to help me move the project along and not have to personally be involved in every detail. Even with a staff of engineers, the magnitude of the project seemed overwhelming. Bob asked probing questions proving he was a well-qualified automotive engineer. As was common knowledge, the company's cash position was near zero so only cost-saving changes could be considered. Even though high labor costs would continue to be a big problem, transfer of sub-assemblies to vendors would be high priority and would help reduce costs in the long run. My first task would be the basic layout of all three lines of new vehicles; the Packards, the Studebakers, and the new Freedom economy car on similar but different-length wheelbases. Toward seven o'clock, we were both getting very tired and hungry so Bob said we could meet again in a couple of days. Before we parted, he admitted that my plan was a big factor in his own promotion. Therefore, for many reasons, the plan had to work and work quickly. I was so distracted thinking about the project, I missed a turn driving home. It was eight-thirty when I finally dialed Mary's number.

"I'd about given up on you, Hans," she said. "Where have you been?"

"The meeting lasted over three hours. It was exhausting. I'm afraid this job is going to be extremely demanding for the foreseeable future. Even so, I'll have to admit, Mary, I feel more alive and useful than I have in a long time. I guess I'm almost as enthusiastic about my new job as you are yours. Unfortunately, it looks like our time together is going to be limited for awhile." I held my breath. I had no idea how she would respond.

I was relieved when she said, "I understand, Hans. I'm sorry I got so upset the other night when you told me you couldn't go to Chicago. I'm human and don't like to be disappointed. Being an only child in a wealthy family, I guess I'm a little spoiled. I'll admit I have almost always gotten my way. I've come to expect it. I've never been a good loser. Show me a good loser and I'll show you a frequent loser. That's just not my style."

"That's part of your appeal, Mary. Plus, you're the prettiest and sweetest girl I've ever met. I feel lucky to even have a chance to be your boy friend. So, how about dinner tomorrow night?"

"Oh, you smooth talking devil. How can I resist such charm?"

"You're teasing me now aren't you?" I said. "I know I'm not very good at romance. I admit it. I've never known how to act around women. I know my way around automobiles, but women, well that's another story."

"Well, you learned to kiss pretty well somewhere along the way," Mary said with a chuckle.

"Hey, how about dinner tomorrow night?" I repeated.

"OK, OK, lover boy. See you at seven."

"Good night, Mary. Sweet dreams. See you tomorrow."

CHAPTER 45

As I think back, there was so much going on in those next few weeks, it all runs together into one big blur. Interviewing engineers, meetings with Bob Nitski, design and construction of the new Freedom prototype, planning and early design work on the 1957 Studebaker and Packard cars and selecting the sub-assemblies to be produced by outside vendors took almost every spare minute and every ounce of energy that I had. Somehow, all tasks stayed on schedule. Most amazing, Mary and I found time for an occasional date. She and I finally got our weekend in Chicago only four weeks from the originally planned date. Those precious days with Mary in the windy city were everything I had hoped for and more. We pledged our love to each other and proved it in almost every way imaginable except one. Marriage was never mentioned. I think we both intuitively knew that good marriages take a lot of work and time which at this stage of our lives and careers we didn't have.

The day after Mary and I got back from Chicago, I got a call from George Burgdorf. He said he wanted to talk to me away from Mary and the family. He said to meet him at the Indiana Café at 7 pm that next night. He mentioned that Virgil Norman would be joining us. When I asked what this was all about, he said he didn't want to go into it over the phone. That night and the next day I was distracted and filled with anxiety. Was Burgdorf upset about Mary and my trip to Chicago? How could that be? He let us use his hotel suite, didn't he? Or maybe he was worried his little girl was getting too serious about a guy who might get killed by someone in the union. And most perplexing, why was he bringing his lawyer along?

When I arrived at 6:55, they were already there. I noticed their drinks were almost empty. A smiling George Burgdorf stood and extended his hand. A wave of relief swept over me like a cool breeze in July. Virgil Norman also stood and shook my hand.

"Well, Hans, I'll bet your curiosity is killing you," Burgdorf said with a chuckle. "Virg and I are not above having a little fun at someone else's expense as long as there's no real harm done. So now you can relax, we'll get you a drink and then we'll talk business. What'll you have?"

I hesitated and finally said, "Whatever you're having, I guess." Burgdorf held up three fingers to a waiter who was watching the table like a sentinel. Shortly, the young man returned with three martinis. They arrived in large frosty glasses. Two green olives on polished wooden stirrers rested just above the edge of each glass. I had never had a martini before but suspected this was my chance to have one of the best. Burgdorf proposed a toast.

"Here's to the future of an up and coming young automotive engineer whose innovations may help save the Studebaker-Packard Corporation." Slightly embarrassed, I clicked my glass against the other two.

"Those are very kind words, sir," I said. Save the corporation? I couldn't believe what I had just heard. I tried desperately to find the right words to reply. After an awkward pause I said, "I hope I can live up to your trust." We all took a sip of our drinks. The gin burned as it slid down my throat, but it tasted surprisingly good. It occurred to me that I could get use to drinking martinis. George Burgdorf cleared his throat.

"Hans, I'll get right to the point of why I asked you to join us tonight. In order for you to reach your potential here in South Bend, there are several things that must be done. First, you've got to become a U. S. citizen. That's where Virgil comes in. If you don't break any laws, we should be able to obtain citizenship for you in about a year. One thing that could kill your chances for citizenship is confrontation with the union. I suggest you stay clear of Mike Levy and all his cronies. We are aware he has it in for you. Our sources have reported that he wants to get rid of you one way or another. For our town's sake as well as the happiness of my daughter, we can't let anything happen to you." I sat quietly, sipping my martini following every word this wealthy businessman had to say. "If you and your colleagues can save the company, I see you as one of the future pillows of this community. But as you have pointed out to me before, the union can ruin the best-laid plans. There are some good people in the union that do a day's work for a day's pay. But there are way too many that follow Mike Levy blindly and seem not to care that they are killing the company with their high wages and poor work habits. Virgil and I agree a more reasonable union president would probably accept the wage cuts that Vance Jamison is planning to implement, but not Levy. So, again, you stay away from Levy. Virgil and I will try to figure out some way to legally get him out of that job."

I was beginning to feel the alcohol and spoke loudly without thinking. "Mr. Burdorf, Mike Levy is a psychopath. And worse, he's a murderer! He just hasn't been caught yet."

"Whoa there, Hans. Be careful what you say," Virgil Norman cautioned. "Even though we are meeting tonight in confidence, any accusation might be overheard."

Burgdorf added, "Hans, I repeat, Mike Levy is not your problem. Let us handle him. And lastly, it is obvious that my little Mary is crazy about you and she usually gets what she wants. She sees your potential just as Virg and I do, so don't let us down."

"I'll do my best, sir." I took another sip of my drink. I was feeling powerful.

"Ever been to an American football game, Hans?" Burgdorf asked.

"No sir, I haven't. I've seen portions of games on movie news reels but never the real thing."

"We'll have to do something about that," he said.

Virg Norman spoke up. "Right here in little ole South Bend we have the best college football team in the country. The team's winning record goes way back. Ever heard of Knute Rockne? The greatest football coach of all time."

"No, sir. I'm afraid I know nothing of American football," I answered. "I do know that Studebaker had a Rockne automobile in 1932, any connection?"

Burgdorf laughed. "Yes, there certainly is. You'll find that most people in this town follow 'the Fighting Irish' of Notre Dame and Albert Erskine, the president of Studebaker in '32, was no exception. But I'm afraid I disagree with you Virg, on who was the greatest coach of all time. Let's not forget that Frank Leahy has the second highest winning percentage of any college coach in history. Hell, Leahy had four national championships and six undefeated seasons."

"Listen to me, George. You remember that '46 game with Army?"

"Do I?" Burgdorf responded. "That was the best game ever. It's still called the 'Game of the Century'. Both teams were undefeated and were rated one and two in the nation. You and I hadn't known each other very long but we traveled to New York together just to see that game. 'Doc' Blanchard, Glenn Davis, Arnold Tucker, God what a backfield Army had. But we had Johnny Lujack, one of the greatest quarterbacks of all time." I sat quietly as these two old friends rehashed that 1946 game. They seemed to remember every major play but never mentioned who won.

"How did the game turn out?" I asked. They looked at each other and smiled.

"Unbelievably, neither team scored. But man, what a game!" Norman said.

"How long have you two been friends?" I asked.

"We met during the war. How about another martini, Hans?" Mr. Burgdorf asked. "Thank you, sir, that would be swell."

Chapter 46

Both the new 1955 Studebakers and Packards were simply facelifts of the '54 bodies. These designs had already been approved before I was employed. Since Studebaker considered the Raymond Loewy Design Agency too expensive, its contract was dropped in early '54 and a young free-lance designer named Vince Gardner was hired to restyle the Studebaker sedans. He only charged $7500 for the entire job that included a full-size clay model and drawings. I thought he did a good job and I planned to use his basic body design for both the 1957 Studebaker and Packard lines. According to my original proposal to Bob Nitske, using Gardner's design was really our only choice. The real challenge was to add styling changes to establish corporate identity without it being obvious that the Packards were simply redesigned Studebakers. Without spending a great amount of money that seemed an almost impossible task.

By January of 1955, cobbled up versions of all three lines were buzzing around the test track at all hours of the day and night. The mechanical testing and acceptance of styling finally convinced the board of directors to approve limited tooling for the three lines of vehicles for the1957 model year. Still, a million details and loose ends plagued the project. Some nights I worked straight through only grabbing a few hours sleep on an army cot Ed had set up for me in the Proving Ground garage. The workload was demanding but the project was moving forward.

Vance Jamison, the new president of the combined Studebaker-Packard Corporation, was unhappy with the high wage rates of the factory employees. Unlike previous presidents, he took a stand. He informed the union that they must take a cut in pay to the level of Detroit autoworkers. Piecework incentive pay also had to be eliminated. In a lopsided vote, Big Mike Levy and the rank and file union workers said not only no, but "hell no!" to Jamison's proposal. On January 20, 1955, Local 9 of the UAW-CIO went on strike. The strike was devastating to S-Ps already poor bottom line. Fortunately, development work and testing on my three car lines continued since Proving Ground employees were non-union. By early February, the worried strikers were getting more militant and aggressive. Although there were never pickets at the Proving Ground, once or twice a week, I was required to attend a meeting at the main office downtown. I usually had no problem entering the Ad building except for one unusually warm and sunny day the second week in February. We got a phone call warning us that angry pickets surrounded the all factory entrances and the main entrance to the Administration Building. Legally, the union was prohibited from stopping salaried workers. But knowing that damage to our personal cars was a real possibility, Ed Reynolds and I rode together in one of the test vehicles. I had not seen Big Mike since I rejoined the company, but there he was along with the group of shouting pickets. Big Mike looking a bit heavier than I remembered was in the center of the steps talking to Willie Wyatt as Ed and I approached. Willie nudged Levy. Mike leaned on his cane as he turned to confront us.

He then shouted to the group, "Well boys, here comes the source of all our troubles! Does the kraut and his sidekick think they can run roughshod over our union brothers without a fight? If so, they've got another think coming, right boys?" The strikers cheered. We started walking up the stairs to the front door. Mike held his cane sideways blocking our way. "Where do you scabs think you're going? It's such a pretty day, why don't you just stay outside 'til the sun goes down? Me and the boys here will keep you company."

Ed spoke up. "Step aside, Levy. You know you can't lawfully block our way into this building."

"Watch me, Reynolds. You know, I use to think you were an OK guy 'til you started hanging out with this fuckin' Nazi." Mike then turned to me. "Have you burned any Jewish people lately, Adolf?"

"Not lately, Mike," I said. Levy's face turned red and veins popped out on his neck. Insults began to spew from his mouth like pent up vomit. I suspected he might explode at any moment. I tugged at Ed's arm and whispered in his ear.

"Let's go get the police, Ed. We're gonna get hurt if we try to force our way through this bunch of thugs." Ed nodded approval. As we left, jeers and vulgar shouts filled the air. I recognized Willie Wyatt's voice.

"Bye, bye scabs! See you in hell!" As we drove away, we heard stones pelting the rear of the car. The police were slow to respond to our call. With police escort we finally got back to the building an hour later. Big Mike and the strikers were gone.

The next day back at the Proving Ground was quiet. Ed and I labored over specification sheets and components alternatives. Ed was curious why my new Freedom car prototype did not perform as well as the Freda prototype of 1949. By this time, Ed and I had become good friends, so I felt close enough to him to reveal the secret power of Freda's heart.

"Could you still duplicate that power for Studebaker-Packard?" he asked.

"Oh, yes, I have remnants of the original battery at my boardinghouse. I restrict its exposure to air to keep its power from growing uncontrollably. When I took this job, I decided to rely only on my skills and knowledge and not depend on some freak of nature that I didn't know how to control. That's why I've used conventional lead-acid batteries in the new prototypes."

"Yes, I understand, but that 1949 prototype car performed so well. If your new four-cylinder Freedom car ran as well as that early prototype, it would be a big shot in the arm for the company. Maybe the zinc-air battery could be used in all our cars. Hell, Hans, we could jump to being one of the big three in no time. Don't you realize you hold the company's future in your hands?"

"It's not that simple, Ed. I just don't know how to control that battery. It's got an organic component you know. It's a living organism! It mutates extremely fast. Over time it has developed intelligence. Don't you remember the difficulties they had just hauling the prototype away from the Engineering Building? Survival is the first priority of all living things. That car, really the car's battery did not want to be destroyed. You wouldn't believe some of the escapades that vehicle pulled when I was living down in Huntsville. It even showed jealousy toward a new Henry J that I bought. And horsepower, oh my God. When I was at Volkswagen, I powered a stripped down VW using the starter motor from a German Tiger tank. The car ran fine powered only by the zinc-air battery and the tank's starter. But I'll tell you truthfully, a lot more research would have to be done before that battery could reliably be used in a commercial application."

That night I dug the canteen that contained Freda's heart out of my closet so I could check its power level. Hoping that renewing my interest in the battery would help me decide what to do next. I figured with Big Mike's hatred for me, I would be wise to take the battery and high voltage coil with me every time I left home. My volt/ohm meter showed Freda's heart still registering six volts with amperage enough to improve the performance of any car. I still did not fully understand how the battery gained its extraordinary power or why a car ran better with Freda's heart under the hood. I figured it had something to do with more complete combustion, but that was an unproven theory.

As the strike dragged on, tempers flared and not just between union and management but within the union itself. When I arrived at the garage on February 20th, Ed ran over to greet me waving the local morning paper.

"Look at this Hans," he shouted. "Looks like Big Mike is in trouble." Ed handed the paper to me and waited for my reaction. The headlines read, *"Union Local # 9 in Turmoil."* The article stated: *"Negotiations between S-P management and the local union had reached an impasse. In a statement from S-P president, Nance Jamison, he emphasized that without major wage concessions from the union, the company could no longer be able to compete in the American automotive marketplace. In contrast, Union president, Michael Levy said there was no chance the members of Local #9 would give up their hard earned wages and benefits to compensate for poor management. Although reporters were barred from entering the union hall last night, even outside they could hear shouts calling for a vote. After the meeting, several union members stated that they would rather be paid less and still have a job. One disgruntled man said, 'Big Mike won't even let us vote on it! That's un-American.' Another union member who asked not to be identified said he wished Levy would resign because his stand on the wage issue was going to put the company out of business."*

"What do you think is going to happen, Ed," I said. Ed squinted as he rubbed his chin.

"It's hard to say, Hans. From what I hear, the union is split down the middle on this, but Levy's refusal to let the issue come to a vote is illegal under union rules. I think its gonna backfire on him. It could even cost him his job."

Ed was right. Less than a week later when it was finally brought to a vote, wage cuts passed. Charges of breaking union rules were filed with the national UAW/CIO and Mike Levy was temporally relived pending a formal inquiry. The strikers returned to work on February 26th.

On the last day of February another news story about Levy ran in the morning paper. This time the headline read, *"Details of 1949 Auto Crash Revealed."* The article went on to say: *"The cause of the one-car accident in early January of 1949 which resulted in the death of Studebaker president and board chairman, Victor Harper involved details not revealed to the general public. The prototype vehicle driven by Union local president,*

Michael Levy left the road near Michigan City and tumbled down a steep embankment before coming to rest against a large tree. Based on an anonymous tip, investigative reporter, Jason Lasko of the South Bend Tribune staff was able to gain access to the Indiana State Police report written at the time of the accident. The report stated that Harper was dead when the police arrived and Levy was unconscious but not seriously hurt. There was little blood. Mike Levy's trousers were around his knees. A police photographer took pictures both inside and outside the vehicle. The interior photographs are no longer in the file. Miraculously, the car sustained little damage. When Lasko contacted Levy to explain the position of his clothing, Levy said it is quite common for shoes to fly off and clothing to change position in serious automobile accidents. Chief Ramsey of the state police agreed. He went on to say, 'The police are not obligated to make all the details of any accident available unless it is requested in writing.'"

After I read the article, I immediately called Virgil Norman. "Mr. Norman, I just read today's paper concerning the Indiana State police report of the 1949 wreck of my prototype car. Why do you think those details are just now being made public?"

"Hans, George and I told you when we had dinner with you a month ago that we would deal with the 'Mike Levy problem' and that you should just stay away from him and let us handle it. That advice still holds. You should concentrate on developing great cars and not worry about Levy."

"I guess I was just curious," I said.

"Well, don't be. Levy is not your problem. Sorry to cut you off, Hans, but I have to hang up now. I have someone waiting." I hung up the phone a bit confused but pleased at how things were progressing.

When two very smart and influential old friends like George Burgdorf and Virgil Norman decide on an objective, there's a good chance they will be successful. They had told me that if Studebaker was to survive, Mike Levy needed to be removed from the union president's position and I was sure they were helping things along. The timing on the disclosure of details of a five-year-old automobile accident could not have come at a worse time for Big Mike. I didn't have a long wait to find out what the two old pals planned to do next. On March 3rd, Ed Reynolds greeted me waving a copy of the morning paper. Again, reporter Jason Lasko of the *South Bend Tribune* had uncovered another problem for Big Mike Levy. Miss Rose Baxter, former Studebaker employee admitted to Lasko that her six-year-old son's father was Michael Levy. She said that up until recently, Levy had voluntarily given her monthly cash payments of $100 to help raise their son. When he discontinued those payments, she decided to reveal their secret affair. Levy was unavailable for comment. Lasko's article went on to say that Levy was well known as being a "ladies man" but had denied any relationship with Miss Baxter, a colored lady.

"You know Ed, it sure looks like the paper is out to get Big Mike. Reporter Jason Lasko had better watch his step," I said.

"Oh, I think he's safe enough," Ed replied. "If something happened to him, Big Mike Levy would be the first suspect. Levy doesn't own this town the way he once did. You're probably in more danger than Lasko is. Remember when Big Mike confronted us at the Ad building a couple of weeks ago and announced to the crowd that you were the source of all the union's problems? Even though there were a number of witnesses to his statement, they were all union members, not likely to rat on him. But the bottom line is he really believes you are his biggest problem."

"Yeah, you're probably right. I guess I should be more careful."

"You know, Hans, since Mr. Jamison, our president, and his family recently moved into the clubhouse here on the grounds, they've doubled the guards at the gate. This is probably the safest place to be in South Bend. You could stay out here until this whole Mike Levy thing blows over."

"Thanks, Ed. That's nice of you to offer, but I can't let Big Mike rule my life. Besides, I have a steady girlfriend now, and if I don't spend time with her, well, you know how women are."

"Do I? I've been married for a long time and have four kids, Hans, and yet I know less about women now than I did when I was in college," Ed said with a smile. "You're dating Mary Burgdorf, right? If you don't already know it, her father is a very influential man in this town. Not only is his real estate business quite large and successful, he owns a large chunk of Studebaker stock and, he's on the board of several local companies, including our own *South Bend Tribune*."

"That explains a lot," I said.

Chapter 47

Since new revelations about Big Mike's problems had started appearing regularly, I made a habit of glancing at Mrs. Kitchall's newspaper before leaving for work each morning. I was shocked as inch-tall headlines of the March 10th *South Bend Tribune* screamed: FORMER UNION PRESIDENT CHARGED WITH MURDER! The news almost took my breath away. I couldn't believe the police had finally caught up with Levy. I had to sit down as I read the front-page story written by none other than reporter, Jason Lasko. *"Deposed union president Michael Levy's troubles seem to have no end,"* Lasko wrote. *"Yesterday, District Attorney Jerry Goldsmith announced Levy's arrest for the October 1946 murder of former Studebaker Engineering Vice President, Roy Branson. Goldsmith said he could not discuss the details of the case at this time, but that new evidence and a witness had come forth to testify as to Mr. Levy's involvement in the murder. After making bond, Levy returned to his employment at Studebaker-Packard although not as head of the union."* I wondered who the witness could be. After thinking it over, I concluded it would have to be Rose Baxter, the mother of Big Mike's son. But if it were Rose, she would be implicating herself as an accessory to the murder. For her to do that she would have to be extremely angry with Big Mike. That could be since he had recently cut off her monthly child-care payments. Another possibility is she got some sort of plea bargain deal with the D.A. as an added incentive to talk. Of course, I was just guessing. In any case, I was willing to bet that George Burgdorf or Virgil Norman had a hand in convincing Miss Baxter to testify. And, I speculated Mr. Norman might even be representing her at the trial. Although the two old pals had forbade me from getting involved, I had to admit I was taking great pleasure in watching from the sidelines as Mike Levy was finally getting what he deserved.

The daily newspaper kept its readers fully apprised of every detail of the Mike Levy saga including his dismissal as president of Local # 9. Although still an employee of the Studebaker-Packard Corporation, he was no longer able to stroll the plant floor looking for trouble and was assigned a lowly assembly line task installing windshields, not an easy job. The urge to see Big Mike working on the line was almost too strong to resist, but I remembered my instructions from Burgdorf and Norman and stayed out of the plant. But I'll have to admit I would have given anything to watch Big Mike struggle with those heavy windshields.

Testing of the prototypes was nearing completion as the cold winter months of 1955 drew to a close. Except for a few shady places, by February of 1956, the dirty patches of snow had melted. I looked forward to spring. This meant Mary and I could go on picnics and I could drive to and from work with my windows down. My '53 Starliner hardtop convertible, looked best that way.

I could not have asked for better progress on my various projects. Permanent tooling for the new 1957 Freedom, Studebaker and Packard models was on order. Advertising photographs of the prototypes and plans for introduction of the new 1957 models were on schedule for the fall of 1956. Interestingly, sales of the German Volkswagen car, now called the beetle, were increasing substantially in the U.S. In a way, this was good news since it showed a latent need for a small economical car such as our Freedom line. But on the other hand, I knew the VW was a good car and would be strong competition for the Freedom.

At about 9 p.m. on March 1st, I received a most unexpected phone call. I recognized his voice as soon as he spoke.

"Hans? That's your name ain't it?"

"Yes, Willie. You know that's my name. What do you want?"

"I want to do you a favor. With all the trouble that Big Mike's in right now, I'd like to talk to you about the Benny Goodall spare key thing. Maybe we can make a deal."

"Why now, Willie?"

"If it comes out in the Roy Branson trial that Big Mike was also involved in Benny's death, I don't want my name to come up."

"As you must know Willie, I still have the recording implicating you and the only way I would let it go would be for you to admit Big Mike gave you the money for the duplicate keys."

"Well, I'm not admitting anything now but I'm willing to talk about it. You know, maybe some kind of a swap. Could you come over to the Jug tomorrow afternoon sos we can talk it over?"

"Why can't we discuss it on the phone?"

"You may be recording what I'm saying right now. If we can't work things out, I don't want no record of what was said, OK? I've been down that road."

"Alright Willie, I'll meet you at six tomorrow." I hung up the phone wondering why Willie had a change of heart. His fear of being implicated in the almost forgotten Benny Goodall case seemed strange. But many things about Willie Wyatt were strange.

The next afternoon when I got home, I strapped on the canteen containing Freda's heart, assembled the switch and high voltage coil and ran the insulated wire inside my shirt and down my right arm. Since predicting Mike Levy's actions was impossible, I wanted to play it safe. The temperature outside was around freezing. My heavy navy P-coat hid the whole assembly well. I hoped it was not too warm in the bar because I planned to keep the coat on so I wouldn't expose my protection.

The Jug hadn't changed much although it wasn't as crowded as I remembered. I stood in the door looking around. There was still that same gray cloud of smoke hanging near the dirty black ceiling. Willie was alone in a corner booth nursing a draft beer when I walked in. He stood and extended his hand when I reached the table.

"Sorry, Willie. I'm not shaking the hand of a man I don't trust. Now what's this all about?"

"I's just tryin' to be friendly, that's all. Have a seat and I'll buy you a beer." Willie signaled for the barmaid to bring me a beer. "Drewrys draft right?"

"Yes, fine," I replied. "Alright, Willie, what are you up to?"

"Hans, we've been knowing each other a long time, right?"

"Too long," I interjected. "Get to the point Willie."

"Come on, buddy. Let's just drink our beers and try to be friendly. We've both got something the other one wants so maybe we can make a trade." I pulled my beer in front of me making sure it was out of Willie's reach. "Here it is in a nutshell," he said. "I could testify against Big Mike if you would give me the recording about me and Bennie Goodall's spare keys. Also, I'd need to get Mr. Virgil Norman to represent me when I testify. Think you could arrange that? You're big pals with Norman ain't you?"

"That's asking a lot, Willie. Mr. Norman picks his own clients. Anyway, how do I know you'd keep your end of the bargain if I handed over the recording?"

"I guess I could sign something." After a few minutes I was getting warm in my heavy coat. Also, I was feeling a little light-headed. I knew I needed to get some air.

"What do you say we finish our beers outside, Willie? It's pretty stuffy in here."

"What ever you say, pal. But we ain't 'spose to take 'um outside. Guess we'll have to chug-a-lug." We both tipped our mugs skyward and headed for the door. I continued to feel a bit dizzy but thought nothing of it. But I knew I needed to have a clear head around Willie. We stood at the door.

"Tell you what, Willie. Why don't you write down what you are willing to do and what you want in return and we'll meet again tomorrow afternoon. I think I'll head on home."

"Alright, whatever. Same time tomorrow?" I nodded and headed for my Studebaker. I turned and watched Willie walk back into the Jug. I pulled the front seat back forward and took a look. Nothing back there. The engine roared to life and I threw gravel as I backed out. My vision was starting to blur as I pulled onto the paved street. I wondered if I could stay awake long enough to get home. After a couple of blocks, I knew I was in trouble. This was very unlike me. Someone must have spiked my beer. It must have been the barmaid. Willie didn't touch my glass. I couldn't see well enough to go on. I bumped into the curb and slumped over the steering wheel. That's the last thing I remember.

CHAPTER 48

Blinding white light shown through the surface of the water. It seemed only millimeters away and yet I knew I was drowning. I couldn't move my arms or legs. The milky outline of Otto's face scowled at me from above.

"Why Otto, why?" I shouted through the water. Pain shot through me like a bolt of lightning when I tried to get away.

A soothing voice whispered, "It's OK, sweetheart. You're just having a bad dream." I tried to look toward the voice but saw only bright light.

"It's me, Mary. Just take it easy, honey. We're gonna take real good care of you." The dream was so real I had trouble re-entering reality. I tried to think straight, but pain distracted me.

"Oh, Mary. Is it really you? I love you so much. Where am I? Why can't I see you?"

"You're in St. Joseph County Hospital. You've been hurt. But, Dad has made sure the best doctors are available until you're back on your feet. And, by the way, I love you, too, Hans."

"Why can't I see you, Mary?"

"Your eyes are swollen shut. We'll talk later when you're feeling better. But now you need to rest and try not to worry. Just know I'm here for you."

"What happened to me, Mary? How bad am I hurt? Tell me now. I need to know. Please!" There was an agonizingly long pause.

"Alright, if you insist. Someone beat you up beside your car two days ago. You have a broken arm and a broken leg. Both your eyes are bruised but the doctor thinks you'll regain your sight when the swelling goes down. Now will you just rest and know I'm here for you."

"What happened to my canteen?"

"Canteen?"

"Yes, I was wearing a canteen, well it really was a battery."

"I don't know. It wasn't with your clothes when they brought you in." Since I trusted Mary completely, I lay silently and tried to recall what had happened to me. I remembered going to the Brown Jug to meet Willie. And I remembered having a beer with him. I remembered driving away in my car, and, and it all faded at that point. Who beat me up, I wondered. Not likely it was Willie. He went back into the Jug. But still, someone must have known I was leaving the bar. And I'll bet that someone knew I'd be groggy when I drove away. Big Mike was the obvious suspect. But Willie had to be involved too. But I didn't see him put anything in my beer. I tried to recall details of that afternoon, but I guess the nurse had given me painkillers. I just couldn't think straight any more.

I looked forward to Mary's daily visits. In two weeks I was starting to recognize her beautiful face as she leaned over to kiss me. Although I worried about the progress of the new car lines, Bob Nitske came by to assure me that superior planning had kept all the projects on schedule.

I knew it was inevitable, but somehow I dreaded my next visitors, George Burgdorf and Virgil Norman. I was now able to sit up in a chair and that's where I was when the two old pals walked in.

"Well, look at you. Looks like you're making real progress," Brugdorf said. "Glad to see you up and about. Are they taking good care of you? I nodded yes. After a few minutes of small talk, Virg Norman got right to the point.

"Who did this to you, Hans?"

I don't know, Mr. Norman. I guess I was passed out when it happened. I suspect Willie Wyatt set it up, but I don't think he was the one who beat me up. Frankly, I don't remember a thing after I drove away from the Brown Jug."

"Well, as soon as you remember anything, anything at all, have Mary call me or her dad. We've hired a private detective to investigate the matter. Since the police are the ones that found you laying on the pavement beside your car, they are conducting their own investigation but I expect our boy will be the first to come up with something. But one thing we already know; anyone who would beat up a defenseless, unconscious man is a cowardly son-of-a-bitch. Let me ask you this, Hans. Why did you go to the Brown Jug in the first place?"

"Willie Wyatt called me at home and said he may be ready to talk about his involvement in the duplicate key that was used by Benny Goodall's murderer."

"Duplicate key? What duplicate key?"

"I had found out that Willie was given money to have a duplicate key made and that's how the murderer got into Bennie Goodall's locked car."

"Why did you think Willie decided to talk about that now?"

"Years ago I made a wire recording of him admitting that he had been paid to get a duplicate key made through the sister of one of his co-workers. I had always held that recording over his head promising I wouldn't turn it over to the police if he would admit Big Mike Levy was the one who killed Benny. We never were able to make a deal so after I left Studebaker I just let it drop. With Big Mike a suspect in the Roy Branson murder, I figured Willie was now ready to talk. That's why I agreed to meet him. I realize now it may have been a ruse to get me into the bar to spike my beer." Mr. Norman rubbed his eyes and turned to glance in George Burgdorf's direction and then looked back at me.

"Oh, Hans. How can you be such a brilliant engineer and such a dope when it comes to common sense and 'street smarts'? Jesus, boy, you should have told us about Willie and the duplicate keys years ago. And the recording, hell, that may be vital! And to top it off, you placed yourself in enemy territory and got yourself beaten to a pulp. You screwed up royally young man. Is there anything else you haven't told us?"

"I know I messed up, Mr. Norman. Believe me I'm suffering right now for my mistakes." I bit my lip, which caused an unexpected pain. George Burgdorf interrupted Norman's cross-examination.

"Ease up, Virg. Hans is not on the witness stand." Norman looked at Burgdorf and then back at me.

"Sorry, Hans. I didn't mean to press so hard. I'm sorry if I upset you. That's enough for today, anyway. You get some rest. If you remember anything else just write it down so you won't forget it until we see you again." After the door closed and I was alone, I closed my eyes and tried to black out the world.

The police interviewed me while still in the hospital. I didn't tell them anything other than the events of that terrible afternoon. Eight days passed and the doctors finally released me from the hospital to go home. My worries about being helpless and alone were put to rest when Mary dedicated all her free time to my well-being. Of all the women I ever knew, including my mother, Mary was without question the most wonderful, caring and yes, loving one of all. Any time that woman wanted to get married, I'd say yes, yes, yes! But we both had our careers and marriage had not been discussed. But my career was definitely on hold until I could get well. Although I was healing, I wondered if I would ever be the same. When Mary was at her office, time passed slowly for me. I read, slept and did some walking using a cane. My hatred of Mike Levy grew with each day. More than anything, I wanted revenge but felt helpless. I was reminded of Burgdorf and Norman's instructions to let them deal with Big Mike. Besides, what could I do?

A week after I was home I got a call from Stan Blackman. He identified himself as a private investigator hired by George Burgdorf. I remembered Mr. Burgdorf had said he planned to hire a private eye. Blackman visited me the next day. He looked more like an accountant than a detective. His oversized horn-rimmed glasses and bulging eyes gave him a comical look. But there was nothing funny about the man. He was organized and thorough and I later discovered very tough. He sat down and took out his spiral notebook. He cleared his throat before he spoke.

"I know I will be covering ground that has been gone over many times before but I feel it is necessary to make sure I fully understand everything about the past," he said.

"I really don't mind spending as much time as required if it would help put Mike Levy and Willie Wyatt behind bars," was my reply. He took page after page of notes about every encounter I had ever had with either man. I hadn't told Mr. Burgdorf about Big Mike tampering with my brakes that night at Susie's house and the subsequent confrontation when I shot the electrical bolt that put him on crutches for several months. But I didn't hold back anything from Blackman. I gave him every detail I could think of. He wanted to hear the wire recording of Willie that told about the duplicate keys to Bennie Goodall's car. He listened several times copying down every word. As he was getting ready to leave, I told him about the canteen containing the high-voltage battery that was around my waist the night I was assaulted.

"I'm pretty sure whoever beat me up, took the battery and high voltage coil before leaving me," I said. "Find that battery and coil and you've found my attacker."

"I'll do my best," he replied. "By the way, how long have you been using your real name and not Van Hoffman?"

"How did you know about Van Hoffman?" I asked.

"Oh, come on Hans, I've been working for George Burgdorf off and on for ten years? Who do you think told George that Van Hoffman was really the name of a dead boy from Ft. Worth, Texas? I even went down there to meet Hoffman's family. Nice people. Before it was over, I knew everything about you, what you did in Germany, how you got to America, even the restaurant you worked for in Dallas before coming to South Bend. Big D Steaks and Chops as I remember. When George Burgdorf wants something, he generally gets it. So, here's my advice to you, son.

Whatever you do, don't ever hurt George Burgdorf's family and don't get on his bad side."

"I remember what it was like," I said. "His good side is much better."

My first day back at work was May first. Ed Reynolds came by to take me to the Proving Ground. Ed had my car towed there from the police lot after that March second night when I was assaulted. I had talked to Ed on the phone several times during those two months while I was incapacitated. He had warned me that all the windows in my car were broken out and many body panels dented. I did not look forward to seeing my beautiful '53 Starliner in that condition. I hobbled into the garage dragging my right leg and its cast. Just being inside that old building made me feel better. I know it sounds crazy, but I enjoyed the smell of petroleum products as much as my mother's fresh baked bread. There in the corner under a tarpaulin was the recognizable shape of my once beautiful car. I dreaded seeing the damage as Ed had described, but when his workers removed the tarp, my car looked like it just left the showroom floor.

"Ed, it looks like new! Who repaired and repainted it and how can I ever repay? I'm sure it cost a bundle."

"Well, my friend, it's like this; I talked to Bob Nitske and we decided that since it was almost certain that someone from Studebaker vandalized your car, it was only right that Studebaker fix it for you. So between testing projects, the guys and I squeezed in some time repairing your car. And you may be surprised to know that much of that work was done after the men had clocked out for the day. The fellows and I feel a great sense of optimism about your new designs. Those new vehicles look really great. We all think the company is going to survive and even prosper thanks to your designs. So fixing your car was the least we could do. And Hans, we have another surprise for you. We know you think your '53 is the most beautiful car in the world and so we thought you might like to meet the car's designer." Ed motioned to his office. Out walked a handsome middle-aged man with a big smile on his face. Protruding casually from his blue blazer's pocket was a red silk handkerchief that matched his red silk tie. The knife-like crease in his gray trousers completed the ensemble. "Hans Werner, this is Robert E. (Bob) Bourke, the man who designed your '53." I shook the great man's hand but was speechless for a moment. Breaking the ice, Bourke began to explain some of the design features and how he had co-coordinated with engineering to make them possible.

"Take this low sloping hood," he said. "That was only possible by using a low profile radiator, an under bumper air scoop and an off-set air cleaner. I went round and round with the production engineers but in the end they made it possible."

As my courage returned, I asked, "What are you working on now, Mr. Bourke?"

"Well, since we designed the 1956 Hawk, our contract was not renewed. I guess we were just too expensive for the new management of Studebaker-Packard. But I've seen your designs for the '57 Packard and that little '57 Freedom car. You'll do just fine without Raymond Loewy Associates' help. Keep up the good work young man. As for me, an old pal of mine, Clare Hodgeman and I are going to New York and start our own design agency."

"Good luck, sir," I said. "Your name is etched in the history books for the great designs you have already done. I hope you do many more."

"Good luck to you too, son. With people like Ed Reynolds on your side, you can't go wrong. You've got a great future with Studebaker-Packard."

After Bourke left, I patted Ed on the back and said, "Ed Reynolds, you are unbelievable! How did you arrange for me to meet Mr. Bourke?"

"It was no trouble, Hans. I knew he was coming by to say goodbye to all the fellows here and I just asked him to stick around to meet you. He's a great guy. He was glad to do it. I'm just sorry you didn't get to know him earlier."

The rest of the day was spent catching up on the progress of the three new vehicle lines. Unfortunately, by three o'clock, I was exhausted. I wondered if I was going to be able to drive myself home. It wasn't easy, but I made it. Upon entering the boarding house, I asked Mrs. Kitchall to bring my supper to my room when it was ready but not to wake me. I ate at ten pm. My first day back was tiring but fortunately, my strength continued to improve with each passing day.

On June the first, steel parts off the new forming dies were delivered to the Proving Ground for assembly into real automobiles. Dozens of engineers and production supervisors from the factory came out and swarmed over the assembly jigs as the new 1957 Freedoms, Studebakers and Packards began to take shape. I was elated when I saw how perfectly the parts fitted together.

Ed Reynolds summed it up. "Compared to the last all-new models, these '57s are coming together surprisingly well. I guess that German thoroughness and attention to detail you learned at Volkswagen is paying off for your new employer."

"Thank you, Ed," I said. "I couldn't be more pleased." Yet in the back of my mind, I wondered if my good fortune could continue.

CHAPTER 49

That night after supper, I received a phone call from Stan Blackman. "Hans, as you know, Mike Levy's murder trial is coming up in a couple of weeks. Virg Norman, said that we really needed to get Willie Wyatt on the stand even though he may not have had anything to do with the Roy Branson murder."

"What? I don't understand," I said. "Willie was involved in the Bennie Goodall murder not Roy Branson's. What's the point?"

"Well, I have spent some time at the Brown Jug lately and observed Willie interact with his drinking buddies. First off, he's a heavy drinker. Further, he appears to be a bit unstable and in my opinion, not very bright. Virg Norman thinks if he can get him on the stand, he might lie about the simplest question. That way we can nail him for perjury. Then, Willie might be more in the mood to make a deal about testifying against Levy. But we have to have some reason to call him up to testify. Can you think of any connection with Willie and the late, Roy Branson."

"I doubt if Willie ever met Roy Branson. But, he knew Branson was pushing to eliminate piece-work incentive which would cut his pay."

"Okay, maybe that's enough. Did Willie ever complain to you about the piece-work thing?"

"Yes, a number of times."

"Now we're getting somewhere. Do you think Branson's anti-union stance and the attempted lowering of union pay was Levy's motive for killing him?"

"I guess so, assuming Big Mike did it," I answered. "Branson was a great guy. So I can't think of any other motive."

"Alright then, I'll tell Virg to subpoena Willie in the Branson murder trial. Blackman hung up without saying goodbye.

It appeared from the effort that Stan Blackman, George Burgdorf and Virg Norman were putting into the case, they were determined to bring Big Mike to justice. But one thing bothered me, wouldn't the District Attorney be the prosecutor rather than Mr. Norman? I had to assume they were somehow working together. If that were the case, it seemed unusual. But Burgdorf and Norman were two unusual men.

Although the changeover of the assembly lines for the new model Studebakers and Packards would not occur before August, the Freedom line setup was planned for June. That was because it was a completely new car and required its own assembly line. Too, the factory had to keep cranking out the1956 models as long as possible.

My work at the Proving Ground was finished so I moved into my new office in the Engineering Building. I loved that old building with its "art deco" facade. Being close to the plant gave me the opportunity to visit the Freedom line and answer any questions that might arise. It was a beautiful sunny Friday so I walked the short distance to the assembly plant. I needed the exercise after so many weeks of inactivity. This was my first visit into the plant in many months. When I approached the line, I was surprised. The Freedom assembly line was placed right next to the old Studebaker line. Even though I was just doing my job, I realized I was going against the Burgdorf/Norman order to stay clear of Michael Levy. But my curiosity was strong and I knew Big Mike was assembling windshields since he lost his position as union president. But when I approached that area and looked around, Levy was nowhere to be found.

"Where's Big Mike?" I asked the foreman.

"Oh, he's on vacation. Preparing for his trial, I heard. I think it starts tomorrow. Did you need to see him?"

"Oh, no. I was just wondering." I walked away before the conversation progressed any further. If I were truthful with myself, I would have to admit I was disappointed. But it was just as well that Big Mike wasn't around. He was unpredictable. I was afraid word might get back that I inquired about him. That might prompt him to come looking for me. My emotions bounced between anger and fear.

After checking the progress on the Freedom line, I walked back to my office to catch up on some paper work before heading home. Since I was now almost back to normal health, Mary and I had been enjoying each other's company with dinners, movies, picnics and an occasional weekend trip to Chicago. But Mary was attending her class reunion in Indianapolis this weekend, so I was on my own.

After supper at the boarding house, I decided to take a walk down to the river. It was only nine blocks and it was such a pleasant evening, I just couldn't stay inside. As I walked along I noticed dark clouds crawling furiously over the western horizon. But I wasn't worried. The cool breeze felt good and I was enjoying the stroll, so on I went. I could hear the rapids of the St. Joseph River half a block away. I hoped the sound of the water would help take my mind off Big Mike and all the things he had done to me. I'll admit, that big mountain of a man frightened me. I knew that he might eventually come looking for me unless he was convicted of the Roy Branson murder and put in prison. With Rose Baxter testifying against him, it appeared Mike might finally have to pay for his crimes. But the trial hadn't started and he was still out on bail. That fact was not comforting. As I walked across the Jefferson Boulevard Bridge, I starred down at the water looking for a reflection. The water was swift and it was getting quite dark so I saw nothing. The sound of the rushing currents splashing against the boulders was strangely unsettling. Should I go back home to the safety of my little room or should I enjoy the cool breezes of the evening? I decided to walk on over to the Mishawaka side of the river and then down the steps into Howard Park. Mary and I had picnicked in the park several times. As one walks south along the river, the path is soon deserted, unlit and a bit unkept. Soon, my better judgment kicked in and I turned around. By this time, the sky was turning unusually dark. There was no doubt a storm was brewing. For some unexplained reason, I have always been a bit afraid of the dark. Having had my last major confrontation with Big Mike in darkness didn't help. On I walked feeling less fearful as the lights of Jefferson Boulevard came into view. I stood on the bridge several minutes knowing nothing could happen to me there. I breathed deeply drawing in the damp air. The smell of the river seemed somehow different, foul and foreboding.

I was nine blocks from home and it had started to sprinkle. Rain had been forecast. Often the forecasters are wrong, but not this time. I knew I'd better get home before I got drenched. I walked briskly down Western Avenue and turned left into Chapin Street getting wetter by the minute. The rain was coming stronger and stronger. The time between the lightning and the thunder seemed short or was that just my imagination? The streets were deserted. No one in his right mind would be out on a night like this. Well, except for this one German fellow with no "street smarts" as Virg Norman put it. I was getting soaked to my under ware and was still five blocks from home. On I walked, hoping some kind person would stop and give me a ride. The only car that passed was a black '55 Studebaker President Speedster that slowed down but didn't stop. By this time, I was running but soon had to slow to a walk. I realized my leg wasn't as strong as it used to be. I guess my fracture was still healing. I was out of breath when I again sensed headlights approaching from behind. I turned and stuck out my thumb, the American hitchhiker's signal to give this poor soul a ride. The black Studebaker passed without slowing. The car looked the same as the one that had passed earlier, but Studebakers of all colors were quite common in South Bend so I thought nothing of it. Only three blocks from home, I passed beside an overgrown vacant lot in an abandoned industrial area. I felt vulnerable. Lightning flashed. I figured if I could make it to the next corner, I would be safe. The closer I got, the easier I breathed. As I neared the corner, a large dark figure suddenly stepped from behind a hedge and blocked my path. He grabbed my shoulders. I wanted to break away and run but my legs refused to co-operate.

"Stand still or you're a dead man!" the man shouted. It was the voice of Big Mike Levy. I had no defense. I knew he could kill me with his bare hands if he wanted to and he probably wanted to.

After an agonizing few seconds, I finally mustered the courage to say, "What do you want, Mike?"

"I could have killed you back in March, but I wanted you to suffer the same way I suffered. And, I'm not done with you yet." he said. "I've been cruising these streets every night for weeks hoping to catch you away from your boarding house. And now I've got you! I brought along your little shock machine to give you a taste of your own medicine." Mike opened his raincoat revealing the palm switch mounted on his belt. He pulled his left sleeve back revealing the insulated copper wire protruding past his fingertips and pointed at my crotch. "Since you're already good and wet, one bolt from this here lightning machine should end your walkin' and your fuckin' for a long, long time," he said. "When I'm done with you, your pisser won't work at all." He let out an evil laugh. If I tried to run, he would probably zap my backside. I tried to think of anyway to delay what seemed inevitable.

In desperation I shouted, "So you're the one who beat me up after Willie slipped me that mickey? If you hurt me again, you know you'll never get away with it. Besides, your trial for the Roy Branson murder starts tomorrow? Attacking me will only add years to you prison time."

"There won't be no prison time, asshole. I'll get away with that Branson thing and I'll get away with what I'm about to do to you right now. There won't be no trial 'cause Big Mike is leaving this burg and headin' for greener pastures just as soon as I fry your Nazi ass. Say your prayers, Kraut!"

"No, Freda, no!" I shouted. Mike hit the palm switch. Nothing. He hit it again and again. "No, Freda, no, no, no!" I insisted.

"Dammit! What's wrong with this thing and why are you shouting Freda? You beggin' for your Mama?"

"How did you know that was my mother's name? Anyway, I don't need to pray. The way you're doing it, you'll never get the arc to jump. Don't you know the exposed wire is sticking out too far?"

"Nice try, bastard. Think you're pretty smart, don't you, trying to trick old Mike Levy? Why would you want to help me fry your ass?" He hit the palm switch again. He then brought the exposed wire nearer to take a better look in the dim light.

"Now, Freda, yes, yes, now!" I shouted. The palm switch moved without being touched and a large deep purple and red arc traveled the short distance to Mike's face and the down the front of his body to the ground. He screamed and fell off the sidewalk into the gutter. The big brave Mike Levy cried and screamed like a baby. Water rushed around his thrashing body. "Yes, Freda, yes, yes, more, more!" The arc of fiery colors was growing brighter as Big Mike's massive frame heaved and quivered. It was a full minute before he stopped moaning. His clothes were blazing and black smoke billowed skyward. The stench of burning flesh was sickening yet somehow I didn't mind. Levy's blackened and burnt body was finally still. The rain stopped and the fiery arc disappeared. Steam and lingering black smoke rose into the cool night air. The glow of Levy's smoldering corpse was the only light. I stood in awe as a million specks of molten zinc sparkled in the dark flowing water. The aluminum canteen containing Freda's heart had melted and the metallic particles inside were being swept to freedom. I wondered if those shiny dots that had saved my life were still alive. But one thing I was sure of, I would never have to worry about Big Mike Levy again. I turned away, took a deep breath of clean air and then continued my journey home, never to tell a living soul about that frightening night on Chapin Street in South Bend, Indiana.

THE END.

CPILOGUC

The *St. Joseph Gazette*...... August 29, 1985......Page 1:

RETIRING V.P. of STUDEBAKER-PACKARD HONORED

A grand banquet was held last evening for Mr. Hans Werner, Vice President of Engineering of the Studebaker-Packard Corporation at the Century Center Grand Ballroom in downtown South Bend. The occasion was Werner's sixty-fifth birthday and the date of his retirement. Many state and local dignitaries were in attendance as honor after honor was bestowed on the proud honoree. Werner has often been called "the man who saved Studebaker-Packard."

He originally came to the U.S. from Germany at the end of WWII. Although trained as an automotive engineer at the Berlin Technical Institute, he was employed for a time by the U.S. Army as one of Dr. Werner von Braun rocket scientists at White Sands, New Mexico. But his real love was automotive engineering so he came to Studebaker and was able to get a job as a time-study engineer. Werner claims much of the credit for his success should go to his recently deceased father in law, George Burgdorf who recognized his potential and supported him in his climb to the top.

Back in 1955 when things looked bleak for the Studebaker-Packard Corporation, Werner designed three new product lines for the 1957 model year. Of special interest was the new Freedom automobile that filled an unrecognized need for a low-cost compact vehicle to compete with the small imports, in particular Volkswagen. Werner had worked for VW during WWII and for a time in the post-war period.

Indiana Governor, Martin Winstead, South Bend Mayor, Victor Smith and S-P President and Board Chairman, Robert Nitske joined Mr. Werner at the head table along with Werner's wife and son. Werner's farewell speech included praise for the support and encouragement of his lovely wife Mary who is presently Director of the Northern Indiana Library System. He also recognized his long friendship with S-P Proving Ground Director, Ed Reynolds who was best man at Werner's wedding in 1959 but due to poor health was not able to attend the banquet.

The festivities were climaxed with Mr. Nitske's presentation of the keys to a new 1985 Packard Hawk for Werner, a new Studebaker Station Wagon for his wife, Mary and a new Freedom compact car for young Hans Werner, Jr., a graduate engineering student at Notre Dame. Hans Jr. is heading up a graduate studies program on zinc-air batteries using an organic component that promises results several times greater than any of today's batteries. This program entitled the "Freda Project" has recently received a large government grant due to its potential as a very promising approach for the first practical all-electric automobile.